THE SHELTER OF EACH OTHER

CATHERINE RICHMOND

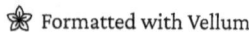 Formatted with Vellum

In celebration of healthcare workers around the world
—we made it through the pandemic!
And in memory of those who didn't.

For thou hast been a shelter for me, and a strong tower from the enemy.

— PSALM 61:3 KJV

CHAPTER 1

August, 1853

"Almost home," Keziah Sirrine told the ill-tempered chicken under her left arm, earning a peck for her trouble. Home to peel off her sweat-stiff dress, wipe the grime from her face, and drop into bed.

Dawn's feeble glow crossed the Mississippi and worked its way through the narrow spaces between the wood-frame houses. Waiting for sunrise would have been sensible. But exhaustion drove Keziah to follow the plume of her dog's tail through St. Louis's dark and muck-filled streets. The hand that usually held her lantern carried payment for the delivery, one leghorn pullet. Her other hand clutched the satchel with her midwife supplies.

Thank you, Lord, for the safe arrival of the baby, and for the quiet and cool of early morn.

As she turned into the alley beside her house, a voice called "*Gardyloo!*" followed by a chamber pot's contents sailing out a second story window.

"You're not in Edinburgh anymore, idiot!" Keziah yelled as slops spattered her apron, already begrimed from kneeling on a dirt floor all night. "How many times must I say it—use the latrine." *Lord, protect my plants from the poison of fools.* She tossed the chicken into the pen, setting off loud squawking, dropped her satchel on the back porch, then grabbed her spade. "Have you forgotten about the cholera four years ago? Thousands died of it in this city because of lazy people like you." With a scoop and a swing, Keziah sent the muck flying. It fell short of the window, but left a satisfying dark stain on the whitewash below.

"Sister Keziah Sirrine." A man barked each syllable as if addressing a wayward child. "That's *not* how we're to love our neighbors."

As if Brother Orrin Butts knew anything about love.

The hair on Finn's neck raised and his muzzle tensed with a growl. He was a large dog, his head as high as her hand, who'd made his mission to protect her. "Whisht," Keziah told him. He quieted on command, but kept his gaze on the visitor.

Where the alley opened to the street stood two men in frock coats, trousers, and cravats. *God save us.* What were Brother Thompson's henchmen, church elders, doing in her alley at the break of day? No use pretending they hadn't seen her with sleeves rolled up and hair falling down. Well, if they wanted presentable, they shouldn't drop in. She raised her chin and gave them a hard stare. "Spreading pestilence isn't kind to neighbors either."

The taller of the two, a man she'd never seen before, closed her neighbor's window. He turned to her with a nod. The corner of his mouth tipped up with a quick smile.

Find me entertaining, do you? Keziah nodded back. *You'll need a grand dose of fun, stuck with Brother Butts as you are.* She straightened her apron, dislodging a flurry of chicken feathers that had been stuck by body fluids. No dignity here. None at all. "Brother Butts and Brother..."

"Duncan Ross." The newcomer nodded.

"Brother Ross." Butts looked down his red nose at her. "If you'd grace us with your presence on a Sabbath, you'd recognize the other members of the Congregation."

Butts knew very well she trained as a midwife, but he disliked anyone having even a smidgen of independence. If she lost her temper, he'd report her as rebellious and headstrong, and rein her in.

Keziah wouldn't give him the pleasure. She kept her tone matter-of-fact. "God determines when babies come." And last night, it seemed the infant never would, even after hours of pacing. Keziah widened her eyes to keep herself awake. "Good morning to you both. And what brings you out this fine day?" Although *fine* put a stretch on it, considering sunrise had thickened the air with flies and the stench of the river.

"You weren't home last evening." Butts clasped his lapels. "It's unseemly for a woman to go gallivanting about at all hours."

"I was helping Mrs. Henderson bring her baby into the world." While keeping Mr. Henderson from drinking himself blind and minding a toddler who seemed determined to set himself on fire. For twelve hours' work, she received one ornery leghorn pullet. And the baby received the questionable honor of being named after the past president. Poor wee Millard Fillmore Henderson. "Scripture says Jesus was born at night."

Butts took a step back as Finn approached with his nose low. "Call off your cur."

Keziah clicked her tongue and the dog returned to her side.

"I returned moments ago. What might you be needing?" A simple remedy, please, then she'd eat a cold biscuit and snatch a bit of sleep. From the next block, the German baker called instructions to his delivery man. At the levee, a steamboat whistled its departure, echoed by a locomotive in the rail yard. Irish stevedores trudged past on their way to the warehouses. The city awakened.

Butts petted his excessive mutton-chop whiskers. "Jehovah's Presbytery of Zion is moving to Iowa."

Iowa? Panic squeezed her throat. The empty prairies of Iowa would provide no hiding place. Fault-finding elders would supervise her every move. She'd have to waste her breath explaining common-sense hygiene to fools like Orrin Butts. "So Brother Thompson is giving up on Joseph Smith's revelation to build in Independence, Missouri?"

Butts scowled, refusing to lower himself to discuss a religious question. He tipped his head toward her home. "A buyer will be moving into this house in three weeks."

The news woke her like a dunking in ice water. "But my garden—"

A wave of his hand brushed aside the work she'd put into cultivating a wide variety of healing herbs. "Iowa has plants."

"Sure and they have the ingredients needed for your rheumatism remedy." Her sarcasm blew past him.

"Ours is not to question the Patriarch."

Patriarch. Yet another title Thompson bestowed on himself, as though *Apostle of the Free and Accepted Order of Baneemy* and *Chief Teacher of the Preparatory Department of Jehovah's Presbytery of Zion* weren't enough. "I'm not finished training with Mrs. Jackson."

He huffed. "That slave—"

"Mrs. Jackson is free. She attended the birth of Brother Thompson's children. He agreed I could learn midwifery from her." Keziah breathed deeply to stay calm, as Mrs. Jackson taught laboring mothers. She braced against the rough-hewn wall.

"You trained to serve the Congregation. You come with us." Butts tipped his head to attempt a benevolent expression. "A woman can't stay in this city by herself."

"Suddenly my safety is a concern of yours? For years I've walked all over St. Louis alone." She nodded at Finn, who kept a watchful eye on the elders. "God provided a dog to guard me."

"You may bring the dog," Butts said as if she required his permission.

Keziah's mind raced. The plants wouldn't survive a move in this heat.The garden wouldn't be ready until after harvest. "I must wait here for Brother Sirrine's return. If he returns and I'm gone—"

"The new owner will tell him where we are."

"The house can't be sold without my husband's permission."

"Brother Sirrine signed it over to Brother Thompson before he left on his mission trip."

What? Without telling her? Of course. Women were too *frail* for such details. Rotten, blasted—*careful.* Was this be legal? There had to be a loophole. "I'd like to see the bill of sale."

Butts shook his head and started down the street. The tall man followed, his head abuzz with enough gossip to start a newspaper. Over his shoulder, Butts called, "Sister, you need to pack."

No, she needed a lawyer...who would take a leghorn pullet in trade.

~

August 1853

Duncan Ross watched Sister Sirrine march into her house and shut her door with firmness just shy of a slam. Serene? Oh the irony of her name. With her eyes flashing the gray-green of a storm cloud, she was anything but calm and even tempered. A true Irish warrior queen, fighting not for land and cattle, but for health. "Who's providing for her?"

"Windows, hinges, door knobs." Brother Butts looked up from his list. "What do you mean?"

"The disciples fed the widows in Acts." Even with her uncommon strength, how had she survived without her husband to bring in money, keep up the house, cut and stack firewood?

"We've no proof she's a widow."

Proof? The man had been gone three years.

The line of reasoning must have seemed weak to the elder, as he shilly-shallied. "She's kin to the Lane family... or maybe Sister Lytle. Suppose they're helping her. And as Brother Thompson says, in Preparation, we can better care for the poor and oppressed among us."

A glimpse of her yard showed a well-populated chicken coop and a garden ready for harvest. Poor? Perhaps. Oppressed? Nay. Full of gumption.

Brother Butts's next words were lost in the rumble of a passing beer wagon.

"Pardon me?" Duncan asked. Had he called Sister Sirrine a shrew?

"If Rufus were here, she wouldn't be mouthing off." The man

rummaged through his coin purse, counting money. "A contentious wife is a continual dripping like a rainy day."

One good proverb deserves another. "Whoever finds a wife, finds a good thing."

"Not one who quarrels with everything you say. You can see why he decamped."

Duncan could point out that asking questions was far from a donnybrook, but then he'd be accused of arguing too. He wanted to join this community, not get tossed out on his ear.

"Sister Sirrine?" A young girl vaulted the fence and raced down the alley, agile as a deer. She spotted the men standing in front of the house. Her eyes widened and she skidded to a stop. Duncan recognized her from Sunday when she'd been sitting between Brother and Sister Butts during worship.

"Malinda Butts." Her father grabbed her arm and shook, making her loose hair fly. "You're supposed to be doing the laundry."

"It's soaking." Her face turned red as watermelon. She raised her chin and scowled at her father. "I want to talk with Sister Sirrine."

Brother Butts handed the list and money to Duncan. "The lumberyard's four blocks east. Count every item. Don't let them cheat you out of a penny." Then he marched off with his daughter. "Home you're going and there you'll stay. Anything you need, ask your mother. You've no business with that crone."

Crone? Duncan considered Sister's clear skin, the thick dark curls tumbling from her straw hat, and her strength in wielding the spade.

This he knew—Sister was no crone. And Rufus had been a gowk to leave her.

~

August 1853

To the full armor of God, Keziah added her best summer dress, a brown and buff gingham, and tied on her straw hat. She gave the house one last glance. It wasn't much. One room, its fireplace serving for cooking and heating. The floor tilted, the windows rattled, and the roof sprung a new leak with every storm. Last week a man offered her nine-hundred dollars for it, leading Keziah to realize how valuable the land was. She could have changed her name, used the money to buy a little house with a garden in another town, and set up her own midwifery practice...if Rufus hadn't closed that door.

"Ready?" she asked Finn, who always was. Anger would have had her stepping out smartly, but muggy heat and her watermelon-filled bag slowed her pace.

"Hello, Mrs. Sirrine. Hello, Finn," called children playing in the street. Finn sniffed their hands, hoping for food. Keziah returned their wave, glad to see their pink cheeks and joyful romping.

Upstate New York; Far West, Missouri; back to New York; Kirkland, Ohio; Nauvoo, Illinois; Voree, Wisconsin; St. Louis. Seven moves, five babies buried along the way.

The business district with its wooden sidewalks and cobblestone streets was nearly empty. Thanks to the heat, no preacher stood on the mounting block, condemning her to hell as the whore of Babylon. The confectioner's was closed until September. The proprietor of the violin shop tested his latest with a few bars of Bach, then segued to *Oh! Susanna!* Carriages lined up at the mortuary, mourners eager to finish the burial and shed their black clothes before the heat of the day peaked.

"*Bonjour, madame*," called the grocer, filling his window display with fresh apples and peaches. "I have the ginger you require."

"*Merci beaucoup*." Keziah set her string bag on the counter. "And I have watermelons for you." Relieved of the weight, she tucked the dried root in her pocket and continued to the center of town.

The Courthouse crawled with German stonemasons, sweating in the heat. Inside, dark shades kept out the sun on the east side, while open windows on the west let in air. Finn's toenails clicked on the checkerboard floor. The hallway opened to a courtroom, a lofty space furnished with dark woodwork and decorated with tall columns. Not a soul anywhere. When would she have another opportunity? Keziah took a deep breath and sang the hymn that had brought her through her darkest days, "Come Thou Long Expected

Jesus." As she finished the line "let us find our rest in thee," Finn growled.

"You have a beautiful voice." A lanky man carrying a stack of thick books, stood in the doorway.

"Thank you." She'd believe the compliment if the courtroom didn't have a dreadful echo. "Might you be a lawyer?"

"Someday." He raised the books. "You won't be finding one today. Court won't be in session until the end of September, on account of the heat."

Her heart sank. "Too late."

"Perhaps I could answer your question."

"How would I find out who owns a house?"

"Ah, that would be City Hall, down by the river. Good luck to you."

Keziah thanked him. She and Finn walked the four blocks to the river, stopping at a pump to wet their throats. The fishy reek increased with each step downhill. They navigated the maze of wagons, stacks of lumber, and bales of cotton to enter City Hall. The mayor's and surveyors' offices were populated solely by dust motes, but one man fanned himself in the waterworks office. An explanation of the problem sent them to shelves stacked with documents. "What year did you say the house sold?"

"1850." Although the sale could have been the year before.

After rummaging long enough for Keziah's stomach to inquire about food, the clerk finally said, "Must not be much of a house. Sold for twenty dollars."

Oh Rufus, what did you do? "Is it all in legal order? Might there be a possibility of contesting the sale?"

"Let's see. Taxes are all paid up."

Taxes she'd paid, scraping every last penny, not knowing it was no longer her responsibility. Money she could have used to replace her worn shoes, buy seeds, and feed herself and Finn. Keziah clamped her teeth closed to hold in a scream.

The clerk shook his head. "Witnessed and dated. Too late to contest the validity."

Too late? "It was sold again this year."

The clerk paged through a thinner pile. "Yes, it was." He whistled. "For two thousand to one of Joseph Murphy's sons."

Two thousand? The Patriarch himself had signed his full and proper name, Charles Blancher Thompson. Brother Butts had witnessed the sale. Keziah thanked the clerk, roused Finn from his nap on the cool floor, and marched back into the humidity.

Anger heats the body, so don't. But she couldn't help herself. The Bible said the laborer is worthy of reward and her work paid the taxes. Steam threatening to burst from her head, she marched to Thompson's office. The door was locked, the printing press silent, the room dark. She thumped the door, earning a sore fist for her effort.

Now what? Keziah mopped her face with her handkerchief. Going to Thompson's house in this high temper, would land her in jail or the asylum.

Finn's wet nose touched her fist. She ran her hands over the dog's soft head. "Dear friend. 'tis hot. One more stop, then home we go."

Over the past three years, rumors had said her husband had taken a Pawnee bride, joined the throngs searching for gold in California, or been thrown off a steamboat for cheating at cards. Fur traders told of a man falling from a cliff and another killed by a grizzly. Evidence of his death, proof of her widowhood, would strengthen her case against Thompson. Even a fraction of the sale price would help her start a new life.

The doorway of the fur trade post led to another empty space. Beaver trade had fallen off with the change of men's fashions, but buffalo hide kept the business going. "Hello?"

A Frenchman with a neatly trimmed mustache hurried from the back room. "Madame Sirrine, how are you? I have just the thing for your companion—buffalo jerky." The fur trader wouldn't meet her gaze.

Finn sat and raised his right paw. He snapped the tossed meat out of the air.

"So, bad news or no news?"

He opened his hands. "*Rien, madame.* I have heard nothing of your husband. I am so sorry."

Of course. Rufus's actions never benefited her. His disappearance wouldn't be any different. She straightened and resumed breathing. "Thank you, monsieur, for your kindness. I bid you adieu." Keziah and Finn trudged home.

Christena Lytle arrived as she hung up her hat. The covered plate she carried attracted the interest of one hungry dog. Her cousin lived close enough to share meals when she knew Keziah had been attending births. Today she arrived for a different reason. "Anyone who locks horns with Orrin Butts needs sustenance." Christena had a year or two on Keziah, but her glossy dark hair, smooth complexion, and trim figure made her look younger. "Although instead of rheumatism, you should have mentioned his piles."

"Heard about the fuss, did you?" Of course she did. Her squabbles with Orrin Butts were the Congregation's favorite theater. And their penchant for gossip would only worsen in Iowa. "I may never count him friend, but I'm not wanting him as an enemy." Keziah peeled off her good dress. "Just once I'd like to speak a word without it leading to a quarrel."

"He says the same about you." Christena laughed, then sobered. "He also says you're ungovernable, recalcitrant, and out of control."

"Out of *his* control. Butts can't control Brother Thompson and whether or not he keeps his position of Chief Patriarch, so he does his best to control me." Keziah washed the sweat from her face and arms, then pointed to the basket beside her stove. "I saved a watermelon for you."

"Bless you. And the Lord." Christena set the table, her flounced skirt swishing as she moved. She tossed a scrap of pork into Finn's bowl, then nodded toward the dress Keziah had hung up, "Never have I seen you wear your Sunday dress on a Tuesday."

"Do you know any lawyers?"

"Not a one." Christena pressed her finger to her chin. "Are you ready to declare him dead or divorce him?"

She slipped on her work dress, the brown cotton chosen to hide both dirt and birthing stains. "Neither. Before Rufus left on his mission, he signed over this house to Brother Thompson."

"You won't need it much longer." Christena shrugged. Her husband had come home. She didn't have to provide for herself. "You know we're moving. Rufus will never see the back porch posts differ from the front."

"Nor the mismatched shutters." Keziah had become adept at picking through debris piles left as houses were demolished and rebuilt after the fires in '49.

Rufus would disapprove. But then, he always disapproved. Nothing she had ever done was good enough. She cut into the meat. "Thompson bought this house for twenty dollars, then sold it for two thousand. I nearly starved to death paying taxes on it. So I should follow him to the wilderness of Iowa?"

Christena sent a worried glance toward the open windows, then whispered, "What choice do you have?"

CHAPTER 2

August 1853

Light footsteps sounded on the front porch, then a tentative knock rattled the door. Finn didn't bother standing, so Keziah knew the visitor posed no threat.

"It's him." Christena tensed to race out the back.

"Would save me from having to hunt him down, but no, it's someone much less weighty." Keziah opened the door and Brother Butt's daughter rushed in. She wore her shoulder-length brown hair parted in the middle, then rolled back at the corners of her forehead, squaring her face. "Good afternoon, Malinda."

"Sister Sirrine, Sister Lytle." Eyes wide, hands clasped in supplication, the girl stepped close to Keziah. A dress of her mother's had been remade to accommodate a growth spurt and the beginnings of curves. Red bumps marred her chin. "I need your help."

Keziah hoped all she needed was a remedy for acne. "Sister Lytle will keep your confidence. What's the problem?"

Christena scrubbed the dishes, pretending to be absorbed in her task.

The girl swallowed. "I need ... a love potion."

Had Orrin Butts sent his daughter here, to trick Keziah in wickedness?

Mrs. Jackson slipped in the back door and gave Malinda a hard stare. "Sister Sirrine is no witch. She don't do voodoo." Her indigo dress and red kerchief announced she was on her way to attend a birth. "Baby on the way. Mama's first three came quick. We best hurry."

Keziah stood to leave, but the girl grabbed her with surprising strength. "If I marry, I can stay in St. Louis." Her voice quavered. "I thought you'd understand. Father said you don't want to leave either."

Sure and he'd been complaining about her stubbornness to any who'd listen.

"You're how old? Thirteen? Too young to marry." Keziah pried her loose, then raced to tie up her hair and don her hat. "Staying here isn't worth being yoked to a man who doesn't love you."

"And is outside the true church." Christena steered Malinda into a chair. "Ask God and at the right time, He will provide for you."

"I love him. He'll come to love me." The girl sniffled. "He's handsome, and has a deep voice, and the most beautiful bay mare. She stands sixteen hands and has a white blaze on her face and he let me feed her a carrot."

Mrs. Jackson sniffed. "Reckon you in love with the horse more than the man."

Christena passed Malinda a handkerchief. "Might he be willing to join the church and come with us, give you time to court?"

"Patrick's business is here, so he can't go with us."

"Patrick Murphy?" Keziah groaned. The girl must have met him when he bought this house. "He's twice your age and Catholic. Your parents will never agree."

Crying proceeded to wailing. Christena waved Keziah and Mrs. Jackson out the door. Keziah pressed her hands together, their sign of praying for each other. She grabbed her bag, and emerged into a day so hot only the cicadas stirred.

"Girl listen to nobody." In spite of her grey hair and wrinkles, the midwife tore across town at a grueling pace, racing through alleys and dirt streets. "Hope she don't get pregnant trying to snare that man."

"Let's pray not."

"So. You leaving."

"Don't supposed you'd... like to move... to Iowa. Hoped I'd ... have more time." Keziah huffed and puffed trying to keep up. "To learn."

"Got the rest of life for that." The older woman glanced over her shoulder. "Someday *you* learn not to lace your corset so tight."

"Went looking for... a lawyer... this morning."

"Meet lots of folks in this midwifing business. I'll give you names." Mrs. Jackson stepped stepped behind her, reached under her waistband, and loosened her corset with a yank.

"Much obliged." Keziah took in a deep breath. "I'd like to deliver this baby."

"Unless you run into something beyond your handling." Mrs. Jackson gave her a sidelong glance. "Now what I'm going to do for simples, when you gone?"

"I'll give you all the plants and seeds you have room for."

"No room for none. I live over a stable, back of a tavern." Mrs. Jackson lifted her face to the sky, a satisfied smile relaxing her face. She wasn't thinking of the flies, the stench of manure, or the noise of travelers. "Thank you, Lord, for freedom."

They turned onto a gravel drive and climbed a bluff overlooking the Mississippi. At the top, a boxwood hedge surrounded a kitchen garden larger than Keziah's yard. Rows of vegetables and herbs showed careful tending. Raspberry bushes, and peach and apple trees hung heavy with fruit. No weed dared mar this perfection. "I covet this garden."

"Got to marry you a steamboat captain." The midwife led her to the back door of the two-story brick house.

"My steamboat sailed," Keziah said, earning a chuckle from Mrs. Jackson.

Before they could knock, a maid opened the door, recognized the midwife, then led them up the back stairs. They passed rooms larger than Keziah's entire house, filled with ornate furniture, fancy woodwork, portraits, mirrors, and patterned rugs. A second maid opened the door at the end of the hall to a dark room. The odors of sweat and chamber pot hung in the air. A woman moaned on the four-poster bed.

"How you doing, Mrs. Bissell? This is Mrs. Sirrine, herb woman and midwife. We together today." Mrs. Jackson pulled back the drapes and opened the windows.

The maid wrung her hands. "Wait! Won't the air cause childbirth fever?"

Mrs. Jackson shook her head. "Overmuch heat won't stop the fever, but will wear out the mother." Not to mention the midwives.

"Glad to see you two." The mother panted as if she too had climbed the hill. "I think the baby's ready. I know I am."

Keziah donned her apron and scrubbed her hands while praying with Mrs. Jackson, "Have mercy on me, oh Lord. In all my actions, grant me skill and judgement, wisdom and sympathy, kindness and understanding. Guide my words and hands that I may ease this mother's suffering and receive this gift of life from you. Amen."

Keziah turned to the mother. "Take slow, deep breaths, ma'am." She lifted yards of lace and lawn, wondering why anyone would give birth in a white gown, and ran her palms over the stretched abdomen. Head down, thanks be to the God of Puah and Shiphrah. Keziah gave Mrs. Jackson a nod. A small body part twitched, then the whole mound tightened. The mother's moan increased to a growl.

Mrs. Jackson had shared what position worked for this mother's other births. Between pains, Keziah pulled a wooden arm chair near the bed, helped Mrs. Bissell into it, and propped her swollen feet on the bed frame. She wrung out a washcloth and wiped the woman's face, smoothing strands of blonde hair from her face.

The maid wrung her hands. "Don't she need a clyster or castor oil to bring the baby on?"

"She's doing fine without it." Over the maid's shoulder, Mrs. Jackson shook her head. Keziah sent the maid and her nervous energy to the kitchen with a paper twist of dried chamomile flowers. She washed between the mother's legs, then rubbed her with oil. The clean smell of lavender covered the foul odors in the room. "You're getting along. Breathe."

By the time the maid returned with the tea, the mother had started pushing. Mrs. Jackson rubbed the mother's shoulders. Keziah kneeled, holding a towel. "You're doing fine. Deep breath. Push again."

A wiggling, slick bundle slid into her hands.

Thank you, Lord. "It's a boy. Healthy and good-sized." He pinked up and voiced his objections as she toweled him off and set him on his mother's belly. Working around his flailing arms and kicking legs, Keziah waited for the cord to stop pulsing, tied the thread two and three fingers from the baby, then cut between the knots. "Rest easy, Mrs. Bissell."

"Mind what else needs doing," Mrs. Jackson said as she took the infant.

Keziah added raspberry tincture to the tea to slow the bleeding, served it to the mother, then kneaded her belly. Soon Keziah wouldn't have the midwife nearby to remind her of her duties. She could no longer rely on her years of expertise and skilled hands. She'd be the only midwife for miles. A cold finger of worry traced her spine.

Fresh air, sunlight, clean linens. No self-destructive children, drunk husbands, or hostile poultry to distract the mother. This infant had an easier start compared to the Henderson baby she'd delivered a few days ago.

May all births be this trouble-free.

With the baby safely arrived, the maid calmed down and helped bathe Mrs. Bissell, dressed her in yet another lacy confection, then tucked her into bed.

"Healthiest little baby you ever saw." Mrs. Jackson cleaned and swaddled him, then settled him in his mother's arms. "Got you a good strong boy."

The maid ran the bell and Captain Bissell arrived, his buttons bursting. He accepted congratulations, paid both midwives, and sent them to the kitchen for supper.

"It's late." Keziah squinted into the setting sun as they crossed the yard to the kitchen. "We arrived shortly after midday."

"You too busy to worry about time."

The cook raised a suspicious eyebrow at Keziah. "Who that?"

"Another midwife," Mrs. Jackson told her. "Captain send us to eat."

The woman set plates on a table by the window, then stomped out with a huff. Mrs. Jackson dug into corn pone and greens cooked with bacon.

"Easy work and supper too?" Keziah dug into the meal. "We should give back half of this."

"No you don't. That makes up for babies take all week to be born and all we get is crust." Mrs. Jackson stared at Keziah. "You do all right."

"Thanks to you." Keziah's smile faded and her appetite dwindled. "What if I don't recognize the plants when I get there?"

"Find someone who got there afore you." She took a bite of peach pie and hummed her appreciation, then looked up. "You no slave. No one can force you to go."

Keziah stared into the dark brown wells of wisdom. She'd managed without Rufus for three years. Could she survive without the Congregation? She'd be labeled apostate and heretic, but Gentiles had called her worse names. "Don't suppose there's room over the stable."

"They ignore this colored woman squatting there, but you..." She shook her head. "Not enough business here for both of us."

"They sold my house out from under me. My husband left me with no money." Keziah jingled the coins in her pocket. "That's all I have. Not enough for a room, not enough for a garden, even if I could find a landlord who'd rent to a Mormon."

"Govenor's Extermination Order still the law."

Keziah's eyes closed as the memory of her burning house overwhelmed her. "I could be killed for something I don't even believe." Her gaze met Mrs. Jackson's concerned eyes. "I follow Jesus. Salvation comes through grace."

Cook called from the doorway. "Either of you know anything about a big old wolf-dog?"

Finn sat in the garden, tongue out and panting.

Keziah and Mrs. Jackson stood. "Our escort. Thank you kindly for supper."

Fatigue set in on the walk home. The impossibility of breaking from the Congregation hovered over Keziah's thoughts. "What woman is truly free?"

"You prayed for freedom?"

"Every day."

"Well, then. Got to think of this another way." Mrs. Jackson laid her palm on Keziah's cheek and gazed straight into the deep places where she hid her worries. "Maybe God wants you with those people, birthing babies, growing simples, making remedies. Saving lives, saving souls. Like Esther in the Bible—for such a time as this."

Keziah shivered. "I'm like Jonah. I want to run away."

Mrs. Jackson chuckled. "I hear of a whale in the Mississippi, I know it swallowed you."

August 1853

"You'll be excommunicated for apostasy and won't see a dime," Christena had cautioned her this morning. "No Gentile church will help you since you're a heretic. Then where will you be?"

Keziah's anger overrode her friend's warnings and propelled her to the row of two-story brick houses on Walton's Court, in the center of St. Louis.

"Starve here or go to Iowa?" She asked Finn, but he had no answer.

The door on the second house banged open and out raced four-year-old Leo Thompson, swinging a doll and laughing. His six-year-old sister Ida followed, raining down curses, braids flying. The pair thundered toward Wash Street. Adding his bark to the racket, Finn took up the chase. Oh, Leo. It's a wonder the Thompsons had more children after him.

"Keziah, I didn't hear you knock." Catherine Thompson let her in, speaking loudly over the crying infant in her arms. She waved at the trunks and crates in the entry. "Forgive the mess. As many times as we've moved, you'd think we'd be more efficient. How can I help you today?"

"Is Brother Thompson in?" Should she call him the Patriarch or one of his other titles? They'd known each other for eighteen years; titles seemed excessive.

Catherine sent a glance toward the closed door. "He's with Brother Powers. They shouldn't be much longer."

"How's the baby?" Under the blanket, Keziah found a round red face.

"Wet and hungry."

"And healthy." Keziah said, thinking of the daughter the Thompsons lost two years ago. "It's hard to imagine in this summer heat, but we'll need fearnought woolens for Iowa's winters. Could you put the word out?"

"Of course. I'll have Charles announce it at our next teaching." Responding to a howl from the back of the house, Catherine hurried off.

Once again Keziah wished Rufus hadn't put her in this position. She reviewed what she wanted to say to Brother Thompson, laying out the facts and asking for reimbursement.

Voices rose from the office, increasing in anger.

"...a full accounting of my expenses..."

"...heresy, lying, calumniating me, misrepresenting the Presbytery..."

"...my wages. You owe me..."

"You are no longer welcome in the Congregation," Brother Thompson proclaimed, as grim as a judge delivering a death sentence. "You may no longer speak to any of us. I withdraw fellowship and cast you into the outer darkness, where there is weeping and gnashing of teeth. And not one dime will you receive, you apostate!"

Keziah chilled. This wasn't a good day to talk to Brother

Thompson about money. Before she could exit, the study door opened and hit the wall.

"Better an apostate than a charlatan and swindler!" John Powers yelled, baring his teeth like a rabid dog. He turned and saw Keziah. "Get out while you can," he told her, then left with a slam of the front door.

After a pause, Brother Thompson said, "Enter, Sister." The Voice crying in the wilderness, the Messenger sent to prepare for the coming and to gather the remnant, the Patriarch of Zion holding the keys of the priesthood, sat at his desk, forehead braced on his fingertips. They'd suffered plenty of tribulations together, but Keziah couldn't count on him as a friend.

He could count on her as a herb woman. "Are you ill? Are you needing a headache powder?"

"Sister Sirrine." He stood and clasped her hands. His gaze held steady on hers. He tilted his head and spoke with warmth and sympathy. "I have every hope the Congregation's move to Preparation will bring us into contact with the Indians and we will receive word of Brother Sirrine. Perhaps even now he is teaching the Lamanites the useful arts of civilization and peace, so they may build the New Jerusalem."

She launched into her speech. "I understand my house has been sold."

"Brother Butts told me you have concerns."

"I paid taxes on that house."

A quick intake of breath showed she'd surprised him, then he resumed his posture as the kindhearted Patriarch. "Dear Sister, you'll never have to pay taxes or worry about money again." He patted her wrist, then lifted his gaze and raised his hands. "The Heavenly Father provided the exact amount needed for our passage and supplies for Preparation, where we will escape the bondage and repression of Babylon, where we will rest in peace and safety, for the gathering and the salvation of the people of Israel, and for restoring the Covenants of Abraham, Isaac, and Jacob. Great blessings are in store for God's people when they are gathered and organized." He steered her through the entry. "We must needs return to preparing.

The steamboat El Paso departs September 9. I will see you then." The door closed behind her.

Her friend Charles was gone, consumed by his role of Patriarch, a leader who held onto authority with a deluge of words. Further questions would gain her no money—all was spent—and lose what little support she had from him.

Keziah stood at the top of the steps. Her head dropped back. She looked at the sky and raised her hands. "Is this Your will?"

I will send you a helper.

"A helper? Since when have I needed a helper?" Ach, she ought not be rude to her Heavenly Father, especially when all He wanted was for her to rely on the Holy Spirit. "Thank you, Lord. Thy will be done."

Her hands dropped to her sides, then she descended to the street. Finn loped from the alley with a tongue-hanging grin. "At least one of us had fun."

They trudged home. Keziah wanted nothing more than to crawl into bed and have a good cry, even at the cost of a headache, but a cart stood in the alley beside her house. On her front porch sat the man who'd accompanied Brother Butts the other morning. His long legs stretched down three steps. His Sunday suit had been discarded in favor of a tan shirt and brown cotton duck trousers. Finn sniffed him without growling, then allowed a scratch behind the ears.

The man noticed her and stood. "Sister Sirrine," he said with a trill of his "r."

"I'm sorry. I'm not remembering your name."

"Duncan Ross. At your service."

"You're a Scot then?"

He nodded. "My parents emigrated from Galloway to New York. I'm from the Cherry Grove School of Faith quorum, near Cincinnati."

"Mine were from Belfast, over the North Channel."

"'Tis good to hear a voice easy on the ears." He tipped his head toward her then turned to the cart. "Brother Butts asked me to help the families whose menfolk had gone ahead. So I brought boxes for you."

Help? No one had helped her during the other moves. "Few possessions means little need of boxes."

"But you have plants. And Preparation is sore in need of a garden." He lifted a crate down.

"Have you been there, then?"

"Nae." He glanced down the alley to her garden. "But hear tell the soil is good. You'll like it."

"As if I have a choice."

He flinched as if she'd shot him.

"Sorry. I meant to say I've no choice of the dirt." She looked away, struggling to get ahold of herself. He didn't deserve her ill-temper. "Uprooting makes me..."

"Crabbit?" he asked carefully, as if she might take another shot. "The Scots word for cantankerous."

"Sure and I'm crabbit." Her jaw had been tight from the words she couldn't say to Brother Thompson, but finally it eased. "This crabbit gardener will bring seeds." The portable part of her garden.

He raised the lid of the crate, showing empty tin cans from coffee, peaches, and oysters. "I'm thinking we could dig up your herbs. Water them along the way. The trip should take a week or so. I found buckets for larger plants and crates for your medicines."

Could he be the helper sent by God? She peered over the side of the cart and found a stack of pails, washtubs, and clothes boilers, all rusty or dented. Four shipping boxes showed signs of recent repairs. Her stock of remedies and a fair number of her plants could be moved. "You've saved cans for years?"

"Folks let me go through their piles." His narrow shoulders lifted. "Not good condition, as ye can see."

"Perfect condition for this work." Faded labels on the crates read cognac, wine, and sherry, but fresh paint said, *Plants. This end up.* "Are you a drinking man, then?" The Mormon Doctrine and Covenants prohibited wine and strong drinks. Brother Thompson also preached against the consumption of spirits—more from concern of the expense than the cost to health.

"Och no. Back of taverns are a treasure trove, although the oyster cans add odor."

The containers were clean. "You've been digging through trash, scrubbing out all these tins." *What might he want in return?*

He showed her open palms. "I washed afterwards." A barber had trimmed his dark brown hair and shaved him.

"You did." She laughed. "And I thank you, for this grand gift. Let me unload." She reached for the nearest stack.

"Allow me." He leaped into the cart and handed down the tinware, then stacked the crates and carried them to the back porch. "I'm thinking, wait a day after tonight's thunderstorm for the dirt to dry out, then we'll dig."

Keziah doubted if she'd see him again. Sure, he seemed like a decent sort. He'd try to keep his promise. But another family would have more need of him. Or Brother Butts, to irk her, would assign the man a different task. "Aye, right."

He must have heard the skepticism in her voice as he met her gaze with a smile. He climbed in the cart and rattled down the road, singing "Will Ye Go, Lassie, Go?"

September 1853

"Hey now, what are you doing up there?" Duncan raced down the alley and past Finn to catch Sister Sirrine as she teetered on a ladder.

"Taking down my herb drying rack." She loosened a rope holding a wood frame beneath the porch rafters. "Out of the way, unless you need a thump on the head."

"On the ground with you. I'll reach it." He kept his hands an inch from her waist. He'd rather steady her, but feared she'd accuse him of forwardness.

The frame swung an inch past his shoulder. "I warned you."

"So you did." Her sure-footed descent made clear this wasn't her first time on a ladder.

"Have we room on the boat for this?"

So, she had decided to go with them. Check that item off his list. Brother Butts had told him to make sure she boarded, even if he had to throw her over his shoulder. However brief their acquaintance, Duncan knew Sister Sirrine would object to abduction. "For such a useful contraption, I'll find room." He reached under the rafters and pulled out the nails. They'd been hammered in halfway, leaving an inch to wrap rope around. Clever. "We've a lot of work before winter. I don't know when we'll build your porch."

"This one wasn't so difficult."

"Your husband built it?" The man had carpentry skills, yet he choose freighting, taking him away from his family. The more Duncan heard about Rufus, the less he thought of him.

She wrapped the rope around the frame. "He's away."

"Who, then? Preparation needs carpenters."

Dark eyes flashed below her brows, one raised.

Duncan's breath caught. "You?" The roof was true, the shingles even, the supports plumb. In fact, the porch looked better than the rest of the house. "You could build porches on all the houses in Preparation. Except the sight of you on a ladder puts the fear of God into me."

"Taking away Brother Thompson's job." Her mouth quirked in a smile.

"Wouldn't do." He turned from her twinkling eyes to her garden. "I've come to dig for you."

"Too late." She pointed toward the crates.

"You're an early riser." Green plants packed every inch, yet the garden held still more. "Should I find cans for the rest?"

"Much as I hate to deprive you of the opportunity to rummage behind all the taverns in town, no." She pointed to the various plants in peeking from the box. "Chamomile, mint, and parsley are hearty and produce plentiful seeds. I've enough."

"Well, then..." No work for him here. No reason to tarry, much as he'd like to stay and get to know this spirited woman. He turned to go.

"May I thank you with a cup of cold mint tea? If you've time."

"I'd be delighted." Going inside would tarnish her reputation, so

Duncan sat on the porch and gave Finn a thorough scratching behind the ears. What else might she need help with? A rectangular basket overflowed with scraps of paper.

Sister Sirrine brought out two ironstone cups. "My remedies. Every winter I promise to rewrite them and organize them, then run out of time."

"I'll look for a box for them."

She shook her head as she poured. "I've room in my trunk for it."

The sweet mint delighted his tongue and the cool liquid eased his dry throat. He saluted her with the cup. "Is such ambrosia allowed?"

Her broad smile and musical laugh had him wishing he could tell jokes all day. "I'll say it's for medicinal purposes."

"Oh, and what might be wrong with me?"

She tilted her head and considered him. "Could be upset stomach, headache, bad breath. But more likely fatigue from packing all of our households."

He covered his mouth and exhaled. "No, not bad breath. Your last diagnosis is correct." He finished the tea, but wanted to linger. "I haven't any teaching on this, but I noticed people in the Congregation don't drink tea or coffee."

"Joseph Smith's *Doctrine and Covenants* forbids the use of hot drinks."

"So cold tea is allowed?"

"Yes." She set her hand on the recipe basket. "Herbs are made into a tea as a remedy. People find a hot drink soothing when they're ill, so I need to get into the habit of calling the remedies infusions."

"So..." How much could he say to Sister Sirrine? He couldn't see her running to Brother Butts for anything short of murder. "A hot cup of coffee on a cold morning..."

"...is a good start to the day. I miss it too."

"Mistress Sirrine, Mistress Sirrine." A barefoot lad raced into the yard, waking Finn. "Mrs. Jackson needs you on Sixth Street, between Chestnut and Market."

"The jail?" Duncan asked. "No place for a lady."

"But perhaps a place for midwife." Sister Sirrine stepped into the house and emerged with the valise she'd carried the other morning. "See you on the boat, Brother Ross." She and Finn followed the boy down the road.

Duncan gave the garden, the plant-filled crates, and the herb rack a last look, then watched Sister Sirrine hurry down the road. He wasn't the only one needing a rest.

CHAPTER 3

September 9, 1853

The sun rose over the Mississippi River, increasing the pungent reek of horse manure, sewage, and fish. North and south as far as Duncan could see, steamboats packed every inch of the shore. Their stacks filled the air with whistles and smoke. Miles of warehouses flanked the river, ready to meet the needs of westward travelers. And in between, barrels, trunks, cotton bales, and people... and rats. A large brown dog shot off, chasing a rat under a stack of lumber.

A voice commanded "come" in Gaelic. The dog whirled around and raced to Sister Sirrine. She'd trained him well.

"Brother Ross." Sister Christena Lytle and her fourteen-year-old son Omer greeted him. They'd arrived in a hired wagon with Sister Sirrine. She didn't glance his way, but Finn paused for a pat. Duncan directed them to their cabins and checked off their names. That left only...

Duncan shifted his feet in the mud beside the landing stage of the El Paso. He'd read last night of Jesus and the disciples caught in a storm on the Sea of Galilee, and asked Him to protect them on their journey. He sharpened his pencil with a twist of his knife, took a swallow of water from his jug, and fanned himself with his hat.

The captain said the boat would leave at dawn, but surely he'd wait for the—

Voices and engines quieted as the Thompson family arrived. The Congregation applauded from the boiler deck. Sister Thompson carried the infant, and the oldest daughter, Amelia, herded the younger children up the landing stage. Duncan held his breath as Leo attempted to dive headfirst into the river, but Amelia caught him in time. The wild lad must keep his parents running.

Brother Thompson paused on the levee and surveyed the stern-wheeler. He raised his arms. His voice carried over the riverfront. "Beloved Brethren and Sisters. Today, Jehovah's Presbytery of Zion embarks for Preparation!" Then he led them in a hymn he'd written. The tune was the Old Oaken Bucket. The Patriarch had given each member a printed copy of the lyrics Sunday. Duncan added his voice, "Now let us rejoice in the day of salvation, No longer as strangers, on earth need we roam." He choked back tears. He was no longer a stranger, and would roam no more. This ordinary shoe-maker was joining the Great Steward and this community to establish the New Jerusalem. God had brought him through the deaths of his children and wife, his house burning down, and failure in farming, and led him to this glorious moment.

The song finished and he followed Brother Thompson onto the boat. The landing stage raised, the whistle blew, and the El Paso backed into the current.

Duncan moved through the crowd at the rail, greeting those he knew. "Sister Lytle, I wanted to let Sister Sirrine know where her plants are stowed."

"Of course." She raised an eyebrow. "She's on the main deck, tending a fireman."

He found her tending half a dozen deckhands. The whole crew had burns, scrapes, or crushed fingers. Instead of relaxing on this trip, Sister Sirrine had gotten right to work. She had a kind manner, respectful to all, confident in her instructions. Duncan would talk to her later, when she wasn't so busy. He nodded to Finn and resumed his exploration of the boat.

The next time he saw Sister Sirrine, she was conversing with Captain Thornburgh beside the pilot house.

"Have you a garden?" she asked.

Duncan couldn't hear his reply.

"A home, then?" Her voice held a certain lilt as if flirting. Being a married woman, he expected she was beyond such silliness, but a steamboat captain's high salary might turn any woman's head.

Duncan returned to the boiler deck and nearly bumped into Brother Butts. "Where's Sister Sirrine?" he demanded, without a "how d'you do?" or a "good afternoon."

"With Captain Thornburgh." He didn't mean to imply they were doing anything untoward. "She's been aiding the crew with medical needs."

"Is she charging a good price?"

Charging the crew who served them? "You'll have to ask her."

Brother Butts stomped up the stairs. His presence would put a damper on any flirting. What was he thinking? Sister Sirrine was a virtuous woman. He had no reason to be suspicious of her...and no reason to send Brother Butts her way.

"Impressive splinter, Mr. Davis." Keziah sat on a crate and directed the fireman to rest his arm on a taller crate. She swabbed his palm with alcohol, then turned it toward the sunlight. "How long has it been plaguing you?"

"Oh I reckon, first run of the year. Haven't been near a doctor since, leastways none who'd see the likes of me. Or any of us."

"We're all God's children." Despite whatever nonsense Brigham Young spouted. "You've been hurting since March, then? It's a wonder it didn't putrefy." She probed the wound with a needle.

The fireman yelped and pulled his hand back. "Sorry, missus. I be still."

Finn gave the man a worried look.

"It's festering and it's got to come out."

"Don't I know it." He set his jaw and frowned at the fields of stumps bordering the Missouri.

"Been on the river long?" Keziah guessed his age between thirty and sixty. His face had weathered tough and dark. His hair bleached to a pale fuzz. As he spoke of working his way up from roustabout to fireman, Keziah figured where the splinter had entered his body and worked it through the hard skin. "Who's cooking this trip?"

"Don't rightly know. New fellow."

Keep a watch on the food, then. "And who's swabbing the decks?"

"Cabin boy is Duke. Second year on the river. He do all right."

Keziah caught the end of the fragment and pulled. "Eureka."

The fireman scooted away. "Oh missus. You done it."

"Not so fast." She applied alcohol again, earning a sharp intake of breath from her patient, then grabbed a jar from her satchel. "Rub this ointment in. 'Twill help the healing. Let me check it tomorrow. And think about wearing gloves."

"Thank you, missus. I'm beholden to you."

She shook her head. "Our lives are in your hands, Mr. Davis. I am thankful for you."

Finn stood, announcing Malinda Butt's arrival. "Sister Sirrine, you've got to see this." She dragged her to the boiler deck's stern and opened a door marked "Ladies." Instead of a dark pit, the hole in the seat led to the bright red paddle wheel, churning the muddy river. A wee one could fall through and drown. The girl's mouth moved, but the noise covered her words.

Keziah shuddered and closed the door. The Saints hadn't travelled by water since leaving New York. Neither the Erie Canal packet boat nor the Lake Erie steamer had anything as dangerous as this. "Thank you for showing me. Stay here and don't let any children in."

Accompanied by Finn, she marched toward the bow and found a young boy sweeping the steps. "Duke?" She introduced herself to the cabin boy. "Might the boat have any chamber pots?"

"Yes, missus, in each room, under a bed." He leaned close. "It's not so bad, using the head when we're underway. The spray gives a wash up." He waved over his buttocks in case she didn't catch his meaning.

"Very good." She thanked him, then spotted a long-limbed shadow. "Brother Ross? I've need of your manifest."

"I've been looking for you, to show you where your plants and chickens are, in case they need watering."

Keziah glanced at the muck-laden river. "They'll wait for cleaner water." She took the passenger list, then hurried to the Thompson's cabin. Catherine opened the door. Keziah leaned close to be heard over the hubbub of family life. "The latrine is open over the paddlewheel. Don't let the children use it. And don't use it while the boat's stopped. There's a chamber pot under the bed."

Brother Ross caught Leo squeezing past his mother's skirt. "Back in with you, lad."

"Thank you both." Catherine closed the door.

"Is it always about the latrine, then?" he teased.

"It's always about health. Trusting God does not give license to carelessness, Brother Ross." Her glare failed to wipe the smile off his face. "Should I recline on a fainting couch with a case of the vapors?"

His smile widened. "Can't imagine that."

Apparently having nothing to do, he followed as she warned the rest of the families.

"The plants and chickens?" He asked when she returned the list.

"One more stop." She headed to the galley. The cook turned out to be an old salt, who'd worked on steamboats and in hotels for years. She offered, "If you need mint, dill, parsley, chives..."

His eyes brightened. "Basil?"

"Sure do." She turned to her shadow. "You may show me to my plants."

"Missus, missus." The cabin boy waved from behind a stack of crates. "Deck passenger took sick."

If the illness was catching, the passenger must be quarantined. Now. "Another time, Brother Ross."

≈

September 10, 1853

Keeping track of people ought to be easy on a steamboat, but it was the next evening before Duncan saw Sister Sirrine again. Even standing still, watching the setting sun from the hurricane deck, she had an energy about her. He approached cautiously. She'd been none too pleased when he attempted to joke about the latrine yesterday. He cleared his throat, but she didn't hear him over the thumping engine and splashing paddle wheel. The ever-watchful Finn noticed and stood, his wagging tail alerting his mistress.

Sister Sirrine waved him closer and gestured toward the bluffs. "Eagles."

A wide-winged bird soared overhead. Another dove toward the river, talons extended, and snatched up a fish. Several more perched in the cottonwoods. Duncan quoted Isaiah: "'Those who wait on the Lord shall renew their strength and mount up with wings as eagles.'"

"'They shall run and not be weary, walk and not faint.'" Sister Sirrine finished the verse. "You're right—steamboat travel is restful. Easier than a wagon train. And the scenery is beautiful."

"I feared you preferred the city."

"I like clean air, forests, prairie." She pointed at a creek joining the Missouri. "Deer. I've seen beavers, a coyote, swallows, bats, turtles."

"I saw a skunk." He paused until she glanced at him. "In the mirror."

A shake of her head set her curls atremble. "Forgive me. Moving is a donnybrook."

"I agree with you about health." He exhaled and braced on the railing. "I lost my children to croup, infantile fever, and quinsy. And my wife to a house fire."

"I'm so sorry." Her warm palm touched his. She glanced at him, her eyes brimming with unshed tears, then turned back to the eagles. "Mine were taken by drowning, stillbirth, measles, parotitis, scarlatina."

He gave her hand a squeeze then slipped his away in case anyone watched. "When I attended the School of Faith, they said the Congregation would share the burdens and joys. None of the others in my quorum could make the trip and I didn't arrive in time to join the men building Preparation, so I'm helping with the move. If you'll allow, I'll share your burden for the health of our community. Let me know how I can be of service." Keziah was essential to the Congregation. If he assisted her, maybe they'd decide he was a necessary part of the group too.

Her head tipped and her eyes narrowed, as if she took his measure. She looked over his head and the corner of her mouth tucked as if she wavered between frowning and smiling. He held his breath until she finally nodded. Not a full partnership, but perhaps probation. He'd do his best.

September 16, 1853

Once Keziah had dressed the crew's wounds and convinced Rebecca Butts that river travel wouldn't make her seasick, she'd time to enjoy the scenery. The further west they went, the wilder the land became. Trees on the banks had been cut to fuel steamboats, allowing a view of golden prairie grass waving in the wind. An occasional hearty soul farmed the cleared land.

Keziah wasn't expecting much from Kanesville, or Council Bluffs as it was now called, so she wasn't disappointed at the jumble of wooden buildings. Absently scratching Finn's ears, she turned away from the town and faced west, toward the Lone Tree ferry landing in Nebraska Territory. A few wagon trails creased the grass, but she saw no other signs of human habitation.

"Praying again?" Christena wrapped an arm around her shoulders. "You're looking the wrong direction."

"Hundreds lost their lives there." Seven years ago, the Saints escaped violence at Nauvoo only to die of starvation and illness in a Nebraska territory encampment called Winter Quarters.

"I thank God you were spared."

Keziah glanced around, to make sure they were still alone, then whispered. "For whatever else he did, Charles Thompson kept us out of Winter Quarters."

"And polygamy in Salt Lake City." Christena shuddered.

The engine quieted and the boat bumped to a stop. Cheers rose from the deck and the shore. Omer tugged on his mother's elbow. "C'mon Mama! Let's go find Papa!"

Christena accompanied her son down the landing stage.

Keziah gathered her satchel and Finn, and followed. "'Remembering not the former things...'"

"Yes, Isaiah 43: 'Behold, God will do a new thing, make a way in the wilderness.' There's Hugh!" Christena ran to meet her husband. Her friend wore yet another new dress today. How many did she have? And when would Keziah have money for fabric and time to sew? She stuffed down her uncharitable thoughts. It wasn't Christena's fault their lives had turned out differently.

Men who'd been building Preparation gathered their wives and children into their arms. Too tall, too shaggy, too dark. No stubby fellow with thin hair complaining about noisy chickens, other people's poorly behaved children, and that only New York knew how to run a state. No Rufus. Her gloom turned to relief.

Outfitters, liveries, blacksmiths, and wagon makers lined a wide muddy street up the hill from the landing. On either side, cabins stood along narrow paths. Would any of the merchants remember the Saints who passed through? Perhaps friends had stayed in the area. Perhaps one who would take her in.

Finn had been sniffing the local dogs, when he raced to her side and gave a low growl.

"Sister Sirrine, no dawdling." Brother Butts snapped at her heels.

"I should see what the stores have for medicinal supplies and if there's a doctor in town."

"Absolutely not. This place is full of saloons and gambling dens. No place for Jehovah's Congregation. Now, load up." He marched away, grumbling about women and shopping.

"Killjoy," she muttered, then glanced around. Finn gave her a tongue-hanging-out grin, but no one else was close enough to hear her.

After a week gliding in the smooth steamboat, riding in a wagon seemed sure to break all the bones in a body and jolt one's teeth loose. They walked for comfort as well as to spare the horses their weight.

They left Council Bluffs and its reek of smoke and waste behind, heading north along the Missouri River. Keziah drew deep breaths, pulling the clean air deep into her lungs. Finn raced along the base of the bluff, stretching his legs after a week of being confined to the boat. He stopped to sniff, then stuck his head into a hole with a dirt pile around it.

"Finn!" She called him back. "Wake a badger, you'll lose your nose." He romped to her side.

The land opened to a wide valley with prairie on either side of their trail. No need to shop with all these plants. Sumac's deep red cones of drupes topped a thicket of brightly colored leaves. Keziah pulled out her knife and snipped off a few for her collecting bag. They'd make a lemony tea, er lemony *infusion*, to settle the stomach, ease breathing, soothe blisters, and could be used for a red dye.

Finn chased a black squirrel up a cottonwood. Keziah discovered a grapevine clinging to the trunk and filled her bag with bunches of dark fruit.

Brother Butts's wife dropped back from the group. Keziah always treated her kindly—after all, Rebecca had to live with Mr. High-and-Mighty. But after a week of their daughter Malinda's chatter, Keziah's patience was exhausted.

The woman glanced at the bluffs to their east and fiddled with the neckline of her dress. "Aren't you worried about getting lost?"

"River to the west, hills to the east, wagon trail in front of me, Finn by my side. No danger of getting lost." Keziah passed her a handful of grapes and hoped she'd take them to her family.

Rebecca rubbed the space between her eyebrows. "We're supposed to civilize the Lamanites, but I keep thinking of the Whitman massacre."

Keziah's heart skipped a beat. Six years ago in the Pacific Northwest, Indians had killed Dr. Whitman, his wife, and eleven other missionaries, then held captive fifty others. Keziah surveyed the empty hills and walked faster. "We haven't seen any Lamanites here."

"I hope we never do." Rebecca shivered. "The newspaper said the tribe near the Whitman mission suffered a measles outbreak and Indians died. They believed Dr. Whitman had poisoned them."

The sumac in her bag took on a blood-red hue. If a Lamanite needed a remedy, dare she give it to him? Would she be blamed if he died?

"What makes us think God will protect us when He didn't protect the Whitmans?" Rebecca picked at lace cuff of her sleeves. "Are Lamanites Gentiles or from the lost tribes of Israel? Angels protected Joseph Smith, so will they keep my husband from a hatchet in his head, keep my children from being taken as a slave? Or will I be tossed out for apostasy for even thinking of it?" She stopped, eyes filling with tears. "Will you pray?"

"You know I will." She couldn't do anything else against this danger. Keziah scanned the hills over her shoulder as they embraced. Would they see the Lamanites on the warpath? "Our Congregation's health and safety are always in my prayers."

Malinda called from the wagon train. "Mama, Sister Thompson needs you!"

"Here." Keziah handed off her collecting bag. "Have one of the children bring me another sack."

Pantalets flashing, ten-year-old Cecilia Hall galloped toward her with a canvas bag. "Sister Sirrine, let's go back to St. Louis. Mother said you'd rather be there."

Another hurting soul. "You don't like it here?"

"I miss Martha." A tear rolled down her freckled cheek.

"Your friend who lived next door."

"Everything's more fun with Martha. We'd make up songs and stories while we did chores. Now all I've got is a stinky brother and sisters too young to do anything."

"You could teach them."

"Huh. I want my friend."

"What about Malinda?"

"No, all she thinks about is boys."

"Boys and horses. How about Amelia?"

"She won't speak to me." Cecilia cried harder. "I want to go home."

"Let's give Iowa a chance." They had to stay. Brother Thompson had spent all their money to bring the Congregation here. And Mrs. Jackson saw God's will in this move. Keziah wrapped an arm around the girl, walking her north, trying to think of another girl close to Cecilia's age who needed a friend. Everyone was either four years older or four years younger, a lifetime to a ten-year-old. "Who else is ten? Moroni Winegar, Joseph Wilding..."

"...are boys. They play with each other, not with me."

"More families are coming. Let's pray for a friend for you." After sniffling and praying, Cecilia returned to the wagon.

A few miles of plant collecting passed before the next worrier joined her. Finn raced to greet Brother Ross. His blue denim shirt and trousers fit better than the brown clothes he'd worn in St. Louis. Had his wife made them for him? How long had he been a widower? "Hello, Finn, Sister. What do you think of this land?" He shortened his stride to keep pace with her shorter legs.

"It's different. The hills are steep, but they're not made of rocks like the bluffs along the lower Missouri. The soil is loose. If Preparation's like this, it will be easy to plant a garden." She handed him a few grapes.

"Thank you. Hmm, delicious." He gave her a glance, then pondered the fruit rolling between his fingers. "Brother Thompson announced we're to call him Father Ephraim, and adults may call each other by first names. I'd be honored if you'd call me Duncan."

She hoped the man didn't become overly attentive. With the way her life went, Rufus would show up to a Congregation bursting with rumors about her conduct. "And I am Keziah."

A straw hat shaded his blue eyes, but couldn't hide the worry. "I joined this group less than a year ago. You've been with Brother Thompson, er Father Ephraim, a while."

"Fifteen years."

"I'm still sorting out a few things." He paused for another grape. "So who is Baneemy?"

Now there's a loaded question. "They didn't explain it in your School of Faith in Ohio?"

"I might have missed the lesson."

"One of Joseph Smith's revelations mentioned God's servant Baneemy."

He stared into the distance. "So... Father Ephraim is Baneemy?"

He'd like the Congregation to think so. "Baneemy is the messenger, sent to prepare us to restore the Kingdom of Israel."

"Is Father Ephraim the successor to Joseph Smith?"

"Joseph Smith has no successor in the church. Anyway, we're not a church. We're a school."

"Does he mean Ephraim from the Bible, one of Joseph's sons?"

She nodded.

He let out a slow breath, adjusted his cap, and wiped his hands on his trousers. "I'm having a bit of a time wrapping my mind around all of this."

Keziah agreed, but she didn't know him well enough to say so. The first time she'd met him, he'd been with Brother Butts, who had the ear of Brother Thompson. Banished in St. Louis meant starvation, servitude. Banished in this empty land meant death. "I hope you'll have a chance to ask Brother Thompson, er Father Ephraim."

"Who am I to question God's servant? I came to naught farming, bookbinding, and running a dairy before I finally learned to make shoes. I've no knowledge of—"

"You've done all those things?" Astonished, she grinned. "Brother Ross, you're exactly what Preparation needs."

CHAPTER 4

September 18, 1853

'Twas a grand and glorious mission they were on, Duncan thought, to build the New Jerusalem. The Heavenly Father blessed them with clear skies. That night, the Congregation camped beside the Missouri. In the morning of the second day, they crossed a small river and followed it inland. Hugh Lytle wanted to call it Jordan, until they learned Lewis and Clark already named it Soldier. Their path beside the Missouri had been flat, but in this glen, the ground rose in gentle steps.

Late in the afternoon Father Ephraim called from the lead wagon. "Jehovah's Presbytery of Zion, welcome to Preparation. There it is, the Lord's House!"

Voices that had quieted in the heat of the day now rose in celebration. Finn howled. Keziah's chickens added to the commotion.

"Finally. I thought we'd never get here."

"Hooray!"

"Mama, I'm hungry." This last from five-year-old Fred Winegar.

A two-story frame house stood on a slight rise, sheltered from the north wind by a hill. Two completed log cabins sat next to it and a few partially-built ones behind them. Duncan quoted the Gospel of John, "'I go to prepare a place for you.'"

"I'll not be calling that a mansion." Keziah spared a glance from her constant search for plants. The house lacked windows, doors, and paint. Much of the roof remained to be shingled. "Preparation is far from prepared."

"Now, Sister, if all were complete, we'd have naught to do in the School of Work." Duncan grinned. There was plenty of work for all.

She scanned the tall grass beside the road and the trees on the hills, all tinted with gold. "The question is how will we do it all before winter?"

"With God's help." He pointed to the plant atop her basket. "Bonny flower you've found."

"Goldenrod. Useful for bee stings, burns, fevers. Makes a calming infusion." She rolled the roots between her fingers, studying the dirt, then turned to him with a smile. "If we can keep from fouling the land, we'll have a grand garden."

Leo Thompson waved his shoes, showing holes in both soles. "Mama, can we stop walking now?"

"And I'm looking forward to using my shoemaker's tools." Duncan scooped up the lad and sat him on his shoulders. "'Make a joyful noise unto the Lord, all ye—'" No one else was singing. "Sorry. Do you not know the song?"

Hugh Lytle turned from leading his wagon. "Psalm 100. Haven't heard it in a while. Just the song for today." He added his voice and the whole group joined in.

Departing St. Louis was a kerfuffle, but nothing matched the chaos of arriving at Preparation. As soon as Duncan set Leo on his feet, he knocked over a stack of wood shingles. Adults shouted instructions and questions. Piles grew as wagons unloaded. Finn and a group of lads chased a runaway pig.

Here in Preparation, Duncan hoped for more opportunity to observe Father Ephraim outside of the Sunday teachings, but the man went upstairs as soon as they arrived. Duncan's eye was drawn to Keziah. In spite of the fifty-five mile trek from Council Bluffs, her energy increased. Satchel in hand, she sought out the lads who'd been serving as carpenters, removing a splinter from an eye, dressing blistered hands, and cleaning a cut from a saw.

"Why isn't the House finished?" Brother Butts yelled at the young workers. "Where are the carpenters you were supposed to hire? What have you been doing all this time?"

Eliza Cobb plopped onto the grass, telling her husband, "I can't walk another step. You'll have to carry me."

"Sister Sirrine, the Thompson's milk cow is eating your plants," Cecilia yelled.

"Make her stop," Keziah said.

Cecilia's eyes widened. "She's bigger than me."

"But nowhere near as smart." Keziah untied the animal from the Thompson's wagon, led her to a patch of grass with a decent-sized tree, and secured her.

Now who needed help? Christena Lytle struggled to pull a trunk off the wagon. Duncan started toward her.

"Put it back," Hugh told his wife. "We're not staying."

Christena blanched and stared open-mouthed at him. "What? Where would you have us go?"

"We have our own cabin." He pointed behind the House.

She sagged against the wagon. "Thank the Lord."

So who got the other cabin? And where would Duncan and the rest of the Congregation sleep?

"You cannot expect me to share that tiny cabin with my brother, his wife, and all our children," Eliza Cobb howled to her husband, drawing the attention of the entire Congregation. "You said I'd have a house."

Orrin Butts stood over his sister, showing her a paper, and the family resemblance was clear. If Eliza had mutton-chop whiskers, they'd be identical. "We'll share until our houses are built. Our older children will stay in the Lord's House."

One of the men announced, "Supper's almost ready. Bring bowls and spoons."

Leo started up the ladder left by the men who'd been shingling. Duncan snagged him, "And where might you be going, laddie?"

"Looking for the latrine."

"It's not up there and you know it." With Leo's squirmy hand in his, they circled the house twice without finding it, but they did find Keziah watering her chickens.

"We can't find the latrine," Leo shouted.

"But we found a place for one." Duncan pointed to a bush behind the House.

Keziah marched up to one of the young men who'd been roofing and grabbed his arm. "Nels Turner."

"Yes, Sister." He spit on the ground.

"Keep *that* up and Preparation will be as foul with illness as St. Louis and Nauvoo. You're old enough to remember cholera." Keziah in action was a force to be reckoned with. "Now, where is the latrine?"

"We've been..." The lad scuffed his brogan in the dirt, then shot a glance toward a thick patch of tall grass. "Haven't..."

"Grab a shovel," Keziah commanded and finally let go of the lad.

"But Sister, it's supper time." He nodded at the cauldron over the fire.

"Be quick, then." She sent him to dig a trench behind a bush. Duncan agreed to start work on a more permanent outhouse in the morning. "Now let's see if anyone remembered to wash hands before eating."

"Yes, Sister, we knew you were coming so we set out soap and water. We use the spring for drinking and cooking." Another young carpenter pointed to the creek burbling past the house. "And the Soldier River water for bathing and laundry."

Strong odors from the other men indicated few had taken advantage of the opportunity.

"Keeping our drinking water safe. Well done." Keziah marched into the house. The ground floor had one large center room and two small rooms on either side. Adults milled about and chatted, while their children ran and yelled. She glanced over her shoulder at Duncan, all the permission he needed.

He rapped a battledore against a laundry boiler, making enough racket to silence the crowd. "Please attend to Sister Sirrine."

With the ease of one used to herding cats, she sent the Congregation outside to scrub their hands. Sister Thompson led the parade, but instead of using the opportunity to eat first, she took control of the soup ladle, then nodded to her husband. Brother Thompson, er Father Ephraim, gave the blessing, then they settled onto the grass for their first meal in their Preparation.

Duncan filled his bowl. The flock had divided into families. Where should he sit? He didn't want to intrude. From the corner of his eye, he saw Sister Sirrine nudge her nephew.

"Brother Ross!" Omer called. "Sit with us."

Duncan sat beside the lad. "How's the stew?"

"What's this?" He picked out a chunk.

"And here I thought a fast-growing boy wouldn't slow down to taste his food."

"It's venison, deer meat," Sister Lytle told her son, then explained to Duncan, "He's not had it, living in St. Louis most of his life."

Finn took the opportunity to slurp the meat from Omer's fingers, earning a chuckle from the boy.

Brother Butts circled through the crowd, consulting penciled notes on newsprint. "The Lytle family will be in cabin two." Hugh nodded. "Brother Duncan, you're here in the Lord's House, in the west room with the other single men. Sister Sirrine, you're with the other single women." He nodded toward the east room.

She raised her chin. "You've news of Rufus's death, then?"

"Nothing of the sort." The man scowled at Finn. "Living in the House, you won't be needing that mongrel for protection. One of the other families can take him."

"The carpenters have seen coyotes and a bobcat. Finn needs to guard the chickens." She spoke with a slow, firm tone. "The wrong amount or wrong mixture of herbs can worsen illness. I need a locked room to store and prepare my remedies, a fenced yard for a herb garden, and a hen house."

"Sister Thompson plans a kitchen garden. And chicken dinner tomorrow will solve the poultry problem."

Hugh stood, arms crossed. "You kill all the chickens, what will we do for eggs?"

Christena joined him. "You won't mind if the herbs for your piles remedy are used up in the soup pot, then?"

Orrin scowled and pointed at Keziah. "We have no time to indulge your fancies." He stomped to the next family.

Duncan glanced around the lawn. The entire Congregation had seen the skirmish, had seen how unreasonable Butts was. The question was...did Father Ephraim? Butts seemed to be his right hand man. Did Ephraim approve of this bullying? Where was the Chief Steward?

Keziah whispered, "If I have to live with his daughter..."

"Perhaps he thinks you're a steadying influence." Hugh wiped his bowl with his biscuit.

"I can't say the sky is blue without him disagreeing." She groaned. "I suspect he asks her to spy on me."

Christena wiped her hands. "Malinda's still wanting a love potion?"

"Chasing every creature in trousers." Keziah peered through her fingers at Hugh. "How big is your cabin?"

He shook his head. "We don't have room for you. Job and Marcia Barnum are staying in our second bedroom while their house is being finished, and Omer's in the loft."

Duncan should stand up to Butts, like the Lytles did. He raised a chunk of venison on his spoon. "No doubt this wasn't the last deer in the area. I'll help you build a fence."

"Thank you." Keziah sent a worried glance toward the wagon carrying her herbs. "Finn and I will sleep under the wagon, keep the deer away from the plants."

Brother Butts had circled to a family behind them. "Such unseemly behavior is not allowed, Sister Sirrine."

Her eyebrows raised. "We all slept outside last night. Was that unseemly?"

"I'll guard the herbs," Duncan said. Sleeping outside would be better than being stuffed in, cheek by jowl, with unwashed lads. He glanced at Keziah. Had he overstepped?

"Very well, Duncan." Brother Butts noticed Keziah had finished her meal. He flapped his hands at her. "Done eating? Go help Malinda wash dishes."

"Not tonight. I'm tending the sore feet of those who walked from Council Bluffs." She raised her chin, managing to look down her nose at the taller man. "Find someone who rode."

Duncan choked back a laugh. The only one who'd ridden the entire way was Orrin Butts.

In the gloaming of their first day in Preparation, the flicker of a lantern drew Duncan to the bank of the Soldier River. Keziah's last patient dried her feet and donned her shoes. "Much better. Bless you, Keziah."

"Try to prop your feet up tonight, Eunice."

"If I can stay awake long enough." The young woman wished Duncan a good night as she passed by.

Finn wagged his tail and herded Duncan to the edge of the water.

"Next." Keziah beckoned him toward her, then refilled the basin. "And how are you still awake, busy as you've been?"

"'Tis better to catch problems small. Slip off your brogans. Did you not bring clean socks?"

"My feet are fine. I'm here—"

"Fine feet? I'll be judging that."

Being too tired to argue, he sat and slipped off his shoes and socks. "And who's washing your feet, then?" Ach, no. He glanced around to make sure they weren't overheard. He intended respect and concern, not flirting.

"I washed mine earlier." She said, all business, as she set his feet into the basin.

"Ahh..." The cool water eased not only his feet, but his whole body. His eyes closed and his toes wiggled. "You'll have me forgetting what I came to tell you." Strong yet gentle fingers worked their way down his heels, arches, and toes. "Pop me in the oven and call me a bread loaf."

Keziah chuckled, a low, musical sound. "Fine feet indeed."

"Ahh…" If only he'd known how this felt, he would have washed his wife Emily's feet every night of her short life, and hope she'd do the same for him.

"All done," Keziah said.

Duncan came back to his senses. He used the cuff of his socks to dry off. "I found a place for you."

"Did you now?" She emptied the basin, grabbed her lantern and valise, and marched up the riverbank. "Show me."

Finn followed and Duncan scrambled into his brogans. "Closer to the Lord's House, past the hedge."

She marched around the bushes, identifying chokecherry, dogwood, and gooseberry, then entered an open field. "The bushes can shade the chicken coop. A gentle slope, good drainage, close to the creek. If you dig post holes, I'll fence it. The kitchen garden can wait until spring."

Duncan caught up to her and helped carry her valise and basin. His choice for the garden met Keziah's approval. Now, for a place to live. "Behind you is an unfinished cabin. It started as a stable, then they realized it was too small. I'm thinking it's the right size for a bothy."

"A gardener's cottage? Aye." The courses of logs rose about six foot high and hadn't been chinked. If Keziah didn't claim it, it would be dismantled for another family's cabin. She stepped inside, stretching her arms to measure the space. "There's only me and Finn."

"And hundreds of plants." He leaned on the window opening, imagining the walls with shelves full of remedies, and drying racks hung overhead. His heart warmed in the glow of her appreciation.

She spun in a circle, graceful as a dancer. "Soon as planting's done, I'll start working on it. Build a roof and a porch. It'll need a door with a lock, windows, and a stove for winter. It'll be…" Her smile faded as a low rumble came from her dog's throat. Finn had a good temperament, only showing his teeth at Orrin Butts.

That very man filled the doorway. He dismissed Duncan with a glare, then fixed his wrath on Keziah. "Sister Sirrine, as a member of this Congregation, you cannot flit about whenever you take a notion, disrupting the rest we all badly need."

"I'm surprised you're not already asleep." She sashayed past him and headed for the House.

Duncan followed, wondering what to say to defuse the quarrel.

Orrin trod after them. "And you certainly can't expect to claim that space when other families are waiting for living quarters."

"Which family do you have in mind? The Winegar family with their six children? Stack them like firewood, will you? The Halls also have six. Or perhaps a family with only four children... like the Thompsons? I'll speak with them in the morning." She took her satchel and basin, entered the House with Finn, and headed to the east room.

"You will not bother Father Ephraim," he called after her.

Adults sorted through belongings in search of bedding. Children had piled in a corner, snoozing like pups. No one waited on Keziah before turning in.

Rebecca Butts spotted her husband and cried. "We have no pillows. Not a one. How am I supposed to sleep without a pillow?"

Duncan found his bedroll and stretched out under the wagon filled with plants. *Who will win the battle of the bothy?* Perhaps he should stay out of the fray and not risk earning the wrath of Father Ephraim. No, he chuckled, Orrin was hopelessly outgunned. Duncan needed a good sleep tonight, since tomorrow he'd be fencing a herb garden and building a bothy...after he finished the latrines.

October 11, 1853

Keziah set the serving bowl on the table in front of Charles Perrin and his three boys. "Where's Hannah?"

"Her time." Charles portioned out the venison stew to his sons.

"We're going to sleep in the Lord's House tonight since Mama's having a baby," the youngest told her. "She wants a girl."

"Don't know why." The middle grabbed his bowl. "You cry like a girl all the time."

"Stop it." The oldest pushed the two apart. "You're gonna miss supper again."

Keziah pulled off her apron. "I'll go."

"Christena's seeing to her." Charles motioned toward the empty chair at the end of the table. "Sit and eat, Sister. You've got plenty of time." He pointed to his boys. "Two days, day and a half, all day."

Keziah gulped a few bites of supper. She didn't want any baby, much less Preparation's first, to arrive unattended. She'd been alone when her first...no. No mucking about in sadness when there's a baby ready to be born. After a detour for her satchel, she hurried through the sunset glow to the Perrin's cabin, trying to remember the prayer Mrs. Jackson had taught her. Nerves had her forgetting most of it. "Lord, have mercy on me... guide me. Amen."

The Perrins had been living in Council Bluffs before moving to Preparation, so Keziah didn't know Hannah well. The air inside smelled of sweaty boys, but not of sickness or blood.

Lodema Winegar, a mother of six healthy children, walked Hannah across the dirt floor. "She's doing well. Pains are a few minutes apart."

"Here's another." Hannah's brown eyes closed in concentration. From practicality, necessity, or both, she wore an old gown. Her fawn-colored hair hung down her back in a braid.

"Towels and rags on the bed. Water's boiling." Christena had the supplies ready. "Since you're here, shall I go eat?"

"Yes. Thank you, dear friend."

The pain eased and Hannah asked Keziah, "Who did you train with?"

"Mrs. Jackson, a midwife in St. Louis."

"Those old slave women really know their birthing." Eliza Cobb stepped into the cabin, ready to stir up trouble.

Keziah glanced at Hannah, trying to gauge her reaction. "Mrs. Jackson is free. Father Ephraim allowed me to train with her since she delivered Catherine's children."

"Good enough." Hannah gave her a wink. "Squatting works best for me."

"Then that's what we'll do." Keziah gave her a cup of water. "Are you a gardener?" Squatting to tend plants stretched the hips for childbirth.

"Sure am. Sorry to leave my garden behind in Council Bluffs. Yours is off to a good start."

"Thanks to our Heavenly Father for the good dirt."

Failing to get a rise out of anyone, Eliza slipped out. Two other experienced mothers, Priscilla Lewis and Mary DeForest, arrived to relieve Lodema.

Priscilla added more water to the pan on the stove. "Is it true a woman in Winter Quarters had her baby in a chamber pot?"

"Would have been the cleanest place around." Mary held onto Hannah through another pang. "What was the name of the midwife in Nauvoo and Winter Quarters?"

"Mother Patty Sessions. I met her on the trail west from Nauvoo. So experienced. Wish I could have trained with her." Keziah had been busy trying to keep her own baby alive.

"Hard-working," Priscilla helped walk Hannah across the cabin. "Delivering babies, tending the sick, always knitting or sewing."

"Especially for Joseph Smith." Mary fluttered her hands. "She liked to hobnob with the Twelve."

"Then her husband married the laziest woman alive. What was her name?" Priscilla rubbed Hannah's back as she groaned.

"Rosilla." Mary snorted. "We camped near them when we crossed Iowa. What a nightmare. She'd wander about, couldn't be bothered to collect firewood, cook a meal, or help with laundry. You were there, Keziah."

Keziah scrubbed her hands. "Rosilla would fill Brother Sessions's ears with lies, then rebuke Patty and disappear. Patty was left to drive the wagon, hunt for their missing cow, bind up the injured, set up their tent, and sleep alone." The confident midwife had been reduced to tears. As difficult as Rufus was, at least he hadn't followed Mormon leadership into polygamy.

"Makes no sense. If Brother Sessions had set Patty aside, all the work would have fallen to useless Rosilla." Mary rubbed Hannah's back.

"Brother Sessions never had a lick of sense. So what happened to Rosilla?" Priscilla asked. "Did she learn to pull in the traces or become Brigham Young's forty-third wife?"

"She left. Far as I know, back to Illinois," Mary said. "That was the week Marcia Barnum made venison stew for everyone. I found poor Keziah under her wagon, her baby only a day old, and realized Rufus had eaten her portion. Marcia scraped the bottom of the pot with a biscuit for Keziah."

Her gut clenched. She wanted to forget that awful night. The next day Rufus had turned their wagon north, leaving their friends and the rest of the westbound Mormons behind, to join James Strang in Wisconsin. And Keziah began to wonder if Rufus meant to kill her.

"Dear friend." Priscilla gave Keziah a hug. "I'm sorry. We shouldn't have brought up those sad times."

Keziah shook off the anguish and dried her hands. "We're blessed to live in a safe community, free from polygamy and persecution. And blessed to celebrate Preparation's first baby."

Hannah gave her a grateful nod. The lines in her face and tension in her shoulders had increased with each pain. "I'm ready."

Priscilla laid a towel on the floor. Hannah held onto the bed's footboard and sat on her haunches. Outside, the women of Preparation sang hymns. Inside the cabin, they cheered Hannah with encouraging words. After a reasonable bit of fussing, fuming, and vowing this was the last time, Hannah gave a big push and the baby slid into Keziah's waiting hands.

Over his hearty cries, Keziah told Hannah, "You have a beautiful baby boy."

"Another boy." Hannah sighed. "Won't have to sew new clothes."

The women burst out laughing. No matter how sturdy the fabric, no clothes survived to be handed down to a fourth boy. The baby howled his objections as Priscilla washed him. "He wants to know what you're naming him."

"David Everett."

Whether learning his name, the end of the bath, or fatigue from his busy day, little David quieted and drifted off to sleep.

"Could you eat?" Keziah asked as she helped Hannah wash, then lie down.

"I'd like a peach pie and a cup of coffee." Hannah grinned.

"How about raspberry infusion and a biscuit with gooseberry jam?" Mary handed her a mug and a plate.

"Close enough."

Keziah stood, stretched her back, and looked around the circle of women tending mother and child. The little community of Preparation had come together with joy. *Thank you, Heavenly Father, for this new member of the Congregation. May we grow in Your grace and peace.*

CHAPTER 5

October 1853

Duncan watched Father Ephraim's six-year-old Ida race from the House, braids flying in the sun. She waved. "Brother Ross, Sister Sirrine has need of you."

Duncan set the rafter onto the ridgepole, then climbed off the roof of the sod house, thinking Keziah would be much more agile on the ladder. He followed the girl as she bounded through the grass like a white-tail deer. Another week or so and the Congregation will have worn footpaths, but for now, the big bluestem made for wonderful games of hide-and-seek.

"Over here," Keziah called from the south side of the House. Unafraid of grime, putrid odors, or gnarled toenails, she scrubbed Luther Cottingham's bare foot. "He's soaked his heel daily in an oak bark decoction and I've dressed the wound with honey, but it keeps opening up. Is there a way to fix his boot so it won't rub?" She handed the brogan to him.

Duncan turned the heavy boot over. The man needed a larger size, but no chance he'd get back to St. Louis for another pair. Small chance a tracing of Luther's foot sent with the next person who went to Council Bluffs would bring new brogans before winter. "Aye. Stretching will be slow, seeing as how the thick leather doesn't have much give. Cutting a hole over the heel would relieve the pressure, but leave you cold and wet all winter."

Luther snatched his boot back. "As much as I paid, you'll not be cutting it."

"Agreed. Do you have another pair of boots, even an old pair of slippers, you could wear while your boot is stretching?"

"In my trunk."

Duncan entered the House, past a group of women discussing methods of cooking venison and the newly built tables and benches, to the single men's room. The trunk reeked, the result of the man's aversion to soap and water. Duncan found a worn pair of brogans, then grabbed his shoemaker's kit.

"These should be loose enough to let your foot heal," he said as he returned, eager to show the skill he brought to the Congregation. "I'll put another sole on with hobnails for grip and replace the laces." Duncan had thought he was too old to blush, but Keziah's nod of approval had his face heating.

Hoofbeats echoed to their south.

"Lamanites!" Luther hissed, but he couldn't run while Keziah wrapped his foot.

Duncan squinted over Keziah's head, curious to see if the Indians here resembled those he'd seen in Ohio and St. Louis. Instead of Lamanites, 'twas Malinda Butts and her older brother Dennis racing a pair of brown geldings on the flats beside the Soldier River.

"Aren't those the carthorses what brought us up from Council Bluffs?" Luther tugged on his beard, releasing a cloud of sawdust and old crumbs.

"I wouldn't have thought they'd run so fast." Holding Luther's ankle, Keziah stood to watch.

Even with feet in the stirrups, Dennis clung to the pommel and bounced like a sack of potatoes as his horse trotted along. Malinda bent over her horse's neck, skirts tucked around legs holding fast, and coaxed the heavy beast into a gallop. After about a quarter mile, Malinda passed a lad who dropped a white flag. She'd won by six lengths.

Luther propped his sore foot on his other knee to keep the bandage clean. "She weighs less than her brother, which helps, but that girl *knows* how to ride."

Such skill as Malinda's wouldn't be appreciated by her father. Sure enough, footsteps thundered downstairs and out the front door. "Get back here right now, you two louts!" yelled Orrin Butts. "I'll tan your hides so you never sit on a saddle again."

Even from a distance, Dennis seemed shame-faced.

Malinda was a different story. She waved and headed for the paddock. "Sorry, Father, got to walk and water the horses."

Luther burst out laughing. "You taught her well, Brother Orrin."

Orrin turned to his audience, his face red with impending explosion.

"Take a breath," Keziah said in an even tone. "And be thankful your children live."

The spoilsport had a wife and three children, all healthy. Yet he was too busy trying to keep other people under his thumb to enjoy his own life. Orrin glowered at each of them, then spat on the ground and stomped off to the paddock.

"Horse race and theater." Luther gave his knee a slap. "Who knew Preparation would be so fun?"

October 1853

A loud thump followed by even louder curses shook the house. Keziah put the pan to soak and hurried upstairs to tend whoever was injured. In the printing office, a red-faced Brother Butts swore and swung a broom at Leo Thompson.

"Out!" the man yelled. "We're behind as it is without you running amuck, destroying everything in your path." He shook the broom at Keziah. "Look what he did." A letter case sat upside down on the floor, thousands of pieces of lead type scattered across the floor.

"Brother Butts, keep your tongue from sin."

The child shot from the printing office. Keziah snagged him, nearly wrenching her shoulder from its socket. "Leo, you made a mess. Clean it up."

"Absolutely not. He can't tell one letter from another. You keep him." Brother Butts slammed the door and turned the lock.

Leo's mother was in the other room caring for her little ones; he'd escape her quick as a jackrabbit. His father had gone to the hills to pray with Baneemy or receive the Keys to the Kingdom or another important work. The rest of the men had gone duck hunting or cutting timber. Christena had already taken her turn with Leo this week; he'd nearly set her cabin on fire. Keziah glanced down at her small charge. He blinked up with wide eyes, his hair rising into a cowlick. How could anyone look so innocent and be so much trouble?

His lower lip drooped. "I want to see how it worked."

"Your father told you to stay out of the printing office." Keziah sighed, battling exhaustion. It had been a busy week of tending sore feet, trying to ignore Malinda's chatter, hurrying to plant her garden before frost, and delivering Preparation's first baby. *Thank you, heavenly Father, for bringing new life to Preparation. May he grow up a wee bit less active than this spalpeen.*

Leo had already demonstrated ironstone wasn't nearly as strong as its name implied, so no dish wiping. "You will help me dry the cutlery." Only the spoons and forks. The Lord knew what havoc he'd wreck with a knife. "First, wash your hands."

Scrubbing with lye soap peeled away layers of muck down to clean skin. She sat the four-year-old at the table with a towel and the utensils, then raced to finish the pans before he lost interest and made a run for it.

"I do so know my letters. See?" He had spelled out his name with forks. "Brother Ross taught me."

Sure and a tribute to Duncan's patience. "Well done!" She sat on the bench beside Leo and pulled a length of string from her apron pocket. "But the tricky thing about type is the letters are backwards. It looks likes a 'b,' but it's actually a 'd.'" She flipped the string over.

He pivoted the letter. "Or it might be a 'p,' no, it's a '9.'" Letters are tricky! Does Brother Butts know? I'd better tell him." He bolted for the print shop.

Keziah caught him and handed him two pails. "He knows. Time to fetch water for the chickens." They stepped out into a sunny day. A gentle wind stirred the golden grass, bringing with it the scents of drying leaves and woodsmoke. They used the well sweep, a lever and pivot, Duncan had built to haul water from the middle of the creek and fill their buckets.

"Why don't chickens get their own water by themselves?"

"They'd fall in the river."

"Can chickens swim?" His eyebrows twitched as he plotted mayhem.

"Yes, but if you put them in the river, they'll float away and we won't have any eggs." He pondered as they filled their buckets, tempted by the adventure of watching a chicken swim. "Those scones you're so fond of require eggs," she told him, trying to tip his decision toward the safety of the hens.

He lifted the full bucket with a grunt. "Water is heavy. Why is it downhill to the river and uphill to the house?"

"Why do you think?" she asked, taking the moment of silence to survey Preparation. The Lord's House and all four cabins had freshly whitewashed outhouses. Women hung out laundry, and children played hide and seek in the tall grass.

"I know." Leo crowed. "Because the water would spill out of the river and into our house and we'd float away."

"Right you are."

Finn had been guarding the hens, but deserted his post when he spotted Leo.

"Chickens make a mess of their water, so first we have to empty their pans."

The boy raced ahead. All of the hens saw him coming and headed for the tall grass, except the leghorn pullet, Keziah's payment for bringing Millard Fillmore Henderson into the world. She stretched her wings and screeched. Leo reared back and tossed the water in her face, which didn't improve her mood at all. She expressed her disapproval with flapping of wings and ear-splitting squawks, inciting the rest to riot. Keziah grabbed the boy and hauled him away from the sharp-beaked mob.

"You were told—"

Leo stopped squirming and jumped behind her. "Lamanites."

"Did you not listen to your father last Sunday? Those who lie—"

He wasn't lying. Two men watched from a dozen feet away. Indians. Keziah's head tingled in readiness for scalping. They wore deerskins decorated with fur. The taller had shaved the sides of his head, then pulled the remaining hair to the crown of his head. His low brow and straight mouth gave him a disapproving expression, but Keziah couldn't tell if his frown was directed toward her or Leo. Probably both. The other man had a full head of hair gathered in braids behind each ear. His mouth quirked in a smile. He nodded at Leo. "Boys."

"You speak English?" Her skin prickled with released tension.

The man nodded.

"Papa says Lamanites need to stop begging—"

Keziah covered the boy's mouth with her palm. "Welcome. Please come with me and I'll introduce you to—"

"Papa!" Leo wriggled away and ran to his father.

Keziah had never been so glad to see Father Ephraim. He must have spotted the visitors from the hilltop. He hurried through the grass, ignoring the child clamped to his leg, which made both men grin. He shook hands with the guests. "Welcome to Preparation."

Ephraim walked the Lamanites to the Lord's House. The visitors moved easily, without disturbing the grass. They were tall and lean, and, to Keziah's relief, carried nothing in their long-boned hands. Where was the rest of their tribe? Her gaze skimmed the golden grass stretching in all directions. No more Lamanites showed themselves...and neither did any of Preparation's women and children. The only sound was the distant chop-chop of Amos Chase and his crew cutting timber.

As Keziah followed the men inside, Finn raced up. His nose quivered at the new scents of the Lamanites. When they reached the steps, she told him, "Sit."

The group assembled in the printing office. Brother Butts glowered from the table where he sorted type. He mustered up a smile for their guests, then closed the door in Keziah's face.

Can't keep out a woman carrying food.

Keziah returned with chokecherry scones and cups of rosemary infusion, and set the tray on the desk. She retreated to the hall, leaving the door open a fraction of an inch.

"...selected a suitable place on the frontier, near you Lamanites, for a door of entrance into the land of Ephraim, and a place of Preparation to enter therein, to establish schools among the Indian tribes of America, to enlighten and civilize you, to teach you the arts of agriculture and science that you may be redeemed from poverty, degradation, and starvation." Father Ephraim was in full teaching mode, complete with gestures and pacing. The Indians ate the food and watched him. "When the Book of Mormon is taught among you, it will bring the Lamanites to a knowledge of their fathers, whereby you may know that the work of the Father has commenced for the restoration of Israel. Then you shall begin to be purified, and in a few generations be a pure and delightsome people. The Gentiles will have no more power over you, and you Lamanites will build the New Jerusalem."

Finally Father Ephraim took a breath and the one with braids spoke. "We are not Lamanites. We are--" The word he said sounded like u-MAHN-hahn. "We don't want to farm. We want to trade venison for corn and fabric."

Butts noticed Keziah and closed the door. From the hall, she listened to negotiations exposing the poverty of Preparation. The Indians left with two bags of corn and the latest issue of *Zion's Harbinger*.

Keziah went into the office for the tray. "What did they say about Rufus?"

Brother Butts scowled. "We have more important concerns."

He hadn't asked, the lazy wretch. Accompanied by Finn, she dashed out the door and caught up with the men at the river. "Please... sirs."

They stood, relaxed but not fidgeting, as Finn sniffed their leggings and Keziah caught her breath. Close up, she noticed their smooth complexions. Their skin shone unmarked by the scourge of smallpox and nearly as dark as walnut.

"Have you seen a man, about my height, heavier, thin hair, round nose? His name is Rufus Sirrine. He came here three years ago, as a missionary."

They shook their heads, then conferred in their own language.

"Ask one who knows many," said the man with one braid. "Charles Larpenteur."

"Mr. Larpenteur, the fur trader? I met him in St. Louis. He's here?"

"North over the hill, then west." He turned his head, indicating the correct direction with his chin. "House at bottom of hill, before small river. Half-day walk."

"The man you seek, he is family?"

"Husband."

Other man said, "We pray he will return."

"You pray?" The Indians continued to surprise her. "Are you Christian?"

"We know Jesus." He glanced back at the Lord's House. "We do not know Baneemy."

CHAPTER 6

Early November 1853

"Duncan Ross," Father Ephraim's voice rang out over the hubbub of breakfast. He stood on the last step and scanned the room, his gaze landing on the oldest Winegar son next. "And Edward. When you two finish breakfast, meet me in the printing office.

Duncan nearly choked on his eggs as queasiness rippled through him. What had he done? None of the other congregants met his gaze. He tucked his biscuit into his pocket, then added his plate to the pile of dirty dishes and thanked Malinda. The girl looked up from the bucket of soapy water and scowled as if personally offended. Young Edward's contribution to the pile earned a fluttering of eyelashes and a syrupy, "Good morning."

At twenty, Edward had yet to grow into his hooked nose. He was a quiet lad, not inclined to say anything as they climbed to the gallows, er, office at the top of the stairs. From his time working as a bookbinder, Duncan recognized the Washington printing press. Dennis Butts sat at table by the window, setting type. Stacks of newspapers covered the floor. Maybe he could work into their good graces by building shelves for them.

Father Ephraim sat behind his desk, Orrin Butts at his side.

"Sister Sirrine would like to visit fur trader Charles Larpenteur, one of our nearest neighbors. You will accompany her."

So he wasn't in trouble. And he got to spend the day with Keziah. The tension in his shoulders eased and he took a full breath.

"Fool's errand." Butts stood, meaty hands on his wide hips. "Waste of time to traipse all over the hills getting lost, wearing out horses, getting chased by bears."

"Isaac Ashton's lived hereabouts five years and seen no bears," Edward said. "But I'll bring my rifle."

Father Ephraim pointed to the map on his desk. "From what the Lamanities told her, sounds like his house may be around here."

"As if you can trust Lamanites," Orrin muttered.

Duncan studied the map. A few lines on paper didn't convey the ruggedness of the wilderness. "I've a compass and a pistol."

"Sister hopes to hear word of her husband." Father Ephraim glanced up at them, his eyes full of sorrow. Were he and Rufus friends?

Orrin grunted. "His fate is in God's hands." And like Pontius Pilate, Orrin washed his hands of this search party.

"We go with God." Once again Keziah had prevailed against Orrin Butts. Munching on his biscuit, Duncan followed Edward to the paddock.

Isaac Swett, one of the laddies, leaned on a pitchfork. "You here to help?"

"No." Edward frowned at the mares and geldings. "We need three good mounts."

"Orrin said no one's taking a horse out 'less he say so." The boy held the pitchfork the way a soldier holds a pike. His pose of authority was marred by fact the pitchfork was taller than him and probably weighed more too.

"We're on an errand for Father Ephraim," Duncan said.

"We'll just see about that." Isaac stabbed the hay fork into the stack and stomped to the house.

"Do you know any of these horses?" Edward rubbed his wisps of chin hair. "I've been bit and kicked, and don't care to repeat the experience."

"The bay gelding with one white sock and the other with the blaze pulled our wagon here." Keziah Sirrine emerged from the stable with three bridles over her shoulder and climbed through the fence. "Who wants to go?" she asked, clicking her tongue and holding out a carrot. Several heads lifted. A chestnut mare was the first to her hand, snatching more than her fair share.

With such an example of energy and courage shaming them into action, Duncan and Edward joined her in the paddock, snagging the two geldings. Duncan saddled Keziah's horse as she put the bridle on. Edward tangled the bridle with the halter. The horse decided he'd had enough nonsense and danced away.

Keziah handed the lad a carrot. "Call to him."

"I'm not good with horses."

"You'll learn." She made the clicking sound again and the horse wandered back to her. "He can't see you if you're directly in front of him, so stand to the side. Let him smell you. Touch his face, neck, ears." Keziah talked him through the bridle, then the saddle as Duncan tacked the mare.

Edward finished with a relieved sigh, "You know a lot about horses, Sister."

"My husband had a freighting business."

"You harnessed draft horses?" Duncan tried to imagine this wee woman hefting a collar over the great head of a draft horse. Such strength.

She hitched her skirt and swung into the saddle without help. "Whatever needs to be done." Her hard life hadn't left her other options.

The two men followed her out, Edward on the other gelding, and Duncan on the tall mare.

"No dawdling!" Isaac yelled as they passed the house. "You're to help with haying when you get back. Orrin says."

No edict from a stern taskmaster could ruin this beautiful day. The sun warmed their backs and tinted the grass gold and deep red. The view at the crest showed at least four lines of hills beyond. Not a cloud or line of smoke marred the sky. A recent frost had banished the mosquitoes and flies. God blessed them again.

"Where's Finn today?" Duncan asked, enjoying the easy gait of the chestnut.

"Guarding the hen house." Keziah adjusted her skirts to cover the loose breeks she wore beneath them. Instead of the useless ruffles sold by milliners, she wore a dark hat with a brim wide enough to shade her eyes. A curl escaped behind her ear. A picture of practicality and femininity. "No doubt a dog or two guards his house. Mediating a fight isn't a good way to start a conversation."

The mare insisted on taking the lead, passing the geldings at the first wide place. "So you know this man, then?"

"We crossed paths in St. Louis," she said, keeping her own counsel about her search for her husband. Keziah rode with confidence, scanning the slopes on either side of the ridge. Wind had blown the leaves off the branches, baring the shape of the glens. She pointed out a cottonwood. "Looks like a bee tree. Help me remember."

"Honey on biscuits." Edward hummed.

"I could use beeswax for shoemaking, to dip the awl in. And there's a birch tree; good source of pegs." He noted the location. "I'll build a hive near your herb garden. Good winter project." They rode in silence for a moment, then Duncan thought of a mystery he'd been pondering. "The Congregation has a few young men adrift without kin. Do either of you know their story? Isaac Swett. Nels Turner. Andrew Haines. James Durfee."

"My brother Mosiah might," Edward said. "He and James are the same age."

Keziah gaze shifted into the far distance. "I knew the Durfee family in Nauvoo. When he was eight, Gentiles burned his house, then his mother died. His father found families for his children and enlisted with the Mormon Battalion to fight the Mexican War. His father and three of the children went to Utah, but James stayed with the Barnums in Kanesville." She steered her horse away from a plant covered with spikes. "I don't know anything about the others."

"Poor lads, growing up without kin. Perhaps the Congregation can fill their need for family."

"I hope so," Keziah said. "Hey, Duncan, sing us a song to scare the beasties away."

"You've no worry about bears, you know."

"You're carrying a pistol and Edward has a rifle, so you're fretting about something. I prefer singing to shooting."

Happy to comply with her request, Duncan launched into "Loch Lomond." Edward and Keziah joined him on the choruses. Scotland's tragedy-laced history yielded more than enough sad songs, but he recalled a few fun ones, like "Ally Bally Bee." Then he switched to American songs, starting with "Skip to My Lou."

The end of the ridge overlooked a broad grass-filled valley. A tree-lined burn flowed toward the Missouri River. Long lines of geese and ducks flew south with a chorus of quacks, honks, and whistles.

Edward gasped. "Never seen so many birds."

"But no people," Keziah said. "I hope we're in the right place."

The horses picked their way carefully down the slope, then, upon reaching the flats, stretched into a canter. Minutes later, Keziah called "whoa!"

Dogs gave warning barks and children scattered. Tucked at the base of a steep hill sat a large white house made of sawn logs. Outbuildings and trellises surrounded the home.

"Impressive place." Duncan estimated forty acres had been fenced and cultivated. "I should try the fur trade."

"Afraid you've missed your chance—beaver hats have gone out of style." Keziah dismounted and led her horse to a hollowed log filled with clean water. Duncan followed.

A woman with brown skin and black hair peeked from the front door, then disappeared.

Edward rested his hand on his rifle butt and watched from horseback. "Did Mr. Larpenteur marry a Lamanite?" His tone carried the mix of curiosity and horror Leo used in describing his baby brother's diapers.

"His wife wasn't with him in St. Louis." Keziah shook her head. "I asked more questions about my spouse than his."

"And Monsieur Larpenteur regrets he still has no answer for you, Madame Sirrine," said a French-accented voice.

They spun, finding two men, the speaker a bit older and shorter than the other. The blocky shape of their heads, deep-set eyes, and prominent noses raised the possibility they could be brothers. Their clothing had been made of fine wool. Both were clean and neatly groomed. And both held rifles.

"Monsieur Larpenteur." Keziah stepped toward the elder, hand extended. "It's good to see you again."

Despite Butts's dire predictions, they'd found Charles Larpenteur.

He shifted his grip on the firearm to shake her hand. "Welcome to Fontainebleau."

"You've built a palace in the wilderness."

He received her compliment with a Gallic smile and raised shoulder. "It's home."

Introductions were made. The younger man was also a fur trader of French ancestry, Theophile Bruguier, but not a relation of Larpenteur's. He too had no word of Rufus Sirrine. Keziah took the news, or lack of it, in stride. Another dark-haired woman in a calico dress called from the doorway in a language Duncan didn't recognize.

"Will you join us for coffee?" Mr. Larpenteur motioned toward the house.

"We'd be delighted," Keziah said, although Edward's grunt as he dismounted told a different opinion.

The central hall led to a parlor with plastered walls, upholstered furniture, red velvet drapes, and a rose-patterned carpet. It was the finest room Duncan had ever been in. He backed into a corner. "I'll not have your furniture smelling like horse."

"Too late." Their host's grin stretched between his muttonchop whiskers. "Have a seat." So they did. The chairs and settee circled a marble topped table. All had matching carved legs.

Larpenteur introduced his woman, Makes Cloud. She dressed as elegantly as a St. Louis matron, with her hair parted in the middle and pinned in back, long earrings brushing her shoulders, and calico dress with lace collar. She served coffee from a china set decorated with blue roses, then left the room. The aroma of the brew had Duncan leaning forward, craving the taste. Was it allowed? How could they resist? Keziah sipped the coffee and pronounced it heavenly. Edward sampled it, then went back for more. Fearing he'd crush the cup, light as an eggshell, it was, Duncan balanced it in his fingertips and took a swallow. The warmth spread through him and the flavor delighted his tongue.

Keziah and the French men discussed acquaintances in St. Louis—she knew several fur traders—and the Congregation's move to Preparation. "I've been growing herbs, so I noticed your garden."

"Mine? No, it's Makes Cloud's." Mr. Larpenteur stepped into the hall. After a murmured exchange in French, he returned to his seat. "She would be glad to show you."

"Thank you." Keziah hurried to join her.

Edward busied himself devouring the rest of the scones, so Duncan carried the conversation. "You have a lovely home. Good farmland."

"I did not think so when I arrived two years ago. It was all under water, up to my chest."

"The Missouri flooded? The water was low when we came up."

"The Big Muddy is capricious." Larpenteur leaned back and crossed his legs. "I dislike farming, so I hire it out. I run a ferry and a tavern."

Bruguiere assumed a similar posture. "I live where the Big Sioux meets the Missouri, about fifty miles upriver."

Children raced by the windows with light steps and giggles. How many were there?

"I do not know if you can do anything about this." Their host leaned toward Duncan, conferring him with leadership by virtue of age and better manners perhaps. "You passed Trading Point, on the curve of the river south of Council Bluffs, on your trip up."

Duncan nodded, recalling the shacks loosely arranged in a square. "We didn't stop there."

"The man who runs the place, Major Matlock, is a drunk and a gambler." Larpenteur paused, watching Duncan closely. "He keeps several Mormon women."

Keeps? Not as wives or hired help, but...

Bruguiere rubbed his beard and muttered to the ceiling, "Nothing wrong with more than one wife." Which could account for the number of women and children they'd seen on arrival.

Gesturing with extended fingers and snarling in French, Larpenteur indicated the women were not wives.

Edward chewed on.

Duncan cleared his throat. "I ... that is we... You think these women are mistreated?"

"I'm sure of it."

No doubt this Matlock would object to any rescue attempt. But Father Ephraim had broken with the Mormons over polygamy, and had proclaimed Preparation would help the poor and downtrodden. Duncan said, "If you have an opportunity to convey a message to those sisters, tell them they are welcome in our community."

"Very well." Larpenteur clapped his hands on his knees, then stood. "Let us see how the gardeners fare."

Duncan hadn't thought a November garden would impress, but Makes Cloud had a nearly an acre, with fruit trees and bushes along the fence, arbors with grape vines, and neatly tended beds. Keziah and Makes Cloud were deep into their tête-à-tête at the base of the steep slope where low evergreens grew. "Berries for pain in joints and flavor meat. Tea from cones is for cough, fevers. Branch smoke stops sickness." Makes Cloud waved her arm in a slow arc.

"Smudge?" Keziah asked, her eyes bright.

"Yes." Makes Cloud cut off a clump from a disreputable mess of twigs. "Tea soothes stomach, quinsy, toothache. Heals skin, itching, wounds." Makes Cloud moved to a plant with spiked leaves radiating from the center. "Braid into cords, start fires, use root for soap."

"Soapweed," Keziah gasped. "I noticed it when we arrived."

"After flower comes fruit. Remove seed and plant in spring." She handed her a paper twist.

"And both grow on hills." Keziah noticed the men approach. She clasped Makes Cloud's hands. "Thank you. You've been a most pleasant and informative hostess."

"Please come again," the woman said, her English as French-accented as Larpenteur's.

"May I? I'll bring seeds for you. And you are welcome at Preparation, although my garden is nothing compared to yours."

The group said *au revoir* and turned their horses north.

Duncan glanced over his shoulder to wave and counted ten small heads peeking out from the trellises. Were there more?

"Makes Cloud knows the local plants and she's willing to teach me." Keziah recited everything she'd learned already. The lack of news about her husband hadn't seemed to dampen her spirits, but then she'd had years to grieve his loss.

They found their way back to Preparation, arriving as the Congregation left the Lord's House after supper. Finn greeted them with a wagging tail, but Hugh Lytle burst from the crowd and ran at them, yelling.

The two brown geldings startled and raced for the barn, hooves thundering, Keziah and Edward scrambling to hold on.

"Horse thief!" Hugh yanked Duncan's arm, loosening his grip on the reins. The mare reared. Duncan shook him off, then grabbed the pommel, leaned forward, and tightened his knees to keep his seat. She kicked and broke into a gallop. Three cabins, the stable, and the barn passed in a blur. Still going like the wind, she headed for the Soldier River.

Help!

"Whoa." Duncan caught the reins and turned her head to keep her on the flats, waited for her to run out her scare. Finally she slowed her to a walk. Her sides heaved and foam dripped from her mouth. He steered her to the stable. "Easy there. Easy."

Edward hauled the saddle off his horse, wide-eyed and breathing heavily. "I thought you were a goner. I thought we all were."

"That's what I call hanging on for dear life." Duncan slid off onto shaking legs, then leaned on the paddock fence. "Why did he yell?"

"Apparently Hugh objects to letting others ride his horse." Keziah hung up the bridles.

"I'll be glad to apologize. I didn't know." His whole body itched. "I thought all property was held in common."

"How'd you get Brother Lytle to let you ride her?" Malinda Butts ran up, and took charge of the mare. "I knew she was fast the moment I saw her, but I didn't know how fast. Have you raced horses?"

"Too tall." Duncan shook his head. "This was my first time galloping."

"You hung on through it all and turned her away from the river!"

Malinda and Isaac Swett curried the beasties and settled them in the paddock.

On the walk back to the House, Catherine arrived carrying Leo. "Duncan's horse knocked the wind out of him."

"I'm not scared." The boy squirmed out of her arms.

"Oh, laddie, I'm so sorry. I didn't see you." Duncan caught Leo. "'Happy is the man who fears always.'"

"'But he who hardens his heart will fall into mischief.'" Keziah finished the proverb as she ran her hands over the child from head to feet. "Anything hurt?"

"Not me. I'm strong." He flexed his arms, showing off his muscles.

Christena rushed up and embraced Keziah, then turned to Duncan and Edward. "Are you all right? I feared you'd fall and be dragged to your death." She glanced over her shoulder. "Hide until Hugh calms down. He's apopleptic."

Finn's growl announced the arrival of Hugh Lytle and the rest of the Congregation.

"Where's my mare?" He yelled at Duncan. "What did you do to her, you thief? I spent a lot of money on her and don't need you ruining her."

"If you had any horse sense at all," Keziah marched toward the man, backing him away with her stern tone, "you'd know better than to raise your voice and run at her. You endangered her, the other horses, and all the people around."

"Don't lecture me. I'm the only one who was hurt." The brown haired man tried to sidestep away.

Keziah crossed her arms. "Where?"

He pointed to his thigh. "Took a hoof to my leg."

She glanced down. "Drop your trousers."

"Absolutely not."

The Congregation chuckled.

"No blood. You can walk. Probably a bruise." Keziah shook her head. "If this is your first time being kicked by a horse, you aren't experienced enough to own one."

Hugh started to argue, but Father Ephraim's voice silenced all others. "Jehovah's Presbytery of Zion. This is the School of Work. Cease this turmoil and return to your jobs." To Hugh he said, "We'll discuss this in my office." They entered the House, Butts following.

The people shuffled away.

Duncan's stomach sent up an inquiry. "Do you suppose there's anything left of supper?"

"Yes, I saved enough for you," Christena said to all three of them, then glanced at the second floor of the House. "Don't worry, they'll be at it a while."

Late November 1853

"Sister, Sister." Leo's small feet thundered on the path. "Strangers came, asking for you. One of them is a Lamanite."

Could it be Makes Cloud? Keziah rolled the willow branch back into the washtub, hoping the weather would hold another day so she could finish weaving the fence. She and Finn raced to the Lord's House, passing two well-built horses, brown with white patches, draped in Hudson Bay blankets. Malinda hauled water for them.

As Keziah hurried up the steps to the office, she heard Father Ephraim expounding on a topic of which he knew nothing, "...to create a School among the tribes of America, to enlighten and civilize them, to teach them the arts of agriculture and science, that they may be redeemed from poverty, degradation, and starvation, which is inevitable with them they are taught unless taught to cultivate the soil."

The Larpenteurs had come to visit. Makes Cloud wore a fur-lined cape decorated with gold braid over a fitted basque and riding skirt in dove gray wool. Her husband had on a fur-lined coat with red braid over a royal blue morning jacket. A white vest, grey breeches, and freshly polished cavalry boots completed his attire. The Larpenteurs' clothing would have done them credit on the finest street in St. Louis, which ought to have given former tailor Charles Thompson a clue.

At Keziah's knock, Mr. Larpenteur gave a relieved smile and stood. "Monsieur, much as I would delight to converse with you on this subject, the lack of sunlight at this time of year limits us. Madame Larpenteur," —Makes Cloud stood and curtseyed to Father Ephraim— "and Madame Sirrine have business to conduct. If you will excuse us."

The pair hurried out, not giving Ephraim time to object. As soon as they left the building, the fur trader spit out a hodgepodge of curses in several different languages. "Madame Sirrine, how on earth do you—"

"Welcome to Preparation." Keziah said loudly enough to cover whatever criticism the fur trader might air. With her index finger over her mouth, she sent a pointed glance toward Father Ephraim's office. The fur trader rolled his eyes. Keziah linked arms with Makes Cloud. "I'm so glad you came."

"Two gardens?" Makes Cloud studied the woven willow enclosures around plowed ground. The smaller was complete, planted with the herbs from St. Louis. The larger was missing a few sections of fence and would be ready for spring planting.

"Food." Keziah pointed to the larger, then the smaller. "Medicine."

Makes Cloud clapped. "Very good."

Finn sniffed the Larpenteurs' coats, but didn't follow them inside—the bothy was too crowded.

"*This* is your home?" Larpenteur took in the bothy with a glance, then stooped to enter. "And that imbecile thinks to save Indians from poverty? Did no one tell him, to save one who is drowning, it's best to have one's feet firmly planted on the riverbank?"

Keziah chuckled at the ridiculousness of the situation. "Cultivate the soil? Makes Cloud could teach him agriculture."

"And we could enlighten him about Indians." The fur trader perched on the edge of the bed.

Soon all three were laughing.

Makes Cloud caught her breath, then pulled out a small sack from her bag.

Keziah caught the scent. "Coffee!" She moved her battered tin coffee pot to the hot part of the stove. "Many thanks. And for you." She gave Makes Cloud a stack of envelopes full of seeds, roots, and dried leaves, a dozen of which were familiar to her.

The woman handed her a twist of purple coneflower seeds. With Monsieur Larpenteur's help, she explained this plant was different than the yellow coneflower native to the area. Tea from the leaves relieved sore throats and cleaned wounds, the root was an antidote for snake venom, and smoke from burning root eased distemper in horses.

The women both used boneset for colds and fevers, but Makes Cloud had good results with it for arthritis and stomach aches. They liked chokecherry for coughs, but Keziah also used it for wounds. They agreed on goldenrod for sore muscles, but Makes Cloud recommended it for piles and consumption also.

Living in trading posts had given Makes Cloud a wealth of education from visiting herb women and numerous patients to practice on. Keziah rejoiced to learn from an expert, becoming so involved in writing notes, she nearly forgot the coffee.

Mr. Larpenteur interpreted between English, French, and Nakota, until he glanced at his pocket watch. "My dear, time to say our goodbyes. Sunset comes too soon." He clasped Keziah's hand. "It has been a delight, Madame, to watch the two of you explore your mutual interest. Makes Cloud has never before found another who shares her passion for plants."

"It's been a joy," Keziah confirmed, then turned to Makes Cloud. "We'll share knowledge and seeds."

On the walk to the horses, Makes Cloud had more to teach. She pointed out a cottonwood beside the creek. "In early spring, wind knock down branch. Gather buds, harvest the resin for healing salve. Leaves, buds, and bark reduce fever.

"Thank you so much for visiting." Keziah dropped her voice to a whisper. "And for the coffee."

Larpenteur shook her hand. "Madame Sirrine, you are always welcome at Fontainebleau. Whenever you want to escape this..." He whirled his hand, "...school of civilization and agriculture." His lips puckered.

Was this her way out? Could she start a new life? A healthy cry from David Perrin echoed across Preparation. No, she must stay for those who needed her. "Thank you kindly, Monsieur." She turned to Makes Cloud. "And we didn't even talk about babies and birthing."

"Next visit," Makes Cloud assured her.

Keziah embraced her. "I look forward to it."

CHAPTER 7

December 1853

Finn's ears pricked. Keziah stopped pounding the pestle into the mortar and listened. Footsteps thumped rapidly, closer with every step.

"Keziah!" Duncan called. "We've need of you."

"So much for our quiet day." She opened the door. "What's the matter?"

"Whole family." He exhaled a white cloud. "Walking since this morning."

"Frostbite." Keziah packed her bag with clean bandages, ointment, and Makes Cloud's juniper infusion.

"Julia Hoyt was fetching snow to rub on their feet."

"Ach, no. It does more harm than good." She moved faster. "Let's go."

Duncan set her cape on her shoulders, carried her bag, and took her arm to steady her on the path. Did he think she was so debilitated and doddery to need help? He knew she could easily climb on and off the roof. She shook free of him to run to the House. "They're too early for the Feast."

"Indians."

She scanned the snow-dusted hills. "Easy tracking in this snow."

"Aye. Since the family escaped without harm, I'm thinking the Indians meant only to frighten them away. Morgan's a trapper. Perhaps he trespassed on their hunting ground." Duncan opened the door to the Lord's House. Keziah pushed through the crowd to the kitchen.

A bulky, bearded man, a woman with straight yellow hair hanging loose, and two wee children sat by the fire. All were dressed in furs, resembling a family of bears. They were too tired to react even when Finn gave them a sniffing.

"Here's snow." Julie Hoyt set a bucket beside them.

"Cold will do more damage. Bring the washtub and fill it with warm water." Keziah handed herbs wrapped in a twist of paper to Sarah Chase. "A mug of warm water with a spoonful of this and another of honey for each of them." Then she turned to the family. Their faces were red, roughened by the wind, and they leaned against each other. "I'm Keziah, the herb woman."

"Morgan." The trapper pointed to himself, then his family. "Wife, son, daughter."

Keziah kneeled by the youngest. Wisps of white hair showed at the edges of her scarf. Cold wind had reddened her cheeks. *Oh dear child. I'll hold you and rock you. You'll be safe and warm in my arms.* But the blue eyes met hers with wariness, not recognition. This was not her baby. Keziah's arms would remain empty. She gentled her voice. "Hello. What's your name?"

"Clara."

"Can I see your hands?"

The little one glanced at her father for permission, then slid her hands from fur-lined mittens. A healthy pink graced her small fingers. She would keep them.

"Now I need to see your toes. Can you take your boots off or shall I help you?"

The boots, also lined with fur, and thick wool socks came off. Her feet were a good color. She giggled when Keziah tickled them. "You've walked a lot. Leave your socks off for a bit, let your feet breathe." She put a dab of salve on the child's hands. "Rub this on your face and ears."

The older child already had his hands and feet ready for inspection. "My name is Wiley."

"Healthy," Keziah declared and spooned ointment onto his palm.

He stuck his tongue out, licked the remedy and grinned, showing a space where he's recently lost two baby teeth.

"'Tis for the outside of you, laddie. Supper's coming soon enough." She turned to the mother. "'Tis beeswax, butter, fleabane, penstemon, goldenrod, and plantain."

"I'm Mary." Her toes glowed red as raspberries. Keziah filled the washtub from the bucket sitting beside the fireplace. The woman gasped when she put her feet in the water.

She moved on to Mr. Morgan. Alas his toes had turned white. Dunking them provoked curses in three languages. His ear showed a previous injury. "Frostbite?" Keziah asked as she passed him the ointment. "Although it looks like a bite from..."

"A drunkard."

"You'll be glad to know," Orrin Butts proclaimed as he joined the gathering, "there are no intoxicating liquors here." He pointed at Sarah. "Supper should have been served an hour ago. And what is that? You'd better not be making tea."

"Medicinal infusion." Keziah waved him out of the kitchen. "We're nearly ready."

"Sorry," Morgan said. "Didn't mean to upset anyone."

She shook her head. "He's easily overwrought." *And as hospitable as a skunk.* She glanced from the Morgan family, green ointment on their faces, to the large room. No doubt there were more people in the House than the Morgans had seen since they'd arrived in Iowa. "Duncan, if you would bring a small table for our guests." She served them first, before they dropped from exhaustion.

"Your furs kept the family warm." Duncan pulled up a stool beside the trapper. "I'm a shoemaker, but I don't know much about tanning hides. Would you be up to answering a few questions? Or perhaps we could talk in the morning."

The Morgans ate and gave a lesson on leather, barely noticing Keziah adding warm water to the tub.

Malinda Butts led two boys her age, Heber Wilding and Mosiah Winegar, into the kitchen. All carried armloads of bedding. "There's no empty rooms, but we found extra quilts."

Extra quilts this time of year and sacrificing their comfort for a hurting family was an act of hospitality. Perhaps the Congregation was making progress.

Malinda readied the children for bed, then settled them on pallets in the corner. The little ones fell asleep instantly. Most days, Malinda nattered and moaned about nonsense: her latest outbreak of acne, the lack of suitable prospects, her wish for a thoroughbred. Today a glimmer of maturity cracked her self-centeredness. Might she grow into a more compassionate adult than her father?

Keziah squeezed the thirteen-year-old's shoulder. "Thank you for loving your neighbor. I'm proud of you."

December 1853

A month had passed since Makes Cloud and Monsieur Larpenteur had visited Preparation. Keziah's pocket crackled with a page of questions for her friend—what did she use to relieve the pain of childbirth, to stop bleeding, to dress wounds.

Keziah surveyed Fontainebleau's grounds in the low winter light as she tied her horse to the fence. No children played hide-and-seek among the outbuildings. The grapevines had not been pruned. Clumps of ice and snow choked the walkways. Fontainebleau seemed deserted...except for a line of smoke from the chimney.

Edward Winegar tapped his saddle with the invitation to the Congregation's Winter Feast. "It's too cold to loiter. Let's leave this and go." His breath made a white cloud in the air.

Duncan dismounted and let the dogs sniff his gloves. "Keziah wants to visit Makes Cloud. She has seeds for her."

"Madame. Messieurs." Theophile Bruguier emerged from the

CATHERINE RICHMOND

house, an old trade blanket draped over a red flannel shirt and drab trousers. His beard had grown and his hair sprouted in unruly waves.

"What's wrong?" Illness? Keziah should have brought her medicine bag. No, Makes Cloud has a better supply of herbs.

The fur trader blinked back tears. "Terrible, terrible. The Omahas killed Makes Cloud."

The ground shifted beneath her feet. Duncan caught her shoulders. "No. No. Why would they hurt such a kind, gentle woman?" *My friend, my friend...*

"She was Assiniboine. They are at war with the Sioux and see her as the enemy." Bruguier nodded toward the house. "Her daughter was with her, but not harmed. Charles watched it happen, but was too far away to stop them."

Duncan asked, "Do you need a minister, help with the burial?"

Bruguier shook his head. "Finished."

"Oh no." Keziah squeezed her eyelids together, but her tears would not be held back. "Is he... would he mind a visitor?"

"Please." Bruguier led them inside. They waited in the frigid hall while the fur traders spoke in the parlor. Then he motioned Keziah inside. "Madame."

The drapes were closed. The dim light of the fireplace showed Charles Larpenteur slumped on the settee. He needed a bath, but, surprisingly, he had not been drinking. Keziah sat beside him. "My friend...I'm so sorry."

Larpenteur murmured in French and reached toward her, his hand cool in spite of the fire.

"How are the children?"

"Old enough to take care of each other. And me." He nodded at an empty bowl and spoon on a nearby small table. He spoke slowly as if pulling each word from its place of pain. "Smallpox took my first wife and our son. And now, this..." He turned to the fire. After a long pause, he asked, "What brought you to me today?"

"We're delivering an invitation to Preparation's Winter Feast on December 27." She squeezed his hand. "Another time, perhaps."

Deep-set eyes met hers. "Will you marry me?"

Keziah shook her head. Decisions birthed in grief led to more sorrow. "I couldn't hold a candle to Makes Cloud."

"And you don't need a second wandering husband." His hand flopped in front of his face. "Especially one of such bad odor."

Bodies could be washed, but wandering souls weren't so easily tamed. "Is there anything…"

"Perhaps…you would remember me in your prayers."

Duncan sat in the chair opposite. "We could pray for you now." He asked God to comfort all who knew Makes Cloud.

They returned to Preparation in a somber mood.

That night Keziah dreamed of holding her son to her heart, willing breath and heat into his still body.

December 27, 1853

When Jehovah's Presbytery of Zion was in St. Louis, Charles Thompson held feasts in April, August, and December, inviting members of the Schools of Faith to join with them for teaching and worship. Now that the Congregation had settled in Preparation, Father Ephraim hadn't considered the difficulties in hosting a large group.

Preparation didn't have enough housing for its usual residents, much less visitors. Winter in northwest Iowa was far less temperate than in St. Louis, making travel perilous. And they hadn't been able to plant, so food would have to be purchased in Council Bluffs. When Keziah mentioned money, Orrin had sided with her, a surprising and unsettling experience.

Father Ephraim dismissed all their objections, eager to show off the progress in Preparation and receive tithing oblations from the worthy. As a result, December 27th found the Lord's House packed with people and Keziah washing dinner dishes.

Malinda set another stack of plates in the washtub. "Sister Sirrine, brown isn't the best color for you. You'd look radiant in ruby red or sapphire blue."

Keziah raised an eyebrow at the child. Did she think money

grew in Preparation's gardens? "I'm a herb woman and midwife, dealing in dirt and blood." With no time to worry about appearance and no fabric for a new dress. "Brown hides stains."

The girl wiggled her fingers by her neck. "A crocheted collar in white would flatter your porcelain complexion."

"I hope your father doesn't catch you reading *Godey's Lady's Book*."

Malinda's face reddened and she hurried back to her chores.

Over the hubbub of Winter Feast, Keziah's ears caught a familiar voice in the main room asking, "I'm a friend of Sister Sirrine's. Does she live here?"

"She lives in a bothy over yonder," Duncan said.

"Go on and visit." Christena Lytle tugged the dishtowel from Keziah's hands. "I'll see to the dishes."

"Make sure they're properly dried." Keziah winked, dodging Christena's snap of the towel. Without another word, because she and Christena had had far too many words on the *proper* method of drying dishes, Keziah stepped out the House.

This year had been full of losses—from leaving Mrs. Jackson in St. Louis to Makes Cloud's death last week. But here was a long-lost friend. "Mercy Jones, you're a sight for my sore heart." She wrapped arms around the woman she hadn't seen since Nauvoo.

Mercy pulled back so they could study each other. Her friend had a few wrinkles and grey hairs, but the twinkle in her green eyes was the same. She asked, "What is a bothy and why are you living in one?"

"It's a small hut where the gardener lives on an estate," Keziah said. "In Scotland."

"Keziah is the gardener hereabouts." Duncan had shaved for the December meeting, showing a firm jaw and cheeks rosy from the wind.

"Mercy, may I present Duncan Ross, who does everything from roofing to taming small boys. Duncan this is Mercy Jones, who I last saw in Nauvoo."

"I believe I met your husband, David." Duncan shook her hand. "If you'll excuse me, I'll let you ladies get reacquainted."

Keziah turned to Mercy and whispered, "You're alive." A tear seeped down her cheek. "I feared to never see you again."

"We didn't have to wait for heaven to have a reunion." Mercy linked arms with her. "David says we're moving here. So show me around." She leaned close. "Let's get away from this racket so we can talk."

"Gladly." Keziah threw on her cape, and, accompanied by Finn, led her out. They climbed the hill behind the house, so steep it seemed they could reach the clear blue sky. The weather continued mild, the temperature cold enough to firm the path and little snow to impede travel. "How is David?"

"More spit and vinegar every day." Mercy grinned. She wore a flounced skirt, a caped jacket with embroidered trim, and a ruffled bonnet, in an elegant shade of emerald velveteen.

Keziah hoped her friend didn't notice the faded scraps of calico holding together her dress. She hadn't found a walnut tree to dye the patches to match. "Tell me, where have you been these past seven years? Did you go to Salt Lake City?"

She shook her head. "David had misgivings about Brigham's... decisions. Fortunately. When we arrived in Kanesville, Job and Marcia Barnum invited us to stay with them. We've been there ever since, running the sawmill with Amos Chase. We rode up together in their buggy."

"Amos and Sarah? I'm looking forward to seeing them again." Sarah was ten years younger, so Keziah didn't know here as well.

At the top of the hill, they turned to Keziah's favorite view. The grasses had lost the golden hue of autumn and dried to pale brown, showing the steep slopes and winding ridges of the Loess Hills stretching north and south. "Working together, we've made progress in three months. One frame house, four log cabins. Three miles of fence enclosing fifteen hundred acres. We planted winter wheat, but the deer ate it."

"And now you're eating the deer. Vengeance is yours." Mercy chuckled, then sobered as she studied the valley. "Father Ephraim said it's laid out like Nauvoo. He must need eyeglasses."

True, Preparation did not remotely resemble the city of painted houses on wide streets crowned by a temple. "He means the houses are grouped together and the fields are on the outskirts of the community."

Mercy pivoted in a slow circle. "No roads. No chimney smoke. Nothing in any direction. There's no one else for miles." A gust flapped her skirts and tugged at her bonnet. "And this wind is dreadful."

"I'm hoping the space and isolation will preserve us from the diseases we fought in St. Louis."

Mercy said in a loud voice, "And in his sermon this morning—"

Malinda Butts led a group of young visitors up the hill.

Keziah squeezed her friend's hand. "Let me show you where I live."

They made their way downhill, past the House, around a sumac bush to a small cabin. Keziah had fenced the herb garden, put up the chicken coop, and started to add a porch when Hugh ran off with her posts.

"Is this the best they can do for you?" Mercy gasped. "No wonder that man called it a bothy. It's tiny."

Tiny, but delightfully free of the chatter of young girls. "It started out as a stable, but then they realized we had more than one horse. With the addition of windows and a door, it was ready for me to move in." She pulled out a key.

"You've had trouble with theft?"

"Let's call it extended borrowing." Hugh Lytle had run off with her firewood in revenge for allowing Duncan to ride his mare, so Keziah moved her woodpile inside. Such a petty quarrel was beneath mention. Keziah explained about her herbal remedies. "I'm protecting curious children. An overdose can be toxic."

"Remember in Nauvoo, when the doorknob fell off in Rufus's hand?" Mercy chuckled. "He stood there on the porch, steam coming out of his ears, yelling at you for being too stupid to open a door correctly."

"I was too stupid to know what to say."

"You were a young wife, shocked speechless by her husband's

nastiness." Mercy held up her fist. "I sent him down to the lumber-yard, where he found out the doorknobs were faulty. I'm guessing he never apologized to you."

"Accurate guess." She jiggled the key.

"You're better off without him, I'd say."

"Much." The lock released and Keziah opened the door.

Mercy ducked to enter, then pivoted to take in the bed across one end, the table at the other, the wood stove in the middle. Dried plants hung from the ceiling, filling the air with their scents. Rows of jars packed the shelves she'd built. "You can barely turn around in here. There's no room to cook."

"Food is prepared and eaten in the Lord's House. Your cabin will be larger, since there's two of you." Keziah had grown fond of her home. She enjoyed the challenge of fitting her few possessions into the space. "This is the perfect size for me. Easy to warm." She added more wood to the stove. "Would you like a herbal infusion?

"No, I would like tea. Hot tea." Her friend handed her a packet. "Don't tell Father Ephraim, but do tell me about him."

Was this a test? No, Mercy's beliefs aligned with hers. Keziah would enjoy the tea. "Thank you."

Mercy plopped on the bed as there was no other place to sit. She fingered the curtain Keziah had pieced together from dyed rags. "You didn't hear this morning's sermon?"

Keziah sat beside her. "From the kitchen it sounded like the same one he's preached since we arrived."

"He started with criticism of Joseph Smith and Jesse Strang, then relocated Baneemy into the Book of Isaiah, then finished with obedience and keeping the commandments. Since when is the tithe supposed to exalt the poor and lower the rich?" She raised her finger and lowered her voice in imitation of Father Ephraim. "Avoid the fate of Ananias and Sapphira, and prove your love of God by tithing."

Two steps took Keziah across the room for to pour the tea into mismatched and chipped ironstone mugs. "We give ten percent of our labor and possessions."

"Of what? You make a church mouse look well-to-do."

"Clothing and household goods. Since he kept sending the men on teaching trips, no one has much. I don't have anything to tithe, so I give of my time and remedies, doing what I can to keep everyone in fine fettle."

Mercy toasted her with a raised mug. "And dishwashing skills. You're all getting along... until you put a wet plate upside down and call it dry."

Keziah returned the gesture. "Wait until you hear our exchange of views on washing clothes and baking bread." She grinned.

"I've been running my household over twenty years. I hardly need anyone sticking her nose in my business, telling me how to do my work." Mercy's mouth turned down and her chin raised. "And what's this about changing the Sabbath to Saturday?"

"It might have to do with the restoration of Israel." Keziah closed her eyes and breathed in the amazing aroma God had made. How could it be wrong to drink it?

"All this time I thought Shiloh was a place, but he makes it sound like it's a person, coming to redeem their inheritances and lead them out of bondage. Who is he talking about?"

"Ask him." She grinned. "I dare you."

Mercy's smile faded quickly. "So you're staying?"

Keziah raised a questioning shoulder. What choice did she have? To be sure, what choice did Mercy have? If David intended to stay, his wife must too. Keziah scanned the rafters, wishing for a remedy to heal a critical spirit, but there was none. "Clear air, pure spring water, beautiful scenery. When winter passes, we'll grow nutritious food. And, my dear friend, I'll enjoy having you nearby." She hoped. "Welcome to Preparation."

December, 1853

Duncan stepped out of the House and listened. With three frame houses under construction, Preparation echoed with hammering. Today a new beat added its rhythm. He followed the sound to the bothy. "Why is it you're always to be found doing dangerous work?"

"Since when is building a porch dangerous?" Keziah sat on the roof, nailing joists to a nicely squared porch. Her skirts were kilted out of the way, modesty maintained by the breeks she wore for riding. Finn had found a spot of dry ground in the sun where he could watch not only his mistress, but the chickens.

Saw marks scored the planks. "Jones and Chase provided the lumber, but not the labor?"

"They're working on their houses." She set another perfectly measured board into place. "And a bridge over the river to Magnolia."

In other words, they had no time to help Keziah. Duncan braced the end of the board. "I thought Father Ephraim got the post office moved."

"No word from Washington yet."

The ground vibrated with heavy steps, perhaps another loose hog or Orrin Butts. But instead Mercy Jones arrived, swinging her fists and breathing heavily. Her shawl and flounces flapped in the wind. "No sooner do I get my house built, the walls aren't painted or papered yet, and Thompson moves another family in."

She could be squeezed in with a pack of lads who didn't bathe.

Keziah set another joist in place. "So where are you to live, you and David?"

"With them. The husband dumped their furniture then disappeared, the boys are tracking mud all over my new floors, and the wife is moaning and groaning." She shot a glance at Duncan, then lowered her voice to divulge a female secret. "You *know* what I've been through. I don't need this. He has to find another place for them to live."

"Is this Guy Barnum's family? Is the elder Sister Barnum with them?" Keziah scrambled down the ladder and stowed her tools. "They were supposed to stay in Council Bluffs until after the baby came."

"If they'd had any sense at all." Mercy marched to the House. "Thompson will hear from me."

"Her green dress puts me in mind of a dragon." Duncan stacked the cut lumbar inside the bothy.

"It's not the dress, it's the fire-breathing." A flash of a smile crossed her face as she shook out her skirt, tied on her rubber apron, and grabbed her satchel. Locking the door, she told Finn, "Stay with the chickens. Keep an eye out for raccoons and the bobcat."

Duncan trotted to keep up with her. He'd met the Barnum family yesterday when they arrived. Miranda Barnum seemed near to bursting, certainly unable to keep up with her sons, and now Keziah believed their baby was on his way. The six-year-old and the three-year-old were as unruly as Leo. "I'll round up the lads, keep them out of your way. What else?"

"Please tell Christena I won't be washing dishes tonight." She glanced at him. "I could use clean water, three buckets, from the spring."

"The lads will enjoy fetching that." Duncan would be pulling them from the water.

David and Mercy Jones's two-story clapboard glowed yellow in the sunlight. Keziah hurried inside and found Sister Barnum hiding in a closet, in the throes of birth pains. Duncan followed a path of pages ripped from a Bible, a broken mirror, and an empty sugar bowl. He tracked the thundering of little feet up the stairs and interrupted the flinging of Mercy Jones's lace collars and underclothing from her dresser. "Come on, laddies. We're on a mission to help your mum." The hellions nearly knocked him over in their eagerness. As the writhing mass tumbled out the door, Duncan called, "We'll hunt down their father. And pray for the Congregation's newest member."

"Bless you."

By sunset, the boys had dried from their dunk in the spring, been dressed in borrowed clothing from the Winegars, and sported several new bruises from stacking the wood pile. Charles and Hannah Perrin had assembled the Barnums' beds, found their cradle, and set the Jones's rooms to rights. The women of the Congregation had sung to celebrate the birth. Christena Lytle had delivered supper for the new mother and the midwife. Mercy Jones sipped from a tea cup and played the accommodating hostess.

And Duncan in his own small way had helped to make it all happen. "Blessings pour out when God's people work together." He lowered his voice and glanced to the woman standing beside him. "Though I'm wondering what's in Mercy Jones's cup."

"Goldenrod, chamomile, lavender. Pray God softens her heart before my supplies run out." Keziah braced her hands on her back and stretched. Her head tipped back, her eyes closed halfway, and her face lost its usual expression of skepticism as she watched Guy Barnum admire his new daughter, Frances. "Behold what manner of love the Father has bestowed upon us."

CHAPTER 8

January 8, 1854

Sunshine reflected off the snow, lighting the meeting room at the Lord's House. Duncan pulled a cut piece of leather from the bucket, thankful the water hadn't frozen this time. In the corner, several women sang as they spun wool into yarn and knitted it into socks. Christena Lytle stirred a fragrant beef stew on the cookstove. Finn napped in a nearby patch of sun. Keziah taught the children at the tables, with constant reminders to sit, raise hands, and wait their turn. All was well with the Congregation.

"Write or draw on your slate three things that are dangerous." Keziah strolled in back of the students, checking their work.

"S is for snake!" Leo stood on the bench.

"Well done." Keziah pressed her hand to the top of his head until he sat. "Dangerous snakes have rattles on the end of their tails. We don't have any like rattlers in Preparation. Raise your hand if you know another animal that begins with 'S', has been seen around here, and is black with white stripes."

"Skunk!" Young Charles Perrin remembered to raise his hand.

"Why is it dangerous?"

"Their spray smells awful," Ida Thompson said. "You'd have to scrub your skin off to get rid of the stink."

"True. Skunk spray stings and can hurt your eyes so you can't see. What do you do if you cross paths with a snake or a skunk?"

"Leave it alone." Young Homer Hoyt said.

"Run away," said five-year-old Mary DeForest.

"Shoot it," said Leo.

"You're not old enough to be touching a gun. And if you miss, it might spray you." Keziah pushed Leo back into his seat. "All of you have fire on your list."

Ten-year-old Cecilia Hall raised her hand. "If you get too close to a candle or stove, your clothes will catch on fire."

"So don't wear clothes. Go naked!" Young Guy Barnum yelled.

"No yelling," Mary DeForest and Mary Lewis said in unison. Their fathers were teachers; they knew how to behave.

"What should you do if your clothes catch on fire?" Keziah touched Ida's hand, reminding her to stop chewing on her fingernails.

"Jump in the river," Mary DeForest said.

"Dump water on yourself," said Leo.

Keziah nodded. "Always a good idea to have a bucket of water nearby. What could you do if you didn't have water?"

"Roll on the ground."

"Roll up in a blanket."

"Yes. Once the fire is out, check your skin. What if you find red or blistered spots?" The students shrugged. "Rinse off in cold water and show me. What if your little brother or sister catches on fire?'

"Pull the baby out of the fire and dunk them in cold water," Young Homer said.

"Enough to put out the fire, but not enough to drown them." Keziah slid the Barnum brothers apart so they couldn't swat each other. "So what do you think about Guy's idea, to stop wearing clothes?"

"You could still get burned, and get frostbite or chilblains," Maria Cobb said. She was eleven.

"So keep wearing clothes." Keziah nodded. "Next write three things to do if you catch on fire."

"I hate this." Leo threw himself and his writing slate on the floor, landing with the muffled thump of a body bundled against winter's bite.

"You broke your slate pencil." Young Guy taunted from his perch at the table. "Leo is naughty."

Duncan glanced up from hammering a sole on his lap stone. Should he intervene or would it undermine Keziah's authority?

"Leo, you may stay on the floor," she told him.

The rascal scribbled with the largest chunk of pencil, making it screech, then flopped like a dead fish as the others worked. Duncan remembered well the challenge of being five, sliding off the bench, the pencil rolling to the floor instead of staying between his fingers, the alphabet letters refusing to go the right direction. He winked at Leo.

"Brother Ross." Aglow in the sunlight, Keziah stood with arms crossed and eyebrow raised. "Perhaps you'd enjoy teaching."

The children giggled, the knitting ladies looked up from their socks, and heat rose in Duncan's face. "I am in need of an apprentice, if you're willing to spare Leo."

Before she could say "all right," the boy shot across the room and climbed onto the bench beside him. Duncan pushed his toolbox beneath Leo's dangling feet, then set the lap stone across his thighs. "'Tis heavy, so you'll have to stay put, not be jumping about like a frog." The boy nodded. "I've cut the sole to fit and set it to soak. Now you need to season it, hit it with the hammer to make it stronger."

Giving Leo a hammer? What was he thinking? Next he'd be asking Keziah for a remedy for smashed fingers. But the boy set to work with a fierce determination beyond anything he'd given to schoolwork.

Slow steps echoed on the stairway. Father Ephraim descended, crossed the room, and handed his son a letter. As always, he wore a matching jacket, trousers, and vest, befitting his calling as Patriarch of Zion. "Leo, take this to Brother Barnum, then come right back."

Duncan relieved the boy of the lap stone. He donned his hat and coat, then scampered out the door.

"Brother Ross, I need to see you in my office."

Uh-oh. Duncan followed him upstairs. "I wasn't meaning to teach Leo the trade, seeing as how factories are taking over shoe-making, but to give him a break from schooling."

Ephraim smiled and raised his hand. "I was hired out at age three after my mother died. There is redemption in work. I appreciate the interest the Congregation has taken in my children, especially in one so indefatigable."

"And clever." Didn't Ephraim recognize how smart the lad was?

"Enough to get himself into trouble. But enough about my rambunctious son." Ephraim unfolded a letter. "When Brother Jones and Brother Chase returned to Council Bluffs to cut lumber for us, I asked them to look into the situation the fur trader mentioned, with the Mormon women at Trading Point."

So, he'd been right to offer help. "What did they find out?"

"Major Matlock died and no one knows what happened to the women." He met Duncan's gaze, then returned to the letter. "The residents of Trading Point are a mix of French and Lamanites of the Pottawattamie tribe. David and Amos spoke to nearly everyone, those who knew English, and none had any answers."

"Then where are the women?"

"If they'd sought help in Council Bluffs, we'd have heard. They could have departed on a steamer for St. Louis or upriver, or joined a wagon train heading west." Ephraim stared at the ceiling for a moment, perhaps asking for a prophetic revelation. Then he grabbed another letter from his desk. "Brother Hickenloper corresponds with an uncle in Salt Lake City. I'll have him make inquiries."

"We don't know their names... or even how many." No woman would admit to being kept by a fur trader. He'd continue praying for them.

Heavy steps pounded on the stairs. Orrin Butts entered without knocking. "The Lewis's cabin is finished. Thomas Lewis will begin teaching tomorrow."

The Lewis family arrived a month after the main group. They had travelled by wagon from southern Iowa with two sons and two daughters. The father, a fellow about Duncan's age, had taught in Nauvoo; the students would benefit from his experience.

"Keziah will be pleased to return to her remedies." Father Ephraim found dried ink on the nib and replaced it.

"And, we have a solution." Orrin crossed his arms.

"To what?" Duncan asked since Ephraim had commenced writing a letter.

"To the noise of shoemaking, hammering, pounding."

"I'm sorry. I didn't realize it bothered you." Duncan ground his teeth. Why hadn't Orrin said spoken to him instead of going to Father Ephraim? The man hadn't complained when Duncan had replaced his soles...although sounds did echo as the meeting room was bare of curtains and rugs.

Orrin pointed to the small building closer to the river. "There's space for you in the store. You'll have safe storage for your tools and can expand your business to those hereabouts who come here to shop. The elder Sister Barnum has been minding the store, but you can do that while you make shoes, freeing her up for other duties." He clasped his hands and grinned as if he'd sold him a bridge in Pittsburgh.

The view out the southern window showed snow stretching unbroken in all directions, except for the line of footprints made by Sister Barnum. Preparation wasn't on the way to anywhere. No one passed by. Sitting alone all day wasn't what Duncan hoped for when he joined the Congregation. He'd enjoyed watching the children with their schoolwork. He slumped on the chair and stared at the floor.

Ephraim mixed another batch of ink and sent Duncan a sympathetic glance. "You'll continue leading singing after supper."

"Thank you." Singing with the Congregation warmed his heart. He managed a smile and went downstairs. Mothers collecting children from school and the knitting women visited by the entrance.

Silas Wilcox, one of their oldest members, hurried into the House. His hair and beard were neatly trimmed, his clothes clean and well-mended. He spotted Keziah and waved. "My wife has need of you."

Wife? Duncan had figured the young woman he saw in Silas's company was keeping house for her grandfather while her husband completed a mission trip.

Eliza Cobb scowled at him, an expression as fierce as any her brother Orrin made. "If you'd kept your *need* in your trousers, she wouldn't be in this predicament."

The man paled, but held his ground.

"It's not a predicament. It's a baby," Keziah pulled on her cloak along with her midwife's authority. "I pass no judgment on their marriage, but I will help their baby into the world. It's my calling as a midwife and as Eunice's sister in the faith."

Rebecca Butts turned on her. "You support him marrying that child? Eunice was thirteen—"

"No need to exaggerate. She was sixteen." Christena Lytle left the kitchen to weigh in. "I've never seen any rules for age differences between spouses. Aren't you younger than your husband?"

"Only eight years." Eliza pointed at Silas. "Eunice is forty years younger than Brother Wilcox," Eliza Cobb said. "Younger than four of his children."

"And now she's seventeen. This is her first baby. She needs our help." Keziah stepped toward the door, but the women closed in on her, their muttering building into a kerfuffle. "I wasn't at Winter Quarters nor in southern Iowa, so I don't know the circumstances of their marriage."

"They lived near us," Priscilla Lewis had arrived to pick up her daughter Mary from school. "Eunice didn't have any other offers. No parents, no land, no dowry."

"None?" Christena asked. "Your son Branson is only two years older than Eunice. Why didn't they marry?"

Priscilla's face tightened and she turned away. "She didn't suit."

Christena dismissed her with a snort.

"So all of you had a choice about marrying? I did not." Keziah stared down each woman until she looked away.

Had this strong and independent woman been coerced into marrying Rufus? Or maybe Keziah had been meek like Duncan's wife Emily, then life with Rufus had forced her to find her backbone.

Keziah spoke quietly, but with authority. "Think about when you had your first baby and those who attended you."

Silas swallowed hard and blinked away tears. "She's hurting and scared."

"We're all outcasts here, considered peculiar by Gentiles. Our hearts should be tender toward our Sister Eunice. We must love her, as commanded by our Lord." Keziah took another step toward the door. The women seemed rooted to the floor, each not wanting to be the first to yield.

How could he distract them? Duncan gulped a big breath. "Another bairn for Preparation! Thanks be to God!. Let us pray." Duncan had never prayed aloud with the Congregation. *Let the words of my mouth be acceptable.* He clenched his hands together to keep them from shaking, closed his eyes, and spoke slowly. "Dear Lord and Heavenly Father, we lift up this new life and ask you to bring this precious wee one safely to his parents' arms. Comfort the new mother, and ease her pains and fears." Could he mention Silas? No, not without stoking controversy. One of the women in the circle sniffled. "Guide the midwife's hands and give her wisdom as she does the work You've given her, the work You deemed so important that it is mentioned in the first two books of your Holy Bible, Genesis and Exodus. And lead us, Jehovah's Presbytery of Zion, in teaching this child and all the children you've blessed us with, to love and follow you with all their hearts, souls, and minds." With all the church meetings he'd attended, he ought to be able to go on for hours, but all he could say was, "Amen."

Duncan opened his eyes. Keziah and Brother Silas were gone.

January 8, 1854

When Duncan had offered to share her burden for the health of the Congregation, Keziah figured she didn't need his help. She'd do what needed to be done, as always. Duncan had surprised her with his resourcefulness, providing supplies for packing her garden, finding the bothy and finishing it, working with the lads to build latrines, and now, praying.

This afternoon, in spite of her best reasoning, the women wouldn't budge to let her midwife Eunice. Then Duncan's inspired prayer had them closing their eyes and softening their hearts. Keziah had slipped through the circle and out the door with Silas.

How was Silas holding up after being thrashed by the women of Preparation? With nimble-feet and erect posture, he hurried down the icy track. He was shorter and stockier than Duncan, with the square shoulders, firm belly, and erect posture of a hard-working farmer. His age didn't worry her, but his wife's did.

"How's Eunice been feeling?" she asked Silas as the path dwindled on the way to the farthest cabin from the House.

"Fine."

No enlightenment there. "Did she eat breakfast this morning?"

"A bit."

"How'd she sleep last night?"

"Fitfully."

"Her pains started last night?"

"Thereabouts."

No sense wasting breath.

"Eeeee! Nooooo!" Eunice, on the other hand, had no difficulty expressing herself. Keziah broke into a run.

"I go." Silas turned back.

Keziah caught his sleeve. "Certainly not."

"Chores." He cringed, shoulders hiking to his ears as a shriek echoed from the house. "Don't need me."

"Your work is here, now." Keziah dragged him toward the cabin. "Your wife needs you. You've had other children. You know what to expect."

He shook his head. "I was away."

Foolish church, sending men on mission trips when they're needed at home. "Well, then, here's your opportunity to fill that hole in your experience, see your child born, and support your wife."

Silas inched the door open.

Eunice stood, hands braced on the small table, her face damp with perspiration. Her round girlish face had been tightened by childbirth pains. "You're back," she gasped, sweat-soaked hair limp at her shoulders.

"Yep."

Keziah shoved him inside and shut the door behind him. "Set water to boil. Put towels on the bed. Light a lantern." She hung her cloak and set a can of lavender ointment on the stove to warm. "Where does it hurt, Eunice?"

"Where doesn't it?" One hand released the table to point to her backside, then low front between her hips. "Worst is here and here."

A good sign, Mrs. Jackson would say. The baby's head was right where it needed to be. Keziah ran her hands over the belly confirming the notion. The womb tightened, setting off another howl.

"Draw a breath. Blow it out." Keziah rubbed her shoulders. "Loosen up. Save your strength. Have you seen a baby born?"

"Winter Quarters. All died." She blinked out tears. "I'm dying."

"You won't." Had the girl watched Silas's first wife die? "We're eating well, living clean here. You're young and healthy and strong. Let's take a walk to the stove, now to the bed, to the table."

"I'll get." Silas made for the door.

"You will not." Keziah maneuvered Eunice between him and the door.

"Don't leave me." Eunice's sharp intake of breath turned into a yell as another wave caught her. When it let go, they resumed pacing. "Malinda wanted to be with me, but Sister Butts wouldn't let her. Phoebe was supposed to come, but between the weather and her also having a baby soon...." She tensed and grabbed her belly.

"Breathe." Keziah rubbed her back. "Slow and deep. In... then out."

Phoebe was Silas's daughter, Eunice's sister-in-law and her step-daughter. Silas would have a child and grandchild the same age. Keziah shook her head, corralling her wayward thoughts. No matter how tangled the family tree, this baby deserved a good start in life.

"Bad one." Eunice eased onto the stool and rested her head on the table. "I'm too tired for this. Maybe tomorrow."

Keziah smiled. She had said the same thing during her first. "Your baby is coming today. Take a sip." She set a cup of cold water beside the girl. She turned to Silas, who, having completed his assigned tasks, took cover in the darkest corner of the room. His wife needed encouragement and distraction. "Sing."

"What?"

"Anything. If you can't remember the words, hum." She prayed the midwife's prayer, remembering most of it, while washing her hands.

His voice, hardly used in conversation, surprised her with a clear tenor. Silas could be the duet partner Duncan had been looking for. He sang "Home, Sweet Home," then "Long, Long Ago." When he moved on to "We Won't Go Home 'til Morning," his wife's head raised.

"A drinking song?" She glared through hanks of damp hair. "That's what you sing for your son?"

"A son? We're having a son?"

"Uh-oh." Eunice's waters splashed onto the dirt floor. "Gotta push."

"Sit on the edge of the bed," Keziah directed Silas into position. She settled Eunice between his knees, her back against his chest. The sun had gone down, so she moved the candle closer. *This baby better come quickly, before the midwife's knees freeze.*

Eunice's groan turned into a shriek. "I'm ripped apart," she wailed. "My bones are breaking."

"Sorry." Silas blinked, working up to crying. "I'll go."

"Hold still. You're where you need to be. Open your hands." Keziah grabbed the can and poured warm ointment onto his leathery palms. The room filled with the calming scent of lavender. "Rub her belly. Keep singing." If the women of Preparation wouldn't sing encouragement to Eunice, her husband would have to do.

You're where you need to be.

Keziah's breath hitched. Hannah Perrin and Miranda Barnum had the support of the Congregation. They would have survived without her. Eunice, though...

Silas hummed and rubbed. Eunice growled, grunted, and pushed. More ointment in Keziah's hands eased out the round head and curled body.

The humming stopped. Silas gasped, "Baby."

"It's a girl."

The new mother flopped back. "Don't even think about trying for a son. Not never going to be no next time. Not never."

The father leaned over her shoulder for a closer look. "Prettiest baby ever."

Little eyes blinked at the world. She inhaled, then let out a cry.

"Aw. Sings like her papa." A smile returned to Eunice's face. She reached back and patted Silas's grizzled cheek. He eased her onto the mattress.

The relieved father scuttled out the door. "It's a girl," he called to the neighbors. "Good singing voice."

Several male voices called their congratulations.

Keziah cleaned the baby, the mother, and the floor. She made an infusion with raspberry leaves, chamomile, and honey for Eunice. Outside, a deep voice crooned a lullaby in Gaelic. *Bless you, Duncan.* Keziah blinked back tears.

Silas returned with stew for his wife and Keziah. He glanced at the bed where his young wife and baby lay in the deep sleep of exhaustion. "Thank you, Sister."

Keziah was where she needed to be today, where God could use her. "'Tis my joy."

CHAPTER 9

February 1854

The creek gurgled beneath the ice as Keziah tromped through the maple grove. At each tree, she removed a full bucket of sap and hooked an empty bucket under the tap. The valley opened to the northeast, so the sun had yet to make its way to the ground. Snow crunched under her feet and currents of cold air cut through her gaiters and wool socks, but a robin called from a high branch. Spring was on its way.

Finn raced up to the ridge, tail wagging, then Duncan Ross hollered, "Need a hand?"

Keziah had asked the Congregation for help. Only Duncan Ross had answered her call. His beanpole shadow stretched before him as he worked his way into the ravine. Grey whiskers covered the lower half of his face and a grey tweed cap shielded the top, leaving only color from his blue eyes and the rosy tip of his nose.

"Watch yourself on the ice."

"I've got tackety boots. You'll be calling them hobnail." He paused to give Finn a scratch behind the ears. "Though I'm a long way from surefooted as you, my friend."

To maintain respect of the Congregation, Keziah conducted herself carefully. She made sure never to be alone with a man, and especially not at a place as distant and isolated as this. Still... Duncan's behavior was above reproach and help was welcome. "Who's minding the store?"

"The elder Sister Barnum wanted a quiet place to write a letter." He reached the base of the slope and scanned the grove. "How do you think these trees came to be here? Did the Indians, Lamanites, plant them?"

"My guess is a storm blew the seeds off a tree north of here and the valley caught them." Keziah emptied the last sap bucket into a five-gallon pail. "The biggest haul yet."

"Glad you borrowed the milkmaid's yoke." Duncan slipped it over his shoulders, steadied the buckets, then lifted with a grunt. "You must be a descendent of Queen Boudicca herself. Or perhaps the Irish warrior queen, Grace O'Malley, if I'm remembering the song rightly."

"Hardly. It took me three trips yesterday." Keziah stomped to keep from sliding downhill. "No, none so fine in my family tree. Only tenant farmers trying to grow blighted potatoes from fields of stone."

"Same." In the sunlight at the top of the ridge, he set down the buckets, glanced back at her, then nodded toward the cabins circling the Lord's House. "Yesterday's sermon seemed useful, practical."

'Twas a relief from all the railing against the Beast of Winter Quarters or the complicated explanations of how the Lamanites descended from the Jews. Keziah gave Duncan a smile. "So you've come to ask me who's been doing all the backbiting and gossiping?"

"We're not to speak evil of another, not to mention faults to a third person, so no." He flashed a teasing grin. "I liked that Father Ephraim used Bible verses to address a problem we all need help with."

"All? You're here to reprimand me for my faults?"

"You've none to mention."

"Now there's a bit of blarney." No faults? That's not what Rufus said. Keziah stopped herself. Why was it she could only remember Rufus's complaints? Surely he must have offered a compliment, offered to help her. And why all this comparing the two men? Rufus kept coming up lacking. 'Twas time to set aside the old misery and enjoy this man's kindness.

Duncan pondered Preparation with a satisfied expression. "We're in the right place, a good place."

She nodded. "'This is the day the Lord hath made; rejoice and be glad in it.'"

"So we shall. And I'm here to carry the sap." Which he did, all eighty pounds of it, to the firepit where laundry was done in summer.

Keziah grabbed a dried corn husk and lit it from the stove.

Duncan laid the tinder and kindling, set the cauldron on top, then filled it with sap. "I'll be back to spell you." He hiked down to the store.

As Finn watched from the stoop, Keziah split a few dozen logs and set a fresh candle in a lantern for later. Steam rose from the cauldron. As it boiled, she added more sap, scooped out a fleck of bark, wedged a fresh log into the fire, and wished for coffee. The last time she'd had a cup was with the Larpenteurs. Dear Makes Cloud... She'd know about the cactus growing near here...

The bell rang and the Congregation gathered for supper.

"Go on and eat." Duncan arrived through the rising steam. "I'll tend the fire."

"Don't let it burn."

Keziah hurried inside, gobbled down a bowl of venison stew and a slice of bread, then raced back to relieve Duncan. The sun set, taking with it every hint of warmth. She lit the lantern and walked in circles to keep from falling asleep and freezing. How tired she would have been had Duncan not pitched in. Had she remembered to thank him? She knew how it felt to be taken for granted; she'd never want to do that to anyone.

Around midnight, the sap turned a golden color. Keziah poured it into a smaller pot and took it inside to finish it on the cookstove. As it simmered, she rinsed the cauldron in the creek, startling an owl, and doused the fire. The house creaked with the wind. Upstairs, baby C.W. fussed, then quieted. As the clock chimed four, the sap finally turned to syrup. Keziah poured it through a wool felt filter into jars, sealed the lids, and stored them on a high shelf. The firepit had cooled.

"We're done," Keziah told Finn, who yawned and stretched. Carrying one warm jar for medicinal use, she shuffled back to the bothy. She stowed the precious jar, climbed into bed, and fell into a deep sleep.

"Keziah! Come quick." Malinda yelled and rattled the door. "Leo fell in the syrup."

The sun had barely inched above the horizon. A mere hour of sleep left her groggy. "Jar's too small for boy to fall into."

"Jar broke. He's bleeding. You've got to come."

No account, useless, troublesome... Keziah shoved her stiff body from the bed, grabbed her satchel, and threw open the door as Malinda started to pound again. "Don't hit me. I'm coming."

She followed the sound of screaming into the house and found Leo howling on the floor in a puddle of maple syrup and broken crockery. No obvious blood or other injuries. The shelf where she stored the jars hung empty from one peg. The entire long week's labor, undone in seconds by one four-year-old. Who was supposed to be watching this hellion? Everyone, which meant no one was responsible. Finn stepped into the stickiness and nearly licked up a shard before Keziah yanked him back. The rest of the wailing came from children of all ages mourning the loss.

"...pancakes..."

"...cornbread..."

"...oatmeal..."

Over the crowd a gangly arm swung a tweed cap. "Yes!" she called. Duncan rang the bell, and herded the Congregation and Finn outside. The noise decreased enough to allow a thought to form.

"David Lee Thompson." Keziah used her sternest voice on his full name. She wanted to tell him to go to blazes, but even in her red-hot anger, she restrained herself. "Stop crying and tell me where you're bleeding."

"No bleed." Leo gulped. "Want syrup."

"Thanks to you, there is no syrup!" He was never ever getting any maple syrup, not ever if Keziah had anything to say about it. "Let me see your hands, palms and backs. Turn your head this way, other way." The rest of his body was bundled in winter clothing. Keziah narrowed her gaze at the Malinda. "He is *not* bleeding."

"Yes, he is. His ear. No, the other one."

"A minor scratch. Next time you pound me out of a sound sleep, it better be more blood than you get on your monthly," Keziah said, too tired to care who heard her. "Get those sticky clothes off him, give him a bath and wash his coat, then clean up this mess before there's a real injury."

"Me? Why do I have to?" Her bottom lip stuck out, warning of impending tears.

Keziah spun on her heel and headed for the door before she could slap the girl into next week. "Because you woke the only bear in these hills."

March 1854

Sunrise woke Duncan, but the lads, needing sleep to grow, would snore on until the bell rang for breakfast. He shrugged into his coat, grabbed his pole and net, and headed toward the mist-covered river.

The ice had begun to break up and melting snow filled the river, turning winter's silence to spring's burble. Duncan crunched through dry reeds and cattails, and climbed down the bank by a cottonwood too crooked for cutting. Three of its roots had ended up in the water the last time the river changed its course, providing a haunt for fish. He speared a bit of cheese on the hook, then let it drift into current.

A thunk of a door had him turning to see who else was up this early, but a white veil of mist hid Preparation. A chill brushed his spine. For the seven months he'd been with the Congregation, eyes watching him every moment. Now he was alone. No, never alone.

"Good morning, Lord." daily practice of gratitude had brought him through Emily's death. Today he thanked God for sunrise, his health, and time to fish.

A bird called from the top of the cottonwood. Duncan leaned back. On the tallest branch stood a full-grown bald eagle. The magnificent creature tilted her head to eye him, then bent to grab of bite of the fish she held.

"You're the expert." His line tugged. He scrambled to set the hook, reel it in, and net the catfish. He'd like to catch a few more before breakfast.

Follow me, and I will make you fishers of men.

Duncan froze. Months ago the Lord had laid it on his heart to read the Bible to lads without families. But there were latrines to dig, houses to roof, and buckskin to tan. And...what if Father Ephraim thought him presumptuous and the lads thought him a fool?

Ach. Bible verses about courage galloped through his head. Duncan pulled the line from the water, said goodbye to the eagle, and took the fish to the kitchen.

Father Ephraim wasn't at breakfast. Figuring to see him at noon, Duncan headed to the store and shoemaking. He'd been working an hour when the door opened and Father Ephraim entered.

"Good afternoon, Duncan. I've come to be measured for moccasins. I'm told they're more comfortable and quieter than shoes."

Stop your quavering and ask, already. "Welcome. Have a seat and take off your shoes." Duncan grabbed a scrap of newsprint and a pencil. The man's brogans were in good condition, the soles barely worn and the laces unbroken. His socks were newly made, without holes or darning. Ephraim worked in the office, not in the fields. "I'm glad to see you. I've been wanting to ask...we've several young men in the Congregation who've no Bible and no kin with one."

"I intend to rectify that situation this spring. I'm traveling east to visit our other Schools of Faith and purchase several items for our needs. I'll add Bibles to our list."

Courage. "In the meantime, with your permission, I'd like to read to them. In the evenings, after work is done. A chapter or two." His hands knew better than to shake as he traced the feet, then folded the paper up and marked the height of the ankle. "I'm no Bible teacher, but—"

"The word of God is powerful." Ephraim raised his arms as if preaching. "The word of God is pure. Blessed are those who hear it and obey." He rested his hands on Duncan's shoulders. "God will bless your reading." He put his shoes back on and headed to the door.

"Thank you." Duncan held up the tracing. "Your moccasins will be ready by the end of the week."

Permission. The tension in his chest eased. Now for the lads. After supper, he found them wrestling in the dirt by the single men's soddy. No wonder they were always filthy. He caught their attention by whistling.

"Scripture says God's word lights our path. Bit of a challenge when you've no Bible to show you the way. So, I'll to read it to you."

James Durfee straightened and dusted himself off. "I'm tired of getting the snot beat out of me. Read away."

Andrew Haines frowned at Duncan's lantern. "The whole thing tonight? You'll need a bigger candle."

"And I'll need another bowl of stew," Nels Turner said.

Isaac Swett whacked his arm. "Always hungry."

Duncan had braced for complaints, but got the usual tomfoolery. God told him to read, so he would.

The sun went down behind the hill. Soon the chill of night would drive them inside. Duncan sat on one of the packing crates outside the soddy's door and the young men settled around him.

What a scruffy bunch. Preparation had no barber and it showed. Nels's hair stood straight up, Andrew's stuck out in all directions, James's waves covered his ears, and Isaac's looked as if it had been chewed on by a goat. Ach, well, Jesus started the church with fishermen, not dandies. He gave them another glance. They'd do.

"Heavenly Father, please help us understand Your word. Thank you and amen." Duncan opened the Bible to three-quarters of the way through. "The Gospel of Mark."

"Why there? You're skipping the rest?" Andrew asked.

"I'm starting with the book that changed my life." And not wanting to put them to sleep with a chapter of "begats."

Isaac wagged a finger at him. "What did you do? Drinking, cussing, fornicating? C'mon man, we want all the details."

"Nothing so scandalous. My wife and children had died, and I wanted to die as well. God gave me a reason to live." The lads silenced and he dove into the chapter before they could distract him again. The first chapter told about Jesus being baptized, calling disciples, and healing. At the end, he closed the Bible.

"Is that all?" Andrew asked.

"For tonight."

"Forty days in the wilderness." Nels tugged on his three chin hairs. "What did He eat?"

"One of the other gospels said He fasted forty days."

"Fasted? Forty days?" Nels barely survived forty minutes without food. "Whoa..."

James stared across the cluster of cabins and dirt streets making up Preparation. "Jesus drew such big crowds, he couldn't go into the city." The obvious question was why no crowds followed Father Ephraim. Instead James's voice softened with wonder. "Crowds followed him to the desert. He must have been..."

"He still is. Until tomorrow." Duncan smiled and stood.

Father Ephraim stepped from the corner of the building into the lantern light. Duncan almost jumped out of his skin. How much had he heard? Had Duncan said anything wrong?

"Well done, Brother Ross." He addressed the lads. "'Study to show yourself approved unto God, a workman that needeth not to be ashamed, rightly dividing the word of truth.' Let me know when you come to that verse. And this one: 'Lay down and sleep in peace, for thou makest us dwell in safety.'." He stepped back into the shadows and was gone.

~

April 15, 1854

The Solemn Assembly reeked of damp wool and bodies unwashed for six months. A wet diaper wouldn't be noticed. Keziah stood at a window behind the last row of benches, swaying to keep the baby asleep. Eunice Wilcox had kitchen duty this morning and her husband Silas was abed with lumbago, so Keziah had volunteered to hold their baby. Her wee neck and ears were clean, her complexion perfect, and she'd put on a healthy weight. No one could fault the young mother's care. Alas, Eunice had named the baby Malinda after her boy-chasing friend.

May you seek God first, Keziah prayed for the little one, *and trust Him for your future.* There, one holy moment for the day.

Outside, children rolled down the hill, yelling and pelting each other with clumps of old grass and snow. Two fifteen-year-olds herded the flock with Finn's assistance. All would sleep well tonight.

When Orrin Butts stood to testify, Job Barnum had a coughing spell. Keziah handed him a rag from her apron pocket.

"What's this?" he asked, his voice loud from congestion.

"Handkerchief."

He frowned at the square of fabric, its stains blended with the faded dye. "What'd you say?"

Brother Butts glared. "Sister Sirrine, you're disrupting the Lord's Solemn Assembly."

Every eye turned to see the source of the commotion.

"I'm keeping gobs from the Lord's floor."

Guy Barnum leaned closed to his father's ear and yelled, "Handkerchief. Cover your cough. Don't spit on the floor."

Couldn't have said it better myself. Keziah accepted Job's thanks.

Several other men gave their testimonies, then Father Ephraim celebrated the growth of Preparation. "Narrow self-interest is beginning to give way to the enlightened policy of seeking the public good and the general interest of all, wherein each person seeks to build up his neighbor, instead of pulling him down, mutually assisting each other in the toils and cares of life."

Keziah looked into baby Malinda's eyes. *Apparently no one told*

Father Ephraim how the women of his Congregation shunned your mother.

"Like the second chapter of Acts," James Durfee said from the front row. "Duncan read it to us last night."

Duncan flinched, but Ephraim continued without reaction. "Peace on earth and goodwill to men is the legitimate result of obedience to the principles of righteousness revealed by Baneemy." He moved on to his favorite subject, the Law of Tithing. "As for the disposition of the Tithe, it ought to be sufficient to know it will be used as directed by the Lord. He appointed an Agent to receive it."

Clever. Keziah turned toward the window, so the Congregation couldn't see her expression. *Who dared to question where the money went or dared to question God's appointed agent?*

"The Tithe is used to establish the House of the Lord," he continued, "so the Son of Man will not have to say He has nowhere to lay his head."

Jesus has a pillow in Preparation? Keziah pressed her lips together. Christena glanced at her, then turned away so they wouldn't burst out laughing.

The Chief Steward planned to raise funds to purchase Mt. Zion, but it wasn't clear if he were talking about Jerusalem or Iowa.

Monona County had been organized. Every office was filled by a member of the Congregation. Charles Thompson added *County Judge* to all of his other titles. And if all that organizing wasn't enough, he ordained new traveling teachers, an evangelical quorum, and a full set of chiefs. *Hope they finish planting before they leave.* With all the men gone, Preparation would be run by women and children. Keziah smiled at the baby. *We'll do a first-rate job, won't we?*

Every time Father Ephraim preached on Baneemy and the keywords, Keziah couldn't make sense of it. Was she the only one who was confused? Heads nodded throughout the room, except one. Duncan leaned forward, chin in palm, squinting at Father Ephraim as if to bring his words into focus. If the meeting grew anymore tedious, Keziah would have to wake the baby.

Finally, Father Ephraim prayed then adjourned. While the men set up the tables for the Feast, Keziah stepped outside. A hint of green brushed the fields and trees. Red-breasted robins had returned. The fresh breeze roused the baby. No crying...yet. Keziah headed down the path. "Let's go see the beehive Duncan made. It's the new design, with removable frames," she told Malinda. "And I've added a few more sections of fence to the garden."

"That's good, because you have more to plant." A man marched toward her, carrying a wooden box with a French label.

Brother Isaac Ashton.

The last time she'd seen him, they'd been running for their lives, trying to escape the Gentile mobs in Nauvoo, Illinois. He'd weathered in the past nine years, his beard nearly gone to grey.

"Brother Ashton, what a delightful surprise! Although if you brought cognac, we're both in trouble."

He opened the crate, showing twists of paper in each compartment. "Larpenteur sent this for you."

"Makes Cloud's seed box." Keziah closed her eyes against a sudden rush of tears, remembering her friend's long fingers sorting through the twists, pressing a special one into her hands, and sharing its use.

He nodded. "I hope you'll be able to figure out the instructions. They're in a mix of French, English, and Sioux, with drawings."

"If Makes Cloud saved these seeds, they're important. Thank you for delivering them." They walked to the bothy. "How is Monsieur Larpenteur?"

Isaac shrugged. "Headed up the river to Fort Union last I knew."

"Poor man." Keziah raised the baby to her shoulder while working the padlock. "And you? What have you been doing since Nauvoo?"

"Farmed in Kanesville, then moved north of here, where I met our fur-trading friend. And now, moving to Preparation, to be the prosecuting attorney for Monona County. Should be an easy job with Father Ephraim keeping everyone in line."

"Your experience farming in this area will be so welcome."

He set down the box and reached for the baby. "Here, let me

take the little one. Is she yours? Oh, I'm sorry. Larpenteur told me Rufus was missing."

She handed him the baby who started gnawing on her fist. They didn't have much time. "This is Malinda Wilcox, daughter of Silas and Eunice."

"My Malinda is almost two years old."

"You had a two-year-old last time I saw you." She locked the seeds in the bothy, wishing she could forgo the Feast and investigate the treasure chest.

"Caroline is now ten."

"Andrew Hall's daughter Cecilia is ten. She's been praying for another girl to join our community, so she'll be glad of a friend." Keziah took back the wee one who lost interest in her fist and let her voice be heard. The bell rang and they joined others hurrying to the House.

Eunice met them on the path and Keziah made introductions as she handed the baby to her mother. "This child of mine never misses a meal. Thank you, Keziah." She carried off the baby for nursing.

Isaac surveyed the crowd inside the House. "There was a time in Nauvoo when I didn't think we'd be old enough to sit with the aged. And now here we are. Orrin Butts still taking charge. Thomas Lewis teaching school again. Homer Hoyt growing a fine head of hair while the rest of us lose it."

And Charles Thompson continues his quest to become the next Joseph Smith.

Isaac greeted Job Barnum as Keziah surveyed the Soldier River valley. No Gentiles here to form a mob...so far. Maybe they'd escape Nauvoo's fate.

CHAPTER 10

May 1854

Homer Hoyt had waved Duncan down after breakfast, asking to use his whetstone to sharpen the clippers, which is how he escaped the solitude of the store for bonny sunshine and a flock of bleating woolybacks, watching the man nearly lop off a sheep's head.

"Lousy lump of lamb," Homer muttered. "Mess of mutton, hunk of haggis."

Duncan showed him the motion. "Here, now, flip her onto her back, keep her from bolting."

Homer released the troublesome animal and thrust the clippers at Duncan. "Why didn't you tell me you've done this before?"

"Didn't want to admit I'd been sacked..." he wiggled his eyebrows "...for *shear* laziness."

Isaac Swett laughed and Andrew Hall chuckled, but Homer asked what was so funny. Which made them laugh harder.

Duncan grinned, happy to have mates to joke with. He let the riled ewe trot away, then grabbed a ram. "Easy there, laddie." Keeping his voice low, he said, "Turn the head, sit him down, roll him, head between your knees." The ram kicked, but gained no foothold. Duncan started clipping. "Down the belly, to the back legs, around the tail. Then head, neck, shoulder, front legs. Work your way around the body, until the whole fleece comes off in one piece." The beastie lounged on the grass, relieved of his hot wool.

Andrew applauded. "As good with the sheep as you are with mischievous little boys."

"This is a job for old men." Homer climbed through the fence.

Andrew grabbed his leg. "You'll be his age by the time we're done."

"Who are you calling old?" Duncan hung his jacket on a fence post. "I've only got ten years on you."

"I'm too young for this, so back to watching the corn grow." Isaac turned to go.

"The corn you planted yesterday will be growing tomorrow." Duncan caught the lad's arm. "These clippers have your name on them. Got a pair for each of you."

Homer examined the clippers. "Burgon & Ball," he read the blade. "Not my name."

Isaac scanned the flock. "Four of us and sixty of them. Fifteen each and we'll be done by dinner."

But the noon bell's ring found the shearing crew down to three men, having sent Homer to Keziah after he clipped the space between his thumb and his index finger, and only six fleeces to show for their hard work.

"Don't worry, lads," Duncan said. "You've mastered sheep wrestling and we'll pick up speed this afternoon."

A high-pitch squeak sounded from the bottom of the hill. Keziah pushed a wheelbarrow down the path toward them. A wide tie kept her bonnet on, but the breeze loosened a few curls. "I knew you wouldn't take time out to eat."

"Wouldn't we now?" Duncan arched his back and stretched. "And how is our three-fingered Homer?"

"He'll live." She unloaded baskets of food and jugs of water. "Stop by the bothy for liniment," she told Duncan.

"Any sign of James Wilding?" Isaac brushed bits of wool and grass off his trousers. "He was supposed to help us."

Keziah paused in filling the barrow with fleeces. "He's gone."

"Gone?" Andrew indulged his sweet tooth with a cookie. "You mean hiding from work?"

She straightened and blew out a long breath. "The Wildings left."

"Left? To their place down in Council Bluffs?" Isaac kneaded his palm.

"The whole family?" Duncan asked. "How many children have David and Alice?"

Keziah counted off on her delicate fingers. "James, Heber, Davy, Joseph, Jeannette, Alice, Thomas, and baby Sarah are on their way... to Salt Lake City."

For a long moment, even the sheep were quiet.

Just when the Congregation had started to pull together... "Why?" Duncan asked.

Her gaze settled on the western horizon, as if wanting to see them safe on their journey. "I can't say for sure, but their two oldest children live there. They joined wagon trains couple years back."

Leave their friends? Trade this beautiful valley for the desert? Duncan shook his head. "What did Father Ephraim say?"

Keziah glanced at the House, then met his gaze with troubled eyes. "Apostasy."

June 1854

Keziah loved the rich scent of growing plants June brought. Unfortunately sunshine and the stove's heat had given rise to less pleasant odors in the Lord's House. She prayed this Sabbath's teaching would be brief.

"Keziah," Isaac Ashton joined her as she ate breakfast. "I've come to say goodbye."

"You're leaving?" Already? He'd only been here two months.

He traced a crack in the table with his thumbnail. "I've been farming on my own for years now. I don't mind telling people what to do, but..."

"...you'd prefer not to take orders from one inexperienced in farming."

"I'd rather do the work myself than argue with a committee." He clasped her hands. "I wish you well." He left.

He wished her well? Not the whole of Preparation? And what fools had he been working with? Isaac's expertise would be missed.

"Who's teaching this morning?" Christena sat in Isaac's spot. "And what's the subject?"

"No idea." Keziah muttered over her bacon and eggs. "Last Sunday Brother Butts read Father Ephraim's thoughts on unicorns. What's next? Dragons?"

"Leprechauns." Christena passed the potatoes.

"What's a leprechaun?" Seven-year-old Mary Lewis asked.

"Balderdash the Irish believe." Her mother Priscilla took the potatoes. "So they can hunt for pots of gold at the ends of rainbows."

Pots of gold under rainbows or plates of gold under a hill in upstate New York. Which was more difficult to believe? Keziah gave herself a shake. Unruly thoughts must be reined in, lest they leak out of her mouth.

Mary tugged her mother's sleeve. "What's a unicorn?"

"Unicorns are a horse with a horn growing from the middle of his forehead."

"Are they balderdash?"

"No. They're in the Bible. But not in Iowa."

Father Ephraim and Guy Barnum had left for St. Louis on June 7th. Brother Butts had alternately pouted at being left behind or strutted at being left in charge. Last Sabbath, he'd read the latest revelation of Baneemy.

Keziah pulled a paper from her apron. "I figured Brother Butts tossed the unicorn in there. But here it is, in Father Ephraim's own handwriting." Keziah read, 'But go ye straightaway and call them to the sacrifice, that they may be left without excuse, in the days that I may send you out into the highways and hedges, where Ephraim and Manasseh is, to compel them to come in, that the number of my house may be complete, that I may send them out as hunters, to push people together as with the horns of unicorns.'"

"Where did you find that?" Christena asked.

"Orrin dropped it after reading it."

"Father Ephraim mentioned unicorn horns when we were in St. Louis. It didn't make sense then either." Christena studied the page. "Did he used to make hats?"

Her friend asked if Ephraim was mad as a hatter. Keziah held back a laugh. "Tailoring is as close as he came."

Mercy Jones's husband David rang the bell. "Brothers and Sisters, since our Heavenly Father has blessed us with such a beautiful day, let's assemble outside. Please bring your Bible." He instructed the men to arrange the benches in a circle.

Bible? Father Ephraim taught from his own revelations. Keziah hurried to the bothy for her Bible. Within its pages she'd met Jesus, and found comfort, knowledge, and peace. What would Brother David say this morning?

Duncan led them in a song with his fine voice. He was one of the few members who'd braved the cold waters of the creek to bathe. He was also one of the few who'd bothered to shave and comb his hair.

David prayed, then sat next to his wife. "Father Ephraim asked me to teach on work."

His next favorite topic after tithing. Keziah and Christena exchanged glances.

"My favorite verse about work is Colossians 3:23: 'And whatsoever ye do, do it heartily, as to the Lord, and not unto men.'" He looked around the group. "Now I have to admit, when I saw lumber for a stranger, my goal is to get the work done fast and get paid. If a board has a knot in it..." He shrugged. "...well, any fair to middling carpenter can manage a knot."

On the grass outside the circle, the children played a quiet game with pebbles. Miranda Barnum changed baby Frances's diaper, wiping her bottom with a mullein leaf. Finn circled the group, accepted a scrap of bacon from Cecelia, then settled behind Keziah.

David motioned toward the newly constructed house where the Jones and Barnum families lived. "When it came time to build my house--"

Uh-oh. All worldly goods were held in common in Preparation. No one had his own house. If David saw the house he lived in as his possession, Father Ephraim was bound to have a problem with it.

"— I picked good logs, tossed out a few bad boards. I hurried to get the logs sawed and move up here to Preparation." He nodded at the large building beside them. "Now for the Lord's House, I picked the best timber, sharpened the saw blade, inspected each plank. Shouldn't we treat every job as if we're working for the Lord? Shouldn't we always do our best?"

"A sow's ear can be more useful than a silk purse." Keziah murmured to Christena.

David's hearing hadn't been damaged by the sawmill. "What was that, Sister Sirrine? Raise your voice. As Father Ephraim says, this isn't church. We can all speak."

We can all speak? Since when? Several people shifted in their seats, others raised their eyebrows, one cleared his throat. Around here, Father Ephraim did the speaking. Even men who'd never opened a Bible knew women were to keep silent. Was David leading her astray? Keziah chose to take advantage of this opportunity. She repeated her comment and added, "For the work we're doing here, clothing made of sturdy twill is better suited than silk."

"So true, Sister. It's not about being fancy. Endless fussing over our work, trying to make it perfect, leads to nothing getting done. Father Ephraim works hard on each issue of *Zion's Harbinger*, yet there's always a typo or two." Realizing he'd slid onto thin ice, David backed up. "Nothing harmful to the message, of course. What other Bible verses have to do with work?"

Duncan read a similar verse from Ecclesiastes about working with all your might. James Durfee reminded them Jesus had reprimanded Pharisees who worked only for show. Orrin Butts quoted a verse in the Gospel of Matthew where Jesus said He shall reward every man according to his works.

David cautioned, "But remember, Ephesians says, 'By grace we're saved, through faith, as a gift of God, not of works.'"

That's it! That's the root of Jesus' message. It's what Father Ephraim had forgotten with his levels of heaven and—

Be still.

Keziah had tensed to stand, ready to shout the truth from the rooftop, but God's firm command kept her seated. She took a deep breath as her heart returned to its usual pace. Should she speak another time, or perhaps another would share this good news, or—

My word shall not return unto me void.

But, look at these people. They're stubborn, slow-witted, fearful... no different from her. His word had changed her life. It was sufficient to change theirs.

Homer Hoyt, relegated to shepherding since cutting his hand while shearing, spoke up. "My work has me been thinking about sheep."

"Psalm 23 comes to mind right away." David opened his Bible to the middle. "The Lord is my shepherd. I shall not want."

"Yep. We are His sheep. We're supposed to listen for His voice and follow Him, but we get lost and He comes looking for us, brings us back into the flock."

"Thank you, Homer." David stood. "This week, as you read your Bible, listen for God's voice and follow Him." He closed with a prayer. Duncan sang "Savior Like a Shepherd Lead Us."

Follow God? Learn from the Bible? Let women speak? Who knew David Jones could be... as revolutionary as Jesus. Could this be the start of a new day in Preparation? Tension seeped out of Keziah's body, replaced by a deep sense of peace.

Christena linked arms with Keziah. "Do you have a remedy for prickly heat?"

"Of course." Keziah raised an eyebrow. The weather had been mild. No one else had complained of heat rash.

When they got out of earshot of the others, Christena tipped her head toward the Lord's House, "You dared to speak?"

She hadn't intended to, but every year she had more trouble

holding her peace. "Maybe the Congregation will have forgotten by the time Father Ephraim returns."

She snorted. "Orrin Butts records every misdeed."

Keziah picked a black-eyed Susan, tucked it into Christena's buttonhole, and recited one of their favorite verses. "This is the day the Lord hath made. We will rejoice and be glad in it."

"I have a reason to rejoice. I'm pregnant."

"Christena!" Keziah embraced her friend. Could it be, after so many miscarriages, so many failed attempts in the years since Omer's birth? Or was it the change of life? "Are you sure? What are you feeling?"

"All the usual—grumpy gut, no monthlies, tenderness." Christena grinned. "I'm hoping for a girl this time. A daughter would be such a blessing."

"And I thought your glow came from a secret stash of coffee." It would never happen for herself, so Keziah would be happy for her friend. She pulled Christena into another hug. *Dear Lord, let her keep this one.* "I'll pray for you every day!"

~

June 1854

"Hellooo, Brother Duncan," Sister Cooley sang at the entrance of the store.

An iron band wrapped Duncan's chest, keeping him from taking a full breath. He didn't look up from cutting deer hide. Lately he'd seen plenty of the woman's round face, arched eyebrows, and smile tipped to the right. "Sister Cooley."

Her shadow darkened his work. "We've known each other long enough to go by first names, don't you think? Still making moccasins? Will you make a pair for me?"

"Sure." He grabbed a pair from the shelf under the workbench. "Try these."

"Oh, made them for me already, did you? Aren't you the kindest man?" She slipped her feet into the shoes. The moccasins flopped on her feet. "Is this how they're supposed to fit?"

"No." He grabbed a pencil and scrap of brown paper, and crossed the room to where she sat on the shoemaker's stool.

She pulled off the loose-fitting pair and wiggled her bare feet. "Aren't you glad I washed this morning? How many feet have you seen since becoming a shoemaker? Do you think mine are the prettiest you've ever seen?" Her skin was smooth and her toes formed a gentle angle.

Wanting neither to encourage nor cause offense, he said, "Yours are fine."

She leaned forward and grabbed his hands. "Are your hands the strongest in Preparation?"

Quick as a wink, he slid his hands from hers and traced the shape of each foot. "Perhaps yours are stronger, grappling with cows as you do." He hurried behind the counter. "Speaking of which, how much butter did you bring today?"

"Silly me, I nearly forgot." She hurried outside and returned with a churn. "I put four pounds in the spring house, then I thought of you all by yourself, how lonely you are, and wouldn't you enjoy my company?" Pumping the plunger, she pierced him with her dark eyes. "You've been having all sorts of interesting thoughts and won't it be lovely to share them with me?"

Lord protect me. "Since you're here to watch the store, I'll be making a delivery." He grabbed a pair of moccasins and dashed out.

"Hurry back, Duncan. I'll be waiting."

How long before she gave up and left? He ran up the hill, wondering where he could hide, and found himself at the bothy. Keziah sat in the shade of her porch, pounding away with her mortar and pestle. "What are you working on?"

Herbs drying overhead and blooming in the garden made a feast for the nose. "Turning dried strawberry leaves into powder. Good for kidneys, bowels, and teeth." She nodded at the bench beside her. "Sit yourself down and have a cup of cold water."

Duncan joined her and the tightness in his chest eased. A wet nose touched his ankle. He reached under the bench to pat Finn, then took a swallow from the cup Keziah offered. "Ah, my favorite, cold peppermint infusion."

She glanced at him, a sparkle in her eye. "For digestive health."

"And to ease the knots." Although Keziah, more than her tea, released his muscles. He leaned his head against the cabin wall. Shoemaking was done with the head bent, resulting in a sore neck and shoulders at the end of the day.

"I've no remedy for the knot Charlotte Cooley's wanting to tie."

"Aye. Last week Julia Scott, before that Sophia Gordon."

Charlotte spoke in questions. Julia complained about every member of the Congregation; Lord knows what she said about him when he wasn't around. And Sophia had the passive resignation—disasters are about to happen and there's naught to be done—his late wife had shown.

Duncan thumped his fist on his thigh. "I don't know why. I'm old, not so elderly as Silas Wilcox, but certainly past my prime. I have naught to offer. Father Ephraim doesn't push marriage the way other preachers do, 'better to marry than burn.' So I don't understand—"

"Naught to offer?" Keziah resumed pounding. "You help anyone in need, you're patient with wee ones, and you're even-tempered. You know several trades and are quick to learn new skills. You sing in tune."

Much as he appreciated her approval, Duncan knew he wasn't anyone special. "The same could be said of Luther Cottingham, Daniel Butts, and others."

"You're healthy and bathe regularly."

Duncan laughed. "Aye, living with this lot of men puts me in mind of the boat from Scotland. 'Twas a right foul reek."

"The single women's room is much the same."

He half turned toward Keziah, breathing in a whiff of warm plants. "They couldn't smell so bad."

"They could. And act even worse. Living close has turned them into porcupines, raising their quills and poking each other with elbows and words."

"Thus the Sabbath teaching against social pollution and filthy conversation." An exhausting thought had him seeking support of the bothy's wall. "Are you saying I'm to expect courting from another *eight*?"

"Perhaps only five. Three seem committed to others."

One lone blue butterfly wandered the herb garden. Did it have a partner or a swarm to share its brief life with? "When I came here, I'd no thought of marrying again, only to be part of a community."

"Ah, but if you marry, you wouldn't have to live with the single men. You'd have a house, a fancy title like 'Head of Family,' and perhaps children."

"Children. No." The iron band tightened again. He bent as his gut twisted. "I couldn't..."

"Oh, Duncan" Keziah's hand touched his shoulder. Her eyes, dark in the shade of the porch, held compassion. She knew his pain. Her other hand pushed the cup into his hands. "Drink."

He sipped and the cool infusion traced a soothing path down his middle. He leaned back and studied the herbs on the drying rack above him.

She nodded toward the store. "When you're settled, best put the dairymaid out of her misery, so she'll look elsewhere."

"Aye. I'll give her a moment to finish her churning, then send her on her way." Duncan took another swallow of the peppermint infusion and reined his thoughts in another direction. "I'm puzzled over another situation. When I joined the Congregation in St. Louis, Brother Butts seemed to be Ephraim's right-hand man, listed in the newspaper as one of the Chief Patriarchs. But now Guy Barnum is a Chief Patriarch and traveling with Ephraim, while Orrin has been moved to the list of Heads of Families."

"Although he's still giving orders." Keziah refilled his cup.

"True." Rolling the tin cup between his palms cooled him. "I've no yearning to be a Patriarch, you understand. But I'd like to know what he did, so I wouldn't trip over the same stumbling block."

The pestle stopped. "Father Ephraim doesn't discuss his reasons with me."

What purpose could there be in keeping them all guessing? Unless Ephraim wanted the Congregation groveling and buttering him up. A growling snort erupted from his throat. "Ach."

Keziah's mouth tipped in a smile. "Agreed."

Duncan recalled a letter read on the last Sabbath. "And who is this William Marks everyone was talking about?"

Keziah refilled his cup. "Brother Marks was a leader of the Saints until he spoke out against plural marriage. Then he followed James Strang who claimed to be a successor to Joseph Smith. Strang even dug up and translated brass plates. Then he, too, promoted polygamy, so Marks left him."

"All the digging I've done and never have I found anything more than rocks."

"Me too." Keziah chuckled. "Then Brother Marks joined forces with Father Ephraim, became a traveling teacher and served on the locating committee. Now he's moving on."

"Isaac Ashton and the Wilding family left." He'd hoped the Congregation would be steadfast, but people came and left before he had a chance to learn their names. They hadn't been here a year yet. His hands, of their own accord, had twisted the moccasins. He straightened them and handed them to Keziah. "Might these fit you?"

Dusty feet with crooked toes emerged from under her apron. "I wouldn't want to try them on, with so much of the garden stuck to me."

His head filled with the image of washing her feet, rubbing away the dirt, soothing her aches. For certain not what Jesus meant when he told the Apostles to wash one another's feet. He turned to hide the heat in his face. "You can try them on when it suits you. Thank you for the infusion and...for listening." He left them on the bench and trudged back to the store, reprimanding his wayward heart for turning towards forbidden fruit.

~

July 1854

"Are you knowing all the letters of the alphabet?" Keziah asked Leo as she examined the gaping wound. The boy had nearly sliced his foot off with a hatchet. He'd lose it if it festered. "What comes after a, b, c..."

"...x, y, z." He scooted away only to be herded back into her arms by Finn.

She pulled him onto her lap. How was she to hold him while dressing his wound? "Spell your name."

"L, eeeeee!" He screamed like a banshee as she poured whiskey over it. He threw himself backward, thumping his head into her chest bone. She nearly upended the bottle and lost her grip on him. He jumped off the porch.

"Hush, lad." Duncan caught him before he'd taken a step. "You're scaring the chickens. Let Sister Keziah tend you."

Even with strong arms pinning him down, the five-year-old squirmed, kicked, and hollered as she cleaned the wound again, and spread the infusion of honey, goldenrod, and plantago on his foot, then wrapped it with strips of muslin and retied his moccasins. "Keep this clean and dry." *Now there's a waste of breath.* "Don't let Finn lick it. Nor you."

"What do you say, lad?" Duncan let go.

Leo raced away, calling over his shoulder, "Thank you, Sister."

"And thank you, Duncan." Keziah rubbed her chest. Would penstemon root ease the head-shaped bruise Leo had left? "You heard his scream at the store?" This man showed up ready to help as often as Rufus was nowhere to be found.

"At the Lord's House." Duncan pulled burrs from Finn's fur. "I'm putting up the new stove and building a pantry, to keep next year's batch of syrup safe."

"We hope." Keziah grimaced, remembering her hard work shattered on the floor. She'd been angry enough to throttle the lad. "Father Ephraim and Brother Barnum brought back type and paper for the printing press, official documents for Monona Country, school books, a grist mill, and a new stove."

"But no Bibles for the lads," he muttered. "Have you heard of vegetarianism?"

She stored her supplies and locked the bothy. "Vegetarians don't eat meat. That's all I know."

"Ephraim brought a book on the subject. Christena Lytle and Sarah Chase are trying to make sense of it, figure out what our meals will look like. I suggested they include the head gardener."

"I'm not the head of anything, but I'm curious enough to help." After a longing look at the kitchen garden, where she'd been weeding potatoes, she walked with Duncan to the Lord's House.

"Lads." Duncan groaned when he spotted Nels and Isaac lounging in the kitchen. "Did I not tell you to saw the boards?"

"And did we not tell you, we don't know how to be carpenters?" Isaac asked.

"If we do not finish, the cooks will not be fixing our next meal."

"All right, all right." Nels held up a screwdriver.

"Lad." Duncan shook his head. "I cannot make it any simpler. To saw a board, you need a *saw*."

Sarah noticed Keziah and motioned her to the table in the corner outside the kitchen. "I've never seen more useless boys."

"Or a more patient teacher than Duncan," Christena sewed tucks on an infant's gown. As her baby grew, the hem could be let out. "Hugh would have beat them with the rolling pin."

Which explained why their son flinched whenever Hugh came near.

"Boys need their father around to teach them," Sarah said.

Rufus was never home. If her sons had lived, Keziah would have taught them to be resourceful and useful...like Duncan.

Christena Lytle handed her *Fruits and Farinacea: the Proper Food of Man*. "I wish this book had recipes. Breakfast of porridge, fruit, and milk, I understand. But what sort of dinner can we make without meat? And supper the same as breakfast? They'll be grumbling."

"Are we allowed to use lard?" Sarah asked.

"We've plenty of lard and no other choice for frying," Keziah answered.

Duncan stepped out of the kitchen. "Are fish allowed? I'd hate to give up my mornings at the river."

Keziah looked up at the man. Was there nothing he couldn't do?

"'Twas you keeping us in fish? I've not seen anything in the book about fish, so your mornings are safe. And thank you."

"No fish for me." Christena groaned, then winked at Keziah. "Your infusion helps with everything but fish."

"For me it was everything but eggs." Sarah turned back to the book. "What about the animals we have now?"

"Meat is selling in the store." Duncan looked up from attaching the pipe. "Homesteaders north and south of here are buying it. And the man running Larpenteur's ferry and tavern picked up a big order."

"Has Monsieur Larpenteur returned?" Keziah asked. Duncan shook his head. She returned to reading. The book seemed poorly organized, a hodgepodge of philosophy, chemistry, and observations of doctors in favor of vegetarianism, but no true plan for changing the diet. "I agree with the author that the shift away from meat must be gradual, to avoid intestinal disruption."

"Lest every day be like the first day of strawberry harvest." Sarah stuck out her tongue and pressed her hands to her belly.

Christena said, "At least we're doing one thing right—making bread from coarse flour."

"Abstaining from meat will be easier in summer and autumn." Keziah pictured the fields of Preparation. "We have corn, potatoes, buckwheat, cabbage, onions, watermelon, wild plums, grapes."

Young boys raced past, taking the path for the swimming hole. Leo's bandage trailed behind him in the dirt. Duncan set down the pipe and gave chase.

"That boy." Sarah shook her head, then returned to the book. "Don't we need meat to make it through winter? What if the children weaken and take sick?"

"I'll measure and weigh them, starting this week then monthly," Keziah said.

"We can make soup, but—"

Orrin Butts, daughter in tow, met Duncan as he returned. "What's the meaning of this?" He pointed to Malinda's footwear. "Why is everyone wearing moccasins? Are you trying to turn us into Lamanites?"

"Remember all the venison we ate when we first arrived?"

"Delicious." The girl smacked her lips. "Wish I had meat now."

Her father glared and shook her arm. "I'll speak with you later."

Duncan continued, "I tanned the hides into buckskin."

"It was a lot of stinky work," Dorman Lewis reported as he hauled in water for the next meal.

How dare Orrin attack Duncan. Keziah stepped forward. "We've had several injuries this year as children grow out of their shoes and go barefoot. Duncan made moccasins to protect their feet. Dorman, show Brother Butts yours." The thirteen-year-old grew like a weed, so he made a good example.

"We don't have pavement or gravel roads here, so no need for hard soles." Duncan balanced the boy as he removed his shoe and pointed at the second set of eyelets. "Buckskin stretches as they grow. They're comfortable enough several adults asked for a pair, including Father Ephraim. I'd be glad to make them for you, Orrin."

"You're too kind, *far too kind*," Keziah told Duncan, then turned to Orrin to nail the lid on this coffin. "If you're really concerned, you're welcome to order shoes for us from back east."

"Never mind." Orrin stomped up the stairs to the office.

Keziah and Duncan exchanged smiles. Tussles with Orrin Butts were less daunting and more successful when they joined forces.

Before they'd caught their breath, Brother and Sister Jones stormed up to the printing office and slammed the door. Oh no. Mercy complained, but David had settled in. Keziah raced to the kitchen and stirred up a pitcher of the soothing infusion.

Voices rose and echoed through the House. Ephraim scolded David over his Sabbath teaching on work, which Keziah had thought was a good lesson.

"...unauthorized teaching...no right to...random Bible verses... failure to follow my written instructions..."

The voices quieted for a time, then David said. "I'm done. I want the title to the land where my house stands."

Keziah carried the infusion and four cups upstairs. The rancid odor of sweat filled the room. She filled the cups.

"It's not your house." Father Ephraim took a sip and nodded his thanks. "As the Chief Steward of the Lord's House, the title is vested in me. As with all buildings."

David ignored her—she could drag a hothead to water, but couldn't make him drink—and flung out his hands. "Buy me out. You bought out the Wildings."

"He can't do that," Brother Butts scowled at her and crossed his arms. "According to the Preemption Act of 1841, we must pay $1.25 an acre when the surveyors come, or speculators will steal the land and all our improvements out from under us."

"You can't buy us out?" Mercy's waved away the offered infusion. "You bought yourself a fancy new suit when you were in St. Louis, but you have us wear rags."

"Now, Sister..."

Mercy dragged Keziah to the desk.

"I have no part of your dispute," Keziah hissed. Unlike Mercy, she didn't have a house in Council Bluffs to return to nor a husband to support her. She relied on Ephraim's favor to survive.

"Look at this," Mercy stretched out Keziah's skirt. "It's shameful. Rags. Patches on top of patches."

"My work is in the garden," Keziah protested. A bead of sweat rolled down the side of her face. "I've no need of fancy clothing."

"I brought back several bolts of sturdy fabric for our Congregation." Father Ephraim told her. "Ask Sister Thompson for what you need."

Keziah thanked him, hurried downstairs, and collapsed with shaking knees on a bench. What if Mercy told Ephraim they drank tea? Or their secret— how, as their faith in him ebbed, their faith in Jesus had grown?

Brother and Sister Jones announced their departure and marched out of the Lord's House.

Duncan watched them stomp away. "They're leaving?"

Mercy's voice had carried to every corner of Preparation. Keziah blinked back tears and nodded. Perhaps those who had much found it more difficult to share their possessions.

"I'm sorry. You've been friends with Mercy for years, haven't you?" Duncan asked.

"We met in Ohio." Christena wrapped an arm around her shoulder. Christena knew her secret too, but she'd never betray her. "Then lost track of each other in the rush of leaving Nauvoo."

The next edition of *Zion's Harbinger* noted, in clear new type, that fellowship had been withdrawn from David and Mercy Jones, the Wildings, and five others for heresy, apostasy, and lying to emigrants on their way to Preparation.

CHAPTER 11

August 10, 1854

"...raise the glorious harvest home!" Keziah sang "Come Ye Thankful People, Come" as she weeded the garden, looking forward to harvest.

Leaves rustled as Finn climbed from his hole in the shade of the chokecherry bush, alerting Keziah to a visitor.

Duncan peeked over the willow fence. "You've a beautiful voice. How about a duet?"

She smiled and wiped the sweat from her forehead. "I only sing while weeding."

Duncan looked up the path. "Another day, I'm thinking."

Two brown eyes peeked through the fence. "You the one help babies get born?"

She stood and leaned over, finding nine-year-old Hiram Winegar. Normally his mother kept her family as polished as a steamboat, but today his hair stood uncombed and purple stains splotched his shirt and trousers. Keziah would like to ask where he found a blackberry bush, but his right now a baby was ready to be born. Every day this week, Lodema had moved slower, with more pauses to hold her belly. Keziah left the garden, fastened the gate, and set Finn to guard the chickens.

"Need anything?" Duncan asked.

She grabbed her satchel. "Let Hannah Perrin, Priscilla Lewis, and Mary DeForest know."

As Keziah and Hiram walked to the Winegar cabin, they passed Andrew Haines and James Durfee returning from the creek, carrying water for the stables. "We're praying," they called.

"Thank you." Carrying her satchel to the Winegars' made known her errand, but offering a prayer was unexpected. Weren't those two in Duncan's Bible reading group?

As they reached the Winegar cabin, Hiram waved and scampered off toward the barn. He'd been three when baby Fred made him a big brother and five when his sister Clarissa arrived. He knew better than to hang around during a birth.

Water simmered over Winegars' laundry fire, to keep from adding heat to the house. Keziah eased the door open and waited until her eyes adjusted to the dark. "Lodema?"

"I'm here," said a voice from the bed. "How did you know?"

"Hiram."

"He frets." She rolled over.

"Are you all right?" Keziah rested her hand on the woman's belly mound. Perspiration had soaked through the gown and waves of heat radiated from her, thanks to August's humidity.

Lodema pushed upright, light brown hair swung down her back in a long braid. "I'm taking a moment to relax before the hard work begins. Christena Lytle took Clarissa and Fred, and I turned Hiram, Moroni, and Mosiah loose. Everything is ready." She grimaced as a pain hardened her belly.

"Including this baby." Keziah scrubbed her hands while praying, then helped Lodema into position.

Hannah Perrin arrived, the first mother Keziah attended to in Preparation, bringing a pail of warm water. "Don't suppose birthing a baby in the river is allowed."

"Cool water would be delightful."

Lodema groaned. "Here she comes."

"You're sure it's a girl?" Hannah asked.

"We'll find out in a moment."

With a push, the baby slid into Keziah's hands. "You're right. It's a girl." *Lord, please let Christena's delivery be this easy.*

Hannah took the infant for washing, earning an earful. "What will you name your darling opera singer?"

"Ovanda. We'll call her Mandy." The exhausted mother slumped back onto the bed. "Clarissa finished diapers last month…"

Keziah pulled Lodema upright and held out a cup. "Cold raspberry infusion. You'll feel better after you wash up."

"I can't do this again. No more babies." Lodema pressed her hands to her head. "I hear Indians know how to stop it. Did…?"

"I had no chance to ask." The loss of Makes Cloud—her knowledge and friendship—hit Keziah again. "Maybe you'll have the change of life. You're forty…"

"Forty-four. Seven children ought to be enough. I thought I was done, then…" She waved toward the baby. Tears rolled down her cheeks. "What can I try? What about those medicines for female complaints in the St. Louis newspapers?"

"Mrs. Jackson, the midwife I trained with, said the best would waste your money and the worst would kill you." Even if Keziah knew one that worked, she'd never get an order past Charles B. Thompson, the postmaster.

"You'd think being squeezed into little cabins with all these children would dampen a husband's enthusiasm." Hannah diapered the baby. "If Father Ephraim sent Frederick on a mission trip."

Lodema groaned and waved her hand to include the entire cabin. "He's not going anywhere lest he takes all these children."

"Can you imagine, Bible teaching with babies." Hannah giggled and rubbed her nose on baby Mandy's. "People would feel sorry for him and donate more."

"I can see it now." Keziah grinned as she rubbed Lodema's belly. "Hiram and Fred racing around, Clarissa looking for a lap to climb into, Mosiah and Moroni eating."

"No one could hear over the racket." Lodema sipped the raspberry infusion as Keziah washed her. She smiled, then shook her head. "I need minutes of quiet, not months." Lodema sent an apologetic glance to Keziah, who'd dealt with the silence of grief for years.

Priscilla Lewis and Mary DeForest brought supper, fresh sheets, and the good news that Christena would keep the younger children tonight. Lodema and baby Mandy were clean, comfortable, and content by the time Frederick returned home.

Departing, Keziah and Finn walked to the river to cool off. She removed her moccasins, thankful for Duncan's gift of comfortable footwear, kilted her skirt, and stepped into the shallows.

She and Lodema were nearly the same age. Seven of Lodema's children had survived. The age span between the first three suggested Lodema had also suffered loss, though not as many as Christena.

Keziah would have given anything—gardening, midwifing—if her children had lived. She would have kept them in food and clothes in spite of Rufus, and taught them to be kind, but wise in the ways of flimflammers. To work hard and not trust their money to silver-tongued devils. To be strong and care for those who are weak. Dear wee babies... Four of the five had had their healthy days, the first smiles and first steps, but all she remembered now was their deaths.

Finn emerged from the river, wet head to tail. He shook. Droplets hit her face, merging with tears. Drying them, Keziah headed back to the bothy.

August 29, 1854

Duncan glanced up from cutting leather as Andrew Hall's eleven- and seven-year-old daughters burst into the store. Their knees flashed below their calico skirts; eating vegetarian hadn't kept them from growing.

"Brother Duncan, you're missing the Gift Oblations." Cecilia wagged her finger, as authoritative as her mother.

Duncan had sat through the Solemn Assembly Sunday and Monday. The Congregation and visitors seemed to understand the preaching, but Duncan got lost when Father Ephraim expounded on the Mormon *Doctrine and Covenants.* So he'd escaped. "I don't have anything to give."

Paralee tugged his arm. "You have to bring your list."

"What list?"

"Your inventory." Cecilia pulled a pencil and blank Bill of Sale from under the counter. "Here you go. Write down everything you have."

"Shoemaking tools, whetstones, photograph of Emily."

"Who is Emily?"

"My wife. She's no longer with us."

"Did she go to heaven? Mama thinks Rufus Sirrine died, but she's not sure if he went to heaven or not."

Duncan's thoughts about Rufus would remain unspoken. "Emily went to heaven."

Paralee pointed to the list. "You forgot your coat, shirts, trousers."

Workman's clothes. Surely Father Ephraim didn't want the Congregation toiling away without clothes. Keziah would have no end of wounds to bandage. Visitors would be scandalized. Duncan finished his list and followed the children up the path.

The Congregation lined up in the shadow of the Lord's House. Keziah stood with Christena and Hugh Lytle and their son Omer. Duncan kept his distance; Hugh still held a grudge over Duncan riding his horse nine months ago.

Duncan followed Cecilia and Paralee to their parents. Andrew motioned him close and muttered, "Didn't mind sitting Sunday. But Monday and now this...Do they not know work's waiting?"

"'The earth is the Lord's, the fullness thereof,'" Sarah Jane quoted, swatting a persistent fly.

"Why are they doing this?" Duncan tapped his inventory with a finger.

"Don't you read *Zion's Harbinger*?" Andrew asked. "Government surveyors are coming. The bill will be due for our land. If we can't pay, speculators will grab it."

Sarah Jane nodded. "Thus the newspaper's request for settlers, saying the Congregation doesn't need as much land as we claimed."

What about the plan to teach Lamanites to farm? To turn Preparation into Zion? To provide for the poor? Thinking of the poor, Duncan glanced at his list. "Like blood from a turnip."

Keziah held up her similarly brief list. "You've company in the vegetable patch."

"Jesus praised the widow who put two mites in the treasury," Sarah Jane said. "Being poor isn't a sin."

"Poverty isn't a sin, but earns no applause here," Keziah said softly.

Duncan hadn't come seeking praise. He sought a place to belong. Although an occasional expression of appreciation would be welcome.

A second story window creaked open and Leo stuck out his head, followed by his arms and a leg.

The adults broke silence to yell, "Leo! Stop! Get down!"

Catherine pulled him back inside, waved, then shut the window. Keeping that child alive was more exhausting than herding chickens. Speaking of, "Where's Finn on this fine day?" Duncan asked.

"Guarding the chicken coop."

"At least someone's on the job," Andrew muttered.

Orrin Butts stepped out the front door and frowned at the crowd. "Sister Sirrine."

"Harvest time," she said with a wink.

Orrin was back in a minute. "Brother Ross."

Duncan followed him past the delicious smells of the feast into the office. Father Ephraim stood behind his desk, hands folded. "Brother Duncan Ross, what do you bring for your Gift Oblation?"

"All I have."

His inventory passed from Orrin to Ephraim, then to Guy Barnum who sat with a ledger.

"Welcome to the Covenant of Sacrifice, Brother Ross," Father Ephraim said, then Orrin ushered him out.

Covenant of Sacrifice? Is that the same as the Order of Voluntary

Sacrifice? He should have paid attention during the teaching. No matter. He had but one turnip and they were welcome to it.

Isaac Swett flagged him down as he descended the stairs. "We're to set the tables in a big square. The husbands will sit on the outside and the wives on the inside."

And whose foolish plan might this be? Duncan asked with a raised eyebrow, earning a shrug from the lad. "Are the sisters to leap over the tables or crawl under?"

He and Isaac arranged long tables on three sides and a short table on the end, leaving an opening for those inside the square. They moved benches into place.

Isaac raised his arms and grinned. "All done."

The Lytle family came through after their Gift Oblations. Hugh pointed his nose in the air. His voice dripped with contempt. "Foolish layout."

Isaac opened his mouth to speak, but Duncan turned his back to Hugh and gestured "stop" so only Isaac could see. He waited until Hugh left. "Not worth your breath. Now, have you no further instructions?"

The lad inched toward the door. "No, that's all I was told."

"Then you'll use the head God gave you to figure out where the rest of us will sit. We're expecting a hundred."

Isaac's mouth dropped open. Nels Turner, another lad from the Bible reading group, started for the kitchen, then saw Isaac hard at work and snuck out. The Hall family strolled through, their girls skipping and singing.

The wind came from the southwest, so the table for the odoriferous single men went in the northeast corner. The single women would sit in the northwest corner and children on the south. Having exceeded his limits of work, Isaac escaped.

Keziah carried a tray of utensils from the kitchen. "A square?"

"For couples." Duncan grabbed the plates and followed, keeping his voice low so those coming and going for their Gift Oblation wouldn't hear. "I came here to be part of a Congregation, but...those in families are held in higher regard. Except you. You're valued for birthing babies and healing."

"Without you, we'd all be barefoot." She glanced over her shoulder at him. "Where's the verse that says not to fuss over the wealthy and despise the poor?"

"Second chapter of James."

Keziah was silent for a moment as she set a spoon at each place on the children's table. "The Bible also says children are a reward from God. Blessed is the man whose quiver is full of them." She kept her eyes on her work, hiding the pain of loss they shared. "So where does that leave us?"

"Thinking every day how old they'd be." Duncan swallowed. "And what sort of people they'd become. I like to imagine my oldest working in the shop with me, my daughter so pretty I'd be scaring away suitors, the next..." His throat clogged and he pressed his fist to his mouth.

"Yours would be as kind and clever as their father. Not a doubt." Keziah emptied the tray and held it over her heart like a shield. "Speaking of fathers, I hear you're holding a Bible study with the single men."

He stepped to the side of the room and lowered his voice. "I'm no teacher, but I do have a Bible and know how to read it."

"Aye? And how's it going?"

He considered their lack of progress, then gave her a sidelong glance. "They're none too clever or eager. Like sheep."

"You're introducing them to their Shepherd. How many in your herd?"

"Andrew Haines, Isaac Swett, Nels Turner, and James Durfee."

"That explains why Andrew and James told me they were praying when I went to midwife Lodema." A smile lit her face. "You are doing a good work."

"God laid it on my heart when we arrived, then I dragged my feet for six months."

"You were building latrines and roofing the bothy." She shook her head. "I'm the one who's dragging feet, arguing with the Almighty about the apprentice He's sent me."

"Aye, more noise from that one lassie than from my entire herd." He chuckled, thinking of Malinda's constant chatter.

The bell rang for the feast. The Congregation lined up to wash their hands.

"Jesus said the kingdom of God belongs to the children. Shall we feast with the kingdom?" Keziah motioned toward the children's table.

He bowed. "I'd be honored."

September 1854

A morning storm pounded the roof, turned the House gloomy, and delayed the Congregation's departure for their assignments, so Keziah lined up the children for weighing and measuring. Duncan and Andrew had suspended the store's steelyard scale from the ceiling, and attached a tape measure to the wall.

Leo climbed onto the scale's sling and immediately pumped his legs.

"This is not a swing. Hold still." All things are possible with God, but holding still wasn't possible for Leo. Keziah moved the weight along the horizontal bar. The five-year-old kicked the wall, slammed into her, and sent her stumbling.

Duncan's arm on her back kept her from falling. "Enough, lad. Cross your legs." He folded the boy's legs into the sling, then turned to her. "Are you all right?"

"Yes, thanks to your good catch." Keziah took the measurement quickly, before the child could pull the building down around their ears. "All right, Leo, stand in front of this tape measure."

The older Barnum boy tried to climb into the sling with Leo. Duncan sorted them out with a firm hand.

Duncan scanned the room, then called, "Malinda, come help Sister Sirrine with measuring. And bring a lantern. Please."

The Congregation gathered around and the size of each child became a competition, an occasion for bragging.

"Hey, Keziah, how much does the scale hold?" Hugh asked. "I want to weigh Christena."

Christena lifted the baby blanket she was knitting, showing off her rounded belly. "I'd break the scale," she said with a proud smile.

"Then weigh my wife," Guy Barnum joked and others joined in.

"Husbands, thou art weighed and found wanting," Christena adapted a verse from the Book of Daniel.

When the laughter tapered off, Keziah reminded them, "We're checking the *children*'s growth as we change to a vegetarian diet." She got the oldest Barnum brother to stop standing on his tiptoes and recorded forty inches in the ledger.

"Keziah?" One of the visitors, a man with a grey fringe beard, pushed to the front of the line. Last Sabbath, William Swett had testified about preaching in Salt Lake City with the Gladdenites. Unable to take the church away from Brigham Young, they'd returned to Council Bluffs. "Keziah... Sirrine? Thought I recognized you. Rufus told me you were dead."

Every voice silenced, replaced by a rush of blood through her head. The ledger and pencil hit the floor. Keziah gasped. "Rufus...is alive?"

"He's building wagons north of Salt Lake City. His wife had twins last year."

Heat shot through her like lightning and her gut drew in as if she'd been punched. The room dimmed and spun. Voices rose and garbled. *Oh Rufus, how could you?*

"Breathe," Christena whispered and wrapped an arm around her waist. "Come."

"This is no circus." Duncan's voice cut through the babel. "Let us pray for our dear sister. With every eye closed..."

She shook so hard her feet dragged. Woodsmoke and dampness hung in the air; they'd moved from the kitchen to the laundry room. Christena pressed her onto a bench. "Sit."

A distant rumble to the east signaled the storm had moved on.

"I didn't realize..." Brother Swett must have followed them in. "I had no idea..."

"Not a thought crossed your mind, blatherskite," her cousin said. Finn growled. The door closed. Christena embraced her, pulling Keziah's head to hers. "Swett is out, but Thompson and Butts are here," she whispered.

Tears would come, but not now. Keziah anchored one hand in Christena's, the other on Finn's neck, then opened her eyes. "You heard…"

Father Ephraim sat on the opposite bench, eyebrows creased with sympathy, chin resting on hands in prayer position. He gave a slow nod, removed an envelope from the inner pocket of his jacket, and handed it to her.

Sister Keziah Sirrine, read Brother Hickenloper's handwriting. The man had left Preparation to join his uncle in Salt Lake City, becoming an apostate and earning pages of invective in *Zion's Harbinger*. She turned the envelope over, finding the seal had been broken.

She exhaled to keep emotion from her voice. "You read my mail?"

Ephraim nodded again. "It is my responsibility, as Chief Steward."

Christena pressed her shoulder. *Careful what you say.*

The letter conveyed much the same news as Brother Swett's revelation. Twins? The news that his wife had birthed and kept alive twins dealt the fiercest blow.

Keziah pushed the letter into her pocket. "You weren't going to tell me."

"I hoped to spare you the pain." Father Ephraim gestured toward the door. "I didn't know Brother Swett had also seen Rufus."

Silence reigned in the meeting room. No doubt the Congregation had their ears pressed to the wall.

Brother Butts crossed his arms and leaned on the wall. "This makes no difference to your life, Sister. You're not going to abandon Jehovah's Presbytery of Zion and take a wagon train to join in the corruption of polygamy."

The tightfist knew she had no means for travel.

"His marriage is illegal, isn't it?" Christena asked Ephraim.

"You could try to seek legal redress." Butts dismissed her

cousin's question with a shrug. "But why? It's not as if you'd remarry and have a family at your advanced age."

Bless Brother Butts's pea-sized heart. His attempts to control her always brought out her fighting spirit. Fury straightened her spine. "I'm two years younger than you, Orrin. Six years younger than your wife." That her body had given up hope of more children was none of his business. "I'm the same age as Hannah Perrin, who had a baby in October, and Lodema Winegar, who had a baby two weeks ago."

"Still...." Butts sputtered. "You've got to understand the economic necessities. The surveyors could require us to prove up any day." He leaned forward, hands extended. "We don't have money to throw at lawyers. Yes, you were right to advise purchase of warmer clothes for Preparation. We wouldn't have survived in Iowa without fearnought trousers, leather gaiters, and woolen coats. But spending money on a lawyer isn't a life-and-death matter."

"I'm so disappointed." Ephraim rubbed his temples. "Of all people, after everything we saw in Nauvoo, I never thought Brother Rufus would yield to the lusts and temptations of that loathsome practice."

Keziah squeezed the hand on her shoulder. *Get me out of here.*

"This has been a terrible shock. I know you'll continue to pray for our sister as she grieves." Christena levered Keziah to standing. Escorted by Finn, they stepped out and took shelter in the corner of the building. The eaves dripped, but the rain had stopped.

Finn leaned against her leg and Christena held her arm. "Thus ends my hope of being a widow."

"You've been alone and conquered every problem without his help. Can't say this will be much change."

What had changed? "No more watching the roads, scrutinizing the visitors, expecting him to show up and shoot my dog." A sunbeam cut through a cloud. Keziah drew in a deep breath. "But if I'm not a widow, not married, then who am I?"

"The independent, hard-working woman you've always been. The survivor. The herb woman of Preparation." Christena pulled her into another hug. "Dear friend, what can I do for you? Do you want to lie down?"

"The bothy is no place to hide." What did she want, now that she'd been delivered from worry about Rufus? "I want to go for a walk."

The storm had settled the dust and blown the humidity from the air, leaving clear skies, comfortable temperatures, and the fresh-washed glory of the prairie in summer bloom. Every plant sparkled as sun lit the raindrops.

"Shall I go with you?"

"Thank you, but I'd prefer privacy as I contemplate murder." She winked.

"That's the spirit." Christena grinned. "I'll leave food in the bothy for you. Go celebrate your freedom."

"Freedom?" Keziah glanced at the Lord's House, then gave a small shake of her head and set out for the hills. "If only..."

September 1854

Duncan swung the flail again and again. It landed on the wheat, breaking grain from chaff. He'd like to land it on the back of Rufus Sirrine. No, a flail was too good for the likes of him. A shillelagh would do. What was the man thinking? Had he left St. Louis intending to rejoin the polygamists? Intending to take another wife? What a fool.

And Sister Sirrine. *Lord heal her heart.* Duncan couldn't imagine the pain. Losing dear Emily and their children had near 'bout killed him. But they hadn't *chosen* to leave. Rufus deliberately—

"Hey man, we've a grist mill now. No need to pound it into flour." Thomas Lewis held out a dipper of water.

Duncan took a gulp, then dumped the rest on his head. "Sorry."

Thomas raked off the straw. They shook the canvas, letting the wind take the chaff, then emptying the grain into a bucket.

"She's better off without him."

For a moment Duncan considered asking "who?" But he figured

most of the Congregation had Keziah on their minds. "I don't understand why..." Even naming the sin was offensive.

Thomas scuffed his boot in the dirt. "He seemed like an agreeable sort. But when Priscilla and I visited, Rufus had set off on an errand for Joseph Smith. He'd left Keziah alone to birth and bury their son... in a shack with no food or firewood."

The fire of rage added to the sweat he'd built. "But...the Bible says a husband should love his wife as himself."

"True. And the church is supposed to take care of each other...if they know of the need." Thomas gave a defeated nod. "When Rufus got back, I took him to task in front of the Quorum. But they didn't want to lose a skilled wainwright."

Why had Keziah been living in pitiful excuse for a house in St. Louis? "Wainwrights make decent money."

"Rufus used it all to climb the church ladder, trying to buy his way into heaven."

No one would try that in Preparation; no one had money.

Thomas stretched out the canvas. "Any time she'd need him, he'd go missing, off on a mission trip, building wagons for new converts. He starved his own children to death, is what he did."

Duncan and Emily had wept together, holding each other through the agony of their children's deaths. When she'd died, he'd felt the loss doubly, wondering if he'd survive grieving alone. How had Keziah endured?

Duncan glanced up at Thomas. "I'm glad she has you and Priscilla." He dropped the canvas and turned slowly until his gaze caught on a pile of logs. "Time to cut firewood."

The sympathy in Thomas's eyes said he understood. "Try not to turn it into sawdust, old man."

"No guarantee, laddie."

CHAPTER 12

September 1854

Last week, the Congregation had been abuzz over Brother Hickenloper's defection to Salt Lake City. This week, Keziah hoped a different event would take their minds off the news of Rufus. Perhaps Father Ephraim would have another revelation and announce all food would be eaten cold to preserve firewood. But no, her arrival in the Lord's House for breakfast was met with a sudden silence, even from the babies she'd delivered. They turned as one to stare at her.

She raised open arms. "Thank you for your prayers. God has blessed my heart with comfort and peace." Peace about Rufus, if not about Preparation. She joined the Lytles for breakfast.

Christena gave her a nudge. "Sounded like you were quoting Scripture."

"That's what I get for keeping company with the likes of you."

Her nosy cousin leaned forward, trying to look her in the eye. "Sleep any?"

"Quite well, actually." Spreading jam on bread always made her long for a hot cup of coffee. "Brother Swett around?"

"Yes. Despite all my efforts to give him the heave-ho." Christena served her the last of the eggs. "He's cutting corn today. Like to shock his sheaves, I would."

"Here he comes." Omer jabbed her with a pointy elbow. "Hide under the table. Too late. He's seen you."

Keziah winked at Omer, then greeted Brother Swett. "Good morning."

He shuffled up to the table, hands clasped at his waist, head tipped toward the floor. "Sister Sirrine, beg pardon for yesterday. I should have realized hearing Rufus was alive would fluster you, what with him married and a new wife and babies."

"Apology accepted." Hiding her irritation with a bland expression, Keziah grabbed Brother Swett's hand and pulled him within earshot of a whisper. "I'll meet you after breakfast. Other side of the chicken coop. Not a word to anyone." She pushed him away and returned to her food. All this forced cheerfulness built an appetite.

"Shooting the messenger is considered poor form, but in this case..." Christena watched him sit with the Butts family. "...count me in."

"Such a helpful cousin." Keziah finished her oatmeal and stood. "But I'd hate to give you nightmares."

Crows called from the roof of the Lord's House as Keziah marched to the chicken coop. "I'll remember your warning," she told them. Anything said to Brother Swett would be repeated to Father Ephraim.

As instructed, the man stood beside the chicken coop. He was one of the rare people in this world who looked worse when he smiled, growing pouches on either side of his face and an extra chin under his jaw. He took a step toward her and Finn growled.

Keziah sank her fingers into the dog's scruff and shook. "Brother Swett. Tell me, how is Rufus?"

"Well enough. Eating plenty. Good coloring."

As many times as Rufus announced his imminent death, he ought to be six feet under. "You said he builds wagons."

"Heavy wagons for all the freighting going through the Salt Lake Valley. He must have a dozen men working for him - wainwrights, wheelwrights, blacksmiths. His wife's brothers breed and raise draft horses across the road."

So her family will see she's taken care of. "Sounds busy. Rufus lives nearby?"

"That he does. Big house behind his shop. Two story, adobe, with a porch around the front and another around back. Good sized garden."

House and a *garden*. Did Utah have poisonous snakes? Did wild parsnip or stinging nettle grow there? "Sounds like a lot for his wife to manage."

"Not at all. She's got help to keep the place up, do the cooking and laundry and such. Comes from money, she does."

Rufus deserved the slowest, most painful death imaginable. Parasitic worms, perhaps. "Where's she from?"

"England. Her brother's married to a cousin of one of the bigwigs."

"Brigham Young?"

He shook his head. "Pillar of the church from one of the Quorums. Can't remember if it's the Twelve or Seventy."

So Rufus had found a way to rise in the Mormon pecking order. "Where did they meet?"

"Her family hired him to take them on one of the wagon trains in 1850."

Ah, after he left St. Louis. A fraction of tension seeped from Keziah's shoulders. "Thank you, Brother Swett. I'll let you get to your work."

Brother Swett's head swiveled, taking in what must look like a shack, a stubble-ridden wasteland, and an ill-tempered mongrel. In comparison to the new young wife, Keziah must appear like a hag, dressed in tatters, her hair greying. He cleared his throat. "Say, if you're thinking of going out there, he's got plenty of room for you."

Shocking Rufus by rising from the dead would be fun, but becoming an unwanted polygamous wife in his household would be nothing short of hell. Keziah's gaze traveled past the bothy with its locking door, the bountiful herb garden, the rippled hills with abundant plants, and the protector leaning against her. A thousand miles from Rufus. Her face relaxed into a genuine smile. "Not on your life."

~

October 1854

Clouds hung low in dawn's light, occasionally releasing a snowflake or two. Keziah lit a lantern, then pulled a branch of dried alumroot from the ceiling rack, and matched the leaves to Makes Cloud's drawing. She put them in the mortar and pounded them with the pestle until they turned to powder. Combined with warm water, it could be gargled to soothe sore throats, or swallowed to relieve dysentery and piles. When the leaves turned into fine particles, she emptied the mortar into a labeled envelope.

"Sister Sirrine." Omer rattled the door. "It's Mother. Come quick. It's the baby."

"Oh no." *Too early. Way too early. The baby's only four or five months along.* Keziah threw on her cape, grabbed her satchel, and blew out the candle. She and Finn followed Omer through the gray day.

The cabin smelled coppery with blood. Soiled sheets had been pulled off the bed and dumped on the floor, leaving a dark stain on the ticking. Christena sat on a towel-covered chair, bent over, holding a tiny baby who wasn't breathing. *No. Not again.*

Keziah didn't want to be here. There was too much blood, too much death, too many painful memories. Someone else—

Thou art here for such a time as this.

The familiar words from the Book of Esther sounded in her head. If not her, then who? Not Malinda with her constant prattle, Rebecca Butts with her worries, or Eliza Cobb with her fault-finding. No one else had trained with a midwife and knew to check that the afterbirth was complete—it was. No one else knew Christena, what she'd been through, how to comfort her, and how to manage Hugh's temper.

The bell rang for breakfast.

"Take the laundry," she told Hugh and Omer, but they left without it.

"Your beautiful baby." Keziah kneeled in front of her. "I am so sorry."

With a sound between a moan and a sigh, her tear-filled eyes opened. "I let my hopes rise..." She paused for another exhale. "You prayed constantly. I had clean air, clean water, good food..."

Keziah wrapped her arms around her cousin and held her as together they wept. When they'd cried themselves dry, Keziah gave her a raspberry infusion, then flipped the mattress over and put clean sheets on the bed. In spite of the enthusiastic fire in the stove, Christena shivered.

"Let's get you clean, so you can lie down." Keziah moved the baby to a folded towel on the table, then washed Christena and dressed her in a clean gown, relieved to see the bleeding had stopped. She stood in front of her cousin, grasped both of her forearms, and hauled her to her feet.

"I'm fainting." She slumped like a sand-filled rag doll, her head on Keziah's shoulder.

"Not allowed." She shifted Christena's weight, then pushed her leg closer to the bed. Then a shift in the other direction, and another step. An extra pair of hands would help, but a crowd would be vinegar on her wounded heart now. "Deep breaths. Three more sidesteps. Here's the bed."

Lying down roused her. "It was the same as the other times. I woke to a fierce--" She closed her hand in a fist. "—spasm. Like a monster grabbed my insides. A puddle of blood. Then she was born."

"I'm sorry I wasn't here for you."

"Even if you'd been here, there was nothing you could do. It happened so fast. Nothing anyone could do. But being here now... you're the balm I need."

"Let me know if the bleeding starts again." Keziah pulled the covers over her. "Rest, dear one."

Her arm shot out and grabbed Keziah's with surprising

strength. "Bury her atop the hill. She didn't get to see the world, so..." She frowned. "Am I insane?"

She shook her head. "No. You're heartbroken. Do whatever provides a wee bit of comfort. Do you have a name for her?"

"Rachel." She started to drift off, then her eyes opened again. "I'm an expert in the terrible job of burying my babies." She cringed. "The shelf by the stove. There's wool dyed with the bloodroot and sumac berries you gave me. A handkerchief to wrap her in. And the blanket I didn't get to finish."

"Those will make a nice bed for Rachel." Keziah smoothed hair back from Christena's face. "You've done all you can. Sleep now."

The bell rang again, this time for dinner. Had Hugh forgotten his wife, and the midwife too, needed sustenance? She'd like to knock sense into his—no, her stomach must not dictate her mood, even if she'd missed two meals. She wadded up the dirty linens and tied them with the cleanest sheet.

Outside, Duncan led the Congregation in singing "Amazing Grace." Christena drifted off.

At the end of the song, Keziah stepped out and caught Hugh. She shared Christena's wishes, gave him the laundry, and reminded him to bring food. He didn't argue, a sure sign of shock. Back in the cabin, she added another log to the stove, prepared more raspberry tea, and heated water for the final grim task.

Dear baby Rachel. So cold and still. Careful with her fragile skin, Keziah rinsed her, then patted her dry with a diaper she'd never use. Fine hair covered her body. Toes, fingers, the shape of her skull, all looked normal. With her head at Keziah's fingertips and her legs stretched out, her feet reached to Keziah's wrist. She wrapped Rachel in the handkerchief, padded her with the wool, then swaddled her in the blanket. Her only fault was her early arrival... like the others since Omer.

And like Keziah's second child, buried along the road... No. That memory would sink her. She'd be no good to anyone.

Crying had given her a headache. In the absence of a hot coffee and food, Keziah leaned her forehead on the window glass and watched Duncan dig the grave. She knew there was nothing more to do for Rachel, but she continued to rock her.

Hugh returned with the coffin, but no food, waking Christena. "Can you walk?"

"No, she's too weak," Keziah answered for her cousin. The east window framed the view of the grave. "She can watch from here. Hold Rachel and I'll help Christena sit up for more of the infusion." She handed the baby to Hugh, then propped up her cousin with all the pillows in the house.

Hugh held his daughter in the window's light. "She's as dark as an Indian and hairy. Is this Lamanite witchcraft?"

The shock had passed and Hugh had returned to his ill-tempered habit of thinking the world was out to harm him.

"It's normal for babies that come early, before they get their fat, before they can breathe."

"The others were the same color." Christena reached for Rachel.

"Oh...I'd forgotten." He handed the baby to his wife. "The Congregation is waiting." Hugh wasn't concerned about inconvenience to others; he just wanted to get this over with. "Take as long as you need, Christena," Keziah told her cousin. "I'll get your dinner, while you spend time with your daughter."

"Sarah Chase is in charge of food." He drummed his fingers on the table. "We're running out of daylight."

"Tomorrow God will bring another sunrise. No need to rush."

Hugh grunted, a sign of impending explosion. Christena met her gaze. She was too fragile to deal with her husband's rage, so she kissed the baby's head and handed her to Hugh. He laid her in the coffin and left.

After giving her another drink, Keziah sat next to Christena, tucking her close to warm her. Beef would build her blood up. If Father Ephraim wouldn't allow it, chicken would do.

A sunbeam slid under the clouds, sparkling the snowflakes over the grave.

Christena gasped. "So beautiful."

"Just for Rachel." Keziah squeezed her shoulders.

The Congregation left the House, climbed up the hill, and stood in a circle. Wind pummeled them, flapping their clothes and spattering them with snow. After a few minutes they hurried back to the House. The bell rang for supper.

Christena had fallen asleep. Pain kept Keziah from giving in to exhaustion. Her head hurt from crying, her heart from sadness, her legs from kneeling on the cold floor, her stomach from hunger, her shoulders and neck from lifting...

Hugh arrived, empty-handed again. *Did the wretch have a thought for anyone else?* He helped pull the sheet to ease Christena into a more restful position. Keziah donned her cape, grabbed her satchel, stepped outside, and stepped on the pile of laundry. *Thoughtless, inconsiderate...grieving father.* She blew out an angry breath, hefted the load, and continued to the House.

Oh Lord, dear Lord. Please heal Christena...and I could use a slice of bread.

Duncan hurried from the House and took the laundry...as if he'd been watching for her. "Your supper's on the table. What else needs doing?"

"Christena hasn't eaten. I need to talk to Father Ephraim about beef for her."

"She hasn't... then you haven't? Sarah Chase said Hugh...." His jaw tightened over a growl in the back of his throat. "Never mind. Sit ye down, before you keel over. I'll talk to Ephraim."

She knew Father Ephraim made him ill at ease, yet he was willing to do this. She gave him as much of a smile as she could manage, then went to eat.

Beneath an upside-down bowl sat stew, cornbread with butter, plum pudding, a mug of water, and a spoon. Tears filled her eyes as gratefulness filled her heart. How different her life would have been if she'd married a man as selfless as Duncan.

~

November 1854

Snow flurries kept Keziah from scouring the hills for new plants and kept the rest of the Congregation away from the bothy.

Today was a good day to finish the last of the tea Mercy had given her. Keziah was grateful she'd returned to Council Bluffs before they learned of Rufus's betrayal. Mercy tended to dig up dirt and spread it. Keziah didn't need more ugly thoughts piercing her heart, poking holes in her gut. What had Makes Cloud recommended for calming? Ah, here it is: pasque flower essence. One drop went into her tea.

Today was also a good day to figure out the remedies Makes Cloud had left. Her seeds had sprouted, then grown into healthy plants which now sat on shelves. Keziah matched them to Makes Cloud's drawings of the leaves. Good thing no one else lived here. Moving herbs around, even with the kind intention of tidying, would throw her whole system off.

And today was a good day to keep her mind in the here and now. Not yesterday with all sacrifices and silences. Not tomorrow with unknowns and questions. Today. She had much to be grateful for, such as Christena's healing. Her cousin had made it to the House for breakfast this morning. *Thank you, Lord.*

Two parts crushed leaves, one alcohol, lid on jar. Sit until the next sunrise. The penstemon leaves crumbled into the mortar and crushed easily with the pestle. Easier than crushing Rufus's head. "No. Back."

Finn blinked with mild offense.

Keziah ran her hand down his thick fur. "Not you, dear friend. Talking to my wandering thoughts."

Next, shrubby cinquefoil— Finn jumped at the door, tail wagging. Rippling curtains of snow hid the outside world, but a gray blur solidified into Duncan, running uphill into the wind. Keziah pulled him inside. "Leo?"

He shook his head. "Sick baby."

She banked the fire, blew out the candle, then packed her bag. "Any idea what the problem might be?" *Please, Lord, not another death.*

He met her gaze, eyes wide. "You're asking me?"

"Best guess."

"He's a cough. Croup, perhaps."

Keziah added another remedy and a yard of muslin to her bag. She pulled on the greatcoat she'd remade into a cape for herself, thankful she'd never have to hear what Rufus thought of her appropriation. "Which family?"

"Jepson. They've been homesteading north of here since June. Baby Thaddeus is a little over a year now. The mother is Elizabeth. The father is Peter. Decent sort, but upset about his baby."

Gentiles... who needed her help.

Finn bounded out in the snow. Keziah locked the door and Duncan took her arm as they slid down the hill. "Mind Finn for me?"

"Glad to. Anything else?"

"No. Thank you." She glanced over at him. Beneath his cap, blue eyes met her gaze. "Yes. Pray."

His mouth widened. "God answered my first prayer, that I would find you."

The horse and wagon appeared through the gloom, parked beside the store. A bulky man raced out, boosted her into his wagon, and they were off.

Keziah braced her legs and grabbed the seat as they bumped along the frozen track. "Tell me about Thaddeus's cough."

The man scowled. "Can't none of you speak good? All youse a bunch of foreigners?"

If it wasn't for the sick baby, she'd jump off the wagon and walk back to Preparation. "I was born in upstate New York."

"Store clerk talk funny too."

"Duncan's from Ohio." She slowed her speech. "How long has your son been coughing?"

"All night. Out a wind. Not eating."

"Can you make the same noise?"

Peter barked, then whistled. Duncan's guess of croup was likely correct.

White smoke rose from the cabin's chimney. The Jepsons didn't have a wood stove. *Dear Lord, please let Thaddeus still be alive.*

Keziah jumped off the wagon as soon as it slowed and raced

inside. The house was so smoke-filled, she couldn't see anyone. "Elizabeth? It's Keziah, the herb woman."

"Here," said a weak voice from the dark corner beside the fireplace. "Baby's sick."

A faint cough-whistle sounded from the same corner. Serious, but not whooping cough. *Thank you, Heavenly Father.*

Eyes watering from the smoke, Keziah shuffled forward until she bumped into the bedstead. She yanked the quilt off the bed, wrapped it around the pair, and hauled them outside. "Thaddeus needs fresh air."

"No. He'll get cold." Elizabeth dragged her feet.

"Your body will keep him warm." She tucked the blanket to let the wee one breathe. "Calm yourself. If Thaddeus cries, he'll have a harder time breathing." Winter's gloom showed damp curls stuck to a round head, a face creased with pain, neck muscles fighting to pull and push each breath. "Stay right here, in the lee of the house. I'll open the windows, fix the fire, warm up cough syrup."

"Windows don't open." Peter trudged around the side of the house. "What's baby doing outside?"

"Breathing fresh air. The house is full of smoke."

The man frowned. "Not sick?"

"He is sick. The smoke's making him worse."

Elizabeth turned so her husband could see Thaddeus. "Breathing better."

Peter charged inside, cursing about wet wood and jabbing the mess on the hearth. His claim had few trees, so they'd been using twists of straw.

With the light from the open door, Keziah found an empty kettle. "Where do I go for water?"

"I'll get it." Peter snatched it from her and stomped out.

Pushing the straw to the back of the fireplace improved the draft. Keziah filled a small pot with honey syrup and set it in the coals. "Don't blame yourself," she told the man when he returned. "You're doing your best to keep your family warm this winter."

He hung the kettle on the crane and grunted.

The child breathed easier. Keziah helped Elizabeth back into the rocking chair. "Hold him on your lap and I'll feed him the syrup. C'mon—" *Don't say laddie.* "C'mon, little one. Time for a taste, soothe your throat." The baby's eyes were shut, but when she touched the spoon to his lips, his mouth knew what to do.

"What you feeding him?" The mother asked, her tone heavy with suspicion.

"Honey infused with penstemon, pasque flower, and juniper." Makes Cloud's recipe. After a few spoonfuls, Keziah filled a cup with warm water, added the rest of the honey and a spoonful of thyme. Thaddeus drank it all. "Good boy."

"He's asleep. At last." Elizabeth let out a long breath.

Keziah folded a shirt to raise the baby's head in the cradle. The mother laid him down and Keziah draped the cradle with a damp muslin. "This will keep the smoke from him and add moisture to the air he breathes." She left a jar of the syrup and an envelope of dried thyme on the table.

"Thank you kindly." Elizabeth's eyes filled with tears. "You be back?"

"If you've need of me."

The woman ran her hands down the front of her dress, shaping the homespun wool around her belly. "Guessing March."

"May I?" Keziah received a permissive nod. She pressed her fingers to the mound and a flutter brushed them. "Lively one."

"Sure enough is."

"The best I can do for you now is let you rest." Keziah nodded toward the bed.

Peter drove her through heavy snow to Preparation and gave her a grudging "thank you." She stepped inside the Lord's House as supper began. Head to toe, she ached with cold. Snow had forced its way through her scarf, icing the right side of her head. Her hands were locked in the shape of the wagon seat. Through her left eye—her right being frozen shut—Keziah saw every member of The Congregation watching her. The aroma of potato soup had her stomach growling. She headed for the kitchen.

Brother Butts stepped in front of her. "Hand it over."

His words pummeled her through a haze of fatigue, hunger,

chills, and worry for a sick child who lived in poverty worse than any in Preparation. "What?"

"Whatever he paid you."

She tried to raise her eyebrows, but only the left one responded. "What happened to our mission to the poor and needy?"

"You don't know how much money those people have."

"Actually, I do." If the Jepsons had money, they wouldn't be cooking on a hearth, shivering under one thin quilt, and wearing homespun. She stepped around Orrin. "What I don't know how much money *you* have."

CHAPTER 13

December 1854

I don't know how much money you have. Keziah's words to Brother Butts echoed in Duncan's head as he replaced the sole on a shoe. Peg-tap-*how.* Peg-tap-*much.* Peg-tap-*money.* The Congregation had drawn in a breath, as quiet as a whisper, then studiously returned to supper. But her words had echoed across the room as Orrin Butts had stomped upstairs.

How much money?

Preparation had begun with each member paying one-tenth of their possessions and services. But when the Land Office announced this valley would be sold to speculators, Father Ephraim instituted a New Order of Sacrifice: everyone had to surrender all property, everything they'd brought with them, and work for him for two years. Thirty families agreed. Seven left.

Neighbor Peter Jepson rattled up in his wagon. "How much is butter?"

"Good afternoon, Peter. Twenty cents per pound. Would you like to try our cheese?" Duncan cut off a chunk and it disappeared into the hole in Peter's beard. "How is young Thaddeus?"

The scowl softened. "Eating."

"Back to good health, then, and hopefully making up for lost time. Will you be needing potatoes? Eighty-five cents a bushel. Oats, seventy-five. White beans, dollar twenty-five. Beef five dollars per hundred pounds."

"Lard?"

"Eight cents a pound. Tallow, ten cents a pound."

The man rolled his hand in his pocket, fingering his coins. After negotiating, he left with lard, pork, potatoes, and beans.

When the Jepsons had moved to the valley, Duncan hoped to invite them to join the Congregation for the Feast. But August's heat brought tempers to match. The December Feast had been canceled —one cannot have a feast without meat, Duncan supposed—to be replaced by a Solemn Assembly. Father Ephraim's teaching on rigid self-denial and the sacrifice of all things wouldn't draw a man like Peter Jepson, who lived as a pauper.

Duncan counted the coins into the money box, then entered the order in the ledger. *How much money?*

The store's windows faced the road, so Duncan stepped outside. No one strode down from the Lord's House. Sun shone on the new snow, showing deer had circled Keziah's garden and a raccoon had investigated the hen house. From the timber claim came the chop-chop of men cutting wood. By the river, a wild turkey gobbled. Otherwise all was quiet.

Back inside, Duncan scanned the columns, adding the numbers in his head. *Whoa, can't be right.* With another glance out the window, he pulled the stool close, sharpened a pencil, and tore a scrap of butcher paper off the roll. He added the figures, once and again. Larpenteur's innkeeper's regular purchases would cover the preemption fees, leaving an abundant overflow. Duncan folded the scrap into his pocket, locked the ledger in the cashbox, and returned to his cobbler's bench.

How much money indeed. Where was it all going?

With free labor and little expense, grain grew and livestock increased...as did Father Ephraim's purse. With this much coming in from the store, why did he need the Congregation's possessions?

Duncan had been allowed to keep his worn clothes, a daguerreotype of Emily, and, of course, his shoemaking tools as they served the Congregation. He hadn't anything else. But others had full sets of silverware, tea sets, furniture, jewelry. Were they stored in the attic of the Lord's House or had they been sold? If so, where had the money gone?

He couldn't ask Keziah. She'd been skittish since the news of Rufus came in. Father Ephraim would blather on about the Sacred Treasury and a British fellow who wrote about the law of right-eousness. Brother Butts would know, but was as tightfisted with facts as he was with funds. So who then?

The last peg tapped in. The shoes belonged to Guy Barnum… who had been privileged to travel with Father Ephraim to St. Louis and had been appointed Chief Patriarch. Before he could talk himself out of it, Duncan tucked the shoes under his arm and closed the store.

He crunched through the snow to the Barnums'. No doubt Guy's wife and the children would be home, but conversation there would be more private than at the Lord's House.

Guy emerged from the latrine as Duncan approached. "Your shoes are done."

"Quick work. Come on in." He started for the house.

"Well, I wanted to ask…" Duncan stopped, which led Guy to take a few steps closer. "I've run a business or two along the way. Might the Congregation need help with bookkeeping?"

Guy shook his head and waved his hands. "Father Ephraim, as Chief Steward, is managing all everything for us."

Aye and that's the problem. "I'm wondering… the store's doing well. Do we still need to sacrifice to pay the Land Office?"

Guy crossed his arms. "Running this place is more expensive than you'd think. The newspaper isn't paying for itself, and we've had to buy lumber since timber's scarce."

First on the list of people he'd rather not see came around the side of the house. "What does it matter to you, Ross?" Hugh Lytle spit on the ground. "You've no horse in this race. No horse at all."

It'd been over a year since Duncan had ridden Hugh's mare. "Hugh, I apologized. No need to flog that dead horse."

Hugh stomped away, muttering about hanging horse thieves.

"Duncan, you old wag." Guy clapped him on the shoulder, an overly-hearty gesture. "Trust Father Ephraim, our Chief Steward, to guide us through to Zion." He took the shoes and headed inside. "Good workmanship. See you at supper."

Where no doubt, the Chief Steward would call him into the office. Duncan passed the cabin he shared with the other single men and climbed the hill. He scanned Preparation, thinking of all the good people he'd come to know. His gaze lifted to the rippled ridges, tall grass dusted with silver snow. Where could he go? He pulled out the scrap and studied the numbers. It came down to a choice: Thompson or Truth.

January 1855

Keziah entered the kitchen and nodded at the pot of oatmeal. "I'll take the rest to those who are ill."

Sarah Chase put the lid on. "I noticed we're missing a few folks this morning. What ails them?"

"Laziness." Orrin Butts set his bowl on the counter and jabbed a thick finger at Keziah's nose. "Do not indulge idlers who shirk their assigned duties."

"Catarrh," Keziah told the head cook, then turned to Orrin. "You are welcome to join me and tell them yourself."

Waving a dismissive hand, he scuttled out. "I don't want to take ill."

His daughter leaned on the doorway. "I'll be glad to help."

Was she defying her father or was one of her candidates for husband sick? Or something else?

Sarah asked, "Are you washing dishes this morning?"

"No, Sister. Moroni and Cecilia are."

"Malinda, I accept your offer." Keziah gathered clean bowls and spoons. "Wash your hands and bundle up."

Duncan put his empty bowl in the sink and tied his cap to his head with his scarf. "I'll bring 'round firewood."

"Will you now?" Keziah raised an eyebrow. Would he deliver

165

wood to Hugh Lytle, who bore a grudge against Duncan for riding his mare?

"Aye."

"Don't take wood from the bothy," she teased. Duncan had been kind enough to replace the wood Hugh had taken from her porch.

"Wouldn't think of it." His wide mouth quirked, trying to hold in a laugh. He gave Finn a scratch behind the ears before the dog raced out.

Keziah and Malinda loaded the sled and pulled it toward the cabins. A scattering of snowflakes wandered through the air.

"This morning you'll see friends in their nightshirts, hair uncombed, houses in disorder. You will not speak of that to anyone. They trust us to help and we must not betray their trust with gossip."

"Yes, Sister."

Keziah softened her tone as they approached the Cobb's cabin. "Keep your scarf up, so you don't breathe in the bad air."

Malinda knocked on the door. "Aunt Eliza? Uncle Rowland? Breakfast."

The air reeked of unwashed bodies. Both adults and their oldest son had managed to get dressed. They slumped at the table, leaning heads on hands. Maria and Harriet were still abed, but roused as the oatmeal was served. All had the glassy-eyes and shiny faces of fever.

Keziah packed their buckets with snow. Makes Cloud's infusion should be swallowed warm. "Do you have a pot to heat water?"

"Don't you remember?" Rowland wheezed. "Father Ephraim doesn't allow hot drinks."

Eliza groaned. "He took our cooking pots."

Did he still have them? And would he allow hot infusions for medicinal use? Steam from boiling water on the stove would help them all breathe. People who know nothing about health shouldn't make rules that impact it. Keziah would have a talk with Ephraim. "When you're done eating, set your bowls on your stoop, and I'll collect them on my return."

The snow drifted over the path to the next cabin, turning the walk into a slog, but Malinda still had breath to speak. "Sister

Keziah, could you do me a favor? Call me by my first name, Tryphina."

"I'll try. Why the change?"

"Malinda is a baby name."

"I wondered if Eunice named her baby after you."

"All she talks about is 'Malinda spit up, Malinda messed her diaper, Malinda cried all night.' She never says anything nice."

"Babies are a lot of work. A good reason to take your time choosing a husband." Keziah wished her younger self had known better.

The girl snorted. "If Orrin Butts was your father, you'd be in a hurry to marry."

Keziah pressed her lips together, holding in her own snort. "I will do my best to call you Tryphina. Why not announce it to the Congregation at our next meal?"

"I will. But if you use my real name, the rest will too. People listen to you."

Did they? It seemed her scoldings on health skated through ears without any change in the hearer's behavior.

Unbroken snow on the cabin's steps announced that neither Johnson nor Matilda Lane had been outside this morning. Both were propped in bed.

"Dear friends." Keziah poured water for them. Matilda took hers and drank it down, but Keziah had to hold the cup for Johnson. Swallowing set off bouts of coughing. While she served oatmeal, Tryphina stirred up their fire and filled their water bucket with snow.

Outside, they took deep breaths of clean air as they walked to the next cabin.

"Now that was foul," Tryphina said.

"The smell indicates Brother Lane is battling more than one disease."

At the Lytle's cabin, Omer answered the door. "Ma and Pa are sick."

"As are you." Keziah couldn't see the boy, but she heard his wheezing. She opened a shutter to light the room, then served the last of the oatmeal. Hugh feigned a death rattle, but his complaints had their usual vigor and he got out of bed unaided. Christena was already at the table. She set aside the sock she'd been knitting and smirked at her husband's theatrics. The Lytles were on their way to recovery.

The path outside the cabin was empty. A sharp bark echoed between the houses. Keziah and Malinda, or rather, Tryphina, followed the sound. Finn sat beside the sled, tongue hanging out, one paw on Leo. The boy flailed like a turtle on its back. "Your dog pounced on me!"

"Because he knows we need the sled." Keziah called Finn. Leo scrambled to his feet and ran away.

"Tell you what I'll do," Ma— Tryphina said as they returned to the Lord's House. "I'll sneak upstairs and get the pots out of the trunks. Sister Thompson won't notice, what with chasing Leo all over."

"Are the pots still there?"

"Last I knew."

Father Ephraim might not know this fourteen-year-old had been snooping in the attic, but he certainly would notice if the Congregation suddenly took up tea drinking.

"I'll talk to Father Ephraim."

"I'll try to keep my father busy."

"Your help is appreciated." Keziah smiled at the girl, then climbed the stairs to the printing office.

The room smelled of kerosene as Dennis Butts cleaned the ink stone and brayer with a rag. The interior walls had shelves packed with newspapers. More papers were stacked beneath the windows. A fire in this room would trap the Thompson family down the hall and burn down the whole building.

"Dennis, where do you put the rags when they're done?"

"Here." He tapped his foot against a metal bucket with a lid. "I empty it every night."

"Well done."

From behind his desk, Father Ephraim motioned her into a chair beside it. "Sister Sirrine, have you come to a decision about Rufus?"

Rufus, who? Keziah shook her head. She had more immediate concerns than her unfaithful husband. "The Cobbs, Lanes, and Lytles suffer from catarrh. Herbal infusions are recommended to ease the symptoms."

"Yes of course." His ready agreement surprised her. "Perhaps we should add beef to today's vegetable stew, to fortify the blood."

"The Congregation will be grateful." She leaned forward. "If the sick had cooking pots, they could heat water for infusions and to add steam to the air."

He pressed his ink-stained fingers together. "I'll ask Catherine to find them."

"I'm concerned about Brother Lane. Is there a physician in Onawa or Council Bluffs?"

Orrin Butts stomped in, brandishing his finger. "Our sheriff is hale and hearty. We will waste no money on such foolishness."

"Johnson works circles around the rest of us," added Guy Barnum who entered with Butts. "He was fit as a fiddle yesterday."

"And today he's too weak to hold a cup of water. Please—"

"We'll pray for restoration of health. And I'll find those items you need." Ephraim hurried out.

Orrin scowled and Guy grinned. No help, either of them.

Keziah returned to the bothy. What else could she do? She went through the recipe box again. In Makes Cloud's notes, she found a recommendation for a plant called biscuitroot. The ground root could be used to treat infections, but harvest yielded only a small amount. *May it be enough.* Keziah added the ground root to her satchel and headed back to the Lanes.

January 1855

"Keziah? What rhymes with Keziah?" Duncan wondered as he worked a mixture of beeswax, turpentine, and resin into the soles and seams of a new pair of boots. "Can't write a song without a rhyme."

As if his thought summoned her, Keziah passed the window and entered the store. Snowflakes decorated her dark hair. She pinched her nose against the stinging odor. "Phew. You've found the cure for catarrh."

"More likely the cause." Could he ask her about rhyming her name? No, he dare not. "Your boots need waterproofing?"

A small shake of her head sent her curls dancing. "What do you do with your rags?"

He held up a metal bucket with a lid.

"Like the one in the printing office." Her eyes widened and she smiled. "'Twas you who trained Dennis to use the bucket, keeping Preparation safe from fires."

He nodded. "I do my best."

"Thank you. You're a good partner, thinking of things I've not considered."

He could bask in the glow of her approval for...forever. Wait... was he falling in love with Keziah? Was that allowed now, with Rufus gone for good?

Keziah brought him back to earth. "I'm needing ten pounds of beef. Father Ephraim approved it for dinner, since so many have taken ill." She put a bucket on the counter.

"What do you think of the vegetarian diet?" Duncan grabbed cuts of salted beef from the barrel until he had a good ten pounds.

"The children are growing. I don't know if they're growing better or worse than those who eat meat. And I don't know how to measure the health of the adults."

Duncan glanced over her shoulder to be sure they were alone, then pulled a slip of paper from the drawer. He looked her in the eye, wrote down the order and the customer's name, and slid it across the counter to her. "I'm to ask for a signature." He met her gaze again. Would she keep his confidence?

"No ledger?" She scrawled her name.

He checked the window again. "Someone." He tapped his chest with his thumb. "Has been ciphering and asking questions."

She stepped sideways, so she too could watch the window. Her fingers jiggled the pencil. After a moment, she said, "The numbers tell a different story than..." She tipped her head toward the Lord's House.

"Enough to pay the Land Office."

"Unless—"

A sharp bark echoed outside, followed by a loud squeals. Leo and the two Barnum boys rode the sled past, heading for the river.

"Second time today." Keziah shot out the door. "Should let them get wet."

"If dunking didn't make them ill."

Keziah dashed through the drifts, moving rapidly in spite of her skirts and petticoats. With his long legs, Duncan passed her and nearly caught up to the boys. Four paws overtook them both and Finn got the capture. The dog snagged Leo's elbow and turned the sled off its course, into deeper snow. Duncan seized a booted foot, putting the brakes on the boys' adventure.

"Hey!" Three angry lads yelled. "Why'd you stop us? We were going to fly over the river. You ruined it!"

"You'd be head-first in the water and drowned, you wee gowks." Duncan caught the sled as it teetered on the riverbank.

"Drowned and frozen to death." Keziah swatted the nearest Barnum, which made no impression as his bum was bundled up in numerous layers. "Ought to put you in jail for stealing the sled I was using."

"No jail in Preparation," Leo sang as he danced away from her spanking arm. "Besides, the Bible says we have all things common."

Quoting the Bible already? The wee lad was as slippery as his father. What manner of trouble would he cause when grown?

Malinda, make that Tryphina Butts, waved from the Lord's House. "Sister Keziah! It's Louisa Paden's time!"

CHAPTER 14

January 11, 1855

This morning, Louisa Paden had plodded into the Lord's House. Her hands rested low on her belly, showing the baby was in position to be born, but she'd had no pangs. She ate a good breakfast. Since this was the young woman's first baby, Keziah didn't rush when word came that her birth pains had started.

"I'll take the meat and these louts." Duncan motioned the boys toward the store.

"And Finn, please." Keziah stopped by the bothy for her satchel, then waded through drifts to the Paden's. The storm had strengthened, hiding the barn behind a white veil.

When she paused to fill her cook pot with fresh snow, the new father burst from the cabin. He grabbed her arm, jerking her off her feet and through the door. "The baby's coming. Hurry. Get in here. It's coming."

Keziah got her feet back underneath her and spoke in a soothing voice. "Yes, Jacob, I know. It will take time. How are you doing, Louisa?"

Jacob shouted, "What are you asking her for? She's in agony, in more pain than her flesh can bear." His spittle hit Keziah's face. "You better get that baby out of her."

"Jacob, I need you to find Hannah Perrin for me. Right away." She pushed him out the door. Keziah didn't know the Padens well as they were twenty years younger, but she hadn't heard Jacob was hot tempered.

Belying the small bones and wispy hair that gave her a delicate look, Louisa bounced out of bed. "I'm having a few cramps. I don't know they're birth pangs or not."

"Walk and let me know when you have another." *Have mercy on me, oh Lord*, Keziah prayed as she washed her hands and heated water. *Calm Jacob and keep him busy so I might ease his wife's suffering and receive this gift of life from you. Amen.*

"I'd rather dance." Louisa hummed a tune and sidestepped around the tiny cabin, then clasped Keziah's hand, "Allemande left, allemande right, promenade. Oh. Here's one now."

The belly tightened under Keziah's palms.

Louisa blinked back a tear. "I wish my mother was here."

Keziah recalled that feeling all too well. "We have a community of mothers to help each other."

The pain eased and Louisa resumed dancing. A reel proved to be too much, so after a few bars, she slowed down to a strathspey, pausing only for pangs.

The door burst open. "Louisa, what are you doing out of bed?" Jacob stuck his finger in Keziah's face. "I thought you were a midwife."

"She is. An experienced one." Hannah Perrin managed to squeeze inside. "She knows it's best for the mother to walk during labor." Hannah pushed Jacob out, with a request to, "Please bring Lodema Winegar."

Louisa taught Hannah how to waltz. When Jacob brought Lodema, they sent him to the Lord's House for food.

"Having a baby is so much fun. Now we have enough dancers for a set." Before Keziah could remind her the cabin had no room for four people to stand, much less dance, Louisa's giggle turned to a cry as another pang hit.

"Making progress." Lodema put towels on the bed.

When the dinner bell rang, Tryphina dropped off bread, cheese, and stew. "Brother Duncan has Jacob cutting firewood."

God bless Duncan for keeping the new father busy. Keziah turned the thought over in her mind. Duncan blessed Preparation in many ways.

"Much appreciated." Hannah closed the door behind the girl and served the food. "Hope chopping will burn off Jacob's fretfulness."

Lodema rubbed the young woman's back. "It's not like living in town, where the new father can hide in a tavern."

Hannah gasped. "Frederick went to a tavern?"

"For the first, last, and only time. We were living in Ohio, on Lake Erie. Mother took a boat from Michigan to help me. I think he was afraid of her. Raising eleven children made her fierce."

"What a blessing to have her help," Hannah said. "We were living in the wilderness of Wisconsin, not a soul for miles around. Thomas came so quickly, Charles and I didn't have time to be afraid."

"You went with James Strang?" Keziah asked. Rufus and Father Ephraim had tested the waters with Strang on their way from Nauvoo to St. Louis.

"No, that was before he started the Voree community." Hannah paused to encourage Louisa to breathe through the pain, then turned to Keziah. "And Rufus?"

"He always had a trip. So inconvenient of me to birth a baby while he was hauling freight for Joseph Smith." Finally she could put Rufus behind her.

"Chamber pot," Louisa grunted, all silliness gone. The pangs came faster and harder.

Keziah gave her a moment, then had her lift up and slid the pot out of the way. "Stay right there. Here comes your baby."

Louisa alternated pushing and cussing. The baby arrived with a healthy howl.

"It's a girl."

And a lot of blood. Keziah cut the cord and passed the wee one to Hannah. Lodema helped her lift the young mother into bed.

"Raspberry leaf remedy in a mug, not too hot. Fill a clean bucket with new snow. Louisa, stay awake. You need to drink this." She was too drowsy.

Keziah kept one hand on the belly. The womb contracted feebly. Was it filling with blood? Would she lose this new mother? What would Mrs. Jackson do? *Heal her, Lord, stop the bleeding.*

Lodema helped Louisa sip the infusion, then brought in snow and Keziah packed handfuls around the lower belly. Her skin, warm from exertion, melted it. A large red puddle formed on the bed. "Towel. More snow."

When Lodema opened the door, Jacob burst in. "What's all this blood?" He cursed. "You're killing my wife!"

Keziah turned to explain, but Jacob grabbed her around the neck and hauled her into the stormy night. He was brawny, muscles thick from farm work, and she couldn't break his hold. She tried to yell for him to stop, but only a croak escaped her throat. Louisa needed her. She must... *Lord Jesus, help!*

"Let go of her now." Hannah said with the authoritative tone used on rowdy boys. "She's the only one who can save your wife."

The world dimmed and went dark.

"Help!" Lodema screamed. "We're under attack!"

Finn snarled. A thump shook Jacob and his grip loosened enough to let Keziah gulp air.

"You all right?" Duncan helped her upright. He and Homer Hoyt took Jacob away.

Save Louisa. Hurry, before she bleeds to death. Keziah sucked in another breath and grabbed handfuls of snow. She tried to stand, but slipped in the deep drift. She crawled into the cabin. Was the bleeding worse? Heart thundering, she pushed snow onto the limp belly.

The young woman muttered, "Cold."

"Close the door. More remedy. Stir up the fire." Keziah told Lodema. "How's the baby? See if she will nurse." Lodema and Hannah raced to help. Was there anything else she could do? Lodema got a second cup of remedy into Louisa. With Hannah's help, the baby latched on. Beneath Keziah's hand, the womb contracted and the placenta released. And finally, at long last, the bleeding slowed.

Lodema slouched in the chair with a deep sigh. Hannah slumped on a trunk and whispered a prayer. The baby's lips made a sound as gentle as an angel's kiss, and the mother dozed. Keziah leaned on the bed frame. Her heart slowed, but neck hurt and her shivers increased. Melting snow and sweat had numbed her, body and mind. Tonight she'd battled with death and nearly lost—lost herself, the new mother, and the child. *Thank you, Lord, for life.*

Priscilla Lewis stepped inside and gasped. Mounds of soaked towels, blankets, and rags covered the floor. Keziah dripped into a puddle. "What happened?"

"Baby." Louisa smiled, then drifted back to sleep. "Rebecca Ann."

Keziah pulled her chilled hands from the mother's belly and pushed off the floor. Her legs unbent enough to allow her to perch on the end of the bed.

Hannah explained, "Louisa bled. Jacob hauled Keziah outside and strangled her. Finn bit him, Lodema whacked him with a shovel, and I hit him with the ax—the butt end so we wouldn't have more blood to deal with. Wish I'd had my cast iron frypan."

"Was he injured?" Keziah asked.

"Not much. Duncan corralled him in the single men's cabin. Oh, Keziah, you'll have quite the bruise," Priscilla checked her neck. She dried and rubbed Keziah's hands, pushed her mittens on, and wrapped her in her cape. "Rebecca Butts is coming and we'll clean up. We saved supper for you. Go on now."

Keziah couldn't move. "Louisa needs more raspberry infusion, as much as she'll take, as often as possible. There's a packet by the stove. Come get me if she bleeds again. She'll need beef. I'll ask Ephraim."

"I'll talk to Ephraim after we put you in bed with a copper bedwarmer." Hannah assisted her to her feet.

Lodema held Keziah's other arm. "You have a bedwarmer?"

"No, but the Barnums will let me borrow theirs."

Keziah looked over these women, dear friends, bound together in this community. "I thank God for all of you."

February 1855

The only place in Preparation with space for laying out fabric was the Lord's House. Sun reflected off the snow and through the windows, filling the meeting room with light. Keziah started to pull one of the tables toward the south-facing windows, but soreness from the Paden delivery stopped her.

"Let me help you." Sarah Chase stepped out of the kitchen and dried her hands on her apron. Together she and Keziah set the two longest tables together. "Finally, time to sew, now everyone's recovered from catarrh."

"Everyone except Johnson Lane, and his wife is tending him." Keziah unfolded the fabric.

"Not a moment too soon. Your skirt is in shreds."

"Finn jumped on me this morning." Only her large apron kept her from indecency.

Father Ephraim's voice echoed from the printing office as he dictated his sermon to Daniel Butts. "Pork is too gross to be palatable. It produces impurities in the system, including scrofula. The raising and butchering of hogs is degrading to man. Their appearance and odor are offensive."

"If he cooked, he'd get used to the look of raw meat," Keziah murmured as she matched the selvages.

"He quotes from that book about a vegetable diet, yet he doesn't mention the prohibition against swine in Leviticus." Sarah smoothed the cloth toward the fold. "This is scratchy."

"Butter is unnatural, gross, and difficult to digest," Ephraim continued. "Eggs are unnatural. They're too nutritious for their bulk and must be corrected by eating apples or potatoes with them."

Does he really believe that? Or was it all about selling meat to fill the cashbox? Knowing he'd grown up in poverty, she was inclined to think money was the issue.

"Sister Keziah." Tryphina emerged fom the single women's room. "Didn't I tell you to choose blue or red? Not tedious brownish green." She continued up the stairs.

Sarah unfolded the end of the bolt. "What happened here?" She held the cloth up to the sunlight. The weaver had switched the weft from green to gray for several rows, leaving an odd stripe. "Ephraim must not have noticed this mistake. It's useless."

"Ah, but the flaw meant I got a high-quality worsted for a woolen price." Father Ephraim said, startling them both. Had Tryphina complained to him?

Keziah hurried to soothe any ruffled feathers. "It will be long wearing and warm."

"Laying out the skirt like this incorporates the stripe into the hem, as a decorative border," Ephraim said. "Or cut out the gray and add a flounce. Or fold the gray into a tuck." He stretched out the cloth, folding and gathering as he spoke, reminding them he'd worked as a tailor before becoming Father Ephraim, Chief Steward of the Presbytery of Zion.

Tryphina stomped down the stairs carrying a bolt of indigo cotton. "This will look better and not be itchy."

Keziah shook her head. She didn't need this girl stirring up trouble. "No. It's all right."

Ephraim took the blue cotton and held it near Keziah. "Yes, even better. It's too light for trousers, but a good weight for a dress. It brings out the color in your face."

Irritation brought out her blush. She didn't want to waste his limited goodwill on clothing.

"How is Brother Lane?" he asked.

"I'm sorry to say there's no improvement."

"I read that medicine is impure, poisonous. Fever and diarrhea remove the impurities."

What impurities? Johnson had a blockage in his throat. "I haven't any medicine to give him."

Ephraim stroked his beard. "He may be feeling the effect of medicine taken years before. Have you tried the water cure? Copious water drinking and exercise will set him right."

"He's not able to swallow water nor get out of bed."

"I'll pray with him while Daniel finishes typesetting." He bundled up and left.

Seeing Johnson so sick should prompt Ephraim to action. Keziah returned to her sewing.

Sarah fluttered her eyelashes. "Decorative border, flounce, or tuck? Which will you choose?"

"None. A week dragging the paths around Preparation will give it a uniform color—mud brown." Keziah laid out her pattern. "I'll ask the question of you: What will you choose to cook?"

"The larder's bare enough this time of year. I don't need further restrictions on ingredients." She winked. "Copious water it is."

"Have you tried roasting prairie turnip?"

"Not yet. We're bored of the usual fare, so prairie turnip will be a welcome change."

Christena's son Omer burst into the House, accompanied by Finn. "Father Ephraim wants you at the Lane's cabin. Right now."

Sarah shooed her away. "Go on. I'll keep an eye on this."

Keziah trotted and slid on the snowy path. What did Ephraim expect of her? She'd tried every herb she had, including biscuitroot from Makes Cloud, but none helped. She knocked on the door and entered. The rattle in Johnson's exhale had worsened, but at least he still breathed.

"Sister. He won't wake. What did you give him?" Ephraim bent over the bed.

"Infusion of biscuitroot, thyme, rosemary, elm, juniper, and honey."

Red-faced, he poked his finger in her face. "Wake him or it's laundry duty for you."

How dare he threaten her? Keziah crossed her arms. If she was relegated to laundry, who would take care of Johnson?

The same thought must have crossed Matilda Lane's mind. "He got the same remedy as the rest of us and we're all awake."

"Johnson, it's time to eat. You must get up." Ephraim shook the man's shoulder. He slumped to the side, saliva wetting his chin. Ephraim turned to Keziah. "Give him a remedy to wake him."

If you hadn't banned coffee... Guilt pricked Keziah. The coffee Mercy gave her should have been saved for medicinal purposes. She asked Matilda, "How was his night?"

"Not well. Restless. Moaning. Uncomfortable."

"When he wakes..." *If he wakes...* "If he can swallow, try the warm infusion and broth again." Keziah added more juniper to the water on the stove, producing a pine-scented steam she hoped would ease his breathing. "We'll let you rest."

"What's wrong with him?" Ephraim asked as they returned to the Lord's House.

She shook her head. "He coughs and is wasting, but doesn't look consumptive. There's a blockage in his throat and windpipe. Please, Charles," she appealed to the man beneath his Father Ephraim mask, "he needs a doctor. Nothing I've done has helped. I fear for his life."

Leo and the two young Barnum boys raced out of the House and headed for the barn. What were they up to?

Father Ephraim didn't respond to her plea or her use of his first name. He watched the boys. "The children are healthy and active. Preparation's fresh air and vegetable diet is good for them."

With supervision, it could be better, but now wasn't the time for that battle. "Yes, Preparation has been good for us, all except Johnson. Please..."

"Enough, Sister. Enough." Patience spent, he hurried to the House and hurried upstairs.

Sarah waved. "I cut out your dress. It's on the shelf with your sewing basket."

"Thank you." Keziah found a spot in the sun and pinned the bodice. She measured a length of thread, but couldn't find her scissors. That last summer in St. Louis, she'd delivered babies and sold herbs to buy a good pair of Wendt dressmaker shears. "Sarah, where did you put my scissors?"

"Right there." The cook pointed to the corner of the sewing basket. The two of them looked through the spools and scraps, then unrolled the fabric. No scissors. "No one came through the kitchen. Daniel stayed in the printing office. All morning I've been here...

Except for my trip to the root cellar." They exchanged looks of dismay. "Oh no. Let's ask at dinner. Perhaps someone found them."

Keziah had a strong suspicion who that someone might be. She bundled up and started for the barn with Finn. Halfway there, a child's scream turned her steps toward the Cobbs' cabin. The Barnum boys pinned Harriet Cobb to the backside of the outhouse as Leo chopped her hair.

"Stop!" Keziah yelled in chorus with the girl's mother.

Whooping and waving her braids, the boys raced for the tree claim. With a whistle, Keziah sent Finn in pursuit. "Harriet, are you hurt?" She bent over the little girl, checking for blood.

"Your hair." Eliza Cobb gasped. "Your beautiful hair."

"They promised to show me a kitty," the six-year-old sobbed. "But there's no kitty and all they did was pull my hair."

Eliza Cobb embraced her child and scowled after the boys. "No sparing the rod this time."

Keziah pulled her shears from the snow, furious with the child, but more so with his father. Ephraim had plenty to say about the care she gave Johnson Lane and what the Congregation ate, but turned a blind eye to his son's wild behavior. "Let's remove a few layers from any bum we want to paddle."

Eliza gave her a grim smile. "Count on it."

February 14, 1855

Duncan kicked snow from his boots and stepped inside the Lord's House. Food! his stomach exclaimed, welcoming even vegetables.

Orrin stomped across the room. "Have you seen Keziah? She was supposed to help cook, but she didn't show and now dinner will be late."

"Aye." Duncan pulled off his mittens. "She's tending Johnson Lane and Sarah Jane Hall." He'd spent the morning shoveling a path between the Lanes', Halls', and Barnum's cabins, giving Keziah a shortcut.

"Sarah Jane's sick too? She has dishwashing duty."

"Find a substitute." He hung his coat on a peg. "Sarah Jane gave birth this morning. To a baby girl. They named her Adele. And Miranda Barnum's having pangs."

"People must remember their obligations, how it disrupts the work when they laze about. Each must do his part." Orrin tapped a pencil on his list. "We can hardly run an organized, orderly community with all this chaos."

Did the man not hear a word he said? Was he deaf as well as blind to the needs of the Congregation? "Then I suggest you remove from your list those who are ill, those ready to give birth, and the only person we have to help them." A plan self-evident to all except Orrin. Duncan stepped around the man and headed for the kitchen.

"Then who..." Orrin sputtered and waved his useless arms. "What about now? Today's dinner? Lodema and Hannah are helping the Halls, so who..."

Duncan turned and gave him a hard stare. So the man *had* known about the birth, yet chose to complain instead of recruiting other workers. "Roll up your sleeves and wash your hands." While he followed his own instructions and set the tables, he heard Orrin asking his sister Eliza and his wife Rebecca to pitch in. What was wrong with the gowk? Did he think kitchen work was beneath his dignity?

Keziah had run herself ragged, back and forth between those who needed her care, with nary a complaint. If Orrin dared call Keziah lazy, Duncan would give him a drubbing he'd never forget.

CHAPTER 15

February 26, 1855

Keziah stopped by the Barnums' table at breakfast, where Guy sat with his sons ages eight and five, and held his toddler daughter on his lap. "How is Miranda feeling?"

Guy ran his hand down his beard, smearing oatmeal cached there by wee Frances. He needed a bib as much as she did. "In fine fettle."

Young Guy Barnum disagreed. "She was crying. A lot."

"I'll check on her."

Guy grabbed her wrist before she could step away. "Mother's tending her." He pulled her arm, trying to catch the spoon before his daughter could grab and fling it. "She's in good hands."

Why was he fighting her? "Always good to have assistance nearby."

"I'll go home soon as we're done with breakfast."

The Barnum brothers exchanged oatmeal cannonballs with Leo.

Keziah hardened her voice. "Keeping the children occupied elsewhere would help."

"Oh... of course, of course." He glanced over her shoulder, searching for anyone who would take his children. Frances, who'd survived fourteen months with two rowdy brothers, took advantage of the opportunity and dove for the toast she'd thrown on the floor. Guy had to release Keziah to keep his daughter from falling. Keziah headed for the door. He stood, holding his daughter, and pointed at the midwife.

"Don't you dare..." He stopped and glanced around. His threat attracted the attention of all. He lowered his voice. "I appreciate your concern, Sister, but it's completely misplaced. Save yourself the trouble. All will be well."

"I'll make sure of it." Keziah threw on her cape and left the House. All well? She snorted. It's not his body in danger of bleeding to death, contracting an infection, or tearing in a tender place. It's not his body twisted with pain. It's not his body worn out from birth fourteen months ago, only to face another too soon.

When Frances was born, Miranda had been exhausted from moving and battered by Mercy Jones's hostility over having to share "her" house. This time Miranda was in her own house, didn't have the other woman's malice, and this was her fourth child. Surely this delivery would be easier. *Easy? Don't count on easy,* Mrs. Jackson's voice echoed in her head.

"Good job guarding the chickens," she told Finn as she retrieved her satchel. She hurried across Preparation, thankful the snow hadn't been too deep this year. Twenty feet from the Barnums' house, she heard Miranda's scream. Keziah broke into a run, raced inside and up the stairs.

Miranda lay flat on the bed, red-faced and howling like a banshee.

Her mother-in-law wrung her hands. "The pain is horrible."

Keziah dropped her cape and washed in the basin. The water was cold. She had to use the soap from her satchel, then shake dry since there was no towel. Miranda continued to scream. She didn't have this much pain with Frances. What could be wrong? Keziah touched her belly. Miranda yelled louder, pinched her hand and yanked her hair. Was this what Guy wanted to hide, that his wife had turned into a wildcat?

Keziah backed away, crossed her arms, and said to Marcia, "I've ascribed the Barnum boys' fighting to their father, but I see now their mother deserves the credit."

"What did you say?" Miranda raised her head.

"This is your fourth time giving birth. You know how your body works. You know to reduce your pain, you must move."

"I can't. The pain is terrible."

"It wasn't bad until Guy took the children for breakfast," Marcia said. "Then she's been awful."

"Guy was supposed to bring breakfast. He forgot about me," Miranda said. "No wonder I can't get this baby out—I'm starving."

"Then don't fight those who are trying to help you birth your baby." What about praying out loud as Duncan did? "Heavenly Father, we lift up your daughter Miranda and ask you to comfort her with your presence, relieve her pain, and—"

"All right." She whimpered. "I'll try."

Keziah helped the woman sit up.

She clamped onto Keziah's shoulder. "No. It hurts too much. I'm going to faint."

Keziah felt a strong pulse in Miranda's armpit. "You're not going to faint. You're going to walk."

"I'll make a mess on the rug."

Rug? Keziah looked down. The Barnums had an enormous oriental rug. Their bed, dresser, and mirror were decorated with elaborate carvings. Embroidered curtains hung at the windows. Fancier than anything here except Fontainebleau. Almost as elaborate as the steamboat captain's house in St. Louis.

Was this why Guy didn't want her here, to learn the Barnums had better furniture than anyone else in Preparation? Did Father Ephraim know?

"I'll try," Miranda said with a whine.

"Up with you." With Miranda's arms braced on their shoulders, Keziah and Marcia dragged her across the floor. "One foot in front of the other. You know how to walk." They circled the room once, then Miranda dove for the bed, landing on hands and knees.

"All right. Stay like that."

The next pang came and went. "The pain moved down. It's not so bad."

"Walking and gravity help the baby shift positions, lessening the pain. Do not lie down. I'm going for hot water." Keziah dashed downstairs, opened the door and spotted the Perrin boys pulling their sled to the big hill. "I need your mother and any other woman. Get help. Hurry." She closed the door, then rushed around, heating water, and finding towels. What would Mrs. Jackson say about this mother?

Back upstairs, Marcia swabbed her daughter-in-law's face with a wet washcloth.

Miranda knelt and leaned on the footboard. "I found a better position, no thanks to you."

Her mother-in-law hissed. "Miranda. Manners."

She grimaced as another pang caught her. "The baby's coming."

Keziah gave Marcia a warm towel for Miranda's back, washed while praying, then rubbed her hands with ointment. Six pushes later, the baby still hadn't come. Squatting set off more groaning.

"Duncan heard you calling for help." Christena and Priscilla rushed into the bedroom.

"You're right on time. Wash your hands." Keziah motioned them into position. "All ready. With the next pang, push the baby out."

The baby arrived, screaming like her mother.

"First rate lungs." Marcia took her granddaughter to the warm water, which didn't make her any happier. "Aw, she looks so much like Guy."

Her bald head looked like Guy's, but fortunately she didn't have her father's eagle-hook nose.

"Where's my breakfast?" Miranda dug her fingers into Keziah's arm as she rubbed her belly. "You promised."

Keziah stared her down until Miranda let go and apologized. What was wrong with her? And was there a remedy for it? "Drink your infusion." She stepped into the hall and wiped the sweat off her forehead. Christena joined her. Keziah whispered, "I'm sorry. I didn't think you'd want to see another baby born."

"I wanted to check out their fancy furniture." She pulled Keziah's head to her shoulder. "Hugh said the Barnums did well in business in Council Bluffs."

"I'm surprised they weren't required to sacrifice it, like the rest of us. Sure and it's worth more than the pitiful stuff the rest of us gave."

"They kept their furniture. Did they keep their money too? If Guy ever falls out of favor, Ephraim could sell it out from under them. What is Guy now, Chief Patriarch?"

"That was last year. Now it's First Patriarch of the Common Treasury."

She motioned for Keziah to turn. "Let me re-pin your hair." Christena ran her fingers through the tangles. "The Bible says women will travail with pain, but that was ridiculous. What happened to our good-natured sister? Was she like this the whole time?"

"Worse before we prayed. I've seen rabid dogs with better temperament."

"Instead of training in birthing, you should have learned wrestling and boxing."

"Miranda wasn't like this at Frances's birth. Although...this baby is bigger. Perhaps the pain was much worse."

"I heard the baby cry." Guy arrived with food, and without his other children. "It's a girl! Her name is Helen."

Helen?

Keziah and Christena exchanged glances and burst out laughing. After the delivery from hell, what else could she be called?

April 1, 1855

Keziah stirred the sap, watching the reflection of the full moon ripple and form on the surface. Mice rustled through the underbrush, hunting fallen seeds, while owls perched on the roof, watching for a reckless mouse. Finn's ears pivoted to the yip-yip-aroooh of coyotes across the river, then his attention turned toward the cabins and his tail thumped on the porch. Footsteps crunched through the snow, coming rapidly toward the Lord's House. Duncan Ross stepped into the firelight.

"Johnson Lane's taken a turn for the worse," he said, reaching for the paddle. "I'll finish the syrup. I'll not waste your hard work."

And he wouldn't. Unlike Rufus. Unbidden an old memory surfaced. As the sap had reached the boiling point, her waters had broken. She'd needed the midwife. The syrup had needed stirring. She'd woken Rufus. He'd pinched the tender skin stretched over her belly, jumped on his horse, and rode in the direction opposite the midwife's. Shock had frozen her in place until a buggy full of German women arrived. They had sized up her situation and helped. She should have left with them, but she'd believed becoming a father would change Rufus. How foolish...

Across the quiet of the night echoed a song in Gaelic, from a man who was gentle and considerate, who could be trusted.

Keziah approached the Lane's cottage. Boiling maple sap into syrup had a good chance of success. Keeping Brother Lane alive, or doing anything to relieve his misery... *Dear Jesus, have mercy.*

Matilda Lane let her in without speaking. The man's irregular gasps, the foul odor, and the bucket of bloody rags told his story. Keziah slid a steaming pot near Brother Lane's face. "Deep breath," she said. "Slow and deep." His pulse raced beneath her fingers.

Oh, Lord...

Together the women rolled Johnson to exchange his dirty sheets for clean ones. He didn't help or resist, bringing the phrase "dead weight" to mind. Not that his bones weighed much.

"I'm going..." Matilda motioned toward the door. "I've got to..."

"Take all the time you need, dear sister."

The chamber pot was empty and Johnson hadn't the strength to reach the outhouse. He needed water. Keziah mixed honey, thyme syrup, and the last of the brandy she'd hidden from Father Ephraim. She propped him on a pile of clothes topped with a pillow. His head weighed heavy in her hand.

"Brother Lane? You need to wake up and drink your tea. Here, now, take a sip." She tipped a spoonful of infusion into his mouth.

Most dribbled down his chin, then he coughed up the rest. Rubbing his throat brought about a swallow for the second spoonful. Drop by drop she continued until the liquid was gone.

His breathing seemed quieter propped up, so she left him upright. She added a chunk of cedar to the steaming pot on the stove to cover the sour odor of affliction.

Christena entered the cabin. "You've been up all night. I'll sit with him."

"Rest well, Johnson" She squeezed his limp hand.

The sun had risen, showing patches of tangled brown grass between drifts of snow. A half-dozen geese headed north and robins chirped in the tree claim. Soon Preparation would bloom again. Would Johnson Lane see another spring?

Keziah entered The Lord's House and washed her hands. Matilda Lane slept at the kitchen worktable.

Brother Butts came down the stairs. "You missed your time tithe this morning. It's a hardship for others to do your work."

Did he not care where she'd been? She'd like to yell, but she didn't have the energy. "Brother Lane is dying."

Father Ephraim followed. "Preparation is the gate of entrance to the land of Ephraim for those found worthy." He pulled on his coat. In a softer voice, he said, "I'll sit with him."

Keziah trudged into the kitchen, but whatever Sarah Chase had prepared was long gone. She joined Matilda, resting her head on her arms. A cup of coffee... a swallow, even...

A hand jiggled her shoulder and she woke. The aroma of fried eggs and potatoes raised her head.

Duncan slid the plate closer. "You missed breakfast."

"Bless you." She glanced around. Matilda was gone. "If you had coffee, I'd—" She'd kiss him. She stopped the words from leaving her mouth, but not the blush heating her face.

"Had I any, I'd share with you." He folded his lanky self onto the bench across from her. "Maple syrup's locked in the pantry."

"Thank you." She dug into the meal, hurrying to get back to Johnson. The tang of cheese gladdened her tongue. "'Tis a grand breakfast."

"When King David was in the wilderness, on the run from Absalom, he ate cheese and honey." He pushed a biscuit with butter and honey toward her.

"I feel so useless."

Duncan shook his head. "You've done everything you can for Brother Lane. You've kept the rest of us hale and hearty. And best of all," he counted on his long fingers, "you brought David Perrin, Malinda Wilcox, Ovanda Winegar, Ella Ashton, Rebecca Paden, Adele Hall, and Helen Barnum to safely draw their first breaths."

She was too worried about Johnson Lane to celebrate the babies. "If anyone passes by the store, tell them we've need of a doctor." Keziah would risk denunciation if it would save the man's life.

Father Ephraim's voice behind her said, "Too late."

Keziah's shoulders slumped in defeat.

~

May 1855

"Do not be scaring the fish," Duncan called to Leo and the Barnum brothers as they raced past the store to the river. The boys waved their fishing poles and filled the spring air with whoops and hollers. Dorman Lewis, a fourteen-year-old, brought up the rear of the parade with the worm bucket. No lassie in skirts and petticoats could keep up with the boys, so the young men of Preparation were given charge on a rotating basis. Keziah reported the arrangement worked well, with minimal loss of blood and, so far, no broken bones.

Duncan paused in stitching a leather upper and lifted his face to the comfortably warm sun, breathing in air heavy with the scent of growing. Perhaps a day off was in order...

"Good morning, Brother Ross."

What had he done to earn a visit from the head fault-finder? "Brother Butts. Have you a shoe in need of mending? Or you're ready for a new pair?"

Footsteps thudding on the wood floor, Orrin circled the store, reading the notice board and peering under the counter. Had Duncan left his bookkeeping notes out? No, they were in his pocket. Orrin stroked his fringe beard, settled into the chair, and finally spoke. "No, I've come about a more troubling matter."

Now what? Had one of the single women complained about him? Had Father Ephraim changed his mind about the Bible reading? Duncan secured his needle and pliers. "Aye?"

"Those who left our community, the apostates, want their tithes and free-will donations back." He braced one leg on the opposite knee, showing a polished ankle-high boot that had not been made in Preparation. "All religious and benevolent societies in this country rely on contributions or dues for support. No church, Mormon or Methodist, returns money when a congregant leaves. It doesn't happen. But these apostates seem to believe they're entitled to it."

Why bring this up? Duncan hadn't contributed any money. "Hadn't Father Ephraim given money to those who left?"

"He shouldn't have. We need those funds for the Presbytery of Zion, to pay taxes, to support those sent on teaching missions, and provide for the indigent. Those individuals who demand their money back have made a shipwreck of their faith, seceded from their church, taken leave of their senses, and are full of the devil." He warmed up to his subject, raising his voice and wagging his index finger. "They're not content to be infidels or to set up their own church. Oh, no, they threaten us with prosecution by the law. Father Ephraim and Brother Barnum are consulting a lawyer in Onawa today, incurring yet another expense."

Which was more upsetting to Orrin—the expense or Ephraim taking his favorite, Guy Barnum, on this expedition?

Orrin didn't wait for a response. "In contradiction of their own testimony last December, the apostates claim Father Ephraim is an imposter."

Imposter? Who did they think he was pretending to be? "So..."

"It's malicious slander. And, in the biggest paradox of all, these men, who as Mormons survived the mob, then pledged everlasting brotherhood here, are now threatening us with violence."

"Ah, last Sabbath's teaching on self-preservation." And Preparation had no sheriff since Johnson Lane's death. *Please don't ask me to replace him.*

"Exactly." Orrin clapped his palm on his knees. "Are you with me...us?"

Duncan considered those who'd left this past year. Keziah's friend Mercy Jones and her genial husband David. Hard-working Nelson Messenger who shingled every roof in the community. Tenderhearted Mary Warner. Quiet Henry Platt and jokester Edwin Briggs who'd helped him build the garden fence. The Winegar family. "The people who left wish to harm us?"

His fist pounded. "We have the right to defend ourselves."

"Not being a soldier nor having any weapon..." The Sabbath lesson echoed through his head and he held up the strip of buckskin trimmed off the moccasin. "Am I to make this into a sling and gather five smooth stones?"

"To slay our Goliaths. Yes." Orrin's eyes glittered with undue enthusiasm toward killing their friends. "We have a few rifles, and more may arrive from Onawa tonight." He stood, his clap on Duncan's shoulder sounding a death knell. "Glad you're with us. Say, how about that Gentile who lives up the river? Might he sound a warning if he sees trouble coming?"

"Mr. Jepson? He and his family left before the river thawed this spring."

"We'll post guards then."

Orrin's footsteps quieted as they left the store for the dirt path, and Duncan hit his knees. Never in his worst nightmare had he imagined this peaceful Congregation would degenerate into a battleground...and no way to stop it. He pressed shaking hands to his face.

"Oh Lord, deliver us from evil," he prayed, "from within and without." Gleeful shrieks and splashes sounded from the river as he left to find Keziah. "And help me protect these children."

≈

June 1855

"Boneset!" Keziah pushed through the underbrush, heading for a cluster of tall plants topped with small buds. Trees and the burbling creek made this valley a cool respite from early summer's heat and the tension of the Lord's House. Duncan had told her about his conversation with Orrin, but neither of them had seen any rifles. The men had been on the lookout, which had the women picking on each other, leading Father Ephraim to teach on the conduct of women last Sabbath. He still hadn't looked her in the eye since Johnson Lane's death. Did he blame her or himself? Or was he preoccupied with another concern?

Christena watched Preparation's children rolling down the hill, herded by Finn and supervised by the oldest Perrin boy. Even the wee ones appreciated being free of cranky adults. "Let me guess," she said. "It's for setting bones."

"Never that simple." She cut off several stalks. "It's a purgative, diaphoretic, tonic. Good for fevers, coughs, and moving the bowels."

"Our bowels move plenty thanks to Ephraim's vegetable diet." Christena leaned over, studying the ground. "Wonder how snake tastes."

"Snake?" Keziah raised her skirts and leaped back onto the path. "Where?"

"Only an earthworm." Her cousin grinned. "Enough weeds?"

"Enough trouble." Keziah swatted her with a stem. "You remind me, I need plantain for snakebite."

"Did you see us, Sister Lytle, Sister Sirrine?" called six-year-old John Perrin. "I won!"

"My head feels funny." Five-year-old Amy Chase wobbled.

"Sit awhile," Keziah advised, but the girl followed the others up for another roll.

Christena pulled a clump of leaves with the root attached from her bucket. "A plantain for your thoughts, dear lady."

"They're rolling like the children." Keziah rested her head on her cousin's shoulder and Christena pulled her close, not minding her sweat. All winter, she'd pondered, prayed, and listened for guidance until a clear path formed ahead. "All those Bible verses about divorce..."

"Rufus was dishonest and committed adultery. His sin destroyed your marriage."

"I'll never know the truth of what happened."

"Do you want to?"

She shook her head. "But I want my life to stand for truth. Brother Lane's death set me thinking. I don't want to die tied to Rufus in any way."

"Nor live with that tie." Christena leaned back to look her in the face. "So you'll write to Rufus?"

"No. Even if I had a stamp, Ephraim is postmaster. I must talk to him, if I can find a time when Orrin Butts is gone."

"I'll pray for that miracle."

The dinner bell rang, sending children and dog racing for the Lord's House.

Keziah straightened. "Thank you, dear friend, for listening." They headed back.

Near the House, the children called to Malinda, er Tryphina. Finn gave the girl a thorough sniffing. No doubt she'd been riding this morning. Sunlight showed the honey and saleratus remedy had helped clear her skin. The girl glanced around, then whispered to Keziah, "Father's helping with the sheep today."

Which meant Keziah could speak to Ephraim in private. Although as slow as he moved, what would Orrin do with a sheep? "Shearing?"

"Counting." Tryphina hurried to the stables.

"Thank you, Heavenly Father for answering our prayer so quickly." Christena took her gathering bags. "I'll set these under your porch. Go on now. Ephraim's late for every meal, if he even comes at all, so this is a good time."

Telling Finn "Stay," Keziah took a deep breath and marched into the House and then up the stairs to the printing office.

"Sister Sirrine." Father Ephraim waved her into the chair. "I've been wanting to thank you for tending Brother Lane this winter."

"I regret..."

The printing press squeaked and thumped, worked by none other than Daniel Butts. Was there no avoiding this family? Orrin Butts would find out her business and impose his opinion soon enough.

Ephraim leaned on the desk. "You have nothing to regret, Sister. You gave him good care. Now he's in the celestial kingdom, free from pain and work."

"Last Sabbath's teaching..."

"Oh, Sister, that wasn't directed toward you. You're the example Preparation's women young and old should follow." He leaned into the sunlight, looking careworn and wrinkled. He could use a skin remedy too.

Keziah cleared her throat. "Yet I find myself unequally yoked."

"Through no fault of your own." He leaned back, frowning at the ceiling. "Rufus knew better. He knew, yet broke his sacred vows."

"And now I know. And the knowledge prompts me to act."

Ephraim's gaze shot back to her. "Sister. You're not leaving."

She couldn't. Not without cash, but, she might have figured out an answer to that problem. "You're still in correspondence with Brother Hickenloper."

He nodded. "Trying to save him from apostasy."

"Would you ask him to consult a lawyer on my behalf?"

"Brother Butts told you we don't have funds for lawyers."

Money was Ephraim's priority, not the state of her soul. "Rufus owns a successful business, employing a dozen skilled craftsmen."

Ephraim tapped the desk, pondering whether Salt Lake City had a lawyer who would take her case and send Rufus the bill. Keziah saw the moment alimony crossed his mind. His fingers stopped and he grabbed an old envelope from the corner of his desk. Keziah had supported herself since Rufus left, but that truth would be ignored in the quest for a hefty settlement. "I'll write Brother Hickenloper right away. Rufus has sinned by abandonment, desertion, bigamy, adultery. He should pay, er, rectify his errors."

"Thank you. And I'd appreciate if you'd keep this between us." Keziah stood, meeting Daniel's gaze.

"Of course." Ephraim said, scribbling on the envelope.

All Preparation would know before sunset.

When Keziah arrived back at the bothy, she found Louisa Paden sitting on the bench, holding five-month-old Rebecca. "Let me guess. A teething remedy?"

"No, her teeth aren't the trouble." During labor, Louisa had been cheerful to the point of silliness, but today she kept her gaze down and patted the bench beside her.

"What's wrong?" Keziah lowered her voice and sat.

"I wanted to thank you. Hannah and Lodema said you saved my life."

"Watching Rebecca grow is all the thanks I need."

Tear-filled eyes met hers. "You won't be able to see her grow. We're leaving."

"Back east?" Keziah would be glad to see the last of Jacob, but she'd miss Louisa and the baby.

She shook her head. "North of here about ten miles, on the Little Sioux River. The men are calling it Belvidere."

Men? Who would partner with hothead Jacob? "Who else is going?"

"I'm not supposed to say until they tell Father Ephraim, but I wanted you to know."

Keziah gave her a hug. "I hope...you'll come back and visit."

"Me too."

But they both knew Father Ephraim would label them apostates and forbid further contact.

The next morning Keziah was in the kitchen garden harvesting snap peas for dinner when twelve-year-old Cecelia Hall slipped through the gate. One look at her face and she knew the Halls were the other family leaving.

"They thought I was asleep last night, but I wasn't. I heard we're moving. Again." She plopped at the end of the row and let her tears fall. "I won't even have any boys to play with. Just babies."

"Babies?" Keziah dropped the peas into the bucket of cold water. "Rebecca Paden..."

"And the Thomas babies. Guess who's going to be washing diapers and minding them." She pointed to herself. "No more school."

"I'm so sorry." Keziah held her as she cried. "I'll pray they change their minds."

"They won't." She sniffed. "Their lumber came."

They had money for lumber?

"They started building today—my father, Jacob Paden, and Omer and his father."

Keziah gasped. There was only one Omer in the Congregation. Omer Lytle. Christena's son. Did she know? She stood and helped Cecelia up, then handed her the bucket of peas. "Please take these to Sarah Chase."

The girl found a clean place on her skirt and wiped her face dry. "Please don't tell anyone. I'm not supposed to know."

Keziah nodded. Chest aching, she hurried up the path to the Lytle's. Why hadn't Christena told her? Did she know? It couldn't be true. How would she survive without her?

"Christena?" She knocked, then pushed the door open.

Her dear friend faced the corner. Moving carefully, she folded a shirt and set it in a crate.

"You're leaving."

She nodded, hands limp at her sides. "Hugh told me last night." She spoke slowly, her voice thick with tears and resignation.

"What happened? Did he hit you? We'll go to Father Ephraim. He's still the County Judge. He'll decree you can stay. We'll live together." Desperation reduced her to babbling.

"No. He said he'd take Omer."

That mean, rotten, spiteful maggot.

Keziah crossed the floor in three steps, pulled Christena into an embrace, and together they cried and pleaded with God.

CHAPTER 16

July 1855

The bell over the shop's door rang.

"Good morning, Duncan." Marcia Barnum entered, carrying her overstuffed bag of mending. "Thanks for asking me to sit in for you. I need a break from those wild grandchildren."

"Oh surely not wee Frances?" Duncan packed his awls, needles, and punches.

"Especially Frances. She's a year and a half now, and tearing around after her brothers." Marcia settled into the chair with a contented sigh. "No one sits when she's about."

"Have a peaceful afternoon then."

After strapping on his knapsack, Duncan strolled into the sunshine. Isaac Swett had told him several saddles and bridles were in need of repair. But instead of an empty building, the stable hummed like a baritone beehive. Duncan took a step back. Was it—

An arm clamped around his neck. "Gotcha."

Duncan threw himself backwards. His weight pushed the knapsack into the man. They went down with a thud.

"Oof!"

Duncan jumped to his feet, heart thundering, hands fisted. Had he been attacked by a Lamanite or an apostate? No. Jacob Paden, the hothead who'd attacked Keziah last winter.

"Jacob?"

"I told you to be quiet." Hugh Lytle stomped out of the stable, hissing. He spotted Duncan. "Ross. I should have known you'd cause trouble."

"I'm here for leatherwork, not a choking."

"Hugh asked Jacob to keep watch." Andrew Hall and a few others emerged from the stable. "Why don't you come back another day?"

Henry Brooke stepped into the light. "We can't let him go. He'll run straight to Thompson."

Thompson? Not Father Ephraim?

"No, he won't. Duncan's a decent sort." Fred Winegar joined their circle. "Besides, we're all in agreement. Let's go talk to Father Ephraim right now."

The men exchanged glances. Hugh crossed his arms and gave a tip of his head.

"We're not going to apostatize. Our faith is still strong." Andrew explained to Duncan. "We prefer to live separately, each with his own family."

Every member of the group had a wife and at least one child.

"You'll stay in Preparation, won't you?" Duncan asked the group as he extended a hand to help Jacob up.

Hugh frowned at the Lord's House. "Depends on what Thompson says."

"All his potato and onion meals are about to kill me." John Thomas held out his waistband, showing a gap of a couple inches. "My trousers are falling off."

"Nobody wants that." Henry's were also loose. "I need meat."

"True. We don't look so dignified with breeks around our ankles." Duncan opened his knapsack, and took out his punch and hammer. "Let me fix your belts."

The men compared the mouth-watering wonders their wives could make with a meat as Duncan punched new holes. "So if he allows meat, and lets your wives take charge of the kitchen once in a while..."

"No, we want to eat in our own homes, with only our family," Henry said.

Had they asked their wives how they felt about cooking? "You'll need to trade your heating stove for a cooking stove."

"I have my eye on land across the river." Fred pointed northeast. "My sons will need their own farms soon. When I die, I want to leave an inheritance for them."

Where would the money come from for that? "We've accomplished a lot working together."

Hugh shook his head. "We can do more as families, without good-for-nothing idlers sponging off us."

Who did he mean? People here worked hard. Not that Duncan spent time watching others work. "Your leaving will mean a lot of acres and livestock for only..." He paused to count. "A dozen men."

"We'll divide up the cattle and fields for each of us." Andrew handed him his belt. "The Congregation will do all right with what's left."

"The Lord's House will be empty without you." Had they spared a thought for the single people? Duncan would miss their children.

"We'll come back for Sabbath teaching and feasts," Fred assured him, leaving unsaid the question of whether Father Ephraim would allow visits.

The men marched to the Lord's House with nary a word of thanks. When they needed his help, Duncan was a member of the Congregation. When a better plan came their way, he was forgotten.

If Hugh Lytle left, his wife would go too. Keziah would be without her best friend...unless she went with them. Heart kicking into a gallop, Duncan packed his tools and hurried to find Keziah.

July 1855
Under a cloudless sky, Keziah and Finn swished through tall

grass up and over the hill. The downward slope led to a valley carpeted with ferns and roofed by small trees. Indigo buntings sang and insects hummed, but otherwise all was quiet. Keziah sat on a fallen tree. The hollow closed in around her, comforting as a hug, easing her heartache.

Blessed are the peacemakers, for they shall be called my children.

If only she knew how to make peace...

Finn stood, ears up, nostrils twitching. He huffed, then galloped up the trail, tail wagging. Friend, not foe. Moments later the dog escorted Duncan into the valley.

Keziah stood. "We've no babies due. Is it Leo chopping off a leg, then?"

"No medical crisis."

"Thank the Lord," she sat and Finn plopped at her feet. "Join us and listen."

Duncan perched on the other end. He'd shaved off winter's whiskers. Summer's heat had his dark hair curling over his neck. He gazed about, took a deep breath, then his shoulders dropped on his exhale. "You didn't bring your gathering bags."

"What I'm searching for isn't of this world."

"Have you found it?"

"Perhaps. If you are the peacemaker." She glanced at him in time to see a muscle ripple in his jaw. "What's wrong?"

He leaned forward to press his forehead into his fingertips. "I kicked open a hornet's nest, when I stumbled on a secret meeting."

"Hugh, Andrew, and the rest?"

"You know?"

"Women talk."

His dark eyes studied her. "And what are they saying?"

"They prefer to stay here."

"I thought they were, if Ephraim changed a few things." Duncan still had hope.

"They've have chosen land on the Little Sioux River, northwest of here, and started building. They're calling the place Belvidere."

"So even if Father Ephraim allowed meat, they wouldn't stay." His hands hung limp between his knees, then his wrists turned as if tossing a thought. "I put new holes in the men's belt loops. Have the children lost weight too?"

He was truly her partner in concern for the health of the Congregation. "No. They're allowed milk and eggs."

He tilted his head and smiled. "Keziah Sirrine. You got Father Ephraim to change the diet. And when we were sick last winter, you talked him into allowing beef broth. *You* are the peacemaker."

"No, I'm a troublemaker. Ask Orrin Butts."

"Never."

"'Tis you. Teaching the children to sing, making moccasins from buckskin, Bible study for the single men."

Duncan straightened, studying the patch of sky. "'Blessed are the peacemakers, for they...' It's us. Both of us." He turned to her, his eyes serious again, his words coming fast. "Orrin still thinks those who left last year might take up arms against us."

"I've had letters from Mercy Jones." Would Christena write? Would Ephraim let her see her mail? "No violence. Only lawyers."

"For one as worried about money as Orrin, the expense of a lawyer would seem violent. But for quick-tempered men like Jacob Paden and Hugh Lytle..."

"...violence is the answer. We need to be about our Father's business."

He pulled her to her feet and took a few steps before he looked down at their joined hands. "Oh. Sorry." He let go and rushed on.

The warmth and strength of his hand had hers reaching for him again, but she tucked it under her apron. She was married until Father Ephraim said differently. They crested the ridge overlooking Preparation and started down the hill at a run.

"Where are the children?" Duncan asked, as ever concerned with their safety.

"Amelia took them on a picnic."

He prayed with every step.

Keziah told Finn to stay outside. The Congregation spilled from the doors, grumbling and bleating.

Hugh Lytle's shouts echoed from the Lord's House. "Every time I turn around, *your* daughter is on *my* horse."

Orrin Butts yelled back at equal volume, "You agreed to shared property. You signed up for it."

Father Ephraim weighed in. "It's the Heavenly Father's plan that all things are held in common."

"Please sit down, brothers." Duncan hurried inside and squeezed through the milling crowd to reach its center. Keziah followed in his wake. He was right—peacemaking would take both of them. "If we limit who can ride your horse, would you stay?"

"It's your fault. Ever since you rode her..." Hugh's glare shifted from Duncan to Keziah. "Here's our local herb woman to tell you it's not safe for girls to gallop and jump."

"The risk is the same for women as men." Keziah breathed through her mouth. The heat of anger worsened the usual odors.

"The Bible says, I will not suffer a woman to teach." Jacob Paden crossed his arms and scowled down at her.

Duncan stepped to her side, ready to protect her.

She raised an eyebrow at the man. "So you'll be midwifing your own babies now. "

Several people snorted and giggled.

Hannah Perrin said, "Start praying now."

His face reddened and he backed away.

"Keziah Sirrine," Christena Lytle's voice echoed across the room. The Congregation silenced. Her friend stumbled forward, chin raised, her pointed finger wavering. Keziah's blood chilled. Would she reveal her secret, her lack of faith in Ephraim? "This is your fault for not praying for Preparation."

"Christena?" Her mouth dropped open, yet it took a moment to find a breath. "*Not praying?* How can you say such a thing? After everything we've been through, all the times we've prayed together." Yesterday morning she and Christena had clung together and prayed God would change Hugh's decision. Did she blame Keziah because Hugh was dead set against staying? Christena was an adult, not an infant in the faith. She knew prayers weren't a street-corner conjuror's trick—say a magic word and a rabbit pops from his hat.

"I know Keziah to be a praying woman. And you know it too."

Duncan's hand rested on her shoulder, steadying her. "Your words are unfounded and hurtful. You've no call to make this false accusation."

"You didn't pray." Christena's eyes were red and the pupils were large. "You didn't pray."

Omer pulled down her pointing finger. "Mama, what's wrong with you? That's Keziah, your cousin, best friend, sister in the church."

Could it be poisoning? "Have you eaten anything different, like mushrooms?" Christena didn't respond, so Keziah turned to Omer. "Try to get her to throw up."

Hugh took her elbow and dragged her out. "We don't have time for this."

Father Ephraim raised his arms. "And I will soften the hearts of the people, as I did the heart of Pharaoh, until my servant Baneemy, whom I have appointed, shall have time to gather up the strength of my house."

"He's not Baneemy," Henry Brooke said in an undertone to Jacob Paden. "Not Father Ephraim either."

Duncan muttered, "Short journey from wanting meat for dinner to questioning Ephraim."

The group complained about money, land, and meat, muttering to no one in particular. Not seeing any way to make peace, Keziah retreated into the far corner and leaned against the wall. *Not praying? If Christena had put a butcher knife through my heart, the pain would be less.*

Duncan brought her a bench to sit on. "Even when you're attacked, you continue caring for them. Might you have a calming herb?"

"None strong enough. I'm thinking a cast iron frying pan applied to each head..."

"Gently, of course." The corner of his mouth turned up, hinting he'd not lost his sense of humor in this latest donnybrook.

Orrin conferred with Father Ephraim, then waved his arms. "Guy Barnum and Homer Hoyt will bring your trunks out."

The group shuffled out, muttering about what was due them,

but loading corn, potatoes, pumpkins, and squashes into the wagons.

Keziah leaned against the wall. "So much for making peace."

"No one was wounded, except Jacob Paden when he tried to strangle me."

She pulled aside Duncan's collar, finding no marks. "Why didn't you tell me?"

"I'm breathing and talking. No harm. The lad, however..."

"Strangling is his way." Keziah watched Jacob heft a trunk into a wagon. "He's fine. I'll be glad to see the last of him. And hotheaded Hugh."

"I'm sorry about Christena."

She blinked back tears and straightened her shoulders. "Thank you for coming to my defense."

"Always," he said.

Catherine Thompson, her loose dress no longer concealing her pregnancy, hurried down the stairs. She held a bloody cloth to the head of her two-year old, and called for Keziah. The boy seemed determined to best his brother's record of injuries.

Keziah sighed. "And I'll trade peacemaking for poultices."

August 1855

Sun lit the Lord's House, but it wasn't heat making Duncan fidget. Nor was it the odor of sweat, since Keziah had gently, but fervently insisted they all bathe before the Solemn Assembly. No, it was Duncan's bones.

Instead of this hard bench, his bones wished to sit on a pillow. With the Congregation so small this year, such indulgence would surely be noticed. Duncan could claim advanced age, except Job Barnum and Silas Wilcox had a couple decades on him and neither sat on a cushion. Orrin Butts was a few years older, yet he sat without complaint. Credit his ample padding.

Duncan leaned to his side for another look. Aye, a good bit of padding. What did the man eat? His haunches were bigger than

Rowland's or Guy's or Homer's. Whisht! Studying others' rumps during the Solemn Assembly surely must be a sin.

Duncan focused on Father Ephraim. He preached while standing, so the size of his rump didn't matter.

"...as long as there's a true Israelite in the labyrinthian wilderness of Gentile Babylon."

Labyrinthian was a good word to describe Ephraim's teachings.

"...pleased to see them gather to the land of Mount Ephraim..."

Mount Ephraim? Was he changing the name of Preparation?

He addressed an unnamed critic who charged him with self-aggrandizement, then, "And now in conclusion..."

Conclusion? The bones of his bottom were ready.

Ephraim raised his voice, "...we would say to all whose affections entwine still around the standard of Emanuel as proclaimed unto the remnant seed of the Church by Baneemy, Patriarch of Zion and Apostle of the Holy Priesthood..."

The man had changed his name. Again. He'd been Brother Thompson in St. Louis, then Father Ephraim upon arrival in Preparation, and now, Baneemy, Patriarch of Zion and Apostle of the Holy Priesthood. A mouthful. Would anyone remember it, much less call him such?

Duncan snuck a glance around the room, but no one reacted.

If one name change was good, then more must be better. The Congregation became the Watchmen of Ephraim. This big room they gathered in was now the Hall of the Sons of Ephraim. Well, God had changed Abram's name to Abraham, Jacob to Israel, Simon to Peter, so change must be all right. Although remembering new names wasn't easy. Malinda Butts' yearlong request to be called Tryphina had met with little success. Humph. Perhaps Duncan should rename himself Doubting Thomas.

Father, er, Baneemy, anointed Guy Barnum the Patriarch of the Sacred Treasury. Daniel Butts was now the Lord's Printer—whose printer was he before? Fancy designation for a young lad. Orrin must be proud.

Abandoning all hope of conclusion, Baneemy dove into "...regeneration of the flesh, being born again into newness of life a second or third time, as many probations as an individual may be entitled to or worthy of..." Was he talking about reincarnation, what people in India believed? As rough as this life had been, Duncan wasn't sure about giving it another try. If God gave him a choice, he'd choose heaven. His bones would enjoy sitting on a cloud.

"...the disappearance of Babylonians, Chaldeans, Amorites, Hittites, Greeks, and Romans." Duncan had met a Greek family in Ohio. Such kind people, inviting him and Emily for supper. He didn't recognize their food, but it was delicious.

Food? Was it time for the feast? Duncan sent a hopeful glance toward the kitchen, yet no food emerged. Attendance was down this year; they should have plenty to eat.

"...Samaritans, Sodomites, and Antediluvians have contaminated the Mormons. Samaritans are attacking the Presbytery of Zion, watching for an opportunity to seize the crown, disputing the keys of authority." Samaritans? Like the Good Samaritan in Jesus' parable? Were crown and the keys of authority here in Preparation? Best guess, locked up in the printing office so Leo couldn't break them.

Helen Barnum started to fuss and her mother took her outside. Next Sabbath, Duncan resolved, he'd hold a baby so he could leave when teaching turned to tedium.

The Baneemy's voice lowered as he spoke of the apostates. "...the problem of rebels leaving the community... a decided partiality for the customary mode of family exclusiveness was soon discovered to be the predominating sentiment without exception to saint or sinner."

Whose fault was that? Better houses went to those in families. Leadership positions went to heads of households—except for young Dennis the printer.

Baneemy folded his notes. "The object of the House of Ephraim is precisely the same as before the incorporation, namely: to build up Zion, a place of rest, a house of bread, a joyful home, and a quiet habitation for the pure in heart, and a place of succor for the worthy and virtuous poor among the Gentiles."

There, that's what he'd been waiting for these past two years, a clear statement of Preparation's purpose. He stood, to his bones relief, and applauded. The rest of the Congregation must have liked the purpose statement too, as they joined in. Or else they'd noticed the tables set with bread, potatoes, squash, beets, watermelon, muskmelon, grapes, plums, and cheese. The feast was ready.

After a week, one thing was clear. No one in the Congregation would be calling their leader Baneemy, Patriarch of Zion and Apostle of the Holy Priesthood.

$\sim$

September 10, 1855

One look at Catherine during supper and Keziah knew her time would come soon. After two sips of soup, the woman inched her way upstairs.

Shortly after falling asleep in the bothy, Finn pawed Keziah's arm and made a sound between an exhale and a full-fledged bark. Keziah rolled upright and straightened her skirt. The knock sounded.

"It's time," Amelia Thompson, the oldest daughter, told her when she answered. Keeping little brother Leo alive had trained her to be calm in every crisis. "The pains are closer together. She's leaning on the windowsill, panting and moaning."

"You know a lot." Keziah tied on her moccasins and grabbed her satchel. "Any thoughts of becoming a midwife?"

"Not a one." Amelia flashed a quick smile. Escorted by Finn, they raced through the night to the Lord's House.

Keziah smiled back. "Raising Leo would have me looking for a convent." A glance at the stars showed several hours before dawn. "The other children?" Mothers should be relieved of their flock during labor.

"In my bed." The single women would keep watch over them.

"You must be tired."

Amelia's eyes widened, as if forcing herself to stay awake. "You have no idea. She's been frantic to clean all week."

"Nesting. Since she can't reach or bend, you're stuck with scrubbing and carrying."

"And ever so much laundry." Amelia opened the door to the Thompsons' family quarters. Fabric hung ceiling to floor, drifting with the breeze from the window. "I'll bring hot water."

The couple stood at the window. Light from the single lantern showed he'd discarded his masks of Father Ephraim, Baneemy, and the rest. He was back to being Charles, father, husband...friend. "Thanks for coming so quickly."

Catherine raised her head from his shoulder. Her face shone with perspiration. "Oh good, the midwife is here. I can have this baby."

"How are you doing?" Keziah set out her supplies, then scrubbed her hands in the ironstone washbowl and said the midwife prayer.

"Wonderful." In spite of the cool September night, Charles had shrugged off his usual vest and sweated through his shirt. "First-rate."

And now the opinion that truly counted. "Catherine?"

"Pains hard and fast." She moaned.

Charles William had come easily, with Mrs. Jackson's help. "Last time you gave birth in a chair. This time?"

She nodded. Keziah put a towel on the seat of the wooden chair and brought the lantern near. Charles sat and held Catherine between his knees. A touch on her belly found the curve of the baby's back in perfect position. "Do you want anyone else here?"

"Let's not wake anyone this time of night."

Keziah moved her supplies closer and sat in a chair facing her. "Especially the children."

"Especially." She groaned. "Here it comes."

"Take it easy, dear." Charles hung onto her. "Easy does it."

Catherine caught her breath. The normally tranquil woman snarled, "Nothing about this is easy. Nothing. And don't call me 'dear,' like you've forgotten my name."

"Yes, darling."

Even-tempered no more, Catherine reached over her head and thumped his head.

Keziah folded back the well-worn nightgown. "Not yet."

"I beg to disagree. I'm so rrrrrr..." Another pain caught her. When it passed, Keziah slid to the floor between her knees. Still no baby.

Keziah bathed Catherine's feet in the hot water Amelia brought, then gave her an infusion of tansy, sage, and pennyroyal. After a half-dozen pains without change, Keziah suggested walking again.

"Too tired." Her head lolled against her husband.

"Come along, sweetheart. Hike up the hill will bring this baby out."

"Hike yourself, slave-driver," Catherine said, but let him lift her to her feet. They shuffled across the bare floor. Keziah stole a glance at the room.

Lengths of muslin were tacked to the ceiling, forming separate areas for Leo and Charles William, and another corner for Ida and Amelia. More muslin was tacked over the window. Clothes hung on pegs, a few sets for each child. The sole bedstead was simple and well-used. She saw no evidence Father Ephraim tapped into the Congregation's possessions to benefit his family, and much less extravagant than the Barnums'.

"I give up." Catherine slumped to the chair. A spasm hit hard and she cried out.

"What's wrong? Why so much pain? Help her!" Charles demanded.

What would Mrs. Jackson do? This was Catherine's fourth, no fifth, birth, including Isabelle who died in St. Louis. Shouldn't it be easier? Surely the baby would come soon. "Squat on the floor, Catherine. Keep breathing. Charles, sit behind her for support. Hold her up."

A few more pains came and went before she had to change positions.

"Here, I'll walk you." Charles tried to help her up.

She pushed him away. "My feet are asleep. I can't stand."

Keziah pulled a pillow close to the edge of the mattress. "Kneel and lean on the headboard."

"Oh this is better."

Charles rubbed her back.

"No. Don't touch me."

He scooted away as if burned. "You want me to leave."

"Stay where you are. This is your—" The rest of her sentence was lost in a sobbing cry.

Charles whispered to Keziah. "I don't remember the others…"

"We forget, lest all be only children." Keziah's hands felt a shift. "Here comes the baby. Push now."

With a grunt, groan, and a wail, the baby finally arrived. Keziah had expected the vegetable diet to result in smaller babies, but this one was a good size, accounting for the lengthy delivery. "It's a girl."

"Thank God," Catherine said. "I wouldn't survive another Leo."

"Some girls are troublesome and disobedient," Charles added helpfully.

Catherine glared over her shoulder and the baby added her protest. "They get that from their father."

Keziah cut the navel string, wrapped the girl in flannel, and handed her to Charles.

"Magnificent work, Catherine. Dear baby, as beautiful as your mother! Welcome to the world, little one." Charles melted into a puddle of cooing and oohing, with occasional snatches of songs. Keziah cleaned Catherine and settled her into bed with a raspberry infusion.

Amelia brought more hot water which Keziah used to clean the infant. Charles pulled back the muslin curtain and rosy light filled the room.

"What will you name her?" Keziah asked. After naming the last one 'Charles,' she hoped they wouldn't name this one 'Catherine.'

"Osneth Effina." The very opposite of a common name. Christena would laugh… No, she thought with a wrench of her heart, Christena was gone.

"We'll call her Ossie." Catherine smiled at the baby.

Charles clasped Keziah's hand. "Thank you for bringing God's blessing safely into this world."

Keziah gathered the soiled laundry and promised to bring breakfast up. She stepped into the hall to find Amelia asleep in the corner. Keziah contemplated joining her, but joyful laughter from the other side of the door energized her.

Keziah smiled and headed to the kitchen.

CHAPTER 17

October 1855

Duncan hammered fence posts around the herb garden to the tune of giggles, shrieks, splashes, and happy barks. Keziah emerged from the river bed, pulling a wagon full of willow branches. Since Christena's departure, other women had joined Keziah in her work. Today it was Mary DeForest and her wee ones. Joseph and William had stuck willow switches in their breeks, and galloped by, pretending to be horses. Young Mary carried wreaths of flowers, one of which graced Finn's neck. Having worn herself out keeping up with her older sister, Mabel whined, "I want to ride in the wagon."

"There's no room for you," Keziah told the lassie. "When we arrive at the bothy, I'll set out a quilt for you to lie on."

"Don't *want* a nap. Not tired." She stomped off.

Keziah raised her sunbonnet, her face pink from the hot day, and spotted him. "Duncan! How did you know I was expanding the garden?"

"You asked me to sharpen your gathering knives and marked off the dirt."

"I award you a crown for hard work." Young Mary held out a circle of purple ironweed and orange coneflowers.

"I'm honored, your highness." Duncan bent on one knee and the girl placed the crown on his hat.

Sister Mary stretched. "I'm done in. We're going back to the cabin for a nap."

Keziah unloaded the wagon. "Shall I keep any here so you can rest?"

"Then you'll not get a lick of work done. No, I've got them trained to nap." She clapped her hands, and the four children followed.

Finn crawled into his hole under the sumac and gave big sigh. Keziah unlocked the bothy and poured cold peppermint infusion for them both. After a too-short rest, she sorted through the branches on the wheelbarrow, chose a thick one, and wove it around the stakes.

"You've done this before." Duncan returned to setting posts. "How long will the fence last?"

"I don't know." Keziah started another row. "We never stayed long enough in one place to tell. Six years in St. Louis, a year in Wisconsin, two in Nauvoo, three in New York, one in Ohio, two in Missouri." She looked south. "That's why I've felt safer here—we're out of Missouri.

"What's wrong with Missouri?"

"A group of us had settled about sixty miles north of Independence." She recited the facts, as if her feelings were too much to bear. "The Missourians got riled up and formed a militia, so the Mormons did too. There was looting, burning, shooting. Murder."

"You were there?" Duncan asked Keziah, but she kept her head down, gaze on the fence. He thought of what others had said about Rufus. "By yourself?"

"Rufus was moving Mormon families into town for safety. I was home with the baby. The mob drove us into the snow, then burned everything. My little boy drowned crossing the creek and, a week later, my baby was stillborn." She nodded toward the House. "Charles's wife died of exposure, leaving a five month old baby."

Duncan wanted to flog Rufus. He wanted to hold Keziah. Since neither was an option, he refilled Keziah's cup and brought it to her. "How you ever survived..."

Her hands clutched the fence, knuckles white. "Our potatoes had baked in the fire, so I had food until the militia came. The next farm north, the neighbors died." She took the cup, drank it down, and resumed weaving. "The governor of Missouri issued an extermination order against Mormons. All our property and possessions were confiscated. We ran for our lives."

Extermination? As if they were insects, not humans, children of God. Keziah was quiet, too quiet. Duncan put his palm on her wrist and she stilled. "There's not enough people in this area to form a mob," he told her. "Hugh Lytle's group is busy building their own community."

Keziah raised her head. Her gaze traveled the garden, circled the houses and cabins along the river, and settled on the Lord's house. "What does it take to make peace?" she whispered.

November 1855

Icy rain turned the footpaths into slushy mud and drove the Congregation to shelter in the Lord's House. Keziah hung her dripping cape on a peg. Finn shook, spattering rain about. The men huddled in one corner. The women sewed in another. And the children, having finished school for the day, romped in the middle.

Keziah had stopped looking for Rufus. Maybe her heart would give up on Christena. She crossed to the kitchen.

"Is Maria ill?" Sarah Chase asked from the kitchen.

Keziah shook her head. "She'll be back tomorrow."

"Ah." The cook nodded. "If you have time, could you help with the peeling?"

"Surely." Keziah rolled up her sleeves, chose a knife, and joined Hannah Perrin beside the pile of potatoes.

"Misery loves company," Hannah said with a smile. Wisps of light brown hair escaped from the rolled braid at the back of her head.

A loud crash and a curse stopped conversation. Leo sprawled on the floor, tangled with a spinning wheel.

"Fool!" Rebecca Butts, Orrin's wife, grabbed the boy and he kicked to escape. "Bungler!"

"Bridle your tongue," Hannah said, her voice calm and quiet.

Rebecca's face reddened, bordering on apoplexy. Keziah pressed her shoulder. "Let go of him."

"Hold still, lad," Duncan unraveled the yarn from the boy's legs.

"He broke my spinning wheel." Rebecca swung her fist at Leo, but the boy dove under the nearest table. "My mother brought it from Liverpool and he broke it."

Duncan returned the bobbin to its place, then turned the wheel. "It's working."

"Get back here and take your punishment, Leo Thompson." Rebecca reached for him, but he dashed up the stairs. "Hide behind your mother's skirts, will you?"

"Duncan set your wheel aright." And tucked it in the corner, away from the marauding hordes. Keziah caught the woman's forearms. "Rebecca."

"It's the only thing I have left." She pushed away, her words hissed past clenched jaw and tight lips. "Everything else—my nice dishes, my pearl necklace, my lace tablecloth—is gone." Her eyes closed, but couldn't hold back tears.

Keziah squeezed her hands. "I know."

"No you don't. You and Rufus were always poor."

Ouch. She didn't need that reminder.

Hannah murmured, "Naked we come and naked we will return."

"And in between, I'm grateful for something to wear." Keziah guided Rebecca back to her stool.

The children resumed frolicking.

Rebecca pointed. "Next one of you comes near my spinning wheel will be beat to an inch of his life."

Without looking up from the potatoes, Hannah said, "'The fruit of the spirit is love, joy, peace, long-suffering—'"

Rebecca turned so fast she nearly upended the stool. "Don't you dare quote the Bible to me, Hannah Perrin."

"So much for a 'soft answer turning away wrath,'" Hannah murmured.

A knife twisted in Keziah's heart as she remembered Christena's Bible quoting. "Aye, making peace is more uncertain than making an infusion."

Duncan clapped and called the children to the empty corner by the kitchen. "Who wants to hear a story?"

The children settled onto the floor and the adults sighed with relief. Keziah returned to the potatoes.

"A friend from Denmark told me about a kingdom of sea folk who lived deep in the ocean." Duncan's voice lowered, sounding mysterious and enchanted. "They were called mermaids and mermen. They swam all day, playing hide-and-seek among the plants growing on the bottom of the sea. The top of their bodies were like ours, but instead of legs, they had tails like fish." He moved his arms and legs to act out the story.

Sarah Chase reached for a potato, and whispered, "Are fairytales allowed?"

Keziah nodded. "Brigham Young tried to ban stories as a waste of time."

Hannah looked up and pushed out her lips. "And we all know how Father Ephraim feels about Brigham Young."

Ida Thompson tiptoed downstairs, followed by her brother, Leo, who asked, "Is this a true story?"

"'Tis a fairy-tale," Duncan told him. "You must use your imagination."

Young Mary Lewis settled three-year-old Amy Chase on her lap. "Leo, hush. We want to hear the story." A throat-clearing from her mother had her adding, "Please."

"The ocean king's daughters had beautiful voices to sing the music of the seas. The littlest mermaid had the best voice of all."

Leo squeezed between the Barnum boys. "Mermaids can breathe water and air?"

Duncan nodded, unfazed by the interruptions. "Every year on

their birthdays, the mermaid princesses were allowed to go to the surface and peek at the people. Then they'd return to the sea palace and tell the others what they saw: churches with steeples, horses pulling carriages, and people walking on the beach. One sister saw swans flying and dolphins jumping. Another saw children swimming."

"I didn't see mermaids when I swim," John Perrin said.

"These children didn't either, but their dog saw a mermaid and guess what he did."

"He barked like Finn!" Amy said. Finn raised his head, but, failing to see the cause of the excitement, went back to sleep.

"The littlest mermaid had listened to all her sisters' stories." Duncan leaned forward on the stool. "She couldn't wait for her turn. She wanted to see green hills and trees. She wanted to hear church bells and thunder. Finally, at last, it was her birthday. Her grandmother wove a wreath of pearls into her hair and the little mermaid swam to the surface. There, right in front of her, was a three-masted ship decorated with flags and lanterns. A band played and people danced. It was the birthday of the prince." Duncan's expressive voice kept the children's and the adults', attention. "Then a terrible storm came up."

The children gasped and clung to each other.

"In the bright lightning, the little mermaid watched the sailors try to keep the ship afloat, but it broke apart. She knew the prince would drown in the ocean, so she dove through the wreckage, found the prince's body, and lifted him to the air."

"So *strong*," Ida said.

"All night she kept his face up so he could breathe. In the morning, she saw land nearby. She pushed him onto the beach, then hid behind the rocks. Girls from a nearby school found him and woke him up. The prince lived."

"What about the rest of the people on the boat?" Mary asked.

"Let's imagine they all caught hold of floating barrels and were rescued." Duncan continued, "The little mermaid returned to the sea kingdom. Every night she swam near the palace and watched for the prince. She wanted to be a human, with legs, and live with him. The only one who might help her was a sea witch who lived in a cave guarded by snakes that would grab a mermaid and squeeze the life out of her. The little mermaid gathered her courage and raced past the snakes into the cave."

"Oh no!" Amy Chase said. "She'll never escape!"

"I'll squeeze the life out of you," the Barnum boys and Leo threatened each other.

"Then you'll miss the rest of the story," Duncan told them and they stopped wrestling. "The witch had a potion to turn the mermaid into a human. The change would hurt like knives slicing her body, but give her legs and a soul to live forever. The mermaid decided becoming a human would be worth the pain."

"I want to swim like a fish," said the oldest Barnum boy. The other children hushed him.

"The witch warned the mermaid could never return to her father's kingdom. If the prince married another, the mermaid's heart would break and she'd turn into sea foam. The mermaid had already fallen in love with the prince, so she agreed to that too. The witch required a payment. What do you think she wanted from the mermaid?"

The children guessed money and pearls.

"In payment, the witch wanted the mermaid's voice. The witch cut out her tongue and gave her the potion."

The children said "ouch," except Leo who asked if the potion tasted as nasty as those Sister Keziah made.

"Much, much worse." Duncan met her gaze and winked. "But the mermaid no longer had a tongue to taste it. So she swam away from her home, never to see it again, to the beach near the prince's palace. She drank the potion. The pain sliced her like a sword and she fainted. And there the prince found her."

"He kissed her and she woke up," Ida proclaimed.

"No, that's Sleeping Beauty," Mary told her.

"Now the mermaid had legs. Even though they hurt, she walked with the prince. They rode horses and danced. But she couldn't answer his questions about who she was and where she'd come from. And she couldn't sing for him."

"Why didn't she write what she wanted to say?" Leo asked.

"She never learned," Mary said. "The sea kingdom didn't have teachers."

"Everyone in the palace, including the little mermaid, went on a ship to the nearby kingdom where the prince's parents found a princess for him. The prince liked the princess and agreed to marry her."

Poor little mermaid. With her misfortune, the princess will probably have twins. Keziah muttered, "So much for loyalty."

Hannah had never met her husband, but the gossiping Congregation made sure she knew all about him. She elbowed Keziah. "Rufus was no prince."

"Understatement of the year."

"The mermaid was sad, knowing she would die in the morning. That night her sisters brought her a magic knife from the sea witch. All she had to do was kill the prince with the knife and she could be a mermaid again."

The children gasped.

"But she loved the prince so much, she threw the knife into the ocean and jumped in after it. Instead of dying, she turned into a daughter of the air. If she does enough good deeds, she'll earn her soul and live forever." Duncan raised his hands. "And that's the end."

Mary announced she would rewrite the story so the mermaid and the prince married and lived happily ever after. Ida wanted to learn to swim and become a mermaid. Leo and the Barnum boys became sea snakes, squeezing anyone they got their hands on.

Earn her soul through good deeds? That sounded familiar. Hannah sat with a dazed expression, then whispered to Keziah, "Are mermaids *Mormon*?"

~

December 1855

Keziah entered the height and weight of the children in her

ledger. All of them had grown. Were they growing as much as if they'd been allowed meat? Were they as tall as they should be?

The floor creaked in the printing office. Two sabbaths had passed and Father Ephraim hadn't reacted to Duncan's mermaid story. Five months without a letter from Christena. Six months since her request for divorce. Was Ephraim holding her mail?

Tryphina stomped into the House on a gust of snow and cold. "Sister Keziah, you need to do help the red dun gelding Dennis brought back from Council Bluffs yesterday. He's wretched."

She closed the ledger. Willing or not, she'd be dragged into the girl's emergency. "Perhaps he's pining away for the pretty mare he shared a stable with."

Tryphina stared at her a moment, then waved her mittened hands. "All right. You want observations. Here you go—runny nose, cough, not eating."

"Sounds like an infection." Keziah threw on her cape and they slogged up the hill. Walking straight into the wind, snow pricked her face. "Where is he?"

"In the stable."

"Contaminating the rest of the horses."

"Oh no. Will it kill them all?"

"Let's pasture the rest. They can handle weather easier than disease. Did you touch the new horse?"

"Yesterday. He was fine. But today's he's disgusting, foul, nasty."

"Did you wash your hands after you touched him, before you touched the others?"

Tryphina wailed, "I've killed them all."

"Did you touch Finn?"

"I've killed Finn." She stopped caterwauling. "No, I haven't seen him all week. Dogs can get it? Can I get it?" The howling resumed. "I'll die a disgusting, nasty, foul, death. My brother bought a sick horse and killed me."

Keziah opened the stable and released the healthy horses to the paddock. "Fortunately the new one is in the back stall, beyond reach of the others. And each has his own water. Don't touch anything." She opened the window. The light fell on the red dun.

Between the white secretions dripping from his nose and the way he held his neck stretched out, he did look wretched.

What could she do for this miserable creature? Instead of treating sick draft horses, Rufus shot them. Goldenrod cleared drippy noses in humans. Would it work for a horse? She headed to the bothy.

"Dennis didn't even find out his name. I'm thinking Smoky or Biscuit. Or Prince. If he lives. If I live."

Letting the blathering go in one ear and out the other, Keziah tried to concentrate on the horse. "People can't catch it, but horses and dogs can."

"You know what it is?"

"It's distemper, otherwise called strangles for the noise horses make when they breathe. Wash anything that horse touched—your hands, mittens, his tack. Now."

Tryphina headed for the House and Keziah enjoyed a moment of quiet. Finn greeted her with a wagging tail. "Stay away from the horses," she told him. He followed instructions better than most people.

Remedies for horses. Not on the shelves, not the herbs hanging from the ceiling. No, Makes Cloud had told her...two years ago.

Keziah closed her eyes as the cold wind of grief swept her heart. Her friend had sat on the stool, sipping coffee, sharing remedies, as she'd written them down.

She grabbed her wooden box and searched through her notes, squinting at the messy writing. One day, she'd have a proper recipe book and put her notes in order. Ah, here it was—smoke from purple coneflower root for horse distemper.

The seed from Makes Cloud had grown well, bursting into large blooms that attracted bees and butterflies. Two years of cultivating had given her about a cup's worth of roots. Would it be enough?

Tryphina arrived wearing clean mittens. "I should name him Red. The worst thing if he dies, is that I haven't had a chance to ride him yet. He looks fast."

Keziah cut the root into pieces, then returned them to the paper twist. "We need to smudge the horse with purple coneflower root,

while not burning down the stable. You take the root and the fan."
Keziah took the lantern and bowl, and headed out.

"This isn't a fan. It's a menu. When did you go to a restaurant?"

"Never. I found it blowing down the street in St. Louis. It's the right stiffness."

Back at the stable, the horse hadn't moved. Keziah closed the door and window, so the smoke would go to the horse. She opened the twist and shook a spoonful of roots into the ceramic bowl Tryphina held. She used a spill to take fire from the lantern to the roots, then doused it. A curl of smoke rose from the bowl. Healing would be slow. Keziah hoped the girl's passion for horses would increase her patience.

"It's not making much smoke," Tryphina said. "Open the gate and I'll move closer to him."

"If he bumps you and you drop the smudge..."

"...I'll set the stable on fire. I should have brought a carrot. No, his throat's too sore for hay, so he won't eat a carrot." The girl clicked her tongue. "Come here, Red, see what I have for you." She tried several more names and sounds. Eventually he turned his head to see what all the racket was about. A gentle wave of the fan sent the smoke toward him.

Dorman Lewis opened the stable door and hauled in two buckets of water. "Why are the horses out and what are you doing?"

"Can't you see this horse is sick and we're smudging him?" Tryphina sneered, making known her low opinion of the boy.

"He's got strangles, distemper," Keziah told him. "The disease spreads easily, so the others are outside, and you need to wash if you touch anything he's touched."

"I'll leave this water for you to give him, then." Dorman peeked over the wall. "Not drinking. Looks bad. Hope the smoke helps." The boy stepped outside.

Keziah turned to Tryphina. "Why are you so rough on Dorman?"

The girl wouldn't meet her gaze. "He's such a bumpkin, always staring at me, trying to talk to me, but never has anything to say."

"He's interested in you."

She made a gagging noise. "He's a baby."

"Only a year younger than you, I'd guess. Much closer to your age than all the other lads you have your eye on. Hmm, I wonder if *they* scorn *you*."

"But I'm not..." She squirmed. "What have they been saying about me?"

"I don't know. But I do know the Bible says we're to be kind to each other."

She pondered the thought. "So, don't turn into my father."

Keziah smiled, but didn't dare comment. "If I'm busy and you need help smudging, ask Dorman. And unless I miss my guess, this spring he'll grow quickly. He'll be taller than you by autumn."

Tryphina shifted her feet. "All the root is burned up. It doesn't seem to be helping."

Keziah sprinkled the root with water to be sure the fire was out, then tucked in the corner. They left the stable. "We'll try again after dinner and after supper."

"For how long?"

The wind had changed, flinging snow into their faces from the east. "Until we run out of root or he's recovered."

Three weeks later Tryphina reported the red dun was healthy again and none of the other horses had caught distemper. She admitted Dorman had been helpful in caring for the horse, even naming him Reynard due to his fox-like coloring. But, the girl assured her, she'd never marry anyone that young and silly.

CHAPTER 18

March 1856

The next rainy day didn't come until Spring.

Leo pulled on Duncan's arm as he finished breakfast. "I want another story."

"Leo!" His older sister Ida wagged her finger, looking ever so much like their mother. "Have you no manners?"

Running his words together, he said, "Please and thank you tell me a story."

Duncan raised an eyebrow. "After you finish your chores."

"What chores?"

"Sister Chase's woodbox is empty. How is she supposed to cook?"

"I dunno." He stomped out and slammed the door. Moments later he returned and flung the wood, making as much racket as a dozen lumberjacks, and startling Finn from his nap.

Duncan caught the boy before his second trip. "This job is too much for a wee lad like yourself. You'd better scrub the latrines."

Leo's face twitched as he considered the merits of each job, the rain changing to sleet, and whether Duncan would actually follow through on his threat.

"Oh *please* choose the latrines," Keziah pleaded. "The smell's ripened so since it warmed up."

Defiance triggered, Leo tiptoed to the wood box and gently set each log inside. He finished the job quietly, the raced up to Duncan. "Story now!"

Duncan raised an eyebrow and held the boy's gaze until he said, "Please tell us a story, Brother Duncan."

The other children echoed his plea and gathered around. Keziah stopped knitting to watch. Duncan was the ultimate storyteller, using his expression, voice, and posture to portray each character.

He settled onto the stool and gestured for the children to sit close. "My Danish friend told of an emperor in a faraway country who loved clothes. He didn't do anything all day long except change into different suits, each fancier than the next, and parade around his city, showing off." Duncan's long fingers grasped the frayed lapels of his coat and he puffed out his chest. Then he leaned toward the children and confided, "All the gold of the empire went to pay for his wardrobe."

"I'd like to have new clothes," said Mary Lewis, echoing what every member of Preparation was likely thinking.

Duncan nodded. "So much money attracted weavers and tailors from all over the empire, including two fellows who bragged their fabric had the most colors and fanciest patterns." He lowered his voice and raised his eyebrows. "And, they boasted, it was *invisible* to anyone who was a fool or unable to do his job."

"Uh-oh," said Amy Chase.

"The emperor heard about this and was thrilled. Now he could find out who in his castle was a fool or couldn't do his work. He hired the flimflammers and they moved into the weaving room."

The adults stopped work to listen.

"After a week, the emperor sent his advisor to see how his new clothes looked. The advisor stared at the loom and adjusted his eyeglasses," Duncan blinked through spectacles made with his finger and thumb, "but he didn't see a thing, not even the silk and gold thread the emperor had provided. How could it be, after all these years advising the emperor, that he was unfit for his job? So what do you think he did?"

"He lied!" said Leo, who was an expert prevaricator.

"You know it. The weavers asked what he thought of the fabric, and the advisor declared it more bonny than any he'd ever seen, and he told the emperor the same.

"Another week went by. The emperor got antsy, like Leo here, and sent his highest official to check on the weavers. What do you think he saw?"

"Nothing!" the children cried.

"Exactly. The official knew he was smart. Was he bad at his job? Nobody must know. He didn't want to be fired. So he asked lots of questions about the weaving, then recited the answers to the emperor."

"The emperor was so excited, he couldn't sleep. The next morning he led the entire court to the weaving room. The two flim-flammers pounded away at the looms." Duncan moved his arms forward and back and his legs up and down as if he were weaving. "The emperor looked, but saw not a thread." Duncan widened his eyes and pressed his hands to his cheeks. "Was he a fool? A bad emperor? His trusted advisor and highest official raved about how beautiful the fabric was, how intricate the pattern, how shiny the threads. The rest of the court jumped in. What do you think they said?" Duncan asked the children.

"I wouldn't lie," Mary Lewis said. "So I'd say I like purple."

Mary DeForest, who was also a teacher's child, agreed. "I'd say I like red."

"Looks good," said the oldest Barnum boy.

"Looks fine to me," said his brother.

Young Homer Hoyt nodded. "It will be comfortable."

"And not itchy," added Amy Chase.

Leo tugged Duncan's arm. "Get back to the story already."

Duncan eyed him, unblinking.

"The story."

Duncan waited.

"Tell the story!"

Duncan tilted his head and lifted his eyebrows, and, like a match striking sandpaper, Leo beamed at him. "Brother Ross, please keep telling the story."

"Aye, lad." Duncan smiled at him and gestured for the children to move closer. "The emperor proclaimed he would wear his new clothes in the parade at the end of the month. When the special day came," Duncan held his arms out, "the two crooks arrived, pretending to carry the new suit. They told the emperor to take off his old suit. One helped him into the invisible trousers and the other into the invisible coat. They fastened the invisible cape to his shoulders. His servants lifted the end and followed him outside.

"Wearing only his undervest and drawers!" Leo said, prompting giggles from all.

"The townsfolk had heard all about this fabric for weeks. They lined both sides of the street, applauding their emperor and praising his new suit. All except a little girl who said..." Duncan nodded at Amy.

"He doesn't have clothes on!"

The rest echoed her.

"Word spread up and down the street—the emperor has no clothes. The emperor realized he'd been tricked, but what could he do? He marched proudly back to his castle."

"Where he found the crooks and chopped off their heads," Leo swung his imaginary sword, nearly decapitating the Barnum brothers.

The adults kept their gaze on their work. Living in Preparation trained them not to react, not to trust, not to tell the truth about the emperor's clothes.

"The story doesn't say what happened next, but I'm guessing the flimflammers grabbed their money and ran away. And now *you* must return to your chores and I must get a drink of water." Duncan carried his tin cup to the kitchen.

Keziah tipped the pitcher for him. "Whoever wrote that story sure knew Preparation," she murmured.

"No, he lives in Denmark. Wait. Do ye mean..." Duncan's eyes widened. He scanned the big room. Everyone had returned to their work. "You think..."

Father Ephraim and Guy Barnum were in the printing office and hadn't heard, but their children would be sure to tell them.

She nodded. "Only in Preparation, the emperor is clothed, while us townsfolk wear naught but a sark."

April 1856

Father Ephraim had called a meeting, inviting only the heads of households. Not that Duncan wanted to attend—he valued fresh air too much to be confined in a small room with all those unbathed bodies. But he did want to know what was said. With the speed gossip spread here, he'd hear about it before nightfall.

Enjoying the warmth of spring, Duncan hiked up to the barn. "Take care of your tools," he'd been told on every job he worked. Sunlight through the barn door showed no one here knew that lesson.

He dug his thumb into the mud caking the plow blade, flaking off to the rust beneath. The blade was in desperate need of sharpening, but the file nowhere to be found. Perhaps whoever was in charge of the blacksmith's forge had it. Or one of those who moved to Belvidere had taken it. Or Leo had lost it in the acres of grass surrounding Preparation. Duncan supposed he should be grateful the plow itself hadn't disappeared.

The traces had been hung, keeping mice from eating them, but not cleaned. Duncan laid them outside on a dry stretch of grass. One of the leather straps had been sawn through a couple feet from the end. He frowned at the surrounding cabins, searching for a culprit wearing a trace as a belt and carrying a dull knife.

Well, lad, you can fuss and fume about lost tools, damaged plows, lazy farmers. Duncan pulled out his kit to sew on a new strap. *Or you could be grateful for the sun's warmth, a full belly, and work for your hands.*

A line of geese honked on their way north. Early lambs called for their mothers. And spring wildflowers popped up through the prairie, giving Keziah plenty of supplies for remedies. What would Preparation do without her care? And he...would be lost without her friendship. She hadn't been invited to the meeting either, none of the women had. They'd compare rumors later.

Hoofbeats pounded as Tryphina galloped along the river. No boy would endure the humiliation of losing to her, so she rode alone and raced an occasional visitor.

Luther Cottingham and Nels Turner arrived carrying shovels. Any other day Luther would be making barrels and Nels had wood cutting duties. They never volunteered for other tasks. "Figured it's a good day to muck out the stalls." Nels said in response to Duncan's raised eyebrow.

They hadn't been at it long when two men, Homer Hoyt and Charles Perrin, left the Lord's House and climbed the hill. The men entered the barn, glancing back to make sure they weren't followed and couldn't be seen.

"Short meeting." Nels emptied the wheelbarrow on the manure pile.

Hoyt and Perrin weighed them with a look and decided they were trustworthy... or harmless.

"That's the good news. The bad is I don't have a dime much less —" Hoyt turned to Perrin. "What's hundred-sixty acres at a dollar-twenty-five?"

"Two hundred dollars."

"Federal government is putting Preparation on the market," Perrin said. "We'll need to buy it or take preemptions lest strangers get hold of it, moving onto our land and taking advantages of the improvements we've made."

Luther hitched up too-large pants on too-thin hips, belted by a frayed rope. "How we gonna pay for that?"

Homer crossed his arms, his elbow poking through a rip in his sleeve. "Recollect those stock certificates we got last year and bills of sale for our cattle? Ephraim says we can trade them for scrip to pay the pre-emption fees."

Luther gave his beard a thorough scratching. "Government gonna accept Ephraim's scrip?"

"Of course not." Perrin muttered.

The scratching moved to the back of his head. "What happened to the money he collected in '54, when we thought the government would show up?"

Hoyt thumped his fist on a post. "Ephraim says it went to pay off the apostates who left and their lawyers. Then he commenced preaching about the common treasury, sacred and holy oblation, school of sacrifice, and all."

So, Duncan wasn't the only one confused about the finances around here.

Perrin shook his head. "I'd like to seek the *common* account books for our *common* treasury."

"I brought that up to Guy Barnum awhile back," Duncan said, "when I got to wondering about the money the store brought in, and was told to trust the Chief Steward."

"And what about the butter and cheese hauled to Council Bluffs every week?" Nels asked. "That's got to bring in a pretty penny."

The men stared at each other.

Hoyt lowered his voice. "How much, you think?"

"Enough," Duncan said. "I think."

After a long pause, Luther said, "Brings to mind that hustler in St. Louis."

Nels chucked a cow pie at him. "Which one? St. Louis got thousands."

"Worked the riverfront, but too crippled to be a roustabout. Had a table made out of a crate, little cups, and a marble." Luther moved his hands in circles.

"Oh, yeah. For a nickel, you could guess which one had the marble." Hoyt said. "Cleaned out more than a few pockets, he did."

Perrin leaned against the doorframe, staring at the house he'd built. "This time we're ones with empty pockets."

"It's like that story Duncan told. Ephraim's the emperor." Hoyt stuck his elbow out of the hole. "And we got no clothes."

~

May 1856

In spite of the perfect spring day, the new Wilcox baby wasn't doing well. *What could be wrong?* Keziah wondered as she hurried to the prairie. No fever, rash, or cough. No one in the Preparation was infected with tuberculosis, dysentery, typhoid, scarlet fever, or diphtheria. Neither mother nor infant had sores in their mouths.

"Keziah! Wait for me!" Wearing a dress of her mother's, Tryphina Butts dashed out of the Lord's House and ran up the hill.

Finn turned and waited for the girl. "Whose dog are you, anyway?" Keziah asked him. "Has she been slipping you a bite of cheese now and again?"

He glanced up with a big, panting grin.

"I'm in a hurry," Keziah resumed her brisk pace as the girl drew close. "I don't have time to talk today." *Nor energy for listening.*

"You're looking a plant to help Eunice's baby?" Tryphina waved a cloth bag and paring knife. "I'll help. I brought my supplies."

"Are you done with your chores?" She'd turned into a grumpy old woman.

"Dinner dishes are done, so I can help until supper. What are you looking for?"

"Motherwort and violet. For Eunice and her baby." *Thank you, Lord, for providing abundant plants this spring.*

"I went to congratulate her, but he cried and wouldn't nurse, so she cried, then baby Malinda cried, and Brother Wilcox cried. Maybe the baby's sad because they haven't given him a name yet."

What would Mrs. Jackson do? "Thank you for taking little Malinda yesterday. She enjoyed playing outside?" And Eunice no doubt appreciated the chance to concentrate on the infant.

"She didn't. She kept running away from me, trying to go back in the house, wanting her mama." Tryphina raced from one side of the path to the other, checking each plant, but didn't wear herself out or run out of breath for talking. "Finally I took her to see the horses and lambs and piglets. We're knee-deep in piglets this year. I don't know what we'll do with all of them. I wish we'd get new horses, but everyone tells me stallions are too much trouble. But if we don't have a stallion, what will we do when these horses get old and die? Malinda liked the horses best, of course. I got her to make animal sounds." The girl paused to demonstrate. "Next time, I'll teach her to bark like Finn." She petted him and asked, "Would you like that?"

The spalpeen wagged his tail.

Keziah followed the fence beside the wheat field. "We're looking for dark green leaves, shaped like maple. No flowers yet. Violets leaves are scalloped."

"There's violets by the barn."

Keziah resisted the urge to let her collect those. "Can't risk tainting by manure."

"How do you know they're bad? What if we don't find any others?"

"They're below the barn. Rain washes impurities down the slope onto those plants."

They circled the corn field, then headed down the hill. The creek burbled full this time of year. Finn raced ahead, startling a rabbit. Tryphina expounded on all the horses she wanted, a slightly less painful topic than her hunt for a husband. Were all fifteen-year-olds so talkative? Christena would remember her as a fifteen-year old. She'd been gone ten months and still hadn't written.

On the bank of the creek, Finn dug into a mole tunnel, spraying the path with dirt.

"Leave it, lest you're wanting a bath." Keziah spotted an unexpected gift and reached for her shovel.

"What did you find? That's not a violet. Is it motherwort?"

Heavenly Father, you can see I lack the patience necessary in a teacher. Please find her another. "It's poke or pokeweed. I didn't know it grew this far north. If Eunice has mastitis, an infection in her breasts, pokeweed root might help."

"An infection in her— How awful." Tryphina winced and crossed her arms over her chest. "Do we need a lot? I can dig."

Keziah wrested a four-inch chunk from the dirt. "Let's start with this and see how she does. Help me remember where we found it."

Tryphina turned in a circle. "Pokeweed grows along the creek where the indigo buntings fly."

"And when the birds migrate?"

"Oh. Silly me." She giggled. "It grows south of the place where the creek widens into a pond. Next to the...is this motherwort? And there's violets. I'm good at this, aren't I? I'll come help you every time."

Please don't. The violet patch stretched along the creek, basking in the sun, blooming their distinctive purple. Was the other plant really motherwort? The leaf shape was correct, with hairs on the back side. The intense odor and taste confirmed her discovery. "You're right. It's motherwort. I'll harvest them and you cut off every other violet." With her sharp eye for plants, Tryphina could scout the valleys for miles around, keeping her away for hours. Keziah sighed. *Lord, forgive my terrible attitude. Create in me a clean heart.*

As Finn herded them back to the bothy, Tryphina expounded on what kind of house and barn she wanted. They chopped leaves, making half into an infusion, and mixing the rest and the poke root with lard to make an ointment. Like a burr stuck to her sock, Tryphina followed her and Finn to the Wilcox house.

Eunice may not have the support of anyone else in Preparation, but she did have Tryphina's. Silas had taken his two-year-old daughter for a walk, so Tryphina collected dirty dishes and diapers for washing, then untangled the young mother's hair and braided it.

Keziah taught Eunice to rub her belly and breasts with the ointment, then tried to get the baby to nurse. The infusion relaxed Eunice and her milk let down, but the baby seemed too tired to benefit. He was a thin little man, with bony legs and arms, and a wrinkled face, whose only interest was sleeping.

Eunice hadn't filled out with this one the way she had with Malinda. Was the vegetarian diet to blame? Should Keziah have requested meat for her? Winter's soup had been thin.

"Keep him with you." Keziah passed her another cup of the infusion. "Try to get him to nurse whenever he's awake."

The Lord's House bell rang for supper.

"I'll bring your meals and help with Malinda," Tryphina volunteered.

Tears seeped from Eunice's eyes. "Would you pray for us?"

"I'll go get Father Ephraim." Keziah stood.

Eunice pulled her back. "No. You two. Right now."

The three women held hands, forming a circle around the baby. Tryphina prayed, "Heavenly Father, please help this baby eat and grow stronger. Malinda wants to be a big sister. Thank you for helping us find the right plants today."

Keziah added her prayers for healing, then silently asked, *Help me guide this student you've given me.*

May 1856

The word came at breakfast the next morning: the baby had died.

Duncan searched the Lord's House, but didn't see Keziah. She wasn't at the bothy either, so he headed for the Wilcox's cabin. A black wreath on their door stopped him from knocking. They shouldn't be disturbed. And if he did see Silas or Eunice, he had no words of solace.

Keziah emerged, blinking, then pausing on the step to stretch her back and arms. She spotted him. "Duncan."

"I heard. How are you?"

"Silas is... relieved the baby's the suffering is over." Her voice was hoarse, barely a whisper. "Eunice is heartbroken. I used the last of my angelica to make an infusion for her."

"No." He set his hand on her arm. "How are *you*?"

Her gaze traced the surrounding hills, finally coming to rest on his, showing her own sorrow. "I wish I could have done more, changed the outcome." She let out a long breath.

He suspected she's been up all night fighting for the wee life. "Sarah saved breakfast for you."

"I should see how Tryphina and Malinda are getting along." She headed for the House.

The door opened and Silas crept out, his body weighed by grief. "Thought I heard your voice."

Duncan wrapped an arm around the older man's shoulders. "My brother. I'm so sorry. What can I do to help?"

"You'd think, after losing my first wife at Winter Quarters..."

"Experience doesn't make it easier to bear."

"You've the right of that." He wiped his eyes and blinked at Duncan. "Could you...would you mind seeing to the grave?"

"I'd be honored." Keziah had given all her knowledge and care for the baby and Eunice. A hole, small and deep, was the only gift Duncan had to give.

"Don't have to be no more than..." His shaking hands spread apart, about the size of a bread loaf. Then he sobbed. "Poor little fellow."

"I'll take care of it." He motioned toward the House. "Did you get breakfast?"

"Malinda, er Tryphina, already saw to it. Thank you." He turned and trudged back to his cabin.

It didn't seem right, burying a child on a spring day. The clear sky, green hills, and bird song spoke of growth and new life, not death.

Duncan found a shovel and climbed the hill to Johnson Lane's and Rachel Lytle's graves. Christena Lytle had chosen a place with a good view. *Yes, Lord Jesus, You bid the children to come to you. He's with You now.* Duncan measured a pace from Brother Lane's and another past baby Rachel's and began.

Each bite of the shovel unearthed a line of Robert Burns' "Lament for the Death of Son." *The arrow sped...all joys are fled... lay me low...With him I love, at rest!* May the Wilcox family survive this blow.

At the sound of voices, Duncan set the shovel in the grass, then stood, hands folded, to watch the procession approach. Silas carried the casket, hiding his tears behind a hard stare and clenched jaw. Father Ephraim led the Congregation from the Lord's House to the top of the hill. He'd lost a child, too, a little girl who'd died in St. Louis. Homer and Julia Hoyt had lost two of their children. All five of Keziah's had died, as had Duncan's three. Every face showed the agony of death, in their own families and with the loss of this child.

When the group reached the hilltop, Ephraim raised his arms. "Heavenly Father, I come before you as a high priest in the order of Melchizedek, to dedicate this grave and the body of this child to you."

Silas and Eunice leaned on each other and tried to hold onto their squirming two-year-old. She yelled, "No!" when Tryphina Butts reached for her.

Keziah handed the girl a biscuit and the little one went to her eagerly.

"How come she gets a biscuit?" Leo asked. "I'm hungry too."

Big sister Amelia slapped her hand over his mouth and dragged him down the hill. Fast as he was growing, she wouldn't be able to wrestle him much longer. His self-control hadn't developed as quickly as his body.

Ephraim set the box in the grave and finished the service with a prayer. Duncan returned the dirt to its place, then helped Keziah plant a violet on it.

"You did real fine," Silas told them. "Both of you."

Keziah enfolded him with arms both fierce and gentle, then Duncan added his hug.

Silas made a sound like a chuckle, if such a thing was possible on this sad day. "Well, it's not the miracle we asked God for, but I'll take it."

Duncan turned and saw the reason he hoped Preparation would succeed: the Congregation's women united to console Eunice, an outcast no more.

CHAPTER 19

June 1856

Nothing better than a garden after a rain, when a quick pass with the hoe removes weeds. Keziah worked her way between the yarrow and horehound. Three years after transplanting and the plants flourished.

From the porch's shade, Finn lifted his head and wagged his tail.

"Good morning, Keziah." Tryphina slipped through the gate.

So much for peace and quiet. "Eunice doesn't have need of you this morning?"

"No, she's up and chasing Malinda."

"You've a new dress."

The girl snorted. "Hardly new. It's mother's. The dress I've worn since St. Louis won't let out another inch." She held out the skirt. "Not as pretty as the red."

"You've pockets. Dark blue hides dirt."

"I suppose." She motioned toward the garden. "How can I help?"

Where would she do the least damage? "Weeding between the rows." Keziah handed over the hoe, then grabbed the trowel to clear between plants. She dug up a seeding and set it aside to transplant.

Tryphina wasn't one for silence. "What'd you find?"

"If it's prickly ash, chewing the bark eases toothaches."

"How can you tell the weeds from the good plants?"

"Remove anything growing between the rows. During harvest, you wouldn't want to mix up plants with opposite purposes, say pasque flower in a salve."

"Which would cause blisters. Or plantain to stop diarrhea and pokeweed to start vomiting." Quick learner, this girl. "But within the rows, how can you tell?"

"If all the plants have thick, upright stems and hairy leaves, except one vine with a skinny stem and smooth leaves—"

"Pull the vine."

"If you're not sure what it's becoming, give it time. A mystery seedling can surprise you by growing into a useful plant."

"Like Heber Wilding, getting so handsome. Wish he hadn't moved to Salt Lake City. And Omer Lytle had a nice horse, but he left with the Belvidere apostates, him and Mosiah Winegar."

Should she share this news? It wouldn't stay secret around Preparation for long. "The Winegar family has claimed land across the river."

Tryphina whipped around to face that direction. "Did Mosiah come with them?"

"I don't know. And I also don't know why you're in such a hurry to marry. You're living in the House with other single women, you're not overly burdened with chores—"

"But the Bible says women are saved through childbearing."

"And women die in childbearing." Keziah rested on her knees, unsure if she had enough energy for a theological discussion. "I've heard that verse refers to Mary giving birth to Jesus, since the apostle Paul says we're saved by grace."

"But Father, mine, not Father Ephraim, says the Bible tells women to be silent."

No doubt Orrin Butts's favorite verse. Keziah yanked out a misplaced plantain and tossed it in the pail.

Tryphina went on. "And women are only mentioned when we give birth—Mary, Jesus' mother. John the Baptist's mother, Elizabeth. Peter's mother didn't even get named."

CATHERINE RICHMOND

"What about Deborah the Judge and Prophet of Israel? And Prophetess Anna who met Jesus in the Temple? And Esther, who saved her people—"

"By having a hundred babies?"

"No. You haven't a Bible? Let me see your hands." Still clean. Keziah grabbed hers from the bothy and opened it to the middle of the Old Testament. "Esther."

"The Bible has a book about a woman?"

Maybe someone—not herself—should read the Bible to the single women. "Two. The other is Ruth."

"Why didn't anyone tell me?"

Why indeed? Keziah motioned the girl to the bench Duncan had made for her. "Read. It's short." Perhaps long enough to finish the weeding, or at least to clear the dill out of the lavender.

Finn moved closer, so he could get his ears scratched as she read. After a few minutes, the girl growled. "Whoa. Vashti wouldn't come when he called, so the king dumped her. What a pompous, overbearing—"

"Vashti made the king look bad in front of his officials."

Tryphina grimaced, then returned to reading. "'Everyman should rule in his own house,' as if men need to be told. I hope this gets better."

"Read on." She yanked out a clump of grass invading the fennel plants.

"Whoa. The king has all these women." Tryphina looked up. "Old Brigham Young didn't invent polygamy."

"Where there's men...." Keziah tried to herd her thoughts away from Rufus.

"Esther tells the king two crooks plan to kill him, saving one life." She held up a finger. "One."

"There's more." Keziah moved to the onions.

"Mordecai won't bow to Haman, so all Jewish people have to be slaughtered? And if Esther goes to the king without being summoned, he could kill her. What a bloodthirsty country." Tryphina looked up, eyes wide. "Like when they tried to murder us in Nauvoo and Missouri."

"We're all sinners in need of God's grace."

Tryphina read on. "The king asks her what she wants and she invites him to a banquet. Not once but twice."

"I wonder if she wanted a private place to make her request, then lost her nerve."

The girl read quietly long enough for Finn to herd a wayward chicken away from the edge of the creek. Then she burst out. "Hah! Haman hates Mordecai, but ends up honoring him. Esther calls out Haman, then he falls on her in her bed. How odd to serve dinner in her bedroom. And the king catches him... and hangs him on the gallows he built for Mordecai."

One more pass through the garden and Keziah set her pail of weeds by the gate.

Tryphina gasped. "Even Esther was cruel—she had Haman's sons hung."

"It was a different time, a different culture." Keziah joined her on the bench.

"What happened to Vashti?"

"It doesn't say. Perhaps she ignored the king's command because she wanted to leave the palace."

"To get away from the tyrant, knowing any moment he could kill her."

Insightful, Keziah thought, impressed the girl could think about something other than boys and horses. "Tryphina, one day you may find yourself in a dangerous situation and hear Mordecai's words, 'you're here for such a time as this.' And you can save lives." Mrs. Jackson had used Esther's story to change Keziah's thinking about coming to Preparation, but that story wait for another time.

Tryphina closed the Bible and gave the village a dismissive wave. "Danger? In Preparation? More likely, I'll talk back to my husband and get tossed out like Vashti."

June 26, 1856

Duncan sat on a bench in the Lord's House, on the last Sabbath in July.

"Congregation of Jehovah's Presbytery of Zion." Father Ephraim raised his arms until they all found a seat, then pressed his hands together as if in prayer. "I recently learned of the demise of James J. Strang."

Several people gasped. Keziah had been rocking Ossie to sleep, and she froze.

His voice rose. "Mr. Strang claimed to be the legally appointed successor of Joseph Smith. I had visited him in Voree, Wisconsin, and had become convinced by candid and prayerful investigation that his claims of authority to preside over and lead the church were not founded in truth, and that it was a false spirit that witnessed to me the reverse, which had come upon me in an unguarded moment."

Duncan had heard mention of Strang, but didn't realize Father Ephraim had known the man.

He paced. "You may recall, I reprimanded Mr. Strang for sophistry, for trying to build himself up on the credulity of the rejected church. He said the penalty of rejection was only applicable to the Church at Nauvoo, and that the penalty for the church abroad was rejection of their baptisms for their dead. But the penalty is one and the same."

The man was dead. Why was Ephraim fussing over an obscure religious detail?

"The Strangites left Voree and located on Beaver Island, ostensibly to convert the Lamanites who dwelt there, but the Lamanites would not hearken to their dogmas. When they attempted to force it on them, they took Mr. Strang a prisoner, and delivered him into the custody of the United States officers." Father Ephraim paced, his hard-soled shoes echoing on the wood floor. "Why did his efforts fail to succeed? Because he did not have the requisite Keys of Authority, without which they could not obtain the requisite knowledge. Baneemy, therefore, having been endowed with the Keys of Authority, and having received the necessary knowledge, will be enabled to present the covenants of the fathers to their children. He will not attempt to establish a church among them, nor require them to adopt the religion or politics of the Gentiles, but will simply establish schools among them, in which old and young will be taught the most common and useful arts of civilization and peace."

Wait...how were they supposed to teach the Lamanites when they hadn't seen any for nearly three years? And weren't the Keys of Authority for building the Temple in Jerusalem? Were they different from the Keys of the Church and Keys of the Mysteries of God and the Keys of the Kingdom?

"In his newspaper, Strang called us imposters. The cry of 'imposter,' however, in any event, would come with an ill grace from *James. J. Strang*," Ephraim's voice rang with contempt, "whose character as a Prophet has been tested, and proved false in so many instances, that there can remain no more doubt, among those who are acquainted with his Prophetic career, in reference to his character in connection with the name 'imposter.'"

Duncan sifted the words, accusations, and complaints. It seemed Strang had questioned Ephraim's authority as Baneemy.

"Mr. Strang owed us twenty-five dollars for books he had sold for us on commission." Ephraim paused for a drink of water.

Catherine stood, earning more gasps. She'd never spoken in church before. "What happened? How did he die?'

Orrin Butts stood. "Strang was shot by an apostate. He was forty-three. Then a drunken mob of Gentiles evicted the Strangites from Beaver Island, robbed them of their money, and dumped them on the shores of Lake Michigan."

"And his wife?" Tears rolled down Catherine's cheeks. "Is she safe?

"Which one?" Her husband glared. "He had five that we know of."

"Oh, no. Poor, poor Mary." Catherine sobbed.

Ephraim dismissed the meeting.

Duncan left the Lord's House. In every direction the hills rolled green with the fullness of summer, a view that normally filled him with peace at the abundance of God. He'd thought to go to the river, but water wouldn't wash his thoughts clean. His feet led him to the bothy. He ducked under hanging plants to join Finn in the shade.

"'Tis a fine thing to be a dog." He scratched the soft fur behind the pointed ears. "And not to have to figure out men."

Finn's tail wagged.

He'd come to Keziah for answers, for understanding this contentious group of people, their peculiar leader, and the bizarre undercurrents rippling through their community. He'd have been lost beyond sanity without her.

"Duncan? You've need of a remedy?"

"Since when is it acceptable to speak ill of the dead?" he muttered.

She shook her head, then headed downhill. "Let's walk."

Finn didn't need a second invitation.

Duncan wished he could hold her hand. "You knew this James Strang?"

"And his wife Mary." She took the path toward the river. Large sumac bushes sheltered them from view. "After we left Nauvoo, Charles and Catherine went to Wisconsin. Rufus and I came along a week later. Charles and James Strang shared interests in the church, writing and publishing, preaching. James taught Charles about being a postmaster."

"They fell out over polygamy?"

"No, he had only one wife then. I think... they were too alike, there could be only one."

"One...successor to Joseph Smith?"

Keziah turned toward him. Her greenish-brown eyes studied him, taking his measure. She gave a quick tip of her head.

The pieces came together. "Both Smith and Strang were murdered. So today's anger...is fear."

Her solemn expression didn't change. "You're catching on."

August 27, 1856

The waning crescent moon provided more beauty in the sky

than light on the ground, but Duncan didn't mind. The path to the stable was well worn and familiar, crickets the only traffic. With the heat of summer hanging on, Dennis Butts had been told to take the cheese to Council Bluffs in the wee hours, before the heat of the day, but he hadn't brought the wagon to the store yet. Duncan expected the lad was having trouble harnessing Reynaud. The gelding had been apply named, being clever enough to escape any fumbled attempts on harnessing. If lad wasn't at the stable, Duncan would rouse him from bed. Not a prospect—

A large bear stood in the deep shadows between the cabins. Two more steps and Duncan would have bumped into him. What kind of hunter was he, having no weapon on him, heedless of his surroundings? Then his nose informed him 'twas no bear. 'Twas a man, a sweat-soaked one.

"Duncan, what brings you out this time of night?" Homer Hoyt's dark nightshift flapped around his legs. A clump of hair stood on end over each ear, increasing his resemblance to a bear. Duncan exhaled, glad he hadn't sounded the alarm.

"Readying the cheese run. And you?"

"Julia's time."

Julia Hoyt had gained considerable weight, turning her oval face into a puffy circle, stretching against her dresses, her feet swelling until she only fit her husband's moccasins, but Duncan knew better than to say he'd noticed. "Summer's difficult."

The man grunted. In the silence that followed, Keziah's voice drifted through the muslin curtains and open windows of the Hoyts' cabin. He couldn't make out her words, but her confident tone soothed and encouraged.

"This is your third?"

"Fifth. The two between young Homer and Cynthia died as infants."

"I'm sorry." Duncan nodded at the cabin. "Are they needing anything?"

"Not that I know of."

"I'll be back."

He hurried to the stable. Dennis stood in the middle of the

paddock, holding a collar. Reynaud had his eyes closed, head down, pretending to sleep. An ear twitched as Duncan crawled through the fence.

"Should have named him Trouble," Dennis said.

Duncan handed him a carrot. "Too smart for our own good."

Reynaud may have been smarter than most, but he couldn't resist a carrot. He circled the paddock once more for good measure, then submitted to harnessing. Dennis loaded up, then headed out with the first rays of dawn.

At the Hoyts', Homer continued to pace.

"Any news?"

He shook his head. "I'd like to get dressed. Can't go to breakfast like this."

Keziah opened the door and pointed to the west side of the cabin. "Julia says your clothes are hanging on the line."

"Need anything?" Duncan asked.

"Spring water." She handed him two tin pails.

Summer had been dry, but the spring-fed burn continued to burble. Duncan followed it into the glen, enjoying the drop in temperature and the morning birdsong.

Long ago, beavers had built a dam here, turning the area behind into a pond covered with wee green plants. The beavers had moved on, not wanting to share the water, but their dam held up in spite of spring floods. Past the pond, Duncan startled a doe and fawn with faded spots. They splashed through the burn and disappeared up the glen. As Keziah said, Preparation was beautiful and bountiful.

He filled the buckets at the spring and retraced his path.

Women, even when sure of their words, added a lift at the end of every sentence, as if turning it into a question. But Keziah spoke with authority. Had it always been so? Or did learning to be a midwife give her the voice of command? Maybe Rufus's departure forced her to stand up for herself. From what others said, the galoot wouldn't look kindly on his wife for speaking out. And he couldn't imagine Keziah holding her tongue or groveling to anyone so bull-headed. Ach, what Rufus intended for evil, meant freedom for Keziah.

Was she free...free to remarry?

Duncan stepped out of the glen into another scorching August day. Thanks to Keziah, Preparation lacked the cesspool miasma of St. Louis. A woman like her, diligent and intelligent, deserved respect. Yet...she deserved love too. Hard as she worked, he wanted to take care of her, help carry her load. Today she let him bring water. A step forward.

What should his next step be? None of the Congregation had married and Father Ephraim never spoke of marriage. Rufus no longer had any hold on her, but the legal status of their marriage was uncertain. Corresponding with a woman he saw at every meal seemed silly. Concerts, carriage rides, and dances weren't an option...although, with the graceful way Keziah moved, she might be a good dancer.

The Hoyts' cabin came into view. Time to stop cogitating. Wait... did his ears deceive him or did a baby cry?

"Here's your water." He set the pails on the stoop. "Anything else?"

Keziah opened the door and gave him a big smile. "Tell Homer to come meet his daughter."

September 1856

At breakfast, Keziah's gaze caught on the lads at the single men's table. Isaac Swett rubbed his legs together like a grasshopper. Dennis Butts dug his nails into his arm, drawing blood. Nels Turner used his fork to scratch his back. Andrew Haines and James Durfee fidgeted in their chairs.

Keziah strode to their table and crossed her arms. "What ails you?"

"Nothing," they chorused.

"Back to your cabin before you infest the whole Congregation."

Minutes later. Keziah knocked on the door of the single men's soddy. It swung open to cave-like darkness. Five young men stood in the middle of the room, trouser legs rolled to their knees. As they looked up, the stench hit her. "Are you storing a dead body in here?"

"What?" Dennis straightened and looked around.

Nels clapped him on the back. "Dennis may not look too lively, but I assure you he is not dead."

Finn stuck his nose in, took one sniff, then backed out. No actual dead bodies, then. Keziah sent him to guard the chickens.

"How do you account for the reek in here? When did you last bathe?" No wonder Duncan had moved out.

"Bathe?" Andrew Haines asked, as if the concept was new.

"We went swimming yesterday." Isaac propped his hands on hips and puffed out his chest.

"Did you use soap? Not according to my nose." Keziah stepped outside, far enough away for a clean breath of air, and motioned for the boys to follow. The simple delivery of a remedy had turned into a day-long lesson in hygiene.

"We're clean enough," Andrew said.

If Malinda, er Tryphina, smelled this, she'd surely give up pursuit of these galoots. "And when's the last time you changed your mattresses and washed your bedding?"

After a bit of scratching and shuffling, Dennis said, "When Father Ephraim went on his trip."

Last summer, then. And the rest slept on mattresses they'd filled two years ago, when the Congregation arrived in Preparation. "Do you not remember my instructions about housekeeping?"

"Well, sure." Isaac shrugged. "But I figured you'd do it, seeing as how we work together and all."

Nels gave him an elbow poke. "Who'd want to clean up after us, eh? Couldn't even talk Dennis's sister into that."

"You making fun of my sister?" Dennis raised his fists.

"No, he's saying your sister is too smart to get roped into keeping house for this crew." Keziah handed each a clean rag. "Dip this in the remedy, squeeze it out, and wipe your legs. The insect bites are from your beds, not from the fields. Empty your mattress onto the manure pile, then bring your bedding to the Lord's House to wash it."

"We have to drag it over to the barn?" Dennis pointed his thumb over his shoulder. "Last time I dumped it outside."

"Then you tracked it back inside." Keziah opened both windows and propped open the door. "I'll get the water heating."

"We don't need to wash the sheets and quilts too, do we?" James caught her raised eyebrow and changed his tune. "I'll bring it all."

Andrew squealed as the vinegar touched a bite he'd scratched into a wound. He cleared his throat and lowered his voice to a more masculine note. "Shouldn't we close the windows? Keep the varmints out?"

"No self-respecting vermin would have anything to do with this place. Although you've had mouse traffic in the past. Are you eating in your cabin?"

"No, Sister," they chorused, guaranteeing they ate in the cabin all the time.

Keziah thanked the Heavenly Father for the sunny day. "While your laundry is drying you'll sweep out the cabin."

"Can't you wash mine, Sister Keziah?" Isaac said. "I'm working harvest today."

"Any lad who has time to swim, has time to do his own laundry." Keziah stared him down. "Make haste."

"Boys, you need to catch yourself a wife," a man drawled behind her.

Keziah turned her glare on Guy Barnum. "They have a lot of scrubbing to do before any woman would come within a mile."

"Congregation of Zion," intoned a deep voice.

Keziah tensed. How much had Father Ephraim heard? Would he side with the single men who provided much of the farming labor? Direct her to clean their cabin?

"The land of Ephraim belongs to those with pure hearts and clean bodies," he intoned. "Do as Sister Keziah told you. Without delay."

The fight left her. Ephraim had agreed with her...today.

∽

October 1856

"'If we say we have not sinned, we make him a liar, and his word is not in us.'" Duncan raised his eyes from reading 1 John 1. The lantern shone on the circle of lads in the single men's cabin. Their reactions and questions were always unpredictable, but they didn't expect answers from him.

"Nice and short," Isaac Swett said.

James Durfee leaned forward into the light. His brow lowered over an intense stare. "Read the part about blood again. If you will."

Duncan found it in verse 8. "'If we walk in the light, as he is in the light, we have fellowship one with another, and the blood of Jesus Christ his Son cleanseth us from all sin.'"

James leaned back and shook his head. The nineteen-year-old favored deep thoughts over quick ones. "Brigham Young brought back the Doctrine of Blood Atonement."

"I've no *Book of Mormon*. Could you tell me what that is?" Duncan asked.

"Well, you see, the *Book of Mormon* agrees with John that Christ's blood is our atonement. But Young says some sins cause a man to become a son of perdition."

"What's that?" Isaac asked, sparing Duncan from exposing more ignorance.

"Well, you see, if you commit a really bad sin, instead of going into the kingdom of God, you go into the lake of fire and brimstone with the devil."

"Even if you repent?"

James nodded. "So to save you from the devil, they cut off your head."

Nels made gagging noises.

Isaac rubbed his meager chin hairs. "So Brigham Young goes against the Bible and the *Book of Mormon* to chop off heads. Sounds like a bad deal."

"Yet people keeping joining him. All summer, hundreds of people pulled handcarts to Salt Lake City. Except some got caught in a blizzard and died." At Duncan's raised eyebrow, James explained. "Newspaper."

"A thousand miles pulling a handcart?" Isaac snorted. "I'd get a horse."

"If you'd money for a horse." Duncan turned back to James. "With this blood atonement, are there trials, lawyers, juries and such?"

"Don't know." James leaned forward again. "Could we pray for them? We got friends out there. James Wilding..."

"You were sweet on his sister Elizabeth," Nels said in a sing-song voice.

"Real pretty and good cook. Who wasn't sweet on her?" Isaac asked. "Guessing we all got friends out there."

The Mormons in Utah, or perhaps just Brigham Young, had gone off the rails. He prayed that wouldn't happen in Preparation. "James, keep us posted on what you find in the newspapers." Duncan said. "And let's pray."

December 2, 1856

Keziah woke to a rumble of thunder. The patter of rain changed to splats of snow. Shivering, she slipped from the quilts, stepped over Finn, and loaded another log into the wood stove.

"You're welcome to take over this chore any time," she told the dog. "Or climb up on the bed and keep me warm."

With a big sigh, he rolled over. He'd tried the bed once. There wasn't room for both of them.

Keziah wiggled back under the covers. A warm husband would be helpful on nights like this. Not Rufus of course. He'd load the stove, then climb over her to sleep against the cold wall. Duncan might be thin enough to fit, if they both lay on their sides and he held onto her. No, the bed was too short for his long legs, the bothy too small for two people.

Well, then, imagine a house with a grand bed. Having no fat, she'd thought Duncan would chill in winter, but his hands were always warm. He'd touched her elbow, supported her back, held her hand, brushed her wrist, and each time his hands were warm and gentle. Always looking out for her, he'd be considerate lover. He'd warm her inside and out.

Ach. Enough nonsense. A bedwarmer would be...impossible. Even if she had money, none were for sale in Preparation. What else could she use? She should have brought a brick from St. Louis. What about a tin pail with hot coals? No, she'd burn the bothy down and end up squeezing in with Tryphina in the single women's room. No thank you.

Off to sleep, then.

Outside, something slid on the ice, then thumped against the bothy. "Sister Keziah." Dorman Lewis, Priscilla's fifteen-year-old son, called over the wind. "It's time."

Add to her list of impossible wishes, that women would birth babies during the day when the weather was pleasant. Keziah threw on her cape and grabbed her satchel, thanking God that babies give plenty of notice of their arrival, and that the Congregation had been so healthy.

"Good morning, Sister," Dorman said, even though sunrise had yet to pierce the storm. "Be careful. It's icy out here."

She took the arm he offered. "I heard you fall. Were you hurt?"

"No ma'am. Fearnoughts protect in more than one way."

They sloshed and skidded, following Dorman's bootprints across Preparation. Mrs. Jackson had warned older mothers could have difficult births. Hannah Perrin and Lodema Winegar's had been physically easy, but Lodema had been distressed. Priscilla Lewis had four children and, like Lodema and Hannah, was over forty. Keziah prayed all would be well.

"Good morning, Sister." Lucretia pulled her into the comfortable warmth of the cabin and hung up her cape. The glow of the lanterns showed a tidy space divided into rooms by tablecloths tacked to the rafters. Both Priscilla and her daughter had combed and braided hair. "Father decamped to the single men's house with Branson. Dorman will join them. Mary's asleep in the loft and won't wake until the bell rings for breakfast. Mother's pangs are tolerable."

"Tolerable?" Priscilla snorted from the bed. "My back is near to breaking."

"Back?" Keziah washed her hands in the water Lucretia had warmed and hurried through midwife's prayer. "Point to where it hurts."

Priscilla rubbed low on her sacrum. "My hips are about to wrench out of the socket."

Keziah palpated her abdomen. "The baby is pushing on your pelvic bones. Try walking a bit."

Lucretia helped her mother onto her feet. As they paced, the girl pointed out freshly washed towels, linens, diapers, and gowns for baby and mother. She had water heating on the stove. Lucretia was calm and attentive. She and Tryphina were both sixteen, yet this young woman never blethered about prospective husbands or fleet-footed horses. Why couldn't Keziah have had an apprentice like this?

Because Tryphina needs you.

Orrin Butts's domineering nature sparked rebellion in his daughter. Rebecca Butts's pessimism made Tryphina embrace danger. With guidance, she would find her own path.

"You're organized." Keziah smiled at the young woman. "Did you help when your sister Mary was born?"

"I was only eight, not much help."

"Dearest daughter, you're always my best helper." Her mother patted her hand. "Oh here he comes."

Priscilla tried squatting, kneeling, and hands-and-knees, without progress. She soaked her feet in hot water and sipped cold water. Still the baby tarried.

"How long did your pangs last with Mary?"

"If you're asking if I always have slow births, the answer is yes. With Mary, the pains started Sunday, during worship, and she didn't arrive until late Monday. With Branson, it was three days. Lucretia and Dorman, two days."

"This is normal for you, so no reason to rush." *Excepting the mother getting tired*, Mrs. Jackson's low-pitched voice warned in Keziah's head.

The faint light of dawn traced the horizon, showing a foot of snow on the ground and more on its way. The breakfast bell rang. Lucretia roused and dressed Mary, then sent her to the Lord's House. "Ask someone to bring breakfast for us."

"In weather like this I wish I had my own kitchen so we could eat at home," Priscilla said. "Although today, the mere thought of bacon makes me queasy."

"Unless Father Ephraim had a revelation last night, we're still on the vegetarian diet." Three years ago, Keziah wouldn't have said such a thing. But living in close quarters had increased her trust in Priscilla, as her faith in Father Ephraim receded.

Priscilla and Lucretia paced and tried the positions again. After about half an hour, Thomas Lewis, Mary DeForest, and Hannah Perrin arrived, covered with snow and bearing breakfast. "We're throwing a welcoming party for the baby."

After two bites of toast, Priscilla turned red, began to perspire, and grunted. "He's coming!"

Keziah greased her hands with lard and confirmed birth was imminent. Her husband supported her back, Mary and Hannah held her hands, and Priscilla pushed. The head slid into Keziah's palm, then progress stopped. Her fingers found the problem.

Dear Lord, help!

"Don't push, Priscilla. Pant like a dog. The navel string's around his neck." Keziah tugged the string, hoping for enough slack to slide it over the head, but it didn't move. What did Mrs. Jackson say to do? "Priscilla, roll to the left. Hannah, hold her right leg up."

"Ow, ow, ow, OW!"

Please, Lord, save this baby and mother.

All at once, the baby moved a fraction of an inch, releasing the cord so it slipped over his head. "Good. Take a deep breath and push." The infant thudded into Keziah's hands, large and heavy and moving all four limbs. "It's a girl. A good-sized girl." *Thank you, Lord!*

"Hallelujah!" Lucretia said.

"A girl? We can't name her Sylvan." Priscilla leaned against her husband.

"You've come up with unique names," Hannah took the baby for her first bath. "Branson, Lucretia, and Dorman."

"And Mary, named after our wonderful neighbor." Thomas wiped his eyes. "Let's name her Sylvania."

Priscilla blinked back happy tears. "I like it."

"Sylvania Lewis. How distinguished," Mary DeForest said.

Her father sang, "Oh, Sylvania" to the tune of "Oh, Susanna." The others joined in on the chorus.

As Keziah helped Priscilla wash up, she bumped into every other person in the room at least once. Fewer people to collide with and privacy seemed desirable during birth, but, for Priscilla, the Heavenly Father sent the support she needed.

CHAPTER 20

December 1856

After a quiet flurry turned into ice, December brought one blizzard after another. Snow filled in the not only the glen of the creek, but that of the Soldier River and the cleft in the hill behind the house. Duncan directed the lads in chopping through the crust covering the snow, then shoveling the three to four feet of snow beneath. After six hours hard work, they'd cleared a path to the nearest latrines.

Father Ephraim stepped up to the pulpit on the last Sabbath of 1856. "Is everyone here?" he asked Homer Hoyt, the new sheriff.

"Yes, and here we're going to stay," Eliza Rowland announced. "About lost Harriet in a drift getting here."

The rest had equally harrowing stories.

Homer nodded. "Yes, all will stay the Lord's House for the duration. No one goes outside alone. After the meeting, the men, working in pairs, will take the sleds to each house, collect firewood and bedding, and bring it here. Andrew, James, Nels, and Isaac try to make it to the stable and barn with water. Do what you can for the stock. Duncan and Amos, bring in whatever's left in the store. Dorman Lewis and Thomas Perrin, feed the chickens and bring in the eggs."

Duncan met Keziah's gaze. They'd be busy keeping the peace with the whole Congregation squeezed into the Lord's House.

"We can have meat and cheese?" Nels asked.

Keziah stood. "More fat in the diet will help us withstand the cold. Also, every time you come in from outside, check your hands, feet and face for frostbite. Come see me if you find any. Keep your socks and mittens dry." She pointed to the door by the kitchen. "To keep the House warm, use the laundry exit. When you've got your fellow worker, both of you step into the laundry and close the door. Bundle up. Then and only then, open the door to the outside. Coming back in, do the same. Don't open both doors at the same time."

Father Ephraim's eyebrows raised. He hadn't expected Keziah to speak—women didn't—but he had enough smarts to let her. And she was smart enough not to wait for permission. She did what was necessary to keep them alive.

"We've no time for stuff and nonsense," yelled Luther Cottingham. "What's next, knitting lessons?"

Duncan stood and faced the blusterer. "Making your own socks might keep you from losing a foot."

"Start with one and stuff it in your mouth, man," Nels Turner told him.

Duncan fought off a laugh. "Luther, thank you for volunteering to shovel the path to the laundry door. With the wind, you'll be shoveling constantly."

"Since we're all gathered here in the Lord's House, this afternoon I'll start a new teaching on the laws and covenants of Israel." Father Ephraim concluded the meeting with a prayer for relief from the storm, and the Congregation left for their tasks.

Duncan found Keziah bundling up. "And where might you be going?"

"Bothy. Have to keep the fire going so the infusions don't freeze."

"After I finish packing up the store, I'll help you move."

"Not necessary. The bothy's close. I'll be fine."

CATHERINE RICHMOND

Stubborn woman. He stepped close and lowered his voice. "If you're needed in the middle of a storm..."

She made a noise in the back of her throat.

"I've heard badgers make friendlier noises."

She turned toward him, and he braced to have his throat ripped out, but instead, she laughed. "I hate when I'm wrong and you're right."

"Not as much as I hate worrying about you." He grinned. "Here's a key for the pantry. There's a shelf for your remedies."

Her cold fingers clasped his. "Thank you for looking out for me."

She slipped away, leaving him wishing he could warm her all over. He lowered his head, lest anyone see the heat in his face.

~

December 1856

"The floor's hard."

"There's a draft."

"When will the snow stop?"

Keziah carried the lantern through the writhing mass of humanity attempting to sleep on the floor of the big room. What did they expect from her? Naught she could do about any of it. All the lavender in the world would not ease their sleep.

An irregularly shaped ball rolled out from beneath the Hoyt's pile of quilts. Keziah knelt beside it. "You'll not be wanting to leave your warm bed, Miss Rachel." She lifted the infant and found her diaper still dry. Four-months-old and already breaking free. She'll keep her parents running. She tucked the little one between them.

Accompanied by Finn, Keziah slipped into the single women's room and closed the door. The complaints on the other side continued.

"He's kicking me."

"Shove me off, will you?"

"Never have I heard such snoring. Roll him over, Rebecca."

Behind her, Tryphina snorted. "Yet another reason why I moved out: Father's snoring."

Lantern light showed Matilda Lane, Sophia Gordon, and Amelia Thompson. The others were already asleep.

Amelia pointed to the bed next to hers. "Cecilia Hall left last summer, so you can take her place."

"Thank you." Keziah blew out the candle, pulled off her moccasins, and climbed under the cold quilt, but before she drifted off, Tryphina whispered, "Nels Turner."

"Not now." Matilda groaned.

"He makes me laugh." Tryphina sat up. Her face glowed in the moonlight. "Here's the joke he told me today: why is a bucket of oysters like an unpaid bill?"

"Hush," said three voices.

"Because a fellow must shell out before he can fork over." Tryphina giggled. "So clever!"

Finn sighed, summing up their reaction.

In the main room, the complaints shifted to intestinal noises and smells. Then a gentle Scottish baritone broke through and soothed the quibbling. Keziah recognized the tune, but Duncan sang it slower, at the speed of a lullaby.

Her weary brain struggled to recall the Gaelic. The song told of a young woman supporting her lover's military career. An odd choice for a lullaby... unless he meant to show support for her battle to keep them alive.

He's said as much on the steamboat ride. Or did he see himself as her lover? Her body warmed.

A lover? Surely not.

And...why not?

January 1857

The door opened then closed. An icy gust blew across the floor of the House, nearly slicing Duncan's feet off. His Bible reading lads returned from watering stock. Finn followed, plopping in the corner and chewing balls of ice from his paws.

"They're all dead." Andrew Haines said through the snow covering his face.

"We're all going to die?" Rebecca Butts wailed. "I knew we shouldn't have come to Iowa."

"Oh stop." Her sister-in-law gave her a shake. "The ground's too frozen for burying, so no one's dying."

"Andrew means the cattle are all dead," Isaac Swett broke enough ice from his face to say. "No sense carrying water for them. Coyotes are having a feast."

"Not all of them." James Durfee said through his crusted beard. "The ones in the barn and stable are still alive, needing water and mucking."

"We're counting on those cattle to pay for this land." Orrin Butts jabbed his finger. "You boys do your job or Preparation will be snatched out from under us."

Nels Turner gave him a tired look. "Yeah, the crowd's lining up outside right now."

"Here we go again," Charles Perrin muttered. "How many times we gonna pay for this land?"

"At least we don't have to worry about bank failures like people out East," Silas Wilcox said as his daughter skinned the cat on him.

"Since we don't have any money in banks," Andrew said.

"Sit." Tryphina Butts carried a steaming pot from the kitchen. The four young men plopped onto a bench and removed their mittens, boots, and socks. She spooned warm ointment onto their palms and they spread it over their faces and feet.

Keziah glanced over her apprentice's shoulder. "Healthy skin. Well done."

"What is this?" Nels sniffed then stuck his tongue in it.

Tryphina swatted the side of his head. "Lanolin and evening primrose. And it's not for eating, you dolt."

"He eats everything," Isaac said.

"As if you don't."

Duncan kicked a clump of ice under the bench. "Next time leave the snow outside."

"Send another then," Isaac said.

James looked at the floor. "We left a trail. Should scrape before we come in."

Isaac moaned as he rubbed his feet. "Will frostbite get me out of hauling water?"

"If you get frostbite, I'll have to amputate. Then you'll get out of hauling water." Keziah returned to the kitchen, leaving the young man clutching his feet.

Eliza Rowland followed her. "Why is it Amos and Sarah got to move upstairs? I can't sleep a wink down here with Rebecca snoring like a steam engine all night."

"I don't snore," Rebecca nearly tread on her heels. "It's *your* brother."

"Orrin never snored before you married him."

"That was twenty-two years ago."

"Ladies." Keziah held up her palm. "The Chase's children are coughing. To keep the malady from spreading to us all, they're staying in the hall outside the printing office. The upstairs floor's no more comfortable than downstairs, so stop your bleating." She pointed to a pot with a fragrant infusion. "Unless you'd like to dose Amy and Asaph."

"And sit up with them tonight." Duncan said, knowing Keziah had all week.

"Oh, no. We don't want to catch sick," The two women backed away, only to be replaced by two others.

"Julia Hoyt stole my mattress," Miranda Barnum said.

"Oh for mercy's sake. We're imprisoned by winter, hardly able to steal." Julia looked at the ceiling and fluttered a hand. "What difference does it make. All our mattresses are made from the same ticking."

"Yes, but I stuffed mine with prairie grass, instead of noisy cornhusks."

Keziah lowered her voice as she stirred the remedy. "Sisters. You need to be a good example to the children and young women of the Congregation. Settle this between yourselves and make peace."

Miranda spun on her heel and marched across the room, no doubt to retake her mattress. Julia lowered her gaze and followed.

"Making peace is wearying." Duncan set his hand on Keziah's shoulder, feeling tension in her muscles. "You worry about illness spreading in close quarters."

"No more than you worry about fire." She glanced up at him. "If this building burns, we've no place to go, no food, nothing to cook with."

"I filled buckets with sand and keep watch." His fingers kneaded. "And pray. What else can I do?"

"I'll add my prayers to yours." She tilted her head as he worked his way up her neck. "Your lullabies help too."

Light pressure on a tender spot had her purring. "I've had complaints about singing in Gaelic, but the words would give them nightmares."

"Oh aye, heads on pikes, robbery, murder. A grim history birthed those songs."

In the main room, Rebecca Butts stood at the window and howled with the coyotes. Marcia Barnum knitted, adding yet another grey sock to the stack beside her, her movements as relentless at the ticking of a clock. Leo somersaulted the length of the room while reciting "eight times eight is sixty-four." The rest stared into space.

"Sure and I'm running an insane asylum. I've remedies for coughs, but none for what ails them."

"Concoct such and the world will beat a path to our doorstep."

She glanced out the kitchen window, the only one not completely frosted over. Wind-blown snow obscured the valley, and every sign of civilization. *Finally... a smile.* "That's what we need - more cranky souls to squeeze in here."

～

February 1857

Wind howled and pushed against the Lord's House, first from the west, then worked its way around all four walls, piling snow against the windows. Amos Chase and Luther Cottingham alternated shoveling to keep the path to the latrines open. Elijah and

Elisha Cobb joined their cousins Dennis and Daniel Butts to keep the surviving stock watered.

Keziah scratched the frost off the window, praying she'd see sun. Sun to warm up the House, to drip into an icicle, to give hope. But more low clouds barreled down on Preparation. Even if they did get a midwinter thaw, she wouldn't be able to reach the maple trees for sugaring.

Sarah Chase stepped out of the kitchen. "The wood bin's empty."

John Perrin put down his slate and donned his fearnoughts He returned in a few minutes with a handful of branches. "We're out."

Rebecca Butts howled, "We're all going to die!" as she'd done at least once a day for the past two months. If she mentioned the Donner Party and cannibalism again, Keziah would stuff a sock in her mouth. She whimpered to a stop.

Duncan shoved his feet into boots, pulled on his coat, and told the teachers, "Let's go find a dead tree."

Josiah DeForest and Thomas Lewis exchanged looks. They hadn't been asked to do chores in addition to teaching, but firewood was essential. "Class dismissed."

The children scattered. Leo climbed to the top of the stairs, and swung a leg over the railing. If he jumped, he's destroy the mattresses and smash his head.

"No!" Keziah raced across the room. Her feet slipped out from under her. Duncan must have been right behind her as he set her upright, then snagged Leo out of the air.

"If you're wanting a nap, laddie, best sleep in your own bed."

"No nap." Leo squirmed as far as he could get with Duncan holding onto his arm.

"Not tired? Then you won't mind chipping the ice off the floor." He handed the boy a bucket and tools. "There's lines of ice below where the laundry hung yesterday. Tap it gently with the mallet, then scoop it up with the dustpan into the bucket. And remember, you've plenty of supervision." Every eye in the room was on Leo. Duncan joined the two teachers and Finn at the door. "We'll be along the river. Send the rest to help when they return."

Keziah could count on Duncan, could trust him in their partnership for the Congregation's health. She didn't have to direct him; he saw what needed doing and did it. Keziah cleared frost off a window pane and peered into the storm. *Lord, watch over Duncan. I'm needing him like no one else.*

March 1857

The Congregation finished their supper of potato soup and Duncan led his four young men upstairs. Keziah took a breath of slightly less fouled air. The men needed a bath. They *all* needed a bath. They all *wanted* a bath. But no firewood could be spared for heating water. The lack of clean clothes and haircuts had them resembling a herd of tramps. Close quarters had them coming unhinged.

Lord, you told us to love one another. I might manage, if we weren't packed in like sardines.

Young Charles Perrin and his brother John entered the kitchen, escorted by Finn. "Are there any cookies?"

"I'm afraid not. We're out of sugar." Last year's maple syrup was a dim memory. The honey was nearly gone and the bottom of the molasses barrel was in sight. "Brush your teeth, then take out the washbasin."

They returned from their chore to report, "Still snowing," as they had every night the past four months.

"Pray for..."

Duncan and his lads clomped down the steps.

"Father Ephraim and Daniel are typesetting," Duncan said. "Could we read down here?"

Eliza Cobb unrolled her mattress with a snap. "When am I supposed to rest?"

Her sister-in-law piped up. "You're always snoring when it's your turn to fix breakfast."

"Let them read," Hannah Perrin said. "Maybe God will bless us all with good dreams."

"'Tis only a chapter," Duncan said. "I'll be quiet."

They formed a circle of chairs near the door of the laundry room.

"Matthew 25," he began, his voice near to a whisper.

"Can't hear you," Homer Hoyt said from his bed.

Duncan faced Keziah and widened his eyes. She addressed the Congregation, "If you'd like to hear tonight's reading, please raise your hand."

Those who were awake heartened and waved.

Duncan returned her smile and, with a loud, clear voice, read Jesus' parable of the wise and foolish virgins.

Isaac interrupted him. "Wait a minute. The ones who had enough oil wouldn't share. Those who ran out had to go to the store in the middle of the night. Then they couldn't get back into the wedding. What happened to helping those in need?"

"We're out of sugar," Young Charles Perrin said. "And can't get to the store."

"Now that's an emergency," Nels Turner said.

"We're not running out of anything at my wedding." Tryphina stood behind him.

"Yes, your highness." Andrew curtsied to her.

Thomas Lewis joined the men. "The wise ones are those who have received the truth and haven't been deceived."

"Deceived?" Nels Turner asked. "Who said anything about deceit?"

"Joseph Smith did." Brother Lewis had been a bodyguard to Joseph Smith in Nauvoo.

"So, we're not supposed to share with those who don't plan ahead?" Andrew rested his hands on his greasy head, spreading more of his odor. Keziah dropped juniper berries in a pan of hot water on the stove, releasing the fragrance of pine.

"You're missing the point." Silas Wilcox, beard wrapped around his neck like a scarf, joined them. "It's about the kingdom of heaven, about being ready when Jesus comes again."

"When is He coming?" Maria Cobb asked.

"That's the whole point," Silas tapped the table. "We don't know, so we have to stay prepared."

"But none of us has oil lamps," Andrew said.

"And you're not a virgin." Nels took a preemptive swing.

"Your mouth could break your nose," Duncan told Nels as he caught both men's forearms before their fists could connect. "Watch your words. Children are listening." He made it through the parable of the talents before Nels broke in.

"Isaac hid his gold in a hole in the ground," he said in a singsong voice. "Now he can't find it."

They all knew Isaac hadn't a penny to his name, so they ignored Nels.

"How are we supposed to use our talents when we're cooped up here?" Tryphina asked.

"What talents are you thinking of, Miss Tryphina?" Nels wiggled his eyebrows.

James Durfee said, "Hardly fair, taking away from the guy that didn't have much and giving it to the one who had a lot."

"Whatever God gives us, his servants, we're to use for his kingdom." Silas pointed to the worn Bible. "Colossians says 'And whatsoever ye do in word or deed, do all in the name of the Lord Jesus.' Like Duncan here, making shoes to keep us all from going barefoot."

Duncan lifted a shoulder. He never sought acclaim.

"You men have been sharing your singing," Keziah reminded them.

"Keep reading," Homer called.

The rest of the chapter told of a shepherd separating sheep and goats.

"'I was hungry and you gave me meat.'" Nels cast a hopeful eye into the kitchen. Finn joined him.

Sarah Chase snapped her dish cloth at him. "Wait for breakfast."

He swallowed hard and asked the group. "We're allowed to eat meat, then?"

"We were selling meat to pay for the land." Orrin Butts sneezed three times, then wiped his nose and coughed. No wonder he snored.

"Paying for the land *again*." Charles Perrin moaned.

"So... Jesus says if we help the least of these, we help Him. And get eternal life. That is..." James stretched out his arms. "Everything."

"But how can we while we're stuck here?" Tryphina had squeezed her chair between Andrew and Isaac.

"Sarah feeds us, so she's getting in." Isaac said. "And we're hauling water for people and the animals. Hope that counts."

"And all the sisters sew and knit to keep us clothed." Andrew nodded at Keziah. "Sister Sirrine helps us when we're sick."

"We're held prisoner by the snow, so are we the least of these?" Tryphina asked.

"Whether you're washing dishes or typesetting the newspaper, your work is holy." Silas's smile emerged from his mustache and beard. "Serve each other like you're serving the Lord."

On that note, Duncan led the singing of, "Nearer My God to Thee."

Rebecca sat up. "Not too bad."

"We could do this every night." Eliza found a rare point of agreement with her sister-in-law.

"Have you been teaching the Bible long?" Julia paced with baby Rachel.

Duncan shook his head. "I'm no teacher. I read and the lads talk it over." He kept saying he wasn't a teacher, but his students' learned much through their questions, and now through tapping into the Congregation's wisdom.

Keziah strained the juniper and took the infusion to Orrin.

"What's this? I'm fine. Don't need your concoctions." He sipped and grimaced. "Terrible. Nasty." Then he inhaled. "Hey...my nose cleared."

Orrin might never respect her, but that wouldn't stop Keziah. "Sleep well."

∾

CATHERINE RICHMOND

April 1857

Duncan leaned forward, trying to pay attention... or at least look as if he was. Father Ephraim read from his newest book, fresh off the Washington Press upstairs, *The Laws and the Covenants of Israel*. Duncan's mind wouldn't hold to the man's words. The text read like much of Ephraim's—too deep for a common man. Occasionally a phrase from the Bible caught his ear, like now: "sent out into all the world to preach this Gospel of the Kingdom." Then, he dove into "three Priesthoods restored, Ephraim regenerated, as the first born of the restitution," and Duncan lost his way again. He could make sense of most of the Bible, but not this.

Chirping sparrows raced past the window behind Ephraim. Jesus said God remembers the sparrows, but the endless winter had the Congregation wondering if He'd forgotten Preparation. Nearly the end of April and storms continued. James Durfee asked if the weather indicated loss of God's approval. The Bible said He makes rain to fall on just and unjust, but what about snow? Snow this deep and heavy would be death to anyone pulling a handcart to Salt Lake City. The lads continued to pray for those on the trail.

"Regeneration brings the dead back to life again," Ephraim said.

Duncan straightened, moving slowly so the bench wouldn't creak. Was the Chief Steward talking about reincarnation? Surely he meant Heaven.

"Sitting under his own vine and fig tree, in the midst of his children."

Oh to be with his children again, to hold them on his lap... Or would they have grown? Duncan glanced at Keziah. She'd be thinking of her little ones too.

Ephraim moved on to his favorite topic—money. Tithing and Sacrifice, the Treasury of the Second Priesthood and the Treasury of the Third Priesthood. Duncan must have missed the First Priesthood. "The Lord's Treasury is now established, over which a faithful Steward is set, whose business it is to test the worthy poor by the covenants of righteousness, and give to them accordingly."

Test the worthy poor? Jesus didn't mention any test. Duncan wouldn't pass as he had no idea what the covenants of righteousness were.

"All men are now called upon to sell all they have, deposit the proceeds in the Treasury of the Lord, if they wish to be perfect..."

Perfect? Only God is perfect. And Duncan had nothing to sell, so where did that leave him? Falling asleep on a warm afternoon.

Warm? He hadn't been warm for six months. Sun streamed through the windows, melting away the frost. Icicles dripped. A loud scrape overhead drowned out Ephraim as a slab of ice slid off the roof and crashed in front of the House.

Leo jumped out of his chair, shoved on his boots, and ran out the door. He returned in seconds, arms held high. "It's spring!"

The rest of the children and Finn followed him outside. Ephraim dismissed the class and the adults joined them. The air brushed Duncan's face, gentle as a baby's hair. After four months of feeble light, the sun shone with fierce strength.

"Will take months to get rid of all this," Isaac muttered.

"Muddy mess it will be," Andrew agreed.

"How did you lads get so crabbit?" Duncan stretched his arms wide and raised his face to the warmth. "'Tis a glorious day!"

"We can move back into our house." Eliza pointed to the wood frame dwelling across the stretch of snow.

"We'll need firewood," her husband said.

"What are you waiting for? Get chopping!" She clapped at her sons, then waved to include the other single men in the community. "You too!"

"What do you think we've been doing all winter?" Nels fluttered back at her.

"Stay away from the south side of the House," Keziah called, ever on the watch. She took Frances Barnum and Miranda Wilcox a safe distance away, whirling around in a dance, looking ever so much like a lassie herself. "Snow, snow, go away! It's time for us to play! Soon 'twill be May!"

Mary Lewis, Amy Chase, and Harriet Cobb joined the fun, circling the child most likely to be hit by ice sliding off the roof, Leo. "No snow today! This we pray! There's a sleigh! Hip-hooray!"

Duncan turned south. A pair of draft horses pulled a large sleigh to Preparation. A well-dressed couple waved from the front seat. It was David and Mercy Jones.

"We were worried about you." David said. "No word from you since October."

Finn broke a path to the road. Keziah followed and hugged her friend. "You're a sight for sore eyes."

"And you're a smell." Mercy wrinkled her nose and scanned the flock. "What a slovenly bunch. Did Ephraim decide cleanliness was too Methodist?"

"Not at all, Sister Jones." The Chief Steward smiled, welcoming them in spite of their status as apostates. "Every stick of firewood went to keeping us from freezing."

She frowned at her husband. "Told you we should have brought wood."

Nels Turner and the Perrin boys peeked into the sleigh. "Did you bring sugar? We're out."

"Yes we did. And other provisions too." David sent the lads inside with the haul. "Any word from the Winegars?"

Ephraim nodded toward the north. "No, but we can see their chimney smoke."

"We'll check on them later." David handed him a pile of mail and newspapers. "Glad to see you alive."

"God provided." Ephraim stroked his beard. "We survived."

"The cattle didn't," Orrin muttered.

"You haven't heard the news, then." David's expression turned grim. "Band of Sioux went on the warpath. Fifteen settlers missing. Troops from Fort Ridgely out looking for them."

Rebecca clutched her chest and scanned the horizon. "We'll be scalped in our beds."

Duncan glanced at Keziah. Her hands were pressed together, praying for Preparation...and perhaps the smaller Belvidere group where Christena lived.

"Where?" Ephraim asked, "And when?"

"Spirit Lake. On the Minnesota border, hundred-fifty miles

northeast of here. March 9th, but the newspaper just reported it April 8th."

"We must leave! Save our children!" Rebecca sobbed. "Where's the fort?"

"Minnesota."

Mercy shook her. "Stop fussing, Rebecca. If the Sioux wanted Preparation, they'd have been and gone already." She turned to Keziah. "Have you any calming tea?"

"I have a chamomile infusion that's calming. Come inside."

Ephraim took the newspapers and mail into the House.

Orrin pointed to the lads. "Arm yourselves and start patrolling."

With what? Two years ago when he was worried about attacks by apostates, he said rifles were coming. Duncan had never seen any.

"So while we protect the community, you'll haul water?" Andrew asked with a skeptical raise of his eyebrow.

Isaac stuck his hands in his pockets. "If we see a Lamanite, should we shoot him or teach him to farm?"

James answered, "We take care of the least of these."

Orrin turned red and steam rose from his bald head. Had they discovered another way to heat the Lord's House?

CHAPTER 21

September 11, 1857

Catherine Thompson sat on the edge of her bed. "I've been thinking so much of Isabelle. She would be six years old."

Keziah ran her hands over the stretched belly. The baby was in a good position. A foot poked. Little, but lively. "I wonder if our children can see us from Heaven."

"I hope so. Perhaps your children are keeping her company." Catherine clasped her hand. "Were any of them baptized?"

"No, they were too young."

Catherine paused for a birth pang. "Remember in Nauvoo, when we could be baptized in the Temple for our dead?"

"'Twas a comfort." Keziah murmured as she prayed and washed.

"Our beautiful temple. Gone, gone." Another pain came and went, then Catherine brightened. "Rufus lives near Salt Lake City. Perhaps he's been baptized for your children."

Or perhaps not, as he'd never seemed impressed with them, and now was busy with twins. "The newspaper said their temple wasn't finished yet." Discussing religious mysteries with the prophet's wife seemed dangerous. Father Ephraim hadn't conducted any baptisms in Preparation, for the dead or for the living.

"I'm glad children may now be admitted to membership."

Ah, yes, Ephraim's latest revelation: *All children between eight days and twelve years whose parents are members, may be admitted to membership by blessing, laying on of hands. Trouble not about your dead.*

Keziah asked, "Where is Ephraim?"

"Onawa. He said he'd be back." Her groaning changed to a grunt; he wouldn't be in time.

Charles enjoyed his children's births. What on earth would take him to Onawa during this important time?

Keziah helped Catherine into position, set out her supplies, and greased her hands. As expected with a sixth baby, the delivery progressed rapidly. "It's a boy." On the small side, but a fine pink color and a full head of dark hair. He filled his lungs with air and let Preparation know of his arrival.

Catherine reached for him. "Such a voice. Are you a preacher like your father?"

Hopefully not, Keziah thought as she washed mother and infant. And yet...Ephraim had brought them to a beautiful place.

"Five children on earth, one in Heaven. An abundance of blessings." Tears ran down Catherine's face. "Perhaps enough babies..."

Another dangerous topic. "You're only thirty-six."

Footsteps on the stairs ended their conversation. Father Ephraim burst through the door. "You didn't wait for me."

"*Your son* didn't wait." Catherine handed over the bundled baby.

Keziah slipped out as Ephraim declared with joy, "Abraham Daniel Thompson, you have redeemed my day."

October 20, 1857

Last night, Hannah Perrin swayed into the Lord's House, arching her back and shifting on the bench during supper. Keziah figured birth would be soon, but morning came and no one had summoned her. Hannah wasn't in the House, her cabin, or the latrine. Keziah called for Finn, telling him to find Hannah, and he led her to the banks of the river. Hannah stood in the shallows, downstream from the creek. Her hands circled her belly. Every few minutes she stopped and tensed.

"Are you thinking of having your baby in the river?"

Hannah laughed. "No. Not on this cool day. I wanted to ease the pain in my feet, but didn't consider how I'd get myself onto dry land and back into my shoes."

Keziah slipped out of her moccasins, kilted her skirt, and stepped into the water. "'Tis warm."

"Downstream it is. Up here, where the creek joins the river is the perfect temperature..."

Wading upstream, a current of cool water rippled under her feet, while warmth still surrounded her ankles. "The creek races out of the hills, staying cool. But the river dawdles across the prairie, picking up heat from the sun."

"Like Preparation. We brought our experiences, our differences, and coming together has changed us."

"Standing in the river turned you into a philosopher."

She grimaced and looked down. "Waters into water. I'm changing back into a mother."

Keziah helped her up the riverbank and into her moccasins. After a moment to check her belly, she helped Hannah to her feet. "The baby's ready."

"The pains woke me at dawn." Another stopped her from moving.

"Are we going to make it back to your cabin?"

Hannah grinned. "If I have this baby outside, will I make *Zion's Harbinger and Baneemy's Organ*?"

"Or the *Preparation News* or *Western Nucleus and Democratic Echo*. The things you do to get your name in the papers." *Zion's Harbinger* listed the patriarchs and heads of families by their full names. Single men and women were listed by first initial and last name. Wives didn't merit a mention. The other newspapers Ephraim printed didn't name anyone in the Congregation.

Hannah's hand tightened in hers for another long pain, then they resumed walking. "I wonder why animals hide when they're giving birth. In Wisconsin, our cow disappeared for two days, then showed up with her calf. The barn cat did the same with kittens." She wiggled her fingers. "Yet even with everything we can do with our hands, we need help. I'm so glad you're here for me, Keziah."

As they passed the store, Duncan emerged. "Might you be needing help?"

"Thank you, but I'm fine." Hannah doubled over. The pangs came closer together.

Keziah nodded, her eyes darting from him to the Perrin house. With labor speeding up, Hannah wouldn't make it home. Duncan gave her a thumb's up and loped toward the stable.

They'd made it ten steps closer by the time Duncan arrived with the largest of his young men, James Durfee and Andrew Haines. "All right, lads, clasp arms. No, not your own. The other fellow. One goes behind her knees and the other behind her back. Lift and off you go to the Perrins'." He turned to Keziah. "What else? Your satchel?"

"At their house. Their sons brought water."

When the next pang hit, the lads stopped, turning wide-eyed to Keziah. "What's going on?"

Keziah waved them on. "Keep going lest the baby be born in the grass."

They hustled along.

All four of the Perrin boys raced to meet them, calling "mama."

"I see where I'm needed," Duncan said and rounded up the boys.

Keziah helped Hannah inside. "Thank you all." She closed the door. This baby wouldn't wait.

Duncan's voice carried. "Thomas, what chores have you? And young Charles? John, you're to watch over David. Come along, then. You, too, Finn."

"That man is a blessing to Preparation."

Keziah nodded, not trusting her voice after dreaming of Duncan's warm embrace again last night. She helped Hannah out of her wet clothes and gave her a sip of cold water, then washed and prayed. "Four years ago David arrived, Preparation's first baby."

Hannah groaned, then squatted at the footboard. "This may be my last."

Priscilla arrived. "You almost gave birth *outside*."

Tryphina followed her in. "But James carried you. So strong."

"Here comes the baby." Keziah got them back on track. She called for her supplies. "Thread. Scissors. Towel. Another towel."

"It's a girl," all three women said together.

Hannah laughed and cried. "Welcome to Preparation, Hannah Malvina."

November 1857

On other evenings, the single men's cabin shook as the lads' fought like cats and dogs. But on this chilly night, Duncan heard no arguing nor thumping. He opened the door, braced for the stinkers to shriek and jump down from the loft as they'd done last month. Instead their faces shone ghost-pale in the lantern's light.

"What is it?" He shut the door behind him.

Andrew Haines tapped the newspaper. "Read it to him, James."

"I brought back the Council Bluffs newspaper from the cheese run." His voice had lost its confidence. "'...the murder of an entire train of emigrants on their way from Missouri and Arkansas, via Salt Lake, at the Mountain Meadows, south of the most southern Mormon settlements. The company consisted of about 130 to 185 men, women, and children.'"

"Oh no." Duncan groaned and sank onto the nearest crate. "Those poor people."

James cleared his throat. "'They were in possession of quite an amount of stock, consisting of horses, mules and oxen. The encampment was attacked about daylight, so say the Indians, by the combined forces of all the various tribes in that section of the country. It appears most were killed in the first onslaught. The emigrants sent out a flag of truce. The savages immediately rushed in and slaughtered all of them, with the exception of fifteen infants. They have since been purchased by the Mormon interpreters.'"

Lord, what would you have me say? "It's been four years since we saw an Indian here."

276

"That we know of," Isaac said.

Nels pointed a biscuit at the newspaper. "The next column says the Army is marching towards Utah, but Brigham Young won't let them in. A newspaper in Kentucky is calling for Mormons to be cut out like cancer."

"Gentiles won't ask what kind of Mormons we are," Andrew said. "They paint us all with the same brush."

"And if the Mormons are behind this attack," James folded the paper, "we'll be in real trouble."

Isaac barred the door. "We need guns."

"Lads." Duncan held out his Bible. "Is there anything we've read telling us what God would have us do?"

Andrew snorted. "There's plenty Brigham Young needs to hear about submitting to kings and governors."

Nels swatted him. "What God would have *us* do, dunce."

Duncan opened his mouth, but Isaac surprised him by quoting from Matthew 5, "'Whoever says *fool*, shall be in danger of hell fire.'"

James opened to 1 Peter. "'Having your conversation honest among the Gentiles: that, whereas they speak against you as evildoers, they may by your good works, which they shall behold, glorify God in the day of visitation."

"We'll be reading more tonight about how to treat others." Duncan took back his Bible. "But first..."

"Let's pray." James bowed his head and began.

The world spun into a tempest of violence, but tonight, in this cabin, God was victorious.

CHAPTER 22

March 20, 1858

Keziah rolled over in bed. Preparation had so much to be thankful for. This winter had been delightfully easy, with no ice, gentle snows, and both a January and a February thaw. Spring came early and the garden burst into bloom. The children grew, free of disease. So why this uneasiness?

She should get up and make a chamomile infusion, but that involved getting out of bed, stirring the fire, lighting the lantern to find the right paper twist, and waiting for the water to heat. She turned onto her other side.

When he instituted the Voluntary Sacrifice, Father Ephraim had promised to divide the land among the members. No one had a title yet. Surely he'd resolve the issue before more members left.

And it had been nearly three years since she'd asked Ephraim about divorce. Had Ephraim sent the letter? Was it lost in the mail? Did Brother Hickenloper find a lawyer? Did Rufus refuse to settle?

Fast hoofbeats, pounding on the door, and a bark from Finn spurred her from bed. "Keziah!" Tryphina called. "The baby's coming."

Keziah dressed, grabbed her bag, let Finn out, and locked the bothy behind her. The weak light of a waxing crescent moon showed only the outline of the girl and two horses.

"Well it was coming." Tryphina handed her the reins. "Aunt Eliza thinks it's stuck."

Where Eliza Butts Cobb trod, disaster followed. *Dear Heavenly Father...* Eliza's daughter-in-law had visited Preparation once. She was in her mid-twenties and sturdily built. Birth ought to be easy. But Mrs. Jackson would say, "what you want and what you get, two different animals." Keziah asked, "How is Alice?"

"Sobbing and overwrought."

Eliza had that effect on many.

"The path is clear," Tryphina said. "Keep your reins loose and your horse will follow mine."

They mounted up and galloped out of Preparation southwest along the river. A flock of geese honked overhead.

Rowland and Eliza's eldest son had sold his lumber business in Pennsylvania and brought his bride to Iowa. Elijah had built a home finer than any in Preparation, complete with kitchen and dining room, and cultivated a good number of acres in his first year of farming. Lanterns lit the house, showing two stories, double chimneys, and shutters at every window.

His younger brother Elisha took their horses. "Elijah's inside."

Wailing echoed from the house, but it wasn't the laboring woman. It was her mother-in-law. Eliza met them on the front porch, eyes red and nearly popping from their sockets. Her cap dangled down her back and her light brown hair had fallen from its pins.

"Lazy Alice has been lying around for a month. Now she's too weak to get the baby out." She fumbled with her cap. "It's going to suffocate and die. Our neighbor in Pennsylvania had a baby get stuck. The doctor yanked it out with a tool, but both the baby and mother died. If Alice dies, it's all Thompson's fault—"

Keziah grabbed the woman's shoulders. "Stop. Now," she said with the voice she used on Leo.

"But it's true. Alice could die."

"Not another word out of you, unless it's helpful, kind, and heartening." Keziah pushed past the overwrought woman.

"Up here," Elijah called from the head of the stairs. In spite of the cool night, sweat soaked the man's shirt. His wife lay flat on the bed, eyes closed, her dark curls wet with perspiration and tears. "Pains started about sunrise yesterday and came regularly until about midnight, when they slowed down."

Tryphina arrived with hot and cold water.

"It's been a long night for you both." The pains should be coming harder and closer together. While praying, Keziah washed and dried her hands, warming them after the ride, then ran them over the tight belly. The baby was positioned for birth, thank the Lord. A foot thumped against her palm. "Still kicking," she said.

"Trying to kick his way out." Alice sniffled as her belly tightened. "I'm dying, aren't I?"

"Certainly not." When the pain passed, Keziah asked, "How long have you been lying down?"

"Mother Cobb told me to stay in bed."

"For the past month." Elijah's mouth twitched beneath his full mustache.

Ridiculous. Keziah clamped her lips together, not wanting to add to the conflict between mother and daughter-in-law. "What have you had to eat and drink?"

"Mother Cobb said not to."

Tryphina wiped Alice's forehead with a cool cloth.

Eliza peeked into the room. "Is that blood? She's bleeding to death. I knew it."

Elijah pushed her into the hall, then yelled down the steps. "Elisha, come get Mother." He backed into the bedroom, closed the door, and locked it.

"There's no blood." Keziah calmed Alice, then had her sit up with her husband's help and drink the cold water Tryphina brought. The pains started again. Alice squatted through a half-dozen spasms without making any progress.

Keziah searched her memories, trying to recall what Mrs.

Jackson advised, praying she wouldn't need to operate. There would be blood...and likely death.

"Onto the bed. Elijah kneel at the headboard. Alice lean back on your husband, knees up." Keziah rubbed her hands with lard. "Elijah, pull back on her knees as far as possible."

"Ouch, ouch, ouch. I'm stretching," Alice shrieked.

"So the baby can come out. Next pain, take your biggest breath and give us your biggest push." Muscles tightened under Keziah's hands. "Now!"

Nothing happened.

Dear Heavenly Father...

Another pain came and went.

What would Mrs. Jackson say? *Lord, have mercy, get those thighs back.*

Keziah pressed Alice's right leg. "Tryphina, left leg, like this. Alice, push. Now."

A round head, dusted with dark hair, popped out. Three more pushes, accompanied by long bouts of grunting, and the baby arrived. His mewl had his parents smiling. Both his arms waved, to Keziah's relief. A tight birth could cripple a baby's arms.

"Hearty fellow." Tryphina bathed him. "Wiggles like a piglet."

"Don't I know it." Alice groaned.

"For all the work it took to birth him, I thought he'd be bigger." Elijah glanced at the window where the sun peeked over the hills. "His name is Wayne."

"Wayne?" Eliza yelled through the door. "You're supposed to name him after your father. Wayne is a surname."

"Thank you, Mother." Elijah looked at the ceiling and counted to ten. "If you bring up breakfast for the four of us, you can see your new grandson."

"Four? It's too soon to feed the baby anything but mother's milk."

"The least you can do is feed the midwife." He glanced from Keziah to his cousin. Tryphina swaddled Wayne. "And her assistant."

"All right." Eliza stomped down the stairs.

Keziah cleaned Alice and the bed, then blinked with fatigue. Dare she ask if this family, living outside of Preparation, had coffee?

"As handsome as your papa," Alice said to the baby as Tryphina put him in her arms. She thanked her and Keziah, then passed him to her husband. "Wake me when the food comes. Your mother is a good cook."

April 1858

The Perrin's cabin hummed with the conversation around the quilting frame. Keziah stepped inside, Finn trotting at her heels.

"The garden's bursting with green. So much better than last year."

"Hope we never again have to go four months without clean clothes." Hannah wrinkled her nose. Beneath the quilting frame, her foot rocked the cradle holding baby Hannah Malvina.

"All that snoring." Rebecca Butts covered her ears.

"I thought I'd never be warm again." Catherine Thompson made a line of tiny stitches in the pinwheel quilt on the frame.

Keziah waited by the door as Finn made the rounds.

"I'm sorry, but there's not a crumb here for you." Hannah held her hand out to be sniffed. "Remember when we'd have tea..." She glanced at Ephraim's wife, to see if she'd caught her complaining.

Catherine sighed. "Tea with pumpkin pie, custard, or cookies. You made the best gingerbread."

"I wonder why Sarah Chase never makes gingerbread. I gave her the recipe." Hannah tapped her thimble on the quilting frame.

"Ginger and sugar are expensive," Keziah let Finn out, then took her place at the frame. "Do you suppose Sarah gets tired of cooking all the time?"

"She likes being in charge," Rebecca said. "The power to set the menu."

"Perhaps we should rotate cooks." Catherine snipped her thread. "I'll speak with Charles."

"Where's Priscilla?" Keziah threaded her needle.

"Right here." The woman slipped through the door and waved a newspaper. "With this week's *Western Nucleus and Democratic Echo*." Father Ephraim's latest publication.

Hannah motioned her to the chair nearest the window where the light was best. "Commence reading, dear friend. We desire to be well informed."

Priscilla unfolded the paper. "Ads for lawyers, one for a land agent, another lawyer, and a forwarding merchant if you have something to sell in St. Louis."

"Why so many lawyers?" Keziah ran her thread across a block of beeswax. Apostates consulted lawyers to get their tithes back. Was Ephraim encouraging the rest of the Congregation to leave? And when would she hear about her marital status?

"Council Bluffs must be knee-deep in them." Priscilla continued. "Next, an article about American Safety Paper. Oh, Keziah, did you know 'It's an established fact that metallic copper carried about the person or suspended in the room has a very beneficial effect in preventing certain diseases.' Hannah, do you have anything copper?"

"Not a penny." She chuckled.

"Beware, 'certain diseases' may arrive at any moment. The rest of the column touts the benefits of Safety Paper in preventing forgery."

Again, why would Ephraim print this? Had he used this paper for the stock certificates and scrip he'd issued?

"Next column notes Charles B. Thompson is a justice of the peace and land agent. Then there's an ad for a lawyer in Magnolia, a banker in Sioux City, and a lawyer without an address."

"Helpful," said Hannah.

"Oh! There's a *store* in Magnolia. Ready-made clothing, dry goods—"

"Instead of scraps, we could make a pretty quilt." Rebecca frowned at the faded, mismatched pattern.

Hannah waved her on. "Not a penny."

Even if it wasn't twenty miles through the hills, none of them had cash for shopping. Keziah hadn't had money since Rufus left, but she enjoyed looking.

"Another store in Council Bluffs. The senator and representative for this district serve an area larger than New England. Someone gave a speech about Kansas. Mexico is on the verge of revolution. Nobody's getting married in Boston—"

"Nor here," Rebecca said. "Daniel's twenty-two and has a skilled trade. I would have thought he'd be married by now."

Left unsaid was the question, *who'd marry a man without a penny to his name?*

The distinctive rhythm of hooves at a gallop passed outside. It had to be Tryphina. No one else could get a plow horse to move so fast.

"Speaking of brides..."

Rebecca snorted. "She knows nothing of being a wife. Sarah won't let her in the kitchen. She won't sit long enough to sew or knit. And she always disappears when it's time for laundry."

"She'll manage," Hannah said. "We all did."

"She's becoming a good herb woman and assistant midwife," Keziah said.

Rebecca looked up from her sewing to frown at Keziah. "What?"

"Oh, Keziah, you'll appreciate this: 'A lady, on separating from her husband, changed her religion, being determined, she said, to avoid his company in this world and the next.'"

"Rufus already changed his religion." Keziah started stitching.

"Don't worry, Keziah," Catherine said. "A sinner like him won't end up in the same kingdom of glory as you."

"He's no longer my worry." *Thank the Lord.* Keziah stitched another line.

"Oh no." Priscilla read a story about the Utah Expedition. The troops sent by the Federal government faced cold weather, and shortages of provisions and provender. Brigham Young intended to fight, then destroy all the Mormon possessions and evacuate to another country.

In silence the women imagined those they knew who followed

Brigham Young. Were they destined to wander, never finding a safe home?

"Let us pray." Catherine bowed her head. "Heavenly Father, guide the army and the Mormon leaders to a peaceful resolution. Thy will be done. Amen."

A prayer as brief as her husband's were long-winded. The women thanked her.

Priscilla resumed scanning the paper. "A tribute to printers. A suggestion to use postage stamps to seal envelopes. An article about enemies and—who'd believe it?—an article about kissing."

"Read it!" they all asked. And she did, in a dramatic voice, to peals of laughter. "'...a rich, hearty kiss, from the plump, warm, rosy lips...'" Why would Father Ephraim include this? Perhaps Daniel had his eye on a bride and instructed himself. Keziah had been dreaming about kissing Duncan. Last night she dreamed she'd kissed his shoulder, his *bare* shoulder. She bent over her stitches to hide her blush.

Priscilla stopped giggling and wiped her eyes. "Next articles about banking and President Polk, a few jokes from minstrel shows. 'Heber Kimball, Mormon, boasts that he has altogether fifty children; and that he is still doing the work of Abraham, Isaac, and Jacob.'"

Rebecca huffed. "Have they no shame?"

"Too busy," Hannah joked.

"The newspaper will include reports from the Traveling and Evangelical Presbyters of the Ecclesiastical Kingdom of Jehovah's Presbytery of Zion, and by the Elders of Israel, including reports from the Bishops of different Congregations scattered throughout the earth." Priscilla looked up. "The men will travel again?"

"First I've heard of it," Rebecca said. "I wonder who's going."

Catherine shrugged and kept stitching.

Hannah moaned. "Better not take my Charles, leaving me alone with four boys and one baby girl."

Better not take Duncan either, or Preparation would fall apart.

"Who are the Elders of Israel? And what other Congregations?" Rebecca asked.

"Find out and let us know," Priscilla said, then resumed reading. "For Keziah, an ad for 'the perfect substitute for lancet, leaches, and blisters.'"

"Procedures skilled doctors no longer use." Keziah motioned with her scissors. "What else does it say?"

"'This new medicine subdues inflammatory disease by restoring the balance between fluids and solids at only $2 per drachm. Dr. Coggswell sent Antiphlogistic Salt to five hundred unbiased editors who subsequently declared it the most valuable medical discovery of this or any preceding age.'"

"Unbiased? Did the editors receive the Salt in payment for advertising?"

"How'd you guess?" Priscilla read on. "We all need to know this: 'The House of Ephraim Hotel practices the strictest temperance principles. Fare is such as the limited variety of the country will afford.'"

"That's how to draw a crowd," Hannah said.

Tryphina burst into the house. "He sent them away!"

"Who?" Rebecca Butts jumped to her feet, tipping the chair over.

"My father. Your husband." Hands on hips, the young woman glared.

"Brother Butts left?" Catherine asked.

"No." The girl counted on her fingers. "He gave traveling orders to James Durfee, Isaac Swett, Nels Turner, Amos Chase, Homer Hoyt, Josiah DeForest, and Elisha Cobb, and Andrew Haines. He sent Uncle Rowland to Virginia and Thomas Lewis to Kentucky."

Not Duncan. Keziah breathed a sigh of relief.

What was Father Ephraim thinking? The past five years in Preparation had been about making a success of farming. Now they'd be so short-handed, they'd barely feed themselves. And why not let the men pack and say goodbye?

"My husband?" Priscilla gasped. "He sent my husband to Kentucky?"

Hannah stood. "We should help them pack, send them with food."

"Didn't you hear me?" Tryphina wailed. "He sent them away. They're *gone*."

Duncan had spent the morning in the store, turning cowhide into a new pair of brogans for Nels Turner. No wonder the lad was always hungry, fast as he grew. His toes had poked through his old shoes, rendering them useless for passing down to another. Last summer, he'd topped Duncan's six-feet, to his great delight and much hooting from the young men.

"Heavenly Father," Duncan rubbed linseed oil, suet, and beeswax waterproofing into the leather. "Thank you for Nels and all the lads, for their vigor, their questions, and their zeal for Your Word. Keep them from evil. May they always follow you."

The bell rang for lunch. Duncan wrapped the brogans in a sheet of newspaper, closed the store, and headed to the Lord's House, where a stramash shook the building. Tryphina wailed, a familiar sound, but several other women howled with her. Duncan guessed it was Leo. The lad hadn't broken anything in a few weeks, so he was due. Yet no blood marred the floor, nor broken crockery. Several women clustered about the stairs, calling for Orrin and Father Ephraim.

Keziah stood on the third step, a hand on each railing to block the way. Finn sat in front of her, ears up, watching the group. Keziah met Duncan's gaze, but before she could speak, Tryphina grabbed his arm.

"They're gone!" She listed Duncan's Bible reading lads, and six others. "Sent on a teaching mission this morning."

"Without a chance say good-bye." Eliza Cobb wiped her eyes.

"They were forced to leave empty handed, without food nor funds to buy any." Sarah Chase scowled. Without funds? But Orrin said they set aside money to support mission teachers.

"Not even a change of clothes," Julia Hoyt added.

How could Father Ephraim have done this? Cruel, heartless, foolish. Duncan looked down at the brogans in his hands. With an

287

hour's notice, Nels could be wearing new shoes instead of tearing his feet apart. And...

Who would shear the sheep? Plow the fields? Repair the back fence? Not to mention all the chopping and hauling the lads did each day. Preparation suffered from a lack of preparation.

"Sisters," Keziah said, her voice quiet, but firm. "Dinner is getting cold. Go and eat. You know Father Ephraim and Orrin won't come down to a row."

What did the women hope? Nothing they said would bring the mission teachers back nor fix this shortage of workers. Duncan grabbed a few slates and a slate pencil, then sat next to Silas Wilcox.

"Homer and Isaac are on a mission." He wrote 'sheep' on the slate. "Who else knows how to shear?"

"No one." The older man rubbed a hand down his beard, nearly as wooly as a ram.

"Dennis Butts, Thomas Perrin, and Dorman Lewis will learn. Good thing those blizzards thinned the herds. I'll send Tryphina with a note to the Winegars, offering to trade a fleece or two for Moroni and Mosiah's help. She's been wanting to visit anyway." He started a new list. "Planting?"

"Charles Perrin. As does Guy Barnum...if he'd be pried away from Ephraim."

Duncan noted the names, then started a third slate. "Wood and water."

"Leo and the older Barnum boy could haul water, but I'd not trust either with an ax. The middle Perrin and the oldest Hoyt could though."

"If Amos Chase was here to run the sawmill, I could repair the fence."

"Let's pray he left behind the boards you need."

Pray? Should start with prayer. Duncan stood and clapped the elder on the shoulder. "Thanks, Silas." The group around the steps had grown as the Congregation arrived for dinner. Duncan rang the bell. "Brothers and Sisters, Silas and I rearranged work assignments...so we won't go hungry." He read the list.

"Impossible," Eliza Cobb huffed in a contemptuous tone like her brother Orrin. "With both teachers gone, the children won't have anyone to run the school."

"The older ones will be planting, so you'll only have the young children," Keziah told her.

"Me?" Eliza shook her head. "I'm no teacher."

"We'll help." Her daughter Harriet stepped forward, joined by Ida Thompson, Mary DeForest, and Amy Chase, all around nine years old.

"Oh all right." Eliza huffed. "But only until I get my son and husband back."

Keziah asked Duncan, "Who might those shoes be for?"

"Nels."

Her eyes clamped shut and her jaw clenched. Duncan guessed she wrestled with God. Slowly her eyes opened. She glanced at the empty steps behind her, the women in front of her, and the remnant of Preparation gathering for the meal. At last she met his gaze, took a deep breath, and asked in a quiet voice. "Tryphina, does the horse have another run in him?"

The young woman straightened. "Ready to ride, Sister."

Duncan had never known a braver woman than Keziah. And her apprentice had progressed more than he'd ever imagined.

Keziah's attention turned to Sarah. "How fast can you have food ready?"

The cook held up a bag. "Bread, cheese, dried apples. Box of matches. Canteen. Tin cups." She glanced at Duncan. "I've got a bag for Nels's shoes."

Keziah nodded, then addressed the other women. "Bring ten wool blankets. Meet at the stable."

Eliza turned to go. "I'll pack for my Elisha."

Hannah gave her a shake. "Blankets only. There's only one horse."

The women hurried off.

Duncan reached over Finn to Keziah, lifting her cold hands from the railings. He cupped his hands around hers, warming them. Standing on the step had her eyes level with his; he saw the fear behind her determination. Ephraim had sent the men into the wilderness with nothing; she made sure they'd have enough to survive. Would Keziah be labeled apostate? Would she be thrown out with naught but the clothes on her back?

She whispered, "No food nor shelter... out in the weather for days."

"We'll pray a wagon picks them up." He brought their joined hands to his heart. "If you suffer any retaliation, I'll stand with you. If you're expelled, I'll go with you."

"I'm so thankful he didn't send you." She bent her head, brushed a kiss on his knuckle, then slipped into the kitchen. But not before he'd seen a blush on her cheeks.

Duncan's heart danced a skip-change. Was that a declaration?

April 1858

Keziah worked the pestle in the mortar, crushing dried cone-flower leaves into a powder. Other women wash their sorrows with tears, but crying only sent the pain from her heart to her head. Pounding out her misery gave her something to show for it.

Preparation hadn't been her choice—Mrs. Jackson showed her it was God's. Surely the Heavenly Father didn't want her expelled.

Thank you, Heavenly Father, for the blessing Preparation had been to me.

The bothy's heavy log walls, the lock on the door, and the willow fence around the herb garden had felt safe, but it was only an illusion. At any moment, a moment that might come today, Charles Blancher Thompson could throw her out.

No sense making it easy for him. She would slip into the Lord's House through the laundry room and bring the food back here to eat. She would spend her days in the hills, gathering plants. She would keep her irreplaceable scissors and gathering knives in her pocket at all times.

Finn scratched at the door. She let the dog out and he raced down the fence, scattering a trio of rabbits. The garden's lush carpet in a hundred shades of green testified to the richness of the land.

A meadowlark whistled its seven-note song. Keziah glanced up, spotting the bird on the roof of the Lord's House. The second story windows of Father Ephraim's room looked down on the bothy and garden. From his office he could survey the hills. Preparation was a small community, unable to keep secrets. Her heart sank. Hiding would be impossible.

If she had to leave...

And go where? Ten miles north, Belvidere was the closest community. Others received letters from friends who'd left, but Christena wrote not a word. No apology for her false accusation, no reminisces of joys and sorrows shared. Nothing.

David and Mercy Jones would take her in, if she walked two days to Council Bluffs.

The bell rang and she followed the Congregation into the House for supper.

Tryphina whispered, "found them." Keziah hugged her, then the young woman joined her parents. Her father waited with arms crossed. Orrin Butts would certainly have words with Keziah for entangling his daughter in her effort to help the traveling teachers against the will of Father Ephraim.

Heavy steps thumped overhead and the Congregation's low muttering ceased. Keziah moved back, beside the door to the laundry room. Duncan joined her. Father Ephraim and Guy Barnum arrived. Instead of standing in his usual place in the midway along the north wall, Ephraim stopped in the shadow at the bottom of the staircase.

He raised shaking hands, showing wet armpits in spite of the cool weather. "Brothers and Sisters of the Congregation of Jehovah's Presbytery of Zion. This morning Baneemy commissioned our traveling teachers, with the intention they would pack for travel, then depart tomorrow in the cheese wagon with our prayers and copies of *The Laws and Covenants of Israel*. Unfortunately they left right away. Several people acted quickly to supply the teachers, others adjusted assignments, and I commend you for working together. Let us pray." He hurried through a prayer with only a brief mention of the traveling teachers. "Amen," he said, one foot on the bottom step.

What? Had Orrin given the wrong instructions?

The Congregation sat in stunned silence, then Eliza Cobb raced toward Ephraim. Guy Barnum blocked her way. "Where did you send my Elisha and my husband? And when will they return? How are they to survive since you didn't send any money with them?"

"The Heavenly Father will provide." Ephraim disappeared up the stairs.

"Let go of me, you oaf." Eliza elbowed Guy. "Ridiculous, insane, foolish—"

Her sister-in-law took pulled her away and spoke in a low voice. "You heard what he said about the cheese wagon. They're going to Council Bluffs. We have friends there. They'll look out for Rowland and Elisha."

Eliza glanced from Ephraim to Orrin. "I'm not sure I can eat a bite, knowing my men are starving." She raised her chin and led the way to the food line.

A voice behind Keziah whispered, "He's lying," Leo kept his gaze on the stairs his father had ascended. "I heard him say the men had to go right away."

Why did he lie? Had he sensed the Congregation teetered on the edge of rioting?

Duncan rested his hand on the nine-year-old's shoulder. "The Bible says we must honor our father and mother."

"It also says not to bear false witness." The boy blinked back tears.

"Only God is perfect. Everyone else make mistakes. Including parents."

Leo's mouth twitched as he studied Duncan. "Since the men in your Bible study are gone, can I join?"

"Certainly. But it's not a Bible study. All I do is read." Duncan scanned the room. "Would Ida like to come too? Perhaps Mary DeForest and Mary Lewis, John Perrin, the Barnum boys?"

"I'll ask." Leo raced off, tipping over two chairs, and bumping Eliza into spilling her soup.

"Out of the mouths of babes, eh?" With a raised eyebrow, Duncan tipped his head toward the stairs. "Relieved?"

"I don't have to hide from Ephraim." Keziah nodded then met his gaze. "So why is he hiding from us?"

~

July 1858

Duncan watched Guy Barnum carry two bowls of stew upstairs. Father Ephraim hadn't come downstairs all summer, even for Sabbath teaching. He was alive; voices traveled through the thin walls of the House, especially his preacher's voice. Keziah had the right of it—he was hiding.

Keziah paused after her last bite of supper to survey the Congregation. "Everyone is scratching."

"Not Finn." Duncan nodded at the dog sleeping under the table, then reached to take her bowl to the dishpan. "Nor I."

"Your head doesn't know what your feet are doing." She faced him, chin down, eyebrows up. "Peel the sock off your right ankle."

"'Tis nothing." He tried to stand on one foot and wobbled.

She pointed to the chair. "Sit. You don't need to be falling over."

He sat and pushed down his sock, revealing a red rash with blisters. "I'm not so old."

"And I'm not so trained in fixing broken bones. But I do have a remedy for poison ivy." She stood. "Don't whistle, lest you spread the itch to your mouth."

Keziah raised her voice. "Brothers and Sisters, if you're itching, raise your hand. You have poison ivy. When you change into your night clothes, wash your bodies with cool water and soap, being sure to clean under your fingernails. I'll be around with a remedy for the itch. Tomorrow, wear clean clothes and wash your tools, lest the poison return to you."

"But I've no clean clothes, don't you know." Luther Cottingham built watertight barrels and kept his cooperage tidy, but spent not a moment on personal cleanliness.

"He could grow potatoes in those ears," Duncan muttered.

Keziah pressed her lips together, holding in a laugh. She narrowed her eyes at Luther, an expression saying she'd not put up with his nonsense. "Do your laundry." To the rest she said, "Try to recall where you've been so we can rid Preparation of this pest. And absolutely no more scratching." She turned to Duncan. "You could apply the remedy to the brothers."

"Glad to." And glad Keziah trusted him for this task, but he had his eye on more of a long-term partnership. "I'll boil water. You bring the herbs."

"Will do." She spun on her heel and was back in two shakes to supervise him. She set aside a brown jar marked with a blue flower, then sprinkled a handful of dried leaves and berries into the water. A delightful aroma filled the kitchen.

"Smells delicious. What is it?"

"Juniper berries, and leaves from red oak, black raspberry, coneflower. Applied to the skin, it dries the rash. The plants are edible, if you'd like to try a sip."

"Perhaps the next time my innards need drying." He hadn't seen Tryphina all day. "Where's your apprentice tonight?"

"Visiting the Winegars. But don't ask me which son she's interested in."

"Aye. Changes with the wind."

She gave the concoction a stir. "We've a few minutes. D'ya have a song for poison ivy?"

"There is one, but it calls for a flute, a bodhran, and a fiddle. Would keep the little ones awake." He couldn't speak of love, but he'd sing of it. "How about 'The Water is Wide'?"

"'Tis a sad one, no?"

"I'll sing it happy."

He sang about boats and flowers. The verse about love growing cold, he changed to growing warm and returning like the morning dew. Keziah ladled the potion through the sieve and into the jugs, her face warming in the steam... or perhaps the song. He finished with "'Someday I hope to love again.'"

"'Tis ready," she said, pointing to the concoction, not her heart.

"And this?" He nodded toward the brown jar with the flower.

"Father Ephraim's infusion, to help him sleep. I'll take it to him while the remedy cools, then we'll go." Moving with the grace and speed of a young girl, Keziah hurried upstairs.

Finn lay in the corner by the kitchen, waiting for his evening bowl of scraps. Duncan joined him on the floor, removing the burs and seeds stuck to his fur. "You've known her longer. Any advice on courting?"

Suddenly the dog looked up, ears pricked. He hurried to the bottom of the steps, listened a moment, shot a glance at Duncan that said "you coming, man?", then broke the rule he'd obeyed for nearly five years and raced upstairs.

"Right behind you." Duncan took the steps two at a time, following loud voices and Finn's growl into the printing office.

Guy Barnum pulled Keziah's arms behind her and backed into the corner. "Call off your cur," he said.

Finn snapped, but wasn't able to reach the thug past Keziah's skirts.

"Let go of me." Keziah commanded, her voice fierce.

"Do as she says." Red heat fired Duncan's body. Two steps took him across the office. Duncan's forearm slammed into the man's throat, thumping his head into the wall. A yank on his wrist released Keziah. "Hands off."

Finn's show of teeth kept Guy cornered.

Keziah moved to the center of the room, rolling her shoulders.

"Sister Sirrine, I'm disappointed." Father Ephraim sat at his desk, face red.

Duncan turned on the leader. "Guy attacks, but Keziah gets your rebuke?"

"Whist," she told Duncan under her breath, then faced Father Ephraim, hands at her side. Her voice was quiet, but firm. "Charles Thompson. Rufus and I were your first converts. Twenty years I've followed you. Yet now, overhearing me address the outbreak of *poison ivy*, you form a notion that I'm poisoning you?"

What? Had he gone stark raving mad?

Keeping his hands above Finn's reach, Guy's shaking finger pointed to the tools on the desk. "You were armed."

She held Ephraim's gaze. "The knife is essential for gathering herbs. Charles, you know how much a good pair of Wendt dressmaking scissors cost. The last time I left them unattended, Leo and the Barnum boys cut off Harriet Cobb's hair."

No one had forgotten. With each retelling, Eliza Cobb expanded the offense from a snip of the braids to near scalping.

Guy waved at the jar. "If that's not poison, you drink it."

"Gladly. But first, before I sleep, I have twenty-three people who need tending for poison ivy."

"I'll drink it." Catherine Thompson, dressed in her robe with her hair down, strolled down the hall. She entered the office and stepped up to the desk. "I could use the rest...from all this noise."

Father Ephraim stood and raised a hand. "Wait!"

"Think of your children," Guy warned.

She pried off the lid and smiled. "Yes, I am thinking of Keziah's gentle care of my babies." She turned to Guy. "And yours." She drank the remedy, then returned the jar to Keziah. "The psalmist says 'I will lay down in peace and sleep, for the Lord makes me dwell in safety.' Thank you, dear sister."

Father Ephraim broke out in a sweat. Guy swore under his breath.

Keziah returned the tools to her pocket, then hurried downstairs. Duncan followed and Finn brought up the rear. "Where's the nearest asylum?" she muttered.

He ran his palms down her arms, finding a slight tremble. "Are you hurt?"

Not looking at him, she shook her head. When she picked up a jug, she winced.

"I'll carry those." He put a hand on her elbow. "I can do this, if you need a rest."

She shrugged him off, and, with her back ramrod straight, stepped smartly onto the path leading to the Cobbs'. *Fearless, dedicated... practiced.* An expert at ignoring her own pain, pulling herself together, and doing her duty. Duncan's fists tightened, endangering the jug handles. Rufus was a thousand miles away, but Preparation's leaders would not attack Keziah with impunity.

Duncan exchanged a look with Finn. "Good dog."

Keziah cleared her throat. "Let's see which of our neighbors can follow instructions."

Eliza's fussing carried across the prairie. "It's bad enough my son is sent away on a fool's errand, now my daughters have caught poison ivy. I suppose hanging about with Leo, they're bound to catch it."

"What if we all catch it?" Rebecca Butts whined. The Cobbs and Butts houses were next to each other; the path between more worn than any in Preparation.

Keziah entered the house without knocking. "Poison ivy doesn't spread from one person to another. Come out in the light, Harriet, so I can see where it got you. Is Maria itching, too?"

"No, but I am." Orrin Butts stepped out, breeks rolled up to his knees. Duncan helped him apply the remedy. "Ah, much better. What's with all the yelling at the House?"

"Ephraim decided the remedy Keziah had been giving him for months was poison, and her plant knife and scissors were proof she planned to harm him. Barnum wrenched her arms behind her."

Open-mouthed, Orrin watched Keziah tend his family, then frowned at the Lord's House. He'd had been Father Ephraim's enforcer, making sure everyone followed the rules. His brother-in-law was Ephraim's biggest financial supporter, paying his debts and buying the printing press. Orrin's troubled eyes met Duncan's. He shook his head and went inside without saying a word.

So it went through Preparation. Itching or no, the Congregation bleated like sheep, fearing for their future. Duncan treated the Perrin boys, then, at last, they were done.

With a hand on a shoulder, he turned Keziah toward the northwest. The sun sank behind the hills, turning the sky rose and purple, setting aglow the fields and Keziah's beloved wildflowers. Beneath his hand, her muscles loosened. He set his other palm on the base of her neck and rubbed. "'He will not suffer thy foot to be moved: he that keepeth thee will not slumber.' 'Let's lift our eyes to the hills,'" he quoted from Psalm 121.

"'From whence comes our help,'" she added the next verse.

"'Our help comes from the Lord, who made heaven and earth.'" He stepped close, eased her head to his chest, and wrapped his arms around her. She rested her hands on his. "'Behold, he that keepeth Israel will not slumber or sleep. The Lord is thy keeper: the Lord is thy shade. The sun shall not smite thee by day, nor the moon by night. The Lord shall preserve thee from evil: he shall preserve thy soul. The Lord shall preserve thy going in and going out from this time forth, and even forevermore.'" Her head rested below his chin, her hands small in his. He wanted hold her the rest of her life. *Guard my beloved, Lord. She's a rare fine woman.*

The river breathed cooler air as night claimed the sky. Swallows chased mosquitos as crickets took up their song. Finn rejoined them after a detour to scare rabbits from the garden. He plopped on the path, tongue hanging out.

She slipped from his embrace. "Thank you."

"Glad to help." He should have picked a longer Psalm, but this was all he could remember. "Always."

"Well, the Lord may not sleep, but I must."

After Ephraim and Guy Barnum's false accusations, could she? He'd offer to guard her door all night, but Finn had the advantage there. She pulled away, took a few steps, then paused. "I"ll see you in the morning."

"Aye. Long sleep." *And may your heart bring you back to me.*

CHAPTER 23

August 1858

Keziah grabbed her gathering bags, whistled Finn from the shade of the porch, and followed the creek into the hills to the blackberries. Moving slowly to avoid thorns and bees, she pulled the fruit off the bushes.

Tryphina plodded through the underbrush, noisy as a cow. She grabbed a handful of berries and popped them into her mouth. "What are you going to make with those?"

"Nothing, as fast as you eat them."

She shrugged. "Father Ephraim and Guy Barnum are gone again."

A relief, to be sure. "Where did they go?"

"To Onawa, but I don't know why."

Onawa? The village of lawyers. What need had Father Ephraim of a lawyer?

Tryphina jumped up to investigate another plant. "Is this wild bergamot?"

"Yes. Harvest the flowers and leaves." Keziah passed her the knife and an empty bag. "Good for fevers, upset stomachs, sore throats. The steam clears stuffed heads. Washes wounds. Makes an ointment for burns and skin infections."

"Such a beautiful shade of purple. My wedding dress will be this color," she said, even though she had no money for fabric and all potential grooms had been sent away. "I know where the mission teachers are. They wrote to their families. Went to talk to Daniel this morning and found their letters on Ephraim's desk. Opened."

As he'd open her letter from Brother Hickenloper. As he'd open her divorce decree, if it ever came. "You're saying the postmaster of Preparation is withholding the letters from their families."

"Yes. For a good month now, according to the postmarks."

Why deny their families this comfort? Keziah called Finn and marched to the House.

"Where are you going?" Tryphina trotted along.

"To deliver the mail." She glanced at the young woman. "You should stay here, in case Father Ephraim finds out."

"I know where the office key is. If Father Ephraim sends me away, I'll throw myself at Mosiah Winegar's feet." She waved her arms. "He'll have to marry me."

"Has anyone told you that's a terrible idea?"

"I'm full of terrible ideas."

Tryphina's thoughts cluttered the air, but fortunately didn't lead to action. Now if the girl would be quiet a moment, so Keziah could think through this plan. Where was Duncan when she needed to talk to him? "If we're caught…"

"We'll say we're cleaning the office."

"No one will believe that." Although the Congregation believed plenty of nonsense. "And when we pass out the mail…"

"They'll be so happy." Tryphina skipped in a circle. She had family to support her; she wouldn't starve.

They entered the House. Tryphina brought the fruit to the kitchen. "We picked berries for Father Ephraim. Is he back yet?"

"Not yet." Sarah peeked in the sack. "Not enough for a pie."

Tryphina took the bag back. "Then I'll give them to Catherine. They're her favorite." She scampered up the stairs, retrieved the key from the top of the door frame, and let Keziah in. She hurried to the desk. "Oh no. The letters are gone."

"Maybe Ephraim and Guy took them to Onawa?" Keziah hesitated in the doorway, twitchy about the office since Ephraim's accusation of poison.

"No, they were here," she patted the empty corner of the desk, "after they left. Who could have taken them?"

"Daniel?" Keziah looked under the printing press.

"Baneemy's favorite printer? Not a chance." She circled the room, checking every stack of paper. "They're gone. Now what? We can't tell families their sons wrote without giving them the letters."

The bell rang for the midday meal. Tryphina locked the office, hung the bag of berries on the Thompsons' door knob, and they went down.

At the bottom of the steps, they both halted. Leo stood at the entrance, handing out letters. "Isaac Swett wrote to Duncan Ross. Thomas Lewis wrote to Priscilla. Rowland Cobb to Eliza. Amos Chase to Sarah." He handed that letter to his sister Ida who took it to the cook. "Homer Hoyt wrote to his family, and Josiah DeForest to his. And Duncan got two more, from James Durfee and from Nels Turner."

"The letters are delivered," Keziah took a relieved breath, "by a nine-year-old postman." Who wouldn't be disciplined. He never was.

"So clever," Tryphina whispered.

"So where'd our young men end up?" Charles Perrin asked.

"In Council Bluffs," Leo said. "Staying in Brother and Sister Jones's barn, working at the sawmill." Ephraim wasn't the only one reading the mail.

"They're safe, then."

"Except..." Keziah spotted Eliza Cobb sniffling in the corner. Her daughters Maria and Harriet looked equally somber. "Elisha didn't write."

Tryphina murmured, "He did. A month ago. His brother delivered it. Elisha headed for Pike's Peak, prospecting for gold instead of souls."

No wonder his family looked so grim. Their second son dared defy Father Ephraim's orders. Would he be welcomed back into the Congregation? Perhaps if he brought back gold... "I'll pray for him."

~

September 1858

All week Duncan had been thinking of the lads and their letters. He pulled a sheet of paper and pencil from under the store's counter. Without any urgent orders for shoes, he'd take this time to write back.

"Psst." Amy Chase's curly head peeked into the store. She whispered, "Mama wants you to bring cheese to the root cellar. Be quiet and don't let anyone see you."

Duncan nodded and she scurried away. Now what sort of cheese might Sarah Chase be needing? And how much? No matter, he decided, grabbing a middling one and locking the door. The turning of the calendar to September hadn't banished August's heat. A visit to the root cellar would be welcome.

He ambled up the hill. Sarah had been watching for him and motioned him inside. He climbed down, ducking to keep from hitting his head on a rope of onions. The cool air smelled of dirt, cabbage, and turnips. Julia Hoyt and Mary DeForest emerged from the shadows. The three were wives of the traveling teachers. He set the cheese on the shelf.

"We think," Mary glanced at the other two for confirmation, "our husbands should come home. School will be starting up again."

"And the harvest," Sarah said.

"And this situation," Julia Hoyt pointed up. Two floors above was Father Ephraim's office. "You being nearest thing to a father for the young men..."

Duncan nodded, glad to be kin of a sort to the four young men in his Bible reading group. The men needed to return...in defiance of Ephraim...because of Ephraim. "Aye. 'Tis time."

"Letters..." Mary shook her head. With Ephraim as postmaster, letters would be read, but perhaps not sent.

"I'll send word with whoever delivers the cheese." Duncan loaded the wagon in the wee hours, long before Ephraim woke.

"Dennis has been driving lately," Sarah noted. His last name was Butts, so his loyalties lay with Ephraim.

"I'll think on it."

"Wait a minute. When they return, what will Ephraim do?" Mary asked.

Sarah crossed her arms. "I doubt he'll notice. He's been sinking, scatterbrained, forgetting to come down for breakfast."

Mary nodded. "He called me Martha yesterday. I figured he was thinking about Lazarus's sister."

"He called me Isabella last week, and there's no Isabella in the Bible," Julia said. "Ever since he accused Keziah of poison, I've thought he's come unhinged."

The slide into insanity seemed to be picking up speed.

"I'd best return to the store. Thank you, Sisters." Duncan climbed into the sunshine and strolled back to the store. The Congregation had fallen into a swamp of mistrust, with secret meetings and questioning loyalties. This morning he'd read God walked with the Psalmist in trouble and stretched His hand against enemies. Had Ephraim become their enemy? Or was the man in need of a doctor for his head? *Heavenly Father, walk with us through this troubled time.*

Duncan laid out a pattern to cut more leather when the door darkened again.

Tryphina shuffled to the counter. "When are the traveling teachers coming back?"

"I don't rightly know." Her last name was Butts, but she often defied her father. Could she be trusted? Was this an answer to prayer? He set paper and an envelope on the counter. "You could ask."

"I could?"

He held out a pencil. "You could."

She grabbed the supplies and waltzed out the door. A half-hour later, she returned, fanning herself with an envelope addressed to James, Isaac, Nels, and Andrew. "Keziah's gathering, so I used the bench you made for her as a desk, and told those boys to come on home." She lowered her voice. "You're not going to turn this over to Father Ephraim, are you?"

"You've no stamp, so it'll have to go on the cheese wagon."

She handed over the letter with a sly smile, then skipped out the door. "September's going to be a good month."

Duncan penciled "Isaiah 51:11" on the corner where the stamp should go, and recited, "Therefore the redeemed of the Lord shall return."

October 1858

Keziah pulled the last of the carrots from the ground. In spite of the clear skies, no children played between the cabins and no laundry flapped on the clotheslines. Even the chickens were quiet. She rinsed the carrots in the creek, then took them to the House. The traveling teachers had returned last week to quiet celebrations with their families. Was today the day Ephraim noticed they were back?

Instead of working, the Congregation waited in the main room.

Keziah leaned close to Sarah while warming her hands over the stove. "What are the men doing?" Harvest chores kept them in the fields in autumn, but this morning Amos Chase, Charles Perrin, Homer Hoyt, and Rowland Cobb huddled around a table.

Sarah started to answer, but was interrupted by footsteps on the stairs. The men stood and met Father Ephraim and Guy Barnum coming down. The room chilled. Every eye turned to watch.

"We want to talk." Charles propped his fists on his hips. "About the land."

"No person can receive land until there is sufficient land owned by the Chief Steward to furnish an inheritance to each family," Ephraim said.

"Give us an accounting," Rowland said through his clenched jaw. "How close are we?"

"I've told you, since we've gotten through the Sacrifice, those who've been faithful and true will receive their land. I'm working to set aside your inheritance."

Guy stepped between the men and Ephraim, and raised his arms. "There's no need for an ambush."

Homer ran a hand through his hair. "I've been trying to talk with you since I got back."

"This isn't a good time." Guy sidestepped toward the door.

"When *is* a good time?" Charles Perrin asked.

Rowland blocked their way. "Let's set up a meeting. Tonight after supper or tomorrow evening?"

"Tomorrow." Guy shouldered him out of the way, letting Ephraim out, then following. Minutes later the two leaders rolled west in the wagon.

Amos kicked the wall. "He won't even listen to us..."

The men stomped off to the fields. Their frustration would boil over if Ephraim didn't act soon. Was there any way to make peace? "We must pray," Keziah said.

Eliza slapped the knife on the table, then stomped out. "It's too late."

Keziah prayed and kept an eye on the Congregation while working in the kitchen. Instead of Father Ephraim and Guy Barnum returning the next day, Hugh Lytle and Jacob Paden rode in from Belvidere. The hotheads stomped into the House, fists raised. Good thing Duncan was gone—they'd use him as a whipping boy.

"Thompson cheated us back in '55. It's our day of reckoning."

Rowland Cobb and Orrin Butts headed upstairs.

"Good to see you." Hoping to defuse the powder keg, Keziah approached the two. "How is Christena? And Louisa and Rebecca Ann?"

"Fine." Hugh and Jacob turned their backs and huddled with the men. Up to no good, Keziah figured.

"Maybe a full stomach will blunt their anger." Sarah Chase served dinner, but the grumbling continued. They sent the children out as soon as they finished.

After dinner, footsteps thumped on the stairs. Rowland descended with a handful of papers. He scanned the room, his expression grim. "Brothers and sisters of Preparation. I regret to inform you that Thompson," the use of his name instead of "Father Ephraim" drew gasps from a few, "has deeded a thousand acres of our land to his wife Catherine and 1,360 acres to Guy Barnum. He set aside forty acres for himself."

The anger boiled over, with cries of "Build a gallows! Hang him dead!"

Lord, help us. Keziah crossed her arms to warm herself. *How can I make peace?*

"Why would he do such a thing?" Silas Wilcox asked.

Charles Perrin shouted, "What about my deed? My land? I've got a promissory note, the bill of sale, a bond, script, and receipts."

"Worthless scraps of paper." Amos Chase banged his fists on the table.

"Only good to light the stove," Andrew Haines said.

"Build a bonfire!"

"No. Don't." Rowland waved his arms and yelled over the uproar. "Keep it all as evidence. We'll get a lawyer and fight for our land."

"Lawyers cost money and Thompson has all of ours," Thomas Lewis's teacher voice echoed.

Orrin Butts stood with his head down, but spoke loud enough for all to hear. "Rowland's right. We need Thompson's account books, his records of our property, all those stock certificates, bills of sale, and titles, to make our case."

Charles Perrin sent two of his sons to the ridge behind the house. "Keep a lookout for Father Ephraim and Brother Barnum. Let us know soon as you see them coming back."

"We're been slaving away, working our fingers to the bone while Thompson sits on his bum. And for what?"

"We've been tricked!"

"No more sacrifice. I want my land!"

"Humbuggery!"

"Brothers and sisters." Keziah needed Duncan's loud whistle, but he'd gone to repair shoes in Magnolia, twenty miles over the hills. Others who could be counted on for calm and good judgement, such as Hannah Perrin and James Durfee, weren't here. She would not allow these gowks to undo her hard work.

Keziah climbed onto a bench. "Brothers and sisters of Preparation! Five years ago we gathered here to show the rest of the world how to live, how God's people work together." No one would meet her gaze. "I've done my best to keep all of you in good health these five years. Do not ruin all my hard work by beating on each other."

"Save the beating for Ephraim!" Amos Chase yelled.

"No fighting." She shook her head. "We took a solemn oath not to murder."

"And not to steal our neighbors' goods, but he stole ours," Charles Perrin said.

"String him up!" yelled Luther Cottingham.

"Would you leave Catherine a widow?" Keziah asked. "And deprive Amelia, Ida, Leo, C.W., Ossie, and baby Abraham of their father?"

A few people looked down, but others called for the noose.

"Ephraim sent my husband and son away all summer!" Eliza Cobb screamed, then pointed at Keziah. "*She* kept me from my grandson's birth. That poison she's been feeding Ephraim has turned his mind against us."

"Eliza, you know better." But she didn't. She was too far gone. "'Do not kill. Love one another, love your neighbor.'"

The Congregation turned into lunatics she barely recognized, with fists raised, faces creased, and teeth bared. The room filled with their shouts. All the lavender in Preparation wouldn't calm these beasts. She tried Scripture again, "'Be angry, but do not sin. Let not the sun go down—'"

The bench tilted. Keziah tipped rearwards, landing on her back, knocking the air from her lungs. She couldn't pull in a breath, couldn't move. The yelling continued, echoing from a distance too far to make out the words. The light dimmed. The voices came from far away. Her shoulders and ankles were grabbed, her body lifted, her head flopped back. She landed on another hard floor and the light went out.

Breathe...

Later, Tryphina called, "Keziah, are you in there?" A door rattled. "I can't find the key. Are you all right?"

The air smelled of bread, molasses, potatoes. Reaching to her sides, Keziah found barrels, a crock, a woven basket. The pantry. She rolled toward weak glow below the door, but the floor tipped and spun like a leaf in the river.

"Keziah? Oh, Heavenly Father, please don't let her be dead."

Dead? She wasn't, but Ephraim would be. She couldn't move, but Tryphina could. "Esther," her voice croaked.

"Esther? No, it's Tryphina." A shadow moved in the light and the voice came closer. "Did you hit your head?"

A whiff of pork inspired her mouth to make spittle. Her tongue loosened. "Esther. Save people."

"I'll get you out, don't you worry." The silly girl fiddled with the lock.

"Warn Ephraim."

The lock fell silent as Tryphina stopped panicking and started thinking. "They want to hang him." She gasped. "A gallows. Like Esther's uncle."

"Ride. Horse. Go."

"I should warn Ephraim." The shadow left. "I'll be back to get you out."

"I'm fine." Safe enough for a nap.

CHAPTER 24

October 1858

At midday, low grey clouds rolled in on a cold north wind. Could it mean an early winter? Duncan shivered and tugged his scarf over his ears.

Lack of ability to predict the weather had kept him from succeeding in farming, but rarely interfered with shoemaking. The morning he'd repaired the Magnolia postmaster's brogans and enjoyed a conversation free of worry about Father Ephraim.

Saddlebags clinking with his tools, he crested the last hill on the way back to Preparation. As Flora started down to the Soldier River valley, she picked up her pace from a plod to a walk. She'd been named after race horse Flora Temple, but other than her liver bay coloring, they had nothing in common.

"C'mon Flora, get us home before the rain starts."

No response. Not even a flick of an ear.

To his left, a flock of geese flew south. A trio of does grazed in the valley to his right. All was at peace... except Tryphina Butts raced by on Reynaud like the devil himself was after her, skirts flapping over bare legs, hair loose. She headed straight for a wagon with Father Ephraim and Guy Barnum, waving and yelling. Duncan couldn't hear her words, but the two men did. They jumped off, unhitched the horses, and, faster than imaginable, leaped on their backs and raced away from Preparation.

He should see if he could help... but Flora refused to increase her speed.

Tryphina watched them for a moment, then noticed him as he crossed the river. "Duncan, hurry!"

"What's going on? Shouldn't we bring the wagon back?"

"Keziah's locked in the pantry and I can't find the key."

Duncan's heart raced, but Flora continued her turtle's pace in spite of his prods. He could run faster than this. "Why doesn't Keziah come out of the pantry?"

Tryphina yanked Flora's halter and got her up to a trot. "She was knocked off a bench and hit the floor. Someone put her in the pantry, which, honestly, was safer than the big room. They're building a gallows to hang Ephraim."

"What?" When Duncan found out who'd hurt Keziah, he'd burst the eejit.

"My father and Uncle Rowland are furious. Ephraim gave away all the land. Well, not all. He kept forty acres for himself. The rest went to Catherine and Guy."

"Who cares about the land? Is Keziah hurt? You left her? Where was Finn?"

"Finn's guarding the chickens. Dorman saw a bobcat last night. Anyway, Keziah was talking. At first I thought she'd hit her head because she called me Esther, but then I realized she wanted me to be Esther. She sent me to warn Father Ephraim."

Dear Jesus...

"C'mon, lazy beastie." He pressed his knees in and leaned forward. Tryphina urged her horse into a canter and Flora followed.

Three men rode toward them from Preparation.

Charles Perrin pointed past Duncan. "I see them!"

Amos followed, scowling at Tryphina. "We'll deal with you later."

Homer, being a giant of a man, rode with his feet dangling by the wee mare's knees. He shook the reins. The mare laid her ears back and bucked him off, then joined the parade back to Preparation, leaving Homer to walk.

Duncan should try to stop them, try to talk sense into them, or at least, delay them so Ephraim and Barnum could escape. But... Keziah...

...please let Keziah be uninjured.

At long last Duncan and Tryphina arrived at the Lord's House.

"I'll take care of the mail and horses," she said.

Mail? Who cared about the mail? He dismounted and ran inside, past the muttering Congregation. "Keziah?" He rattled the pantry door. Locked. "Keziah!"

"Duncan," she said in a weak voice.

Alive. Was she hurt?

"Can you reach the door knob?" Dumb question. If she could, she'd come out. "I'll get the hatchet and break the lock."

"It'd be faster to unlock it." Eight-year-old Amy Chase handed him a key.

"Thank you." Another time he'd ask how she came by it and why she hadn't let Keziah out earlier. Duncan pushed it into the lock, turned, and opened the door. Keziah lay on her side, forearm over her eyes. No blood as far as he could see. "What happened? Did you hit your head?"

"My hair cushioned my landing." Her curls pooled under her head. The hairpins had been lost in the scuffle.

"I've always liked your hair." Saying so was out of line, but it was all he could do to stop himself from declaring his love. He wrapped his arm around her shoulders and helped her sit up.

"The room's spinning."

"What should I do? How can I help?" He slid behind her, knees on either side of her hips, his chest supporting her back and head. He'd stay like this forever, as long as she needed.

"It's slowing." She leaned on him, limp but warm. "Did Tryphina reach Ephraim and Guy in time?"

"They're racing back to Onawa." He wouldn't tell her about the men chasing them. "How long have you been in the pantry?"

"I don't know. What time is it?"

"Almost supper."

"I had a nap."

"You fainted?"

"Can you help me get back to the bothy?" Keziah never asked for help. She must feel shaky, afraid.

"Shouldn't you stay here where someone," preferably himself, "can keep an eye on you?"

"It's not safe," she whispered. "I don't know who made me fall or who put me in the pantry."

"I do." Eunice Wilcox leaned in the doorway, then kneeled to clasp Keziah's hands. "I'm so glad you're awake."

"You saw what happened?" Duncan asked.

The lass nodded. "There was a scuffle between those who wanted to burn everything in the printing office and those who thought to save the papers for a lawsuit. The bench couldn't hold up against the pushing and shoving."

"So it wasn't deliberate?"

"No, but their blood was hot. So Sarah Chase, Lodema Winegar, Hannah Perrin, and I hid you in the pantry. Sarah gave the key to Amy for safekeeping." She squeezed Keziah's hands. "Seeing you hurt gave them pause and they calmed down."

Duncan clasped her hand. "Thank you for saving Keziah."

"She brought our babies safely into the world. We'll keep her from harm." Eunice kissed Keziah's cheek then left.

"Supper's ready," Sarah Chase told them.

Keziah groaned. "No food."

"If I'd spent half the day in a faint, you'd be having me eat and drink." Sarah helped Duncan get Keziah on her wobbly feet then settled at the closest table.

The rest stared. Duncan scowled at them and they returned to eating.

Sarah put a bowl and mug on the table. "I made you an infusion from the dried linden and blue vervain blossoms you gave me, with honey of course."

Keziah took a sip. "Perfect. Thank you, dear friend."

The last person Keziah would want to see stomped across the

room. She straightened, bracing for another rebuke. Duncan put up a hand to stop Orrin Butts, but the man would not be deterred. "Sister Keziah, about sending Tryphina to warn Thompson..." he said to the air over her head.

"She's our fastest rider."

His head made a slow path back and forth. "I never thought our Heavenly Father would put her riding to any good use." His mouth twitched, battling between pride of her equestrian skill and shame of her defiance. "I'm sorry you took a fall. I tried to stop the fight, but they were enraged."

"What did I miss?"

"Rowland stopped them from burning the Congregation's records. He's sorting through the office now." Orrin pulled an envelope from his coat pocket. "He found this. No sign of your money. Save those papers for court." He looked her in the eye. "Keziah... thank you. For everything." He trudged across the room and up the stairs.

She glanced into the envelope, muttered an Irish curse involving severe itching, then stuffed it into her pocket.

Duncan put a hand on her back. A thunderbolt of tension shot through her. "What's wrong?"

"Divorce papers," she said, her whisper fierce. "From *two* years ago. Not a word to me. Thompson took all my money, just like St. Louis."

The money didn't matter. Keziah was free of Rufus. Free to marry him...but in no mood for a proposal.

Tryphina peeked out of the laundry room, then tiptoed to Keziah. "Are you hurt? I didn't want to leave you, but..."

Keziah lowered her voice. "Did Thompson and Barnum get away?"

She glanced around the room. No one was close enough to overhear. Her face creased with worry. "If their pursuers didn't catch them. Hugh Lytle and Jacob Paden left."

Lytle and Paden had been here? No doubt they were responsible for her fall. Duncan should never have left her. "Who cares about that scoundrel, that charlatan?" The words exploded from Duncan's mouth.

He'd spent the past five years trying to show he was good enough to join this Congregation. All the haver and skulduggery from Ephraim, all the madness of Preparation rolled to a boil and burst forth, fueled by his worries for Keziah. Father Ephraim couldn't throw him out now. The rest of them might, but Duncan no longer wanted to be part of this stink hole. His fists hit the table, attracting the attention of everyone in the large room.

"What's wrong with us? We turn into savages, abandon everything the Bible teaches about loving each another and living together in peace? And hurting the one who's done so much to care for us?" He gestured toward Keziah, then thumped the table again. "What's wrong with us?"

Silas Wilcox shuffled to the table and laid his hand on Duncan's shoulder. "We're sinners, all of us, in need of God."

~

October 1858

Keziah awoke to aches such as she hadn't felt since Rufus left. Her foggy head had her wishing for coffee. Instead she counted the chickens—all present and suitably irritable—and gathered eggs, set Finn to guard them, then headed to the Lord's House. She opened the door. If the bleating of the flock hadn't told of their disquietude, the odor would have. No one had taken the time to wash.

"I need to be close to town, so I can continue teaching." Thomas Lewis set wood chips marked with initials on a hand-drawn map. "And Charles Perrin wants to be north of the creek."

"He might be in jail for killing Thompson," muttered Isaac Swett. "No sense dividing the land before we know the how many people we got."

"Put me as far from Preparation as possible." Andrew Haines stomped off, muttering, "If single men are allowed to have land."

"Almost three thousand acres. Ought to have enough for each of us," Josiah DeForest said. "Since I'd rather teach than farm, don't know as I'll need a full section."

"To be fair, everyone should get a section. If you don't want to farm, sell it or rent it to a neighbor who does." Silas Wilcox tapped the map. "Put me close to town, too."

"What if each person got a town lot and a section?" Josiah asked. "How do they do it in Belvidere? They own their land."

Homer Hoyt shook his head. "Those hotheads. Remember Hugh Lytle attacking Duncan because he rode his mare?"

"And Jacob Paden nearly killed Keziah while she was helping his wife," Eunice Wilcox said.

And then there was Christena Lytle, who had destroyed their friendship by accusing Keziah of not praying. Her heart still ached with the loss.

"Let's move to Council Bluffs. We wouldn't have to worry about being scalped by Lamanites." Rebecca Butts tapped her fingers on the table. "And we could go shopping."

"If you have money." Priscilla Lewis rubbed her eyes and stretched. "Well we can't go to Salt Lake City after everything Thompson said about Brigham Young."

"As if Brigham cares what a clod in Iowa says about him, busy as he is with all those wives." Luther Cottingham leaned back in his chair. "He gets dozens of wives and I get none."

Priscilla pinched her nose. "He bathes more than once a year."

"Bit of a fuss, is he?" Luther scratched his beard, unleashing a flurry of crumbs. "If God wanted us to spend time in water, He'd have made us fish."

The young men in Duncan's Bible reading group huddled in the corner.

"Here it says 'every man shall sit under his own vine and fig tree,'" Andrew Haines read from Thompson's *Laws and Covenants of Israel*. "There it is - we should own our own land."

Duncan shook his head. "It's not a prophecy. It's the history of King Solomon in Israel."

"Thompson refers to Jesus as a prophet, but not as the Son of God or our Savior." James Durfee gestured toward the small book. "That's what's wrong with his religion."

Thanks to Duncan's Bible reading, the lads knew the truth.

Duncan noticed Keziah and followed her into the kitchen. "How's your head this morning?"

"Wondering why no one's in here cooking." She set the eggs on the work table and stirred the fire. "If you'd please ring the bell."

"Can't find it." He banged the shovel against the ash bucket, and whistled.

Before they'd fully quieted, Keziah asked, "Has anyone seen Sarah Chase this morning?"

"I did," Hannah said. "She's spent."

Aren't we all. "Starving and dealing with hungry children won't cure that. Julia, would you please start the oatmeal, and Rebecca, please cook the eggs. Has anyone seen to Catherine and the children?" The poor woman and her children had hidden upstairs from the mayhem yesterday.

"She has all the land!" Eliza pounded the table.

"Hush." Her husband put his hand on hers. "You know that was none of her doing."

"Leo came looking for food a while back," Duncan said.

"I visited Catherine and Miranda Barnum this morning." Eunice knew the pain of being the target of gossip; she chose discretion. "I'll take breakfast to them."

"Thank you." Keziah said. "Brothers and sisters, none of us know what tomorrow—or this afternoon—will bring. No matter what happens, we'll be better off finishing the harvest than leaving all our hard work rotting in the fields. Let's not be weary of doing good."

"Not doing any hard work lest I get paid." Isaac Swett crossed his arms over his chest.

"As if you ever work hard. My belly's shrunk into my backbone. I'm helping the sisters cook." Nels strutted into the kitchen. "Need water? Firewood? Someone to taste the eggs? I'm your man."

Several people chuckled and a few applauded. The promise of food motivated Mariah Cobb and Mary Lewis to set the tables.

"What might you need me to do?" Duncan asked.

Keziah studied him. Strain and weariness tugged at his eyes, yet no foul temper marred his kindness. Behind her, Nels crowed like a rooster as he stirred the eggs. "Wish I could be silly..."

"The yoke of the Congregation has been on your shoulders." His warm hand rubbed the soreness at the base of her neck. She leaned into his strength.

She scanned the large room. Who's missing? "Where's Orrin and Rowland?"

"Going through Thompson's books, trying to figure out how much each of us put in." He steered her to an empty spot next to his at the table. "Sit ye down. You're the one Jesus thought of when he said 'Come unto me, all ye that labor and are heavy laden, and I will give you rest.'"

"Only a moment."

"Whatever's on your list will wait until after breakfast," he said in his soothing way. With a twinkle in his eye, he added, "Then you'll hand your list to me, so I'll know what to do with myself and the lads."

From under the table, Leo tugged Duncan's pants' leg. He unwrapped the rag he carried, revealing the bell. "I'm sorry I took this. I was afraid someone would hurt Mother, and thought to ring it to get help."

"Oh, laddie, so very smart of you, but I'll not allow anyone to hurt your fine mother." Duncan smoothed the hair back from his forehead. "We could use your help today. You've got a good view from your upstairs windows. If you see anyone coming, up the river road or over the hills, ring the bell."

The boy nodded.

"But first," Duncan patted the bench. "Breakfast."

October 1858

With Keziah's heartening, they finished the onion harvest, set a pig to roasting, and made good headway with the other chores. Sarah Chase resumed her place in the kitchen, and the midday meal was served on time. Before they returned to the fields, the bell rang upstairs. Duncan and the rest of the Congregation raced out of the House.

"Two men in a fancy wagon," Homer said.

"With fine looking horses," Tryphina noted.

"Followed by Chase and Perrin in our wagon," Homer said. "No sign of Thompson or Barnum."

The men were greeted with shouted questions. Keziah cut through the hubbub and motioned them all inside. "Please, come in out of the cold."

Once settled and served one of Keziah's warm infusions, the men introduced themselves as Judge Whiting and Sheriff Pierce. The Judge turned out to be a young fellow, in his mid-thirties Duncan guessed.

"Mr. Thompson and Mr. Barnum arrived safely in Onawa last night," Whiting said. "We met with them, then with Mr. Chase and Mr. Perrin. Both sides have agreed to negotiate a legal and orderly settlement." He paused, his gaze touching each man. "If you also renounce violence and promise to seek legal redress, say 'aye.' If you disagree, say 'nay.'"

A chorus of 'ayes' sounded.

The Congregation silenced as light footsteps sounded on the steps. "Thank you, brothers and sisters." Catherine's eyes were dry, but swollen from tears and fatigue. Her hand clutched the railing. She cleared her throat and addressed the judge. "I would like safe conduct for myself and our children to Onawa. We are packed and ready to leave."

Whiting nodded. "Mr. Thompson requested we bring his family to him. We'll take the Barnum family too."

Miranda Barnum and the children slipped out. Keziah went into the kitchen and began making sandwiches.

Catherine addressed the Congregation. "First, I would like to return your trunks. Duncan, perhaps your Bible reading men might help?"

"Certainly." He saw the wisdom of her plan. The small group would keep the rest from clogging the stairs. And in returning their belongings, the Thompson family would be allowed to escape with their own. Even Isaac needed only a wee bit of prodding to join in.

"Butts…" Andrew Haines announced the first trunks down. Daniel and Dennis carried the luggage to their home.

"Where's mine?" Eliza demanded. "Or did the thieving wretch—"

Andrew stopped her rant, "Yours comes after the Chases'."

"Butts, Chase, Cobb," Keziah murmured to Duncan. "Alphabetical. Sirrine will be a while." She gathered a stack of dirty dishes and headed to the kitchen.

"As will Ross." Duncan cleared another table and followed. "So… Baneemy?" He shaved soap into the dishpan. "The Keys to the Kingdom?"

She added hot water. "Nonsense."

"All of it?"

"Most. In the first century, Christians lived together in one accord, sharing possessions. Joseph Smith tried with his United Order and it fell apart." She dropped the utensils into the water. "Maybe it's us, too sinful to live in harmony. Instead of working toward healing, I'd like to knock a few heads together."

"Yet you didn't. Not even during the winter of 1857, when we were held prisoner by winter." Duncan scraped the plates into the slop pail, then slid them into the soapy water. "When did you realize it was bunkum?"

"Shortly after we married. Rufus crossed paths with Charles Thompson and Joseph Smith. He swallowed the blarney about gold plates coming and going, and other convenient revelations. There was no reasoning with Rufus." She shook her head. "My jaw ached with the effort of keeping silent."

More proof Rufus was a thickhead.

Keziah attacked the pie tin. "Why can't we accept God loves us and makes salvation easy?"

"All we have to do is believe. We're saved by grace, a gift of God." Duncan poured hot water into the rinse pan. "My search for a community blinded me to how different Thompson's beliefs were. Thousands of people in Cincinnati and St. Louis…I mattered to none." He held his breath, waiting for Keziah to say he mattered to her.

"In Preparation, you matter to all."

He'd fished for honeyed-words and come up empty. "Everyone who needs shoes."

"Ach, more than that. You led the Bible study during the blizzards."

"Only reading."

"God's word does not return void. You've prepared soil, planted seeds and watered them in the hearts of all. And showed them how God's people should act."

So, Keziah thought highly of him as a member of the Congregation. Yet...as more?

With the cleanup finished and the Lord's House nearly empty, the young men brought down the Thompsons' worldly goods. For all the larceny Thompson had been accused of and for the size of his family, he hadn't much in the way of belongings. None of them had much, according to the parade of battered trunks. Except the land, which they would now fight over.

Lord, You told us not to lay up for ourselves treasures upon earth, where moth and rust corrupt, where thieves break in and steal, but lay up for ourselves treasures in heaven. Please guide us in Your way.

Carrying out her duties until the end, Keziah loaded the bag of food and jug of water in the wagon, then met Thompson's family as they came down the steps. "I'll be praying for you." Keziah's anger over Thompson's theft didn't keep her from loving his family.

Catherine shifted baby Abraham to embrace her. The bag at her wrist clinked, not of coins, but perhaps the jewelry the sisters whispered about. "I treasure your prayers, dear friend."

The rest of the children—Amelia, Ida, young Charles William, and Ossie, were quiet. But Leo grabbed Duncan's waist. "I'll miss you."

"I'll miss you too, lad. And pray you grow into the man God made you to be."

He smiled. "Mama said she'd let me read her Bible."

The judge looked over the handful of people remaining and

settled his gaze on Duncan. "I trust the Congregation will finish its business in peace and distribute its assets in an equitable manner."

Duncan squirmed. Did the judge think had any influence over this band of troublemakers? He took a deep breath. "With God's help."

The judge nodded, then, wagons loaded, they headed to Onawa.

Jehovah's Presbytery of Zion had ended. Duncan looked around for Keziah. It was time for a beginning.

CHAPTER 25

October 1858

Keziah slid the bench to the sun-warmed corner of her porch. She sat and leaned against the bothy, soaking in warmth, and closed her eyes. Roasting pork scented the air—no need to worry about supper tonight. No babies due. No one needing a remedy. No Tryphina chattering like a sparrow. Charles Blancher Thompson had escaped with his life and Jehovah's Presbytery of Zion had escaped his clutches. *Thank you, Jesus.* Finn rested his head on her knee and her tension melted. She sank her fingers into his fur, finding the spot behind his ear. His foot thumped against something hollow.

Ach, her trunk. She'd filled it with quilts and bedding, then dragged it over half the country. Keziah raised the lid. 'Twas empty, save a remnant of purple paisley. The cotton sateen slid across her fingers, the softest fabric she'd ever touched. She would remember Christena's kindness in sewing a beautiful dress with it, even if her cousin had accused her of not praying. She'd remember how the round neckline and tucked bodice flattered her figure, and how fashionable the ruffled sleeves were. She'd forget Rufus's insults and threats had forced her to trade the dress for a rooster and hen.

Keziah reached to close the trunk. The envelope in her pocket crinkled. She pulled out the decree and read it again. Divorced on grounds of husband's desertion. The court had mandated Rufus pay her support. Tended carefully, the amount would have let her start over, keep herself in food and clothing, and find the freedom she'd prayed for. But the money was gone.

Charles Blancher Thompson. Rufus Sirrine. She'd been ground under the thumb of larcenous men. But now...

Finn raised his head, and his tail swept the dried leaves from the porch. Only one person merited such a welcome. Keziah shoved the envelope back into her pocket.

Duncan sat next to her on the bench and pressed his warm, strong fingers into her neck. "How's your head?"

"Hmm, much better now, thank you."

"Our friends are leaving for Council Bluffs." He listed off his Bible reading lads and several families.

"You've a new shirt." A white one with blue stripes. He'd shaved and, her nose told her, he'd bathed.

"From my trunk." Duncan perched on the bench, bristling with energy. Finn leaned against his leg. "So what treasures did you find in yours?"

She held out the remnant.

"Pretty collar for tonight's dance."

"A... dance?" She raised an eyebrow.

"Aye. Silas Wilcox had a fiddle in his trunk and he knows how to make it sing. We'll dance long as his fingers hold up." He grinned and raised his moccasin-clad foot. "I'll try not to step on your toes."

If Father Ephraim allowed... No, there was no more Father Ephraim. *Hallelujah!*

Duncan looped the fabric around her shoulders. "Let's forget those things behind and reach forth..." His eyes sparkled like sunlight on the creek. "Council Bluffs needs a shoemaker. I could open a shop. And the general store has coffee."

"Coffee..." Would Council Bluffs have a lawyer who would accept a chicken in trade? And a minister?

He clasped her hand, sending a flutter through her middle. "Come with me. They need a midwife too."

"The garden..." As much peace as she'd found in her garden, more had come from Duncan.

"I'll help you dig up the plants and take down your screens. I'll put in post holes for the fence. If there's maple trees, we'll make syrup." He put a dark-blue book in her hands. "You can organize your recipes."

"What's this?" The title page read *Keziah's Complete Herbal: Consisting of a Comprehensive Description of Herbs with their Medicinal Properties and Directions for Compounding the Medicines Extracted from Them. Preparation, Iowa. D. Ross, Publisher.* He'd used the wording from the distinguished *Culpeper's Complete Herbal*, as if Keziah, the herb woman of Preparation, might belong in such erudite company. He'd made the binding so the pages lay flat when the book was open, for ease in writing. Tears blurring her vision, she ran her fingers over the spine. "You said you'd worked as a book-binder, but you didn't say you were a gifted craftsman. This is the best gift I've ever received. Thank you."

"You're so welcome."

She set the book between them so she could hold his hands and look into his deep blue eyes. "You've worked hard for this Congregation, pitching in whenever needed. Sure and I'm grateful for the many times I've received your generosity." Worry creased his brow, so she hurried on. "Beyond *what* you do, is *why*. God's love powers your actions with gentleness, kindness, patience... faithfulness. I can trust you with my love. I'd like to continue our partnership, if you'd be willing to marry me."

He blinked. His mouth dropped open. "I'm working up to proposing."

"Make haste. We're no spring chickens." She smiled, then leaned forward, brushing his warm lips with hers.

Thundering feet of the lads pounded down the hill. "Duncan, we need you!"

He pulled away, releasing her lips and hands slowly. "Let's hide in the hills." He grinned and whispered, "More. Soon. I love you too."

Keziah grinned back, joy filling her heart. "I'll see you at the dance."

He hurried off.

Before Keziah could bask in the glow from the best kiss of her life, Tryphina emerged from behind the chicken coop. "You proposed! Why didn't I think of that? I don't have to wait for these men to speak up."

"What did I say about eavesdropping?" Keziah said, too happy to put heat into her reprimand.

"How else would I find out what's going on?" She put the muslin-wrapped package she'd been carrying onto Keziah's lap. "Guess what Catherine left for you!"

Keziah found her long-lost purple dress, as beautiful as the last time she'd seen it. "How..."

Tryphina waved her into the bothy. "Hurry and change. I'll be back to fix your hair."

"You, dear sister, have grown into a high-handed young woman." Keziah hugged her.

Tryphina grinned. "I learned from an expert."

October 1858

Duncan stopped the lads on the path. "Why the caterwauling?"

"You need to teach us to dance." Nels spun in a circle. Their manes had been tamed, trimmed to the collar and around the ears, and parted on the side. They'd shaved and dressed in clean clothes.

"Are there enough people left for a dance?" Duncan had more kissing to do. "Have you ever seen a dance?"

They looked at each other and shrugged. Five years in the wilderness of Iowa had left a few holes in their education.

"Come on, then." A quick teach, then he'd get back to kissing Keziah.

Duncan let them into the store where they'd have room to practice. "Oftentimes the gathering starts with a march. Look each other in the eye and smile. Bend your arm like this and she'll put her hand on your elbow." Although the lassies in the Congregation might be as lost as the lads. "Follow the first couple, walk in a circle at a dignified pace with the music. At the end of each dance, thank the lass—"

"Apologize if you step on her toes," Nels said.

"Indeed. The Virginia reel is a popular one. Make two lines facing each other, hold hands, pretend Isaac and Nels are women."

"Oh, James," Nels fluttered in imitation of Tryphina. "You'd be a perfect husband if you only had a horse."

Duncan stifled a laugh. "Thomas Lewis will call the steps." He walked the lads through several common ones. "The reel is a challenge." He steered them through alternating turning partners, then turning the next dancer. "Now sidestep to the top, let go of your partner and cast off, the rest of the line follows. At the bottom of the set, the head couple forms an arch. Other couples join hands and go under. When everyone's through, the first couple stays at the bottom of the set, and the second couple leads."

The lads gawked as if he spoke Gaelic.

"What if we botch it up?"

"Keep dancing and catch up to where you're supposed to be. If everyone gets lost, the caller will stop and review the steps. What others? The Quadrille requires four couples. The waltz, two—"

The supper bell rang and they headed to the House.

They met Hannah Perrin on the path. Earrings dangled from her lobes, an elaborate comb held up her hair, and a gold locket adorned her neck. How had she kept her jewelry from Thompson? She joined lassies visiting with a woman with braids crowning her head. Purple trim formed a V from her shoulders to waist, accenting a trim figure. She turned with a swish of petticoats, showing a long neck and smooth shoulders.

Duncan's breath left his body. It was Keziah. The queen who wanted to marry this commoner. He bowed. "Your majesty."

"Dearest Duncan." She curtseyed.

He swallowed. "Fairy magic turned your scrap of fabric into a beautiful dress."

"Fairy magic? A better story than what really happened." Silas

Wilcox sounded the first notes and she reached for Duncan. "Shall we?"

"I'd be honored." He slipped his hand in hers, then tucked it under his elbow. They entered and circled the room, followed by James and Tryphina, Andrew Haines and Lucretia Lewis, Isaac Swett and Eunice Wilcox, and Nels Turner and Sophia Gordon. And, no doubt drawn by the aroma of meat, Finn.

The marched ended and Thomas Lewis called, "Line up for the Virginia reel."

Duncan and Keziah led as head couple. The dancers managed the steps, even keeping time during the reel and casting off. Keziah stood on tiptoes to form an arch with Duncan. The other couples passed beneath.

"You're a good dance partner." Keziah pulled him as close as she could with Finn underfoot. "And an even better partner for life."

Duncan's heart shifted. Could he be dying? No, the weight of grief lifted, letting him live again, filling him with joy. He put his hands on Keziah's waist and touched his lips to hers. She tipped her head and wrapped her arms around his neck.

"A fine new variation to the reel." Tom Lewis clapped and their friends cheered.

Silas played a jaunty version of "Scotland the Brave."

They broke the kiss as their friends shouted "Congratulations!" and formed a circle around them.

Rowland Cobb said, "None of us wants more long speeches, but this might be our last night together. We'd like to send you off with our prayers and gratitude."

James Durfee said, "Duncan Ross, you read the Bible to us. You introduced us to Jesus, who leads us in the way, truth, and life. He saves us by His grace. We thank you."

Duncan smiled. "'Twas God's idea."

Priscilla Lewis held her two-year-old. "During the fracas, Sylvania got away from me and fell into the coals of the laundry fire. Young Charles Perrin was right behind her and yanked her out, then washed her with cold water. No damage done. Thank you for teaching our children to keep each other safe." She showed Keziah the girl's hands, her skin pink.

"Keziah, I've been the biggest boil on the backside for you." Tryphina said. "In spite of that, you taught me about herbs and delivering babies. And how to propose." She grinned and the lads scrambled to hide behind James.

Parents thanked them for caring for babies, for moccasins, for patience with their children. Children thanked Duncan for telling stories and Keziah for bandaging wounds. Each friend told how Keziah and Duncan had made their life safer and healthier.

Sarah signaled supper was ready. Nels hollered, "Let's eat!" and Finn woofed.

A lump in his throat kept Duncan from speaking. He wrapped his arms around Keziah. Her warmth and energy soaked into his heart. *Thank you, Jesus!*

"As the Irish say, 'we live in the shelter of each other.' Much as I want to hide in the hills, God brought us here. We need to be part of a community." Keziah wiped her eyes and smiled up at Duncan. "Together."

The end.

AUTHOR'S NOTE

This story started with a hike. I found a state park in Iowa called Preparation Canyon. Can't you just hear James Earl Jones saying that name? My legs were stretched by the Loess Hills and my imagination stretched by the history of Preparation.

The leader, Charles Blancher Thompson, was a prolific writer. Close to a thousand pages of his publications are available on the internet. In an era when writing was florid, Thompson's prose was "pressed down, shaken together, and running over." He never used one word when twenty or thirty would do. Unable to dazzle his Congregation with brilliance, he baffled them with bull.

Unfortunately this abundance of words provides little insight into Thompson's mind and even less about Preparation. His newspapers named many people, but told little about them. If your ancestor was a member of the Congregation, I'd love to hear from you.

Charles Larpenteur's account of his wife, Makes Cloud, is recorded in his book, *Forty Years a Fur Trader on the Upper Missouri.*

The court case against Thompson was settled in 1866, when the Iowa Supreme Court declared his real estate conveyances were fraudulent. The Perrin family had continued farming in the area and donated the land that became Preparation Canyon State Park. None of the buildings remain, but I hope you'll enjoy these beautiful hills as much as my dog and I did.

ACKNOWLEDGMENTS

A big thank you to my cousins Kay Dobie and Lisa Dobie for the trip to Greenfield Village. Their print shop has a Washington Hand Press, just like the one used at Preparation, and a knowledgable docent to answer my questions.

Many thanks to Megan Elford, who put her conducting experience to work, using her spider-banishing baton to clear the trails at Preparation Canyon. And to Becki, my hiking buddy.

Dr. Marcie Richmond confirmed that yes, delivering babies can be a wild experience.

Writers shelter with each other. Nebraska Novelists transitioned to Zoom and kept me writing during the pandemic. A.C. Williams put the joy into developmental edits. Katherine Barnett set aside her work to proofread mine. Of course, any mistakes are my own.

With her *Anne of Green Gables* Read-Along, Stephanie Ludwig reminded me of the power of a good story to transport readers to a beautiful place.

All glory to God, for "Whoever dwells in the shelter of the Most High will rest in the shadow of the Almighty. I will say of the Lord, 'He is my refuge and my fortress, my God, in whom I trust.' Surely he will save you from the fowler's snare and from the deadly pestilence." -Psalm 91:1-3 NIV

ALSO BY CATHERINE RICHMOND

Spring for Susannah

Through Rushing Water

Third Strand of the Cord

Gilding the Waters

Off the Ground

Two Hearts One Piano

I love to hear from readers! Please write to me through my website CatherineRichmond.com or Facebook.com/CatherineRichmondFans.

If you enjoyed *The Shelter of Each Other*, a review would help other readers find this book. No need for long and complex - leave that for Father Ephraim! - a sentence or two is fine. Thank you so much - I'll celebrate with chocolate!